A German
Love Story

Rolf Hochhuth

A German Love Story

Translated by John Brownjohn

LITTLE, BROWN AND COMPANY · BOSTON · TORONTO

FIRST AMERICAN EDITION

LIBRARY OF CONGRESS CATALOGING IN PUBLICATION DATA

Hochhuth, Rolf.
    A German love story.

    1. Germany—History—1933–1945—Fiction.
I. Title.
PZ4.H68525Ge 1980 [PT2668.O3] 833'.914 80–13077
ISBN 0–316–36765–6

PRINTED IN THE UNITED STATES OF AMERICA

Contents

Brombach in the far south of South-West Germany . . .

This village on the German–Swiss border is familiar to local literary historians from *Die Vergänglichkeit* (Impermanence), a poem by Johann Peter Hebel. Subtitled 'Conversation on the road to Basle between Steinen and Brombach', it was probably written in Lörrach, the municipality of which Brombach now forms part. 'Gruesome as Death in the Basle Dance of Death' is how the majestic ruins of Rötteln Castle seem to a passing wagoner's son who views them by the awe-inspiring light of the moon. Troubled for the very first time by a dread of mortality, the boy plies his father with questions which prompt the wagoner to tell him that 'in time the world will be consumed by fire'. He says it in Swiss German, for father and son both speak Alemannic, but the Basle poet, who also penned the words 'Take heed, misdeeds there be o'er which the grass ne'er grows,' produced a standard German version as well. I, too, am avoiding dialect although, except for a lawyer, all the surviving contemporaries and witnesses of this story likewise addressed me in Alemannic when I ran them to earth in Brombach and Lörrach. A dialect is a linguistic birthmark which belongs to us from childhood or not at all; to acquire one artificially is as much of an imposture as camouflaging ourselves in leather shorts on the pretext of a trip to Bavaria.

And because no narrative should resemble a tape-recording or saddle its readers with the homework involved in learning a dialect not their own, it is irrelevant that Pauline, a native of the Black Forest, spoke dialect as a matter of course to her children, her husband, her parents – who owned a hill farm – and the customers in her greengrocer's shop. She also spoke it, time and again, to the Polish prisoner of war who helped her with her chores in the evenings, only to notice after a few words that he had either misunderstood or failed to understand altogether. Unpalatable as she found it, she would then switch to standard German because the youngster – he was only twenty-one – had learnt it for a couple of years at his secondary school in Lodz. He had also improved his knowledge of the language since September 1939, when the Germans captured him but soon discharged him from camp and assigned him to local farmers as a field-hand or driver.

With alarm, if not horror, in her eyes and voice – emotions that made her speak too fast for him to follow – Pauline told Stasiek Zasada, 'Rosi Lindner over at Lehnacker – she's gone and hanged herself. They say there was a child on the way, from the Pole who worked for her – and her with three of her own already. It's terrible!' Then, when his intent expression told her that he had only half understood, if at all, she burst out, 'You know who I mean – the landlord's wife at the *Swan* in Lehnacker. She's dead – hanged. They say she got herself pregnant by the Polish prisoner who worked there, and her with two girls and a boy. Stackmann told me in the shop just now, when he was buying some potatoes, and the way he said it! Watch out it doesn't happen to you – that's what it sounded like.'

Her agitation had caused a swift relapse into dialect. The Pole looked puzzled. 'Stackmann?'

'The law,' she explained. 'The one who's always nosing around.' Zasada's face cleared. 'Ah, policeman.' His German suffered from the Polish absence of any words for 'a' or 'the'. 'That woman give me beer. I bring coal to her one time. Pretty, she was, and friendly. Why – why hang herself?'

Mournfully, Pauline replied, 'Because she was pregnant and her husband's away at the war. No woman round here would find a doctor to help her. Doctors who do that are killed – executed – and that's what they'll do to the Pole, too, the one who gave her the child. He's gone already.' Zasada nodded. There was another silence. Then he said, 'I hear he sent away to other work.'

She said dully, 'All right, maybe they haven't killed him yet, but they will. Rosi only hanged herself yesterday. Now they'll get the Pole, for sure.' She didn't voice the thought that had struck her in the meantime – she even kept it from herself: that it was asking too much of a woman whose husband was away for months or years on end to work and eat and share her home with a man who was forbidden to touch *any* woman – who couldn't even date one because he had to be in his room each night by ten o'clock sharp. Pauline didn't venture to ask herself

9

the obvious question – whether she herself could have remained faithful to her husband in Rosi's place – but, being as honest as she was, she knew that living under different roofs was the only possible safeguard. And even then . . . Zasada said, 'Who say woman get baby from Polish prisoner? Did she write to say goodbye?'

But before Pauline could answer, he went on, 'How I find out where Pole go?'

Ah, thought Pauline, he wants to warn him to run for it before they come for him. 'They'll have picked him up by now, even if they didn't do it yesterday,' she said. Then, when he preserved a thoughtful silence, she added, 'Maybe some of the other prisoners over at Lehnacker know where he's been taken.'

Abruptly, Zasada hurried out.

She remained sitting for a moment with her son, not yet four, on her lap. The light was already fading, the more so because the little kitchen window was obscured by the flowers in the window-box outside. When had she last seen Rosi Lindner the innkeeper's wife, always so poised and self-assured? How terrible for her not to have found another way out. A way out of the family way . . . Pauline banished the uninvited play on words. Not that she had any cause for self-reproach, it had never seemed so alarmingly apparent to her that human beings were the slaves of circumstance, not its masters. Poor thing, she thought – or told herself she did. In reality, to the extent that anyone can be sure of reality, Rosi's suicide inspired her with fear rather than compassion. Her son sensed how far away her thoughts had strayed and became jealous. 'Mama sing,' he commanded, although Pauline never sang but usually hummed a tune and rocked Herbert in time to it when she took him on her lap towards six o'clock, as soon as the last customer had left the shop.

Today she clasped him to her as if clinging to the child would exorcize a danger which she herself could easily and accurately have defined. That such a threat should exist was one thing. It was another that matters had reached the stage where a woman had to hang herself because a foreigner got her pregnant. Pauline could not have explained why things had come to such a pass

because she knew nothing of psychiatry. 'We live in sick times
...' That much she did sense. The way the customers in the shop
– two women – had reacted just now, when the policeman
announced that Rosi had hanged herself and told them why,
brought it home to Pauline that people were sick beyond a shadow of a doubt. She'd known both women for years. If, instead
of commiserating with the universally popular mistress of the
Swan, they now voiced malign approval of her desperate act, it
must mean that their minds had been ravaged in a way that sickness alone could account for. 'Serves her right!' one of them had
exclaimed, with a satisfaction which conveyed that Rosi had just
paid off a long-outstanding debt to the speaker. Human beings
are a scary lot, Pauline reflected, so as to evade the thought that
her own position – her close daily contact with the young Polish
boy she found so appealing – was also a thing to be feared ...

If normally inoffensive housewives could exult at the news that
a neighbour had hanged herself, no matter why, what could one
expect from the village Nazis? And if ordinary folk so harshly
condemned an unhappy woman, what attitude must the high and
the mighty take? We live in sick times, she told herself again,
without reflecting that time exists solely on the face of a clock
whereas 'the times' are people and what they think and do.

Yes, people were sick, and because the story of Pauline and
Stasiek cannot be rendered intelligible to anyone, even the narrator, without at least some attempt to analyse the mental illness
that occasioned it, our account must necessarily embrace 'the
high and the mighty' whose minds – whose sickness of the mind
– engendered the tragedies of the Hitler years. This is regrettable,
because they are more aptly condemned than any human beings
to date by a couplet coined a century before their baneful influence took effect:

> Let them not be called to mind,
> Not in book nor yet in song.

Two Ph.D.s . . . The younger, born in 1913, had just completed his doctoral thesis, 'Don John of Austria and the Battle of Lepanto', to be published in book form a year later. The elder, born in 1897, owed his doctorate to a thesis on Schütz, a Romantic dramatist, and had been Reich Minister of Public Enlightenment and Propaganda since 1933. (He originally opposed this choice of official title because of a lingering recognition that propaganda negates enlightenment. Although he made every effort to ensure that his ministry did just that, he instinctively thought it maladroit for the lettering on his door to proclaim the purpose of his work.)

The youthful historian Felix Hartlaub, whose father had been hounded out of his job as director of Mannheim Art Gallery by the man who conferred office on Joseph Goebbels the philologist, was a student in Berlin when Jewish stores and synagogues were vandalized in winter 1938. He noted: 'A sense of shame and humiliation in everyone I spoke to . . . As time goes by, though, I've grown a sort of shell which has something rather beastly about it. That one can eat and sleep at all is compromising enough . . . I have to pass the French travel bureau every morning and see the faces of the people who queue there from an early hour. That's enough for me.'

The elder Ph.D. was one of two Germans whose speeches had pioneered the indoctrination of those tens of thousands of bully-boys who, representing every strand of society from chauffeur to physician, hustled their Jewish fellow-citizens out of bed during the night of 8–9 November and carried off the menfolk.

Here is the younger, writing to his father eight months before Hitler swooped on Poland: 'Who knows how much time there is left and when we shall finally be fed to the cannon?' From an earlier letter dated September 1937: '. . . this increasingly presumptuous gamble on the thickness of Britain's skin strikes me as criminal in the long run. We already have the makings of three world wars. How much longer can it go on?'

The elder Ph.D., whose Führer had packed him off on a trip to Athens and Rhodes so that his wife could mentally digest the latest and most spectacular of his adulteries, noted on 4 April

1939: 'Newspapers arrive from Berlin. Chamberlain has announced a commitment to assist Poland in the Lower House.' And although it was this same commitment that led, after almost six years of war, to the destruction of the diarist and the regime he served as a minister, his comment on the news from London was 'It's uproarious.'

The most potent lie about Goebbels – that he was a man of superlative intelligence – was not of his own devising but has outlived him by more than thirty years. The development which he then found laughable – or 'uproarious', to use the current Berlin vogue-word for something peculiarly mirth-provoking – had in his view been disarmed or neutralized because Hitler had dealt the British prime minister 'an extremely sharp retort in his speech at Wilhelmshaven . . . Threatens to abrogate the Naval Agreement. That cuts more ice than anything with the gentlemen of England.' Uncanny how it sometimes occurs to the spirit of the age – whoever that philosopher's figment may be – to warn those who sail on, heedless of such warnings, to their doom. Still more uncanny, for the innocents who are towed along in their wake, is the failure of those who steer a course for the maelstrom to see what everyone else does: the storm warnings which, as in this case, can sometimes be discerned with ease.

Hitler delivered his riposte to Chamberlain beside the sea because he was there to name the world's most powerful warship – the *Tirpitz* – after someone who had done more than any other single German to magnify the war of 1914 into a world-wide conflict. Every naval attaché present at the launching could tell at a glance that the battleship's displacement, far from corresponding to her official specification, was so immense that the building of her hull alone must have torn up the Anglo-German Naval Agreement . . . Just as the man whose name she bore played an even less active role in 1914–18 than the battle fleet he had built, whose very existence drove Britain into the Franco-Russian camp after two centuries of Anglo-German amity, so the *Tirpitz* sallied forth only once – to bombard the shores of Spitzbergen – and then lay berthed almost throughout the war until she ignominiously capsized beneath a salvo of British bombs. These are circumstances steeped in symbolism. And although no one on that first day of April 1939 could guess that this awe-inspiring leviathan would never take part in a sea battle – any more than did the man whose name she bore, though he was largely responsible for engineering the biggest naval clash the world had ever seen, the Battle of Jutland – all present at the launching could sense that no man seriously intent on peace with Britain would name a ship *Tirpitz* and arm her more formidably than any British ship afloat . . .

Whom God would destroy . . . One week later, on 10 April, Goebbels passed another comment on the mutual assistance pact between London and Warsaw, which was actually to result in the partition, not of 'that' country, as Goebbels 'presciently' referred to Poland, but of *a* country; to wit, Germany. 'History isn't there to be learnt from,' he wrote. 'That doesn't apply to Germany alone, but also – and more so, praise be! – to her enemies.'

Being Hitler's propaganda expert, Goebbels should nonetheless have learnt from history that it betrays a lack of instinct to name a militant nation's most powerful ship after someone who, though he invested the bulk of his unrivalled energy in promoting a lost war, never saw a day's fighting himself; a man whose handiwork, the second most powerful fleet in human history, vanished from the arena, almost to the last ship, after being seized and then scuttled in the main anchorage of its victorious foe . . . Few sailors could have found it heartening to sail in a vessel of that name, for if names have any value at all, what is it if not symbolic? But *that* name, Tirpitz, stood for provocation without political discernment, for dynamic failure – for a man who looked on while all his compatriots fought . . . Embittered by premature retirement, Tirpitz churned out inflammatory speeches which were largely to blame for his country's bombastic declaration of unrestricted submarine warfare and America's counter-declaration of war on Imperial Germany in 1917 – not, it may be added, that the Kaiser's U-boats managed to sink even one of the countless American troopships bound for France . . .

Twenty years later, in 1937, like any intelligent person whose judgement was unclouded by the emotion that ruled all Nazis, however intelligent, the Berlin student Felix Hartlaub could tell that enough tinder had accumulated for 'three world wars'.

As for his senior by sixteen years, the propaganda minister who had long since subjected the less prominent of his fellow-Germans to a ban on reports from abroad, but could and did have personal access to political intelligence of every kind, he behaved as if exemplifying Erich Kästner's dictum that those on whom God bestows office He also deprives of reason.

Goebbels, who had 'naturally' seen to it that this poet's works, too, were consigned to a bonfire outside Berlin University, had time to read a book during his Hitler-prescribed visit to Greece – something he very seldom did in Berlin, as his diary attests. Despite this act of self-indulgence, however, he soon relapsed and succumbed to the callous clichés which he peddled so persuasively to others. This was because his own speeches, of which he himself said that they 'galvanized' him, had transformed them into personal articles of faith: it was his audiences' 'storms' of acclamation that encouraged him to believe what he had planned to make them believe without believing it himself beforehand. Even in Rhodes, and receptive though he was to the aura of the ancient world, he only threw off his master's morbid and criminal ideas for brief and isolated spells. After touring the town in a horse-drawn cab, he commented: 'A modern quarter, most of it laid out by the Fascists. A Jewish quarter, impoverished and fetid with garbage and filth. Ugh! A Turkish quarter, not much better. So they are human beings too, the people who live here. But there are master races . . .' He then read a book capable of humanizing even him – temporarily. 'I have, with profound melancholy, finished Somerset Maugham's *Of Human Bondage*. Heart-rending pessimism, magnificently written and splendidly conceived.' Our hopes revive for the man who, in Rhodes, numbered even Jews among the human race, but by 2 November of the same year, 1939, Poland's eighteen-day defeat had dispelled his last inhibitions. 'These aren't human beings, they're animals,' he wrote of the Warsaw Ghetto, entirely forgetting how lower-middle-class penury and chronic unemployment had once consigned him to a semi-ghetto and kept him isolated in his parents' humble terrace house.

Compare Hartlaub, observing the Berlin Jews who persevered until the outbreak of war in their largely fruitless endeavours to extract travel permits from foreign agencies and embassies, as though they already guessed that they and their families would all be murdered unless they obtained an entry visa before the fighting started: 'I firmly believe that suffering is communicable. Anyone who possesses imagination and strives to be a historian, a writer, has a duty to embrace the suffering of others.'

Being twenty-six years old, Hartlaub was called up at once. As on those who vainly tried to emigrate, so on him, the war descended like a trap-door. Posted to a barrage-balloon unit stationed at Ploesti in friendly Romania, which had still to enter the fray, he wrote: 'What I dislike is the bigotry of most of my comrades, who dismiss this place as a "gipsy dump" and are quite incredibly insensitive to the archetypes of human misery who are legion here.' His comment on the Poles, six months after Warsaw's enforced surrender: 'The Biblical afflictions of this nation are the only aspect of this war that has really moved me so far.' Members of the Leibstandarte, Hitler's household regiment, had told him: 'If a village offered stubborn resistance, the armoured troops drove their heavy tanks at the corners of the buildings. The mud walls collapsed to disclose the interiors and their defenders – men, women and children. They could not escape and were mowed down at leisure. If a German soldier was found mutilated near a village, the tank men used this procedure among others: the heavy steel cables tanks carry were unloaded, tied on behind and wound round thirty or forty villagers, all higgledy-piggledy. Then the tanks roared off, hell-for-leather, with their appendage, "not a shred" of which was left after a short distance. Alternatively, the villagers had to dig a pit – a pit like a yawning crater – and were herded into it. Then came a concentrated explosive charge, ignited and thrown in on top.'

So much for a soldier's view, but here is how the Propaganda Minister saw Poland when he toured Warsaw, that 'hell-hole', some five weeks after Hitler's victory parade: 'Our bombs and shells have done a thorough job. Not a house intact. The inhabitants look stupefied and wraithlike.' Six years later, a visitor to Berlin could have applied the same description, word for word, to the one-time capital of the Reich which Goebbels helped to rule. But not the following lines – they are unmistakably his: 'People crawl through the streets like insects. It's revolting and almost beggars description. In the citadel. Everything here destroyed. Not a single stone left standing. This is where Polish nationalism underwent its years of tribulation. We must eradicate it completely or one day it will rise again . . . A visit to Belvedere Palace, where Poland's Marshal lived and worked. The room where he died and his deathbed. One can learn here what to expect if the Polish intelligentsia are allowed to develop unhampered . . . A drive through the Ghetto. We get out and inspect everything closely. It's indescribable. These aren't human beings, they're animals. That's why our task here is surgical, not humanitarian. Incisions must be made here – really drastic incisions, or some day Europe will perish of the Jewish disease. Driving along Polish roads. One is already in Asia. We shall have our work cut out to Germanize this area.'

Next day he reported to Hitler. 'I presented a report on my trip to Poland . . . My account of the Jewish problem, in particular, met with his full approval. The Jew is a waste product. More of a clinical (?) than a social matter . . . Question: ought we to release pictures of the devastation in Warsaw? Advantages and disadvantages. The shock effect an advantage. The Führer wants to see the pictures himself first. He is closing the Pilsudski Museum on my advice. It might otherwise become a focus of Polish aspirations.'

Reading this, one can only marvel that there are still some historians who believe that the Allied demand for an unconditional Nazi surrender could have been avoided or was actually misguided. Even discounting the pressure on Roosevelt and Churchill to formulate this war aim as a means of pinning Stalin down and averting the threat of a separate peace with Hitler, how could they have negotiated with men like this compulsive diarist and ardent exterminator? However many anonymous inhabitants of the Third Reich may have thought and felt like Hartlaub the soldier, all who spoke out were beheaded, hanged or shot ... Hitler, who was no more a German than Napoleon a Frenchman, treated 'his' Germans better than other nations, but only 'his'. Not all Germans were that ...

Twilight

The offenders' circle of acquaintances is . . . manifestly restricted by chance and opportunity alone. Women who have relations with prisoners of war are brought into close permanent contact with them by their work on farms or in factories. Those involved are far from all women of easy virtue, though the latter probably constitute the majority. Among the accused are country girls of good family and unblemished reputation who have never previously had intercourse, as well as soldiers' wives of whom some have been very happily married for years, including women with several children. As soon as Frenchmen are employed in more senior positions, shorthand typists, housekeepers, estate secretaries and members of the intelligentsia figure among the accused. The extent to which the *apprehension and prosecution* of offenders proves wholly successful cannot be deduced from reports . . . It further appears that prisoners of war and women, too, grow more and more reckless as a liaison progresses, so that exposure ensues in due course, be it only in consequence of malicious denunciations.

The Chief of the Security Police and Security Service, 13 December 1943.

Crepuscular . . . The very word has a sinister ring, a hint of menace and inscrutability, yet twilight lurks in every dwelling, every evening, just as it hovers between those who meet outside its walls. 'Have a care, keep watch, be wary!' warns a poet, as trees stir eerily in the gathering dusk, and adds, 'If there be one deer you favour, leave it not to graze alone.'

But how can one watch over those whom one loves above all others, and how can one protect them even from a friend? For it is also written of friends that one should 'Trust them not when that hour comes!'

Who can tell what rhythm in the depths of our corporeality makes us spiritually more susceptible, more and less obedient to conscience – defenceless, too, quite often – during the half-hour or hour of twilight than at other times of day? Twilight also coincides with moments of daydreaming – they are never more than moments – simply because that is when the day's first relaxation brings its first disinhibition; when words escape the speaker – irrevocable words which he never meant to utter, though their target is more vulnerable to them than at any other hour . . . And war, because it separates more people for longer than all else, is the strongest spur to betrayal.

As she always did when she had shut up shop and was drinking her coffee substitute, Pauline took Herbert on her lap. This was his great moment, the one he yearned for all day long. It was then, before she switched on the light, that she perched him on her knee and sat alone with him in the almost darkened little shop whose door had at last been closed to customers, while twilight still glimmered through the windows: the light beloved of lovers and traitors.

But today – not for the first time – Stani was there. The Pole had half-endeared himself to the boy with the corn-coloured hair by plying him with such gifts as he could muster: model boats, cocked hats and aeroplanes of folded newspaper, a horseshoe, a miniature catapult (a forked twig with a rubber band and little paper balls) for use on sparrows and chickens – even a willow-wood flute that wouldn't play. Herbert also knew that Stani was now making him a drum with a rabbit drumskin. (A more dexterous fellow-prisoner was going to whittle the flute into a playable condition.) Even so, Herbert stared coldly at Stani, the interloper. Not even the laughter they shared when Herbert rode-a-cock-horse on the Pole's knees and plunged into the 'ditch' between them could assuage his resentment of the visitor whose presence almost invariably spoilt his evening cuddle with Mama. Whenever Stani was there – the Pole's name was Stasiek, but everyone called him Stani – Mama talked to the man instead of him, whereas her usual custom at this hour had been to talk to Herbert alone or commune with him in silence for the first time since lunch, hugging him to her and rocking him to and fro. He liked that almost as much as he relished the smell of her – provided they were alone. Sole ownership is the sole guarantee of absolute possession: that thought was still beyond the boy, but he could speak and he did so defiantly.

'Stani go away!'

Pauline looked reproving. 'What ever do you mean?'

The child made no reply, just nestled closer. Pauline said, 'Stani's your friend.'

Herbert conceded this with a single word: 'But – but Stani go away!' The Pole gave a wry smile. Pauline said quietly, 'Did you hear that, Stani?' She sounded depressed as well as earnest. 'Children and fools speak the truth – do you say that in Poland too? What happened at lunch-time, you mustn't ever ...' She broke off and looked away, but it was enough for him that she had called him *du* for the first time – and he had a right to the familiar form of address after those two minutes in the cellar today.

Herbert, of course, knew nothing and everything. He could sense that a new intimacy enclosed the other two like a cocoon, shutting him out. Mama smelt even more wonderful today than usual, and if the accursed man hadn't been there he might almost have been able to forget that his little sister was also there – for good. The stork had brought her when snow lay on the ground, and the sledge Father Christmas had given him was no compensation for the loss of his mother. He had almost completely lost her to his sister and was only gradually winning her back now that the baby girl spent so much time asleep in her basket. She couldn't walk yet, thank God, though she already had legs. And because she couldn't talk yet either, Herbert sometimes stole over to her when Mama was in the shop and pulled her hair as spitefully as he knew how ...

But Mama was talking to the man again, not him. Worse still, she sent *him* away by saying, 'Go and see if the hares have run out of carrots.' And Stani called after him, 'And not get fingers bitten again!' Herbert grabbed two handfuls of carrots from the shop and came trotting back through the kitchen into the yard, which was only small – just big enough to beat a carpet in. Pauline stood up as soon as the child had left the kitchen and shut the door behind him, and the Pole stood up too. The kitchen was even smaller than the shop, so they were very close together. That was why she spoke quickly and reverted to the formal *Sie* – a defence mechanism. 'You'd better go too now, Stani. They'll be waiting supper for you over the way.'

Over the way meant at Melchior's, the coal merchant who owned the premises that backed on to hers and employed the Pole as a carter and coalman. Pauline had turned to face the stove. He was so close that she could feel the coming and going of his breath on her neck. His hands were on her hips again, hot and heavy. She bowed her head as he buried a kiss in the nape of her neck, then blurted out, 'I'm so afraid for you!'

She drew away from him and swung round. Neither of them could speak, they were breathing so fast. He stepped back, smiling gravely. 'Afraid – only for me?'

She was holding a bowl and a wooden spoon against her smock, motionless. 'For both of us – they'd arrest us both. I'm never going into that cellar again when you're down there stacking crates. You'd better go now, really you had!' Again, with an intensity that made her feel almost ashamed for him, she glimpsed the cowering, abject ghetto-look of a prisoner as he stood there obediently with his hand on the latch. 'Please,' he said quickly, 'please let me come ... tonight!' And when she stared at him as if he were mad, he tried to talk her protests away. 'Nobody see me, Frau Pauline – nobody. I come over wall, yard very dark, all sleeping very loud ... always, yes – ' he searched for the word ' – always snorting. I wake up, they snorting so much.'

She laughed. 'Snoring,' she corrected him. 'We say snoring.'

Abruptly, he spoke into her laughing face. 'You – you are beautiful ...' He said it in a choking voice, and she could see how convulsed he was with desire and desperation. And she contradicted him because it was only proper. 'Me, beautiful? I could almost be your mother, I'm fifteen years older than you.'

'My mother very beautiful too,' he replied. To him, what Pauline had said seemed the contrary of an objection. And now came his grand avowal: 'I here at Melchior's only because of you.'

Because of her? It transfixed her, deep down inside, that this big strapping boy should think her beautiful. She was already blind to his terrible imprudence in telling her so.

Stani had originally been assigned to the local dairyman, who dressed him up in a smart white linen jacket and sent him round the village with his one-horse cart and his gentle one-eyed bay gelding, which was unfit for military service, to dole out rationed milk and collect the takings. Relieved to be able to give his confession a factual gloss, Stani explained, 'I quarrel with first boss on purpose, make trouble on purpose so he glad to get rid of me, because I know coal merchant looking for another prisoner. I know he pleased to have me because my friend work for him. My friend tell him I strong – strong for coal sacks.'

Pauline tried to distract him from his confession. 'But coal's dirty and milk's clean. Coal's heavy, milk's light. Why didn't you stay at the dairy?'

Now he had to say it again. 'Because of you. Only because of you.'

Again she strove to turn a deaf ear. 'But it was risky, picking a quarrel with the dairyman on purpose. Poles who quarrel with Germans get punished.' Just to hear it once more, she said petulantly, 'Why did you make trouble?'

'Because always, Pauline, I think you beautiful – always! I

think so every time I bring you milk, and always know I can never, never come to you if I live with milkman at end of village, where we have to be in room by nine o'clock. Melchior's house next to your house. I must live in that house if I want to come to you, Pauline.'

She was touched but tried not to show it. 'And weren't you scared to work next door? You may have to cart a coffin around some day.'

He didn't understand. 'Coffin?'

She translated: 'You know, a box for dead people. Your new boss drives the village hearse. If Herr Melchior gets called up or falls sick, you'll have to drive the bodies to the cemetery.'

Zasada brushed this aside, laughing. 'Who can think of a – how you say? – coffin when he think of you, Pauline?'

She smiled too, though the fear inside her far outweighed the pleasure. She wanted nothing that this – this 'boy here' – wanted, but the speechlessness that gripped her foretold that she wouldn't be able to resist his urgings and entreaties. Not able? Why not? What could be easier than to lock the door at night, as she always did? This admission made her so angry with herself that she took it out on him. With unprecedented brusqueness she snapped, 'No, I don't like this. I've got a good husband, Stani. Now go!'

Her tone warned him to *Sie* her again. 'Talk, please – *only talk* to you, Pauline. Why else I live? Get up at five, six o'clock and work till night-time, and at ten I must be in my room – why? It is only life if I can talk to you.'

Pauline said, 'We're talking now. All right, sit down for a minute, but if you come back in the night – well, it won't do. People can already see the way you look at me in the day-time – you shouldn't really come here in the day-time either.'

While speaking she stroked his hair, which was short, fair and bristly as a field of stubble, but thicker. Still earnestly, his German made more fluent by obstinacy, he said, 'Let all people see! Herr Melchior, he say I can come to you after work and chop wood and carry empty fruit and vegetable crates outside and full crates into shop and sacks of potatoes ... And that shirt you give me, – he let me wear it on Sundays, and even the cravat.'

'Tie,' amended Pauline, and added quickly, 'You know the woman who often comes here in the evenings, the one who keeps my books for me? She's a good sort. I think of her as a friend, but her husband's away too and I don't like the way she looks at me when she finds you still here after closing time. She often stays on late because otherwise – well, she'd just sit there alone like me ... So take care you don't ...' She broke off because his forehead, as he sat there in front of her, was level with her hips. He buried his head in her overall, which smelt of what she sold – of ripeness, freshness, fullness, of fruit, flowers and vegetables – which smelt, too, of her, after twelve long hours of work on a hot summer's day. No one could see them through the shop window – it was shuttered – but just as Herbert had run out into the room-sized little yard, so he might easily come running back. And for that reason – that reason alone, perhaps – she broke away from Stani when his fingers closed on the cool, smooth hollows behind her knees in a way that made them both feel faint. 'Get up this minute,' she gasped, knuckling her hair out of her eyes. Then she said wearily, 'Where will it end? You want me to do what Frau Lindner did – you want me to end up hanging myself?'

He swallowed hard, unable to speak. All the blood had rushed to the epicentre of his being, so he drew up one knee and clasped it in both hands rather than let her see his agony of excitement. She wasn't wearing much beneath that linen overall ...

In his discomfiture, he vainly echoed what both of them and all the villagers for miles around were discussing, 'Nobody could know she make child with Pole.'

Silence. It was pointless, repeating conjectures. Had they already killed the man? Surely not, because they would have done that on the spot, publicly. But where was he, and had it been the woman's confession that led to his arrest? The poor creature must have lost her nerve and talked, thought Pauline. She had a sudden vision of the two snapshots – two of many – which her husband had sent home from Holland tucked between Delft gingerbread and dress lengths and children's toys. They showed him carrying a Dutch girl into the sea on his shoulders, both of them in swimsuits and both laughing like a couple fresh from bed. And because Pauline felt a renewed pang of annoyance at the photos, she was doubly on her guard against Stani in the knowledge that these two snaps, which she hadn't really resented at the time – in fact she had almost forgotten about them – were now obtruding on her consciousness as a pretext for retaliation. 'A half-naked female and him half-naked too, even in the photos …' Not much doubt about the rest of their *un*photographed goings-on! Pauline felt simultaneously touched and exasperated.

'Look, Stani,' she said abruptly, 'I can't help you, however much I understand and however grateful I am. Ten hundred-weight of peaches you shifted today, did you know that? Ten hundredweight, and they're all gone bar fifty pounds or so. I've never done such business in all my born days! I'm not allowed to give you money, but you know where it's kept, so take what you need to get you home – I'd never tell a soul it was missing. Then there's my husband's suits – you know where they're hanging and they don't have any names sewn in. Take one and get along home to your mother, my lad, or we'll both be in trouble.' And she kissed him quickly, but before she could turn back to the stove he caught hold of her. She slumped against him, powerless to free herself because she felt that her 'problem' was resolved when he said, falteringly, 'Tonight – once. Only tonight! Then I run away, but not to Poland.'

Herbert came in from the yard. While Pauline was moving something around on the stove to steady her trembling hands, Zasada said, 'No, not to my home. I never reach Poland – I look like man of your country, and in trains are soldier-policemen with silver plates on chains round neck. All people look to see if I German deserter.'

'Switzerland, then?' she murmured, still bent over the saucepans on the old black cast-iron stove with its long legs and wood-or coal-burning grate.

'Not possible, they give you back.' Then, looking at Herbert, 'Alsace, Vichy France … People there send men to England.

Herbert, bring me flute, I give it to my friend. He carve it good – repair, make nice music. Fetch it.'

Herbert said stubbornly, 'Don't want to make music.'

'Fetch it,' Zasada insisted. 'You not want flute, I give it to Max next door. He very happy!' He turned to the boy's mother. 'Much to think about. For instance, is horse too dangerous? I ride good, but I never, never see man on horse in Germany. Nobody ride here. Why nobody ride here, Pauline?'

She said, 'Anyone who can ride is in the army. Anyway, they've commandeered all the saddle-horses. The old men left at home don't ride. A horse would only give you away.'

Zasada nodded silently. He had absolutely no knowledge, only a vague idea, of the inordinate penalties of recapture: at best, committal to a concentration camp for 'destruction by labour'; more probably, summary execution on the gallows. In any case, he felt no urge to leave. To head for Poland would be suicidal, even if he got there. It would mean risking his parents' lives and spending his own in permanent hiding because there were no partisans to join, not in 1940. England was a long way off, but still ... There was always a chance of sneaking into Spain or North Africa from Vichy France, which the Germans had left unoccupied. And yet, not that he admitted it to himself, this woman held him back. It was many months since his eyes had first devoured the hard brown curve of her upper arms – the sight had smitten him like a thunderbolt – when, that spring, for the first time since winter, Pauline came to the door to collect her milk-can in a sleeveless dress. Miraculously, her skin was still pale walnut, not winter white. She had raised one arm to secure a stray wisp of hair, and there, almost within kissing distance, she had innocently proffered the dense dark luxuriance of her armpit to Zasada's famished gaze. It was that which had first tormented and incited him to pitiable one-man excesses at night – nightly excesses, for her armpit seemed the quintessence of everything denied to a prisoner. Today in the cellar was the first time he had taken possession of those bare shoulders, those arms, those armpits, for a minute, two minutes – he didn't know. He only knew that he would lose his reason, burn up inside, if the woman sent him away. But she wouldn't, or she'd have done so by now. He felt a joyous certainty: scared she might be, but she wanted him.

To run *to* this woman, not away from her: that prospect now made any risk seem acceptable. So he said – casually, because the topic had lost all immediacy, 'I many times think how it would be to escape with horse. Melchior's mare fine for ride – I always ride her bareback, even in river, if river what you call so little water. Also, I know where Melchior keep saddle. I can fetch saddle and hide it in cart when I go to woods. I always go at four, alone at first. Melchior never follow till nine, sometimes not till midday, sometimes not at all. On day like that perhaps he not find out I gone till evening – fifteen hours! Leave cart in wood, tie horse to tree for graze, and hupp!' He laughed as if already galloping off on the mare. 'Ride other horse to Alsace! Except ...' His voice trailed away and became subdued. 'Every child, every people I meet see saddle-horse and stare at me. Every policeman stare at me too ...' He laughed ruefully.

Impatient at these futile dreams, Pauline said, 'So forget the whole idea. Not a horse, a bicycle. Take mine – take my bike!'

He shook his head. 'Never, Pauline – never. Dangerous for you. If you give me suit of husband, that is *very* kind. Money too – yes, but not bicycle as well, never! Finding bicycle very easy. Not necessary I take from you.'

The cuckoo-clock, a wedding present from Pauline's Black Forest relatives, began to strike seven. The Melchiors, who supped at this hour, defied regulations – like every Brombach household which employed a prisoner – by eating with Stasiek Zasada. The first of the innumerable Nazi ordinances governing the treatment of prisoners of war insisted that no German should eat at the same table as a foreigner, but everyone in the village, whether Nazi or not, ignored it. Zasada rose as the cuckoo made its final appearance. Herbert had returned to the kitchen and silently handed him the flute. The Pole took it and ruffled the boy's hair. 'Soon ready,' he said, looking at Pauline. 'Goodnight.' Then, seeing that her face was as unclouded and friendly as ever, he quickly removed the key from the yard door and stuffed it into the pocket of her overall. Before she could object – she had glanced at Herbert, but he was busy with something – he said, 'If not, perhaps from habit, you lock it after all.'

'No!' she said, but he was out of the door so fast that she had no time to explain what she meant by the word.

Case History No. 1: the spirit of the age

Paranoia (Gk.) : Insanity, a form of mental illness construed as an independent 'mania'. Discounting their particular mania (erotomania, megalomania, persecution mania), many sufferers have intact personalities. As a rule, the mania develops into an inherently logical system and cannot be invalidated by counter-argument.

Lexikon Editions Rencontre, Lausanne.

All fish start smelling at the head ... So runs a popular German adage, and Goethe's *Urfaust* contains the following couplet:

> What you the spirit of the age do call
> Is truly theirs who hold that age in thrall.

One of the masters of this age – the second most powerful in the country after Hitler – was Minister-President Field Marshal Hermann Göring, Commissioner for the Four-Year Plan and Chairman of the Ministerial Council for the Defence of the Reich, to quote only a very modest selection of the posts he held in 1940. Chairman of the Ministerial Council ... It was more characteristic of Göring than anything else that although he garnished himself throughout the war with that resounding title – and probably had it printed on upwards of a hundred thousand letterheads and directives – the Ministerial Council never held a single war-time meeting ...

On 8 March 1940 Göring dictated the basic decree governing the treatment of those Polish civilians, not prisoners of war, who had come to work in Germany, some as volunteers and others as deported conscripts. Although it ran to many pages, Göring's decree was only the precursor of countless police ordinances designed to ensure that 'impeccable conduct' reigned among the Poles. Much correspondence was, for example, devoted to such niceties as whether a Pole should be permitted to use matches or carry a pocket-knife when employed on the land. The fact that German civil servants had become quite as mentally deranged as the Reich's most prominent Nazis is confirmed by the following letter, dated 6 May 1940, which Heinrich Müller, the Gestapo chief who ran amuck under Himmler and Heydrich, felt constrained to write to the 'Herr Regierungspräsident' or senior government administrator in Potsdam. In it, Müller stated:

'I consider the proposal to ban the possession and carrying of matches and pocket-knives by Polish civilian workers to be impracticable because

(a) pocket-knives are frequently used in agricultural work and

(b) a ban on the possession of matches would have in prac-

32

tice to be amplified into a ban on smoking. It is not, however, intended to impose a total ban on smoking by Polish workers...'

The Gestapo chief's letter went on to fill a printed page, just as Göring's edicts and the directives issued for their implementation by Himmler, Heydrich, Kaltenbrunner, Müller and a host of underlings filled many bulging volumes of print. Among the 'problems' debated was whether Poles should be permitted to attend divine service, why they should 'categorically' be refused time off to get married, and why children of agricultural labourers should rate as 'fit for work as soon as they attain their twelfth year'. It was also laid down that no Pole, not even one who had volunteered for employment in the Reich, could ride a bicycle ... 'Requests that the children of Polish civilian workers be permitted to receive religious instruction or attend classes in preparation for confession or Communion are likewise to be categorically rejected.' That these same children should be forbidden to attend school seemed equally 'reasonable' to those who had lost their reason but aspired to win the war ...

Pursuant to Göring's decree, civilian workers from Poland had to wear 'an identifying badge affixed to their clothing. This regulation will be implemented by police ordinance.' Göring gave notice that Party Member Heinrich Himmler, the so-called Reichsführer-SS and Chief of the German Police at the Reich Ministry of the Interior, would enact 'the requisite legal and administrative provisions'.

Göring's edict further ordained: 'Where Poles are employed in towns, in commercial, industrial and large-scale agricultural concerns, every possible effort must be made to house them on their own in special buildings such as harvesters' hutments, so that separate accommodation appropriate to given circumstances need only be provided for workers in small agricultural concerns ... Abuses must be combated by making it clear to the Poles, through restrictions on their freedom of movement, that their sole purpose in coming to Germany is to work ... Suitable measures, *inter alia* an absolute compulsion to reside at one's place of employment, tighter registration controls, the introduction of a curfew and curbs on the consumption of alcoholic beverages, are to be instituted forthwith ... It has already transpired, for example, that unrestricted use of public transportation facilities such as railroads, bus routes, et cetera, encourages Poles to leave their places of work without permission and roam the Reich unchecked, and should thus be speedily terminated ...'

Those responsible for such matters were burdened by their racial paranoia, and its manic emphasis on the superman-subhuman distinction, with a 'duty' to apply themselves more zealously to 'GV' (*Geschlechtsverkehr*, or sexual intercourse) between Germans and 'aliens' than to any other so-called offence. This led to mountains of official correspondence, exemption from active service for countless able-bodied men, and a series of executions whose precise number has never been ascertained.

As early as 8 January 1940, for example, a confidential circular was dispatched from Berlin by the Chief of the Security Police and Security Service (SD), Party Member Reinhard Heydrich. Addressed minus commas but with underlining, as reproduced here, to 'all Gestapo (regional and district) headquarters *for the information of* Senior SS and Police Commanders Inspectors of the Security Police and SD Criminal Police bureaus SD regional headquarters', this circular (No. IV 98/40) stated:

'Pursuant to an agreement concluded on 6 January 1940 between myself and the Armed Forces High Command, all Polish prisoners of war who have had relations with German women will in future be discharged as prisoners of war and transferred to the relevant local Gestapo (regional or district) headquarters. Prisoners of war transferred in this manner are initially to be placed in preventive detention. The fact that they have been placed in preventive detention must be reported to me without delay by teletype, together with a detailed account of the attendant circumstances. Further instructions will follow in due course. Signed: Heydrich. Witnessed: Hellmuth, Administrative Secretary.'

Sarcastically termed 'protective custody', the transfer of prisoners of war from Wehrmacht camps to the police was invariably followed in the case of Poles, Russians and Serbs by execution, alias 'special treatment'. Where Frenchmen were concerned, this rule was later relaxed, and from 5 July 1941 onwards even a Pole stood some chance, subject to several provisos, of surviving denunciation for 'GV' with a German female as long as he was adjudged 'fit for Germanization' – but more of that anon.

The term 'special treatment' had been clearly defined as the stock euphemism for execution on 20 September 1939, only three weeks after the outbreak of war: 'At issue in the latter case are the sort of circumstances which, in view of their propaganda effect or reprehensible and dangerous nature, must be eliminated without regard for individuals by means of the most ruthless action, that is to say, by *execution*.' On 31 January 1940, even before Göring dictated his ukase relating to the proposed recruitment of Polish civilians, too, for work in Germany, Himmler had addressed himself to the POW problem in a peculiarly typical vein: 'German women and girls who consort with prisoners of war in a manner grossly offensive to wholesome public sentiment are to be placed in preventive detention until further notice and committed to a concentration camp for at least twelve months ... Should the women and girls of a locality decide to subject the woman concerned to public obloquy or cut off her hair before she is transferred to a concentration camp, the police are not to intervene.'

Illustrative of such influence on everyday life in Germany is the following letter from Potsdam dated 12 December 1940 and headed 'Secret State Police, Regional Headquarters, Reference No. 6890/40 IIE.' In it, one Herr Dr Husmann reported of an eighteen-year-old girl, 'currently detained in Berlin-Moabit', that 'the above-named repeatedly engaged in sexual intercourse with an ethnic Pole at Neumecklenburg, Kreis Friedeberg, although she was cognizant of the relevant prohibition and well aware of his Polish nationality. The name of the Pole is not known here.' (Presumably because the girl did not betray her lover.) Dr Husmann went on: 'Once the incident became known in Nauen, the inhabitants of Nauen took self-defensive measures against the girl Riske in concert with the district headquarters of the

NSDAP. During the afternoon of 12 November 1940 she was dressed in sacks and led through the streets of Nauen with her head shaved. She wore a placard bearing the inscription: "I am a depraved creature because I had relations with a Pole. I am therefore leaving this town in disgrace and going to jail." '

Later on, even the authorities found this treatment unacceptable. On 15 November 1943 the Chief of the Security Police embodied the following remarks in an SD Internal Affairs Report adorned with a 'Secret' imprint: 'Isolated voices may also be heard pointing out that it cannot benefit Germany's national resources if, for example, an otherwise blameless country girl in the full bloom of youth is sent to a penitentiary, there to be corrupted and led astray for life, because of one act of self-forgetfulness committed while men are in short supply. Rigorous punishment is often greeted with particularly scant comprehension in rural areas, where such problems are far more marked than in towns. Furthermore, areas with a predominantly Catholic population adopt an attitude all their own. Under clerical influence, people there are prone to regard Polish or French Catholics as co-religionists to whom they feel closer than to persons of their own race who do not profess the Catholic faith. This attitude also exerts a strong influence on the attitude of women and girls towards prisoners of war.'

Two years before this statement was made, Hitler had personally forbidden what Himmler approved in 1940: the terrorizing of German women and girls by their female neighbours before committal to a concentration camp. On 31 October 1941, Hitler directed Heydrich to revoke Himmler's edict. It must have gratified Heydrich to be able to correct his boss in front of all the ten Reich authorities to whom Himmler's circular had been addressed: Regional and District Gestapo Headquarters; Security Police and SD Commanders in occupied territories; the Chief of the Regular Police; Senior SS and Police Commanders; the departmental, divisional and desk chiefs of the Central State Security Bureau; Security Police and SD Subgroup Commanders in the occupied territories; Security Police and SD Inspectors; SS and Police Commanders; Regional and District Headquarters of the Criminal Police; and Regional Headquarters of the SD.

I have enumerated these ten different *kinds* of police agencies without actually knowing how many departments each of the ten comprised, merely to illustrate the terrible density of the police net which enshrouded Nazi Germany. This net excuses much of what the régime's underlings did beneath it and much of the treatment they meted out to foreigners and each other. There was not a citizen whom the system failed to debase into a dog, not a dog without a watchdog trotting along beside it ... On 31 October Heydrich transmitted Hitler's cancellation of Himmler's edict: 'Where proof of sexual intercourse with prisoners of war exists, dishonoured German women have often been subjected to public abuse. By the Führer's command, no such measures will in future be undertaken. NSDAP authorities have received corresponding instructions from the Party Chancellery.'

Party authorities too! To the great good fortune of the Allies, many hundreds of thousands of able-bodied German males – complete potential army corps – were engaged throughout the Reich and the occupied territories in spying on each other and their fellow-citizens and covering tens of thousands of tons of paper with communications like those quoted here. Heydrich concluded his circular: 'The directive issued by order of the Reichsführer-SS and Chief of the German Police, 7 May 1940, Para. 4, to the effect that public obloquy is not to be prevented by the police, is rescinded as of now. Paragraph 4 of the said directive is to be deleted. Kindly notify all personnel of this ruling.' The directive originally quoted was sent at the end of January 1940, so it seems that Himmler had reverted to the subject on 7 May...

Even at this stage, therefore, German civil servants must have accounted it work of national importance to write or dictate such letters or pass them to their subordinates for action. (Oswald Spengler called Hitler's party 'the organization of the unemployed by the work-shy'.) Similar missives continued to be written even at the end of October 1941, when the Russians, in alliance with an undefeated Britain and the harshest winter for a century, were preparing to destroy Hitler's forces outside Moscow ... The mental disease with which Hitler and his most notable germ-carriers had infected the nation may best be defined, perhaps, as a murderous refusal to face the facts. Mercifully, he and his henchmen were more direly afflicted with it than anyone else, for he *must* have known that a racial 'policy' stultifies any policy of conquest because it transforms the subjugated into rebels, not subjects.

But no such realization could prevail against that most salient of Hitler's impulses, the urge to hate. His intelligence and erstwhile flair for sensing what was acceptable to his neighbours in the field of foreign policy were powerless to restrain the promptings of his mass murderer's soul.

Hitler planned to exterminate the Slavs and annex Slav territories which were larger than his own domain. Even his most exalted advisers failed to perceive that this line of thought was itself frustrating all his efforts to win the war, though his generals at least should have known – and had the guts to tell him – that racial policy and a policy of conquest are mutually exclusive. Successful conquerors have always been at pains to marry the daughters of defeated nations to their soldiers; Hitler was at pains to round them up for 'destruction by labour'. The emperor whose subject Hitler became by birth in 1889 not only ruled Austria but contrived to be King of Hungary as well. He remained so for almost seventy years because, having brutally quelled the Hungarians with Russian help after their insurrection in 1848, he at once restored them to full and equal citizenship. He even pardoned rebel leaders who had been condemned to death *in absentia*. One of these – Gyula Andrassy – he appointed premier of Hungary and, later on, foreign minister of Austria–Hungary itself, although he had sentenced him to be hanged in effigy in 1851...

The fact that Hitler ignored this elementary knowledge of how best to pursue a policy of conquest – and there is no doubt that he possessed it – again poses the question of why emotional constraints should be so infinitely much more cogent and compelling than common sense or even self-interest. Like everything irrational, this problem defies solution. Hitler gave free rein, from the very first, to his hatred of all that was *fremdvölkisch* – alien, foreign, outlandish – perhaps because he felt, whether rightly or wrongly makes no difference, that he himself was no 'true' German, no pure 'Aryan'. And because this detestation of alien peoples, of Jews and Slavs, was the motor of his very existence, Hitler was *incapable* of suppressing it, even in the interests of his plan to absorb racially alien countries into the German Reich.

The man thinks

Expectations that Britain's *coup de grâce* is imminent, that it will result in universal peace and bring relief from the inconveniences of a second war-time winter, the blackout, fuel shortages and so on, have waned ... So far, only two infringements of the prohibitions on consorting with prisoners of war have come to light. At Plankenfels, an unmarried farmer named Klötzer offered a French prisoner of war a cigarette and the wife of Rödel the baker gave French prisoners of war some bilberry juice. Charges were laid with the director of public prosecutions at Bayreuth District Court.

Dr Niedermayer, senior administrative officer, rural district of Ebermannstadt. Monthly report dated 31 August/2 September 1940.

If I drop off now ... That's all I need – make a date with her and then oversleep! It's true, though, I really am dozing off ... I'm going to count in time to that damned great noisy alarm clock, every tick ... Still, why shouldn't I go to sleep? I'm bound to wake up – I lie awake every night between one and three, more or less ... I'd risk anything for the sake of a normal night's sleep at last. Anyway, there's no risk, not now. Trying it on in the cellar today – *that* was risky. Strange, all the phrases connected with hands. Getting someone in your clutches, laying hands on them ... That sounds bad, when it's really the most natural thing in the world. How ready she was for *my* hands! The way she leant against me – I could have counted three, slowly – before she tried to push me away. She'd have fallen if I hadn't hung on to her ...

And the way she couldn't conceal, and didn't even try to, how ... how natural she found it when my fingers slid into her ... Blood oranges, the last of the season, when you have to open them with your thumbs because you don't have a knife – *they* spurt out over your hands like that. If I keep on imagining what she must look like down there I won't need to go at all...

I'm more in danger of losing my mind if I don't have her – which I will – than of losing my life if a German catches me with her. Polish proverb: a good friend you meet at the right time, a beautiful woman at the wrong ... Be damned to that! Why work like a slave, why be young, if you spend years bottling up the most human side of yourself till you turn into a neurotic?

Just as long as the boss didn't take the key out before he went off for a good night's snore ... Funny, that duet of theirs. You can always tell if it's him or his wife, and they always seem to follow a – a sort of marital counterpoint: he never joins in till she's gently purring away ... Even if they were lying awake down there, which is highly unlikely, they'd still hear snoring coming from up here when I was – with her. Joseph snores enough for the two of us. How he can sleep as soundly as he does when he's known for the past fortnight his wife's sharing her bed with a German back home in Lublin ... I really feel sorry for the poor devil. Charming of his mother to write and tell him, I must say!

And yet, there's nothing I want more – nothing I feel a stronger *compulsion* to do – than to spend tonight treating a German the way a German's treating Joseph back home. It isn't the fault of us human beings if people commit adultery – it's the war, turning us into prisoners and keeping married couples apart. If there was *one* unmarried girl around, one I could get within arm's reach of, I wouldn't go to Pauline – yes I would, she's the one I'd go to. I couldn't leave her alone, even if her husband was waiting for me with his finger on the trigger. August and March, that's the difference between her and those schoolgirls in the old days. March can be a lovely month but August is high summer, and when I think how ... No, not that again – it's embarrassing enough with Joseph in the room, having to send myself to sleep, night after night, because I can't get Pauline out of my mind. That's why I couldn't stop myself going over there tonight even if I had to crawl through the machine-gun fire at Kowno again, when the Germans shot me in the shoulder. I reckon they only treated me decently because I was wounded when they captured me – wounded but not badly. If it had been serious they'd prob-ably have left me lying there and shot me, the way we often did with them ... Right, stop thinking about the war and start think-ing what to do if Melchior really has taken the key. Thinking? No point, better go and look – it'll stop me falling asleep. Still, it isn't very smart to go blundering downstairs twice when once will do – why *should* he have taken it when he never does? I could climb out of the window but I'd never get back. It'd be just my luck if he's ... I can't stand this any longer, I'm going to look! What about my shoes – should I take them with me when I go? Of course, I can't go sneaking across a dusty coal yard bare-foot, think of her sheets ... Who said anything about sheets? Don't be too damned sure you'll see the inside of those! There's Herbert and the baby to consider – she sleeps in the same little room, so we'll probably have to use the couch in the kitchen...

These doors creak like mad. Pity I can't oil the hinges, but what would I tell the Melchiors? I could only do it without them notic-ing, which would mean oiling my door but not the one to the yard. Listen! No, everything's all right, they're asleep – sound asleep, and the key's in the lock, thank God ... Why not go right away, now I'm safely downstairs? They say the first sleep's the soundest ... All the same, it's only half-past ten. I might get Pauline into trouble if I turned up and – who knows? – that pretty, sharp-eyed book-keeper friend of hers might still be around. Stupid of me not to have asked Pauline how long she's been known to stay. After all, she's another of these grass widows with time on her hands at night, and considering how often she comes round late she could still be there. I'm a fool not to have told the Melchiors, straight out, how often I feel like sitting in the yard at night, or even the paddock, because I lie awake for hours without being able to read because the light disturbs Joseph. I'll have to bring it up tomorrow – tell them I'd sooner stroll round the yard and the paddock these warm nights than lie awake upstairs. They could hardly refuse, even if regulations do say prisoners of war have to be kept indoors at night. Kept ... The Germans usually reserve that word for their livestock – the Melchiors 'keep' two horses and a brace of prisoners! Well, things will be different some day ... Where are they taking them, I wonder, all those people they're carting off back home? All the professors and high school teachers to begin with, and now the Jews ... Six weeks, that's all the time they took to smash the one great ally we've always had – six weeks to smash France like a fake chandelier ... But Britain will carry on. I could skin my knuckles on every prisoner who repeats that lousy joke about the British fighting to the last Pole. They've never lost a war yet, the British – that's a fact, though whether their allies have always won as well I wouldn't know...

It certainly was a blow when they guaranteed our country and then didn't fire a single shot into Hitler's backside while he was finishing us off in three weeks. Still, who made the British give us a guarantee? Nobody, but they gave it just the same. Besides, what have *we* done for the British, who declared war on Hitler just because he attacked *us*, not them? All right, back to bed, get some sleep in first. 'What? It's only me, Joseph, who do you think it is? I've been outside, go back to sleep. Eh? Just before eleven, that's all. I haven't been to sleep yet. Goodnight.'

Two or three hours' proper sleep now, otherwise I'll stagger around and bump into something and make an ass of myself. Don't worry, I'm bound to wake up at my usual time, around two ... But wouldn't it be better if I slept through – if I missed my chance and ran no risks? No, it wouldn't. I'd sooner get myself shot than sent to a madhouse. Anything, rather than go on vegetating without a woman – without *that* woman. Why take yourself so seriously? Other men don't go crazy because they can't have a woman – no, but they're in camps, and it's easier to do without women in a camp. For one thing you never see any, for another you're always so hungry all you ever hanker after is food, and for another you never speak to one, smell her, touch her, get the feeling she likes you ... Silly of me to have woken Joseph – no, I didn't, he woke up of his own accord. Anyway, he'd never breathe a word if he spotted what was going on. Would the Melchiors keep quiet too? I mustn't let them catch me, that's all. And now I'm going to sleep so I'm really awake when dawn comes – really awake and, let's hope, a normal human being again. I want to be able to sit on the box and drive the cart without the sight of those firm, glossy haunches bobbing up and down in front of me, without Pauline's sun-tanned skin, her glorious bare neck, her strong, smooth, rounded arms, her swelling calves and the curve of her bottom when her skirt goes taut as she bends down to take some vegetables off the lower shelf and put them on the counter – without my starved and per-verted senses rolling all those mental pictures into one. Sodomites ... That's what this war is making out of people like us – normal as the next man, but our pricks quiver like compass needles when we rub down a horse and feel its warmth beneath our hands, as if we were holding the cheeks of a girl-friend's bottom ... It's twice as exciting for me, of course, because I've never done that. The only girl who ever let me undress her was Esther. Twice I had her before I was drafted – even then under protest and not properly – and she was so unutterably coy and Catholic she'd sooner have submitted to murder than do it with the light on or let me *see* her bottom, far less hold it, would Esther, though I whimpered in vain for permission...

44

Any modern story-teller should be strong-minded enough – I myself am anything but – to flout a fashion which Emil Preetorius, the painter, stage designer and collector of orientalia, once derided as follows: 'Modern works of art stand in signal need of comment. One sometimes feels that artists produce their comment first and then a work to go with it ... especially in Germany. The Germans have a peculiar relationship to seeing. They do not feel competent to judge what they see until they know something about it. This is mistaken.' Preetorius thought it equally mistaken – he was eighty years old and rich in experience when he said so – for artistic media to become objects of representation because aesthetes disseminate the fad that art no longer has content. His Spanish friend Ortega y Gasset entitled a whole collection of essays *La deshumanización del arte*. Once man is reintroduced into art, however, the question of content becomes superfluous because there is no human being devoid of a fate worth recording. Or, to put it more gingerly, since we don't know what fate is: everyone comes equipped with a face worth painting or a story worth telling. We should hold fast to that knowledge and defend it ...

But the telling of Pauline's and Stasiek's story is one thing. Another more immediate task is the process of recording my investigation of their story, because there is little resemblance between the people who now discuss this tragedy of almost forty years ago and those who enacted the story and inflicted death on its protagonist. Anyone who cares to devote a little attention to this endeavour to exhume a long-buried tale will learn a great deal about the difficulties posed by believing stories in the first place and telling them in the second!

To begin with, I made a discovery which I not only found surprising – and I doubt if I'm unique in this – but would have disputed before it was brought home to me: that it is very much easier to tell a story when its human mouthpieces are dead than when they are still alive. This seems odd, and the reasons for it are well worth exploring in themselves. What I actually found was that most people are far more readily reduced to silence than induced to talk by someone who questions them with a view to recording incidents which they witnessed, provoked or helped to bring about. It is, in fact, far easier to employ our imagination in constructing a person whom we have never seen than to portray one whose living presence has just impinged on our eyes and ears. If anyone doubts this, let him try it for himself.

I was aware, for instance, that the ex-mayor and ex-district director of the local Nazis, Josef Zinngruber, now eighty, had been given five years for denunciation by a French court, though he did not serve them all. Had he been unable to present me with such an eloquent account of how the perjurious statements of three female villagers and a local police sergeant were all that had put him behind bars, I could easily – and facilely – have produced a straightforward woodcut of the man. After sitting at Zinngruber's table with him and his invalid wife, however, and after looking into his great big glacier-blue eyes, which shine with redoubled sincerity when he lies point-blank, I found it infinitely hard to discover just how he behaved and what action he took when, thirty-six years earlier, someone reported to him that Pauline Krop the greengrocer was sleeping with the Polish prisoner of war who worked for Melchior the coal merchant...

There is no doubt that stories buried deep in the past are easier to tell because less is known about them. 'Reality,' sighed Heinrich Mann, 'is a prop and a burden!'

What he really meant was the present, for the present alone is reality; of historical reality we know next to nothing. Anyone inclined to doubt this should try and explain to his children, let alone his grandchildren, the *atmosphere* in which he fought for or against someone, somewhere, thirty years ago. Alternatively, let him read ten pages from *The Charterhouse of Parma*, a novel set in the present-day world of its author. He will then concede that no one now, a century and a half after the events it describes, would be capable – discounting the events themselves, which are secondary – of reproducing a single social detail, far less a dialogue between two prominent contemporaries who have been personally and politically involved for years, or of 'reconstructing' a single one of the atmospheric influences prevailing at the time. In view of this impossibility, one is bound to contend that the horrors of history are surpassed in horror only by the so-called historical novel...

Nobody can convey the atmosphere of a vanished age, which is more illustrative of that age and possesses more intrinsic truth than the facts. Atmosphere *alone*, which can never be transmitted, is what differentiates the largely similar facts about various human epochs. Adultery with a prisoner of war, for example, has been an established fact at other times and in other climes. It was not punishable during the first of the world wars to date, and although facts – that is to say, the laws of Hitler's Germany – were later to make it a capital offence, only the atmosphere of the police state can account for its lunatic effect on an entire village and the neighbouring municipality. Only that could have prompted hitherto inoffensive neighbours – a forester, a woodman and a smallholder – to improvise a gallows for the 'alien' who had slept with a woman of their race.

Today these men have no comprehension of what they did; then, they found it normal. Atmosphere is probably just the insanity of a period as Nietzsche understood it – a realization indispensable to the would-be chronicler of any period, not only of Hitler's twelve years and the Inquisition, but of comparatively wholesome and innocuous decades like that which succeeded the Franco-Prussian War: the realization that insanity, though very rare in individuals, is *habitual* to nations and ages.

Given that a period's atmospheric influences are wholly imperceptible to the third generation, however vital their effect on every member of the first, and given that a host of facts become permanently obliterated, tales of the present would be truer – *if* we could tell them.

But that is just what we can't do. Even Melville had to make the following admission in the last, and perhaps the greatest, of his novellas: 'The symmetry of form attainable in pure fiction can not be so readily achieved in a narration essentially having less to do with fable than with fact. Truth uncompromisingly told' – and here, like Heinrich Mann, he means the reality of the present – 'will always have its ragged edges; hence the conclusion of such a narration is apt to be less finished than an architectural finial ...'

And because no writer, not even Melville himself, can bear such a burden of reality, he pronounces it ballast merely to justify the fact that he has jettisoned it – that he has been *compelled* to do so by the requirements of form! In that case, what can be said to remain of events that is any more precise or palpable than the reflection of a ship in the swirling water over which it passes?

Shouldn't we therefore nurse the suspicion that a story becomes more spurious the more readable and vivid it is? How else can vividness be achieved than by limiting the action to our own range of vision? Drawing implies omission ... Perhaps, but it irks one when this hackneyed art historian's dictum is constantly trotted out as if omission were a mark of quality rather than a product of necessity. Isn't it *regrettable* that we can draw only by leaving things out? If anyone thinks otherwise, let him accompany me when I call on my sources of information, in other words, the ex-abettors of Hitler's enforcers. Let him listen to their protestations of gratitude as soon as I promise – as promise I must or my story would never be written – to *leave out* this or that aspect of what they tell me and, more especially, to omit their names from this account ... Omission an art? Perhaps, but it is nonetheless a breach of faith and an act of falsification.

So it remains doubtful whether the story of this crime can be told at all, given that nearly all its witnesses and participants are still alive. Most of them are liars, of course. I estimate that half of all they say merits credence, but who is to tell me which half? They speak with consummate conviction, these deliberate liars, because they have been retailing their version since the end of the Hitler era. The practised lie not only attains perfection, it poses as the truth and imposes itself on those who tell it. The worst of them now believe every word they utter. Their accounts are triumphs of will-power over memory: I did it, said their memory; I can't have done it, said their self-esteem; you shouldn't have done it, said the laws that invalidated Hitler's laws after his death. And so, memory abandoned the struggle ...

I do not, of course, mean that this story would emerge without detriment to the truth if it remained untold till everyone involved was dead. It would very probably not come out at all – or, if it did, its narrative cohesion and literary density could only improve to the extent that it strayed from the truth. This is a distressing fact and grudgingly conceded. When Bismarck was serving as a diplomat in St Petersburg, he once belittled a rival by broadcasting a tall story which that gentleman had allegedly recounted of his prowess at hunting. The British ambassador, who had heard it before, retorted drily, 'The story has improved!'

I have no idea how to guard against this danger.

It is remarkable enough that the story should come out at all, having been suppressed for thirty-six years by all concerned – and I mean all. Five years ago, 'Pauline' destroyed every relevant document issued by Gestapo headquarters at Lörrach and the authorities at Ravensbrück concentration camp, where she did two-and-a-half years' forced labour with her hair shorn. Her 'reason': the conversion of a lumber-room into a bedroom left no room for the papers – no room for one little folder, even though she owns a small terraced house! Glad as she now is that I offered to get her a photo of her lover – her immediate reaction was to decline – she was almost as perturbed when I first appeared as those who had helped to murder him ... I never traced *her* tormentors, the people who guarded her during her term of forced labour at Ravensbrück. Pauline herself is quite uninterested in them and free from any spirit of revenge. She even says, 'We had to build roads when it was thirty-five degrees below, but I wasn't beaten as often as most of the others.' She cannot understand why she was so fortunate in her misfortune ... Nor, in point of fact, does she speak of herself when she discusses the tragedy – though her silences outweigh her words – so much as of the Pole whom she has 'on my conscience'. Her eyes fill with tears when she speaks of him.

No, nobody wants to know the truth with the possible exception of the Pole's parents – if they are still alive. I have never met them, but they used to run a service station at Lodz before the war.

As for the regional authorities, they are less interested than anyone in apprehending those who murdered Stasiek Zasada and countless other similar 'offenders' by amateurishly hanging them – that is to say, strangling them. Zasada's murderers still live and draw their pensions in Baden-Württemberg, the West German *Land* whose ex-premier, Dr Hans Karl Filbinger, was so fearsome an upholder of the law that, even while imprisoned by the British after Hitler's death, he continued to hound German sailors with the Nazi penal code.

The woman thinks

Frau D. of Bramberg, an innkeeper's wife, had illicit relations with a French prisoner of war ... When summoned to the Party's district headquarters, D. was seized by a number of female compatriots who shaved her head, hung a placard inscribed 'I have sullied the honour of German womanhood' round her neck, and led her some distance through the town. The police then intervened and took D. into custody, where she still is. News of this incident spread through the district like wildfire. Where public opinion is concerned, it may be stated that a sizeable section of the population approves of such measures and that many people went so far as to call for corporal punishment as well. The action has, on the other hand, been condemned by most of the womenfolk, Party members included. They did not reveal their true feelings at once, but declared – though they went white in the face when they saw the woman's shaven head – that it served her right. Discussing the matter later among themselves, however, they expressed disapproval of the action. A few individuals also questioned whether similar measures would be taken against men who had had relations with Frenchwomen in France. The said action has met with particular disapproval among religious-minded sections of the population, notably Catholics. One recorded comment was: 'All we need is thumbscrews and torture-chambers and we'll really be back in the Middle Ages.'

Report dated 14 March 1941, SD Outstation Ebern, Gau Mainfranken.

The wind against me, that's all I need. It's going to rain, too, and cycling one-handed so my skirt doesn't flap round my ears would be tiring enough even if I'd slept between two and four instead of...

It's a comfort, though, cycling. Sitting at home all through the lunch hour I'd feel scared the way I was this morning, before the first customer looked at me just the same as usual – the same as I looked at her, let's hope. Till she turned up I honestly had a hunch they'd all notice... You can tell with a woman – at least, that's what men say, but maybe it's their vanity, pretending they can tell when we've done it for the first time in ages ... Well, maybe they *can* tell when we're happy, but who'd be happy with a bellyful of butterflies like me? I don't even know if he got back to his room without being spotted – he sleeps right on top of the Melchiors' bedroom!

He sneaked over far too late, which was why he was so late leaving – almost light, it was. Still, if anyone suspected anything they'd have hawked it round the village bright and early. They all like digging the dirt, and you can bet somebody would have come out with a personal remark in the shop ... There's another truck coming, better hold my skirt down or the soldiers'll whistle like last time ... Well, at least it shows they don't think I'm pushing thirty-six. Everyone takes me for a lot younger, except my husband, who has to play Tarzan with a half-naked Dutch girl in a two-piece swimsuit – yes, and even sends me a couple of snaps of the little tramp!

It always riled me, but I'm only telling myself that now because I'm scratching around for an excuse for last night. He's a good sort, Günther, and you can't expect them all to be saints when they're stationed abroad somewhere with nothing to do but hang around and make eyes at those dolled-up city girls. It may be more dangerous, granted, but I'd sooner he had a girl he can take to the beach than use the air force brothel, like most of them do. Who knows, maybe he does that too!

All right, stop running him down just because you've got a bad conscience. Never a week without a big fat parcel, though God knows where he gets the money – he surely can't afford all those lovely things he sends us, me and the children, not on his lousy pay, and last time he came he put down four months' rent on the shop and upped his life insurance. He's a decent man, and it's downright mean of me to treat him this way. I shouldn't have done it the first time, I know, but it won't be the last. Awful of me, pretending to nip off to the dentist, which I don't need to, instead of the chemist's ... Do other women ever have to buy those things? The shopgirls will snigger at me. Let's hope the boss serves me himself – no, he'll be in the army by now but his wife'll understand if I tell her I want some just in case: 'If my husband comes home on leave without any, that'll be that – and two children are quite enough these days...' Rubbish! Don't say anything, just: 'Heil Hitler, I want some shaving-cream and a packet of contraceptives.'

I've got the ration coupon for the shaving-cream.

Anyway, they'll think my husband's home on leave – or will they? A man who comes home on leave doesn't expect his wife to buy those things, he goes and gets them himself ... Give the subject a rest, it only makes you nervous! Just make sure there's no one from Lörrach in the shop who knows you, that's all. Stani isn't allowed inside a shop ... Even if he did go it would have to be in Brombach, and then the whole village would wonder who he needed them for.

Would they think it was me? Frau Melchior's husband's at home and there isn't another woman in the house, not counting Frau König, and she's the head of the Women's League. I'm still pretty easy on the eye and I'm often alone with him in the evenings – and the children are too young to get in the way. Oh yes, *I'm* the one they'd suspect if Stani bought the confounded things himself – impossible! Unless they'd think I was too smart to risk it after what happened to poor Rosi Lindner ... Too smart? That's a laugh! What more of a warning do I need? She must have been desperate, doing that to herself and the children. She sometimes lets rooms, doesn't she – didn't she, I mean? Why couldn't she have pretended it happened with a soldier who was passing through? Maybe it was somebody else who went and told the Party – a relation of her husband's or the barmaid. What am I thinking of! That woman was far too proud to tell a pack of lies ... But can a person be so proud she'd sooner hang herself than answer a few questions? Hardly ... There must have been more to it – something nobody knows about.

I'm not worried about Elsbeth. She didn't suspect a thing when I asked her to mind the shop this afternoon, till I got back from the dentist ... She's a friend of mine, but what does that signify? She'd go peeking at the sheets like a shot if she had the faintest idea! Of course she would, but as for giving me away, *that* she'd never do ... She wouldn't in any case, but apart from that, I pay her quite enough for the spot of book-keeping she does. She usually asks for something off the shelf instead of cash, but that's up to her. She's never made any cracks about Stani giving me a hand in the evenings, carting the empty crates away and carrying in the stuff from outside. All she ever said, once, was, 'He hangs around here because we're both young and he has to spend the whole night sharing an attic with the Pole across the way. Another thing: he comes here because he's homesick for his mother. You remind him of her – he's told me so a couple of times.'

Let's hope it helps a bit, Stani saying that about me and his mother, because who'd do it with his mother! Maybe I didn't like hearing it – maybe it stung me, and that's why it knocked me sideways when I first found out he didn't look at me the way a son does. Myself, I've never thought of him as anything but a man – no son could seem so ... so strong! I can't explain what I mean. It's that sort of ... heaviness without being fat, that rugged look, which makes him so – so virile, so ... well, like a young bull! Now it's happened I can be honest with myself – admit how I've always gone out of my way to be near him, how my heart used to thump at the sight of him. And yesterday in the cellar, when he touched me for the first time, I didn't play coy for a moment or even pretend to fight him off. That's because I always felt so ... so weak at the knees whenever he came near me. Just the nearness of him was like a furnace, the way it feels when you're working at the top of a hay-loft in August, right under the tiles. It was risky from the start, which didn't help.

They always say stolen apples taste sweeter. Like that time at home on the farm, when I suddenly got scared of the young bull while I was milking – the one Father bought when they called up the first batch of lads and sent them marching into Austria – no, the Rhineland, 'thirty-six it was. God, I'm getting old! He didn't scare me inside the stable, being chained up, and they penned him in by himself when the cows were out, but I always had a feeling the fence wouldn't hold. I was the only one that did. It gave me the creeps whenever I had to pass him in the meadow, and I said so often enough, but Father told me nonsense. Then it happened, just the way I'd said – he broke out, and the trouble they had before they cornered him in the wood!

What's really surprising about Stani, considering how tough and strong he is and the way he hauls sacks of coal around with those great big paws of his and has to wash them all the time with pumice and usually just with cold water or that fat-free war-time soap, which is enough to skin your fingers, is how gentle he is with his hands. They're just as gentle and affectionate as he is, by nature. And how grateful he was, as if I'd given him a present! Which I have, I suppose, when you look at it from his angle, being cooped up like that. He says he'd have lost his self-respect, sneaking glances at me the whole time and not being able to do more than undress me with his eyes – he says the shame of it was driving him insane ... And then I had to tell him, just for fear of getting pregnant, that I'd only be a disappointment to him ... but I wasn't, and I promised him I'd take it on myself, this trip to the chemist's, even though it's worse than going to the dentist to have my gum lanced that time ... Stop telling yourself that or you'll start gibbering when you come to ask for the bloody things ...

Except that it's a mistake, him coming to the house, it's so shut in. If anyone turned suspicious and checked, where would he go? There's no way out, least of all the windows – they face the street ... The forest – I could meet him in the forest when he's there by himself, cutting wood! Firewood, because he's never alone when he's hauling timber. But how could I get there without being spotted? At four in the morning, when he starts out – yes,

I could spend an hour with him then, say between five and six, but I'd never get back without someone noticing, and I'd *have* to be back to see to the children and open the shop. Besides, Stani hardly ever knows for sure whether somebody from Melchior's won't be with him or following on later – yes he does, lots of times . . . If I went to my parents' on a Saturday and left the children there and caught the first train back on Monday and got out the stop before and met him somewhere in the woods – he'd be there by six . . . But it'd be just as dangerous as in the house, however we managed it, because somebody would be bound to see me on the way home. Anyway, it isn't so much being scared at home that attracts me to the idea of making love with him in the open – it's wanting it to happen, if it's got to happen, where there's nothing to remind me of Günther and the children. That's what makes me feel so guilty. In the woods I could tell myself I was no more at home than Günther and just as free to do what *he* does when he's away . . . Meeting in the woods at night is out, though. They can fire without warning, being so near the frontier – they'd shoot Stani like a fox with the rabies. Day-time would be safest, of course. Safest for *him*, but how could *I* get away then? Only like now – only if I told Elsbeth I was going to the dentist, but I'd really have to go there then. Somebody in the shop might ask a question, something important, a supplier or somebody from the Party, and Elsbeth could call the dentist and ask to speak to me . . . No, I'd really have to go there on a day like that. Then, while I was cycling along – there are woods either side of the road, after all – I could nip off into the trees with him for half an hour and make love . . . How it *relieved* him – there's no other word for it, even though I only helped him with my hands the first time in case he gave me a child! And all those words he found to describe me – nobody's ever spoken to me like that before. The only awful thing was what he said after the second time: if only he could thank me properly he wouldn't be so afraid of having to pay the price, because no prisoner could expect the sort of happiness I'd given him in the middle of a war, not without paying for it. That's what he said, and it's catching, his fear. You can't pin the feeling down, which is just what makes

'Like unto Zeus in guile,' says Homer of red-haired Odysseus.

Though red-haired too, Churchill hadn't since his salad-days possessed much in the way of hair above the 'vast brow' described by his personal physician, Lord Moran, who wrote: 'At the summit of his forehead two wisps of hair went their several ways, and gave an impression that he had more hair than was actually the case.' Churchill became the Odysseus of the year 1940 because, during the six months that followed the British escape from Dunkirk, he outsmarted 'that man over there', as he derisively referred to Hitler, on three separate occasions.

The first of these stratagems, all of which helped to decide the outcome of the war, robbed the Germans of any chance – if chance there was – of landing in the British Isles. The second lost them the Battle of Britain by luring Göring's aircraft away from RAF fighter stations and diverting them to London. The third fomented a popular insurrection in Belgrade, thereby upsetting Hitler's timetable for the invasion of Russia and ensuring that his tanks ground to a halt before Moscow, defeated by slush and snow, while countless German soldiers froze to death ...

Churchill only succeeded in this third *ruse de guerre*, as in the second, because of something that had happened before the outbreak of war. Working on Britain's behalf (and, of course, their own), a handful of Poles discovered and purloined a specimen of the cipher machine which Hitler blithely used throughout his six-year war. Thanks to this brilliant Polish feat, every order he sent his armies was translated into a code which held no secrets for the British from autumn 1940 onwards.

Thus the most triumphant of all Poland's twentieth-century sagas merits a place in this account of the sad end of an unknown Pole – not for his nationality's sake alone, but because it would be too monotonous and dispiriting for any narrative to confine itself to portraying the trio whose crimes snuffed out his life, among others, with a brutality sufficient to deter one from the study of history in general. No story-teller should quit the stage like the mad dictator from Braunau, who left nothing behind him, anywhere, but scorched earth ...

We are entitled to question the purpose of human existence

when human beings like Hitler, Göring and Goebbels have the power to transform a continent into a charnel-house and millions of their fellow creatures into pitiful zombies, but we must never leave it at that. Although the sun that rises above a battlefield can do nothing for the dead, it cheers the living to see how a night of tyranny may be withstood by the resolution, cunning, intelligence and tenacity of those who were so much weaker, if not wellnigh defenceless, when darkness fell. But for the knowledge that Hitler and his cronies were ultimately confronted by those who (like Churchill) had warned the world against them for a decade, and that they were lured into a position where they could be vanquished by the concerted efforts of millions upon nameless millions, any historian would be limited to the sad and soul-destroying functions of an obituarist. All that makes wartime stories tolerable is that, even in the twentieth century, their retelling can be a hymn to heroism as well as a dirge.

It is, however, characteristic of songs, even folk- or *national* songs, to tell of individuals, for individuals alone are visible to the eye and each of us claims the human right to be regarded as one. Politicians dislike this: they prefer to deal with national *assemblies*, which are easier to control and delude than lone individuals. Writing in the first of the two world wars, the Viennese physician Arthur Schnitzler referred to 'the old politician's knack of ignoring the individual and counting in masses, as opposed to the artist, who resolves the mass into individuals'. Bourgeois and Marxist scholars are at one in happily disseminating the notion that an individual is effective, at best, as the catalyst of a collective will: those who propel him also determine his line of advance! Ernst Robert Curtius wrote: 'It is forgotten that a man never becomes socially effective in consequence of his personal attributes, but because of the social energy which the mass reposes in him. His personal talents are merely the basis on which social dynamism condenses within him.' It is of course true that it was the British *Labour* Party which, when Hitler's tanks were racing for Paris, enforced Churchill's premiership on the King and on the Conservatives who had kept him out of office for a decade. He was the only Conservative with whom the

Socialists declared their readiness to work in harness, but why did they settle on *that* true-blue Tory? 'His personal talents,' says Curtius, almost contemptuously, were 'merely the basis ...' Perhaps, but that was just what made him so irreplaceable. Labour might otherwise have endorsed the royal and Conservative choice of Lord Halifax to be the nation's Noah (Noah means 'Man of Peace') during the cataclysm of 1940. Marxist historians contend that the helmsman's person did not decide the issue, and that it was social 'preconditions' which stationed him on the bridge. This is naturally true to the extent that many millions of voters were as much responsible as Churchill himself for ensuring that he, and no one else, took the helm and ruled the destinies of countless people in his sphere of command – but *how* he wielded the helm was as much dependent on his character and intelligence as on circumstances. Anyone who argues that individuals are interchangeable should ask himself, for example, whether Stalin's show trials would have taken place had Lenin survived ...

It is an instructive and revealing fact that people whose yea or nay can be proved to have unleashed wars or prevented them take special pains – if they have any conscience at all – to stress the insignificance of their role. In language almost identical with the phrases he so often used to allay his conscience in private and public, Bismarck told the Reichstag: 'Although my influence on the events that have sustained me is considerably overrated, no one, I feel sure, will accuse me of making history. That I could never do, gentlemen, even in association with you. We cannot make history, only wait for it to come to pass.'

A grotesque excuse, but Bismarck trailed his conscience like a ball and chain. He forbade the General Staff even to discuss a war against Russia while he was in office on the classic grounds that, even in the unlikely event of total success, the Germans would always have such a war ahead of them, never behind them. He also alluded to the maimed war veterans who would hobble down Wilhelmstrasse and point at his window, cursing him for being the author of their misfortunes ...

He was right, too. On 3 March 1940, nine days before Hitler dispatched troops to Norway by sea and five weeks before he overran France, Churchill matter-of-factly stated that an avalanche of steel and fire might descend on neutral Scandinavia at any moment, and that the decision rested with a single man whom the deluded German people worshipped, to their undying shame, like a deity.

This fact – and it was one – becomes no more tolerable if we also accept the truth of Hegel's often-quoted platitude: 'Governments are the sails and the people the wind.' Wind and sails notwithstanding, we must remember that a ship's course is determined by very few men, if not one man alone. In this case the German helmsman was opposed by at least one Briton who unswervingly, and to the benefit of civilization, held his vessel on course – a *warlike* course. Although Churchill's cabinet contained a minority who thought it expedient at least to parley with Hitler after the British Expeditionary Force had fled the beaches of Dunkirk, Churchill never seriously entertained this idea for a moment. Instead, he merely *simulated* a readiness to talk and forged it into a terrible weapon. A year later, when British and American generals were privately betting on whether Russia would hold out against Hitler for eight weeks or three months, he dismissed their predictions as idle chatter. It was no accident that victory went, not to Hitler the burner of books and Jews, but to an intellectual who could console the French in their darkest hour, on 21 October 1940, with the sarcastic announcement: 'We are waiting for the long-promised invasion. So are the fishes.' His intimate knowledge of history enabled him to console them further: 'Remember how Napoleon said before one of his battles: "These same Prussians who are so boastful today were three to one at Jena and six to one at Montmirail."' Nor was it an accident that Churchill, the most thoroughgoing anti-Communist in Britain, should have been the first and only British politician – the first and only because of his genius – to grasp the truth of what had happened in Poland. On 1 October 1939, just after the Red Army had occupied eastern Poland by arrangement with Hitler, he publicly assured the Kremlin how well he understood the reasons for this step. Guided by the expectation that he would be able to embrace Stalin as an ally when Hitler attacked him too, he told Parliament: 'Russia has pursued a cold policy of self-interest. We could have wished that the Russian armies should be standing on their present line as the friends and allies of Poland instead of as invaders. But that the Russian armies should stand on this line was clearly necessary for the safety of Russia against the Nazi menace. At any rate, the line is there, and an Eastern Front has been created ... It cannot be in accordance with the interest or safety of Russia that Germany should plant itself upon the shores of the Black Sea, or that it should overrun the Balkan States and subjugate the Slavonic peoples of South-Eastern Europe.'

Churchill was alone in referring publicly to this threat – after all, Stalin had a non-aggression pact with Hitler. Two years later, when Hitler had torn it up like almost every other treaty he ever made, Churchill made a radio broadcast on the day Russia was invaded. He had, he said, warned Stalin, and he hoped that his warnings had not gone unheeded. 'No one has been a more consistent opponent of Communism than I have for the last twenty-five years. I will unsay no word that I have spoken about it. But all this fades away before the spectacle which is now unfolding ... I see the Russian soldiers standing on the threshold of their native land, guarding the fields which their fathers have tilled from time immemorial. I see them guarding their homes where mothers and wives pray – ah, yes, for there are times when all pray – for the safety of their loved ones, the return of the bread-winner, of their champion, of their protector. I see the ten thousand villages of Russia where the means of existence is wrung so hardly from the soil, but where there are still primordial human joys, where maidens laugh and children play. I see advancing upon all this in hideous onslaught the German war machine, with its clanking, heel-clicking, dandified Prussian officers, its crafty agents fresh from the cowing and tying down of a dozen countries. I see also the dull, drilled, docile, brutish masses of the Hun soldiery plodding on like a swarm of crawling locusts ... Behind all this glare, behind all this storm, I see that small group of villainous men who plan, organize, and launch this cataract of horrors ... I have to declare the decision of His

Majesty's Government ... but can you doubt what our policy will be? We have but one aim and one single, irrevocable purpose. We are resolved to destroy Hitler and every vestige of the Nazi régime. From this nothing will turn us – nothing. We will never parley, we will never negotiate with Hitler or any of his gang. We shall fight him by land, we shall fight him by sea, we shall fight him in the air, until, with God's help, we have rid the earth of his shadow ... Any man or state who fights against Nazidom will have our aid. Any man or state who marches with Hitler is our foe.'

Only a cynic would call such a man 'interchangeable' or contend that he owed his position to chance. The individual who presided in Downing Street at this fateful hour was also one of the very few historians to acknowledge that Russia had saved France in 1914 by sacrificing two armies at Tannenberg, and that the West had never repaid its debt ...

Churchill played three tricks on Hitler within the space of six short months, each of them as subtle as the notion of whetting the Trojans' appetite for booty by leaving a wooden horse outside their city gates. Then sixty-six years old, Churchill was at the zenith of his 'public' career as a journalist, author and politician, which had already spanned four-and-a-half decades and ended when he was ninety. His last recorded words – 'It's all so boring' – were quite as characteristic of him as the following remark, made in middle age, which his countless political detractors have always cited as evidence of a thirst for aggression in this warrior turned national redeemer: 'I like it when things happen, and when they don't happen I make sure they do.' But Churchill's warlike instincts had no need of 'proof' because he never disguised them, even in peace-time, which he dismissed with pained contempt as 'the bland skies of peace and platitudes'. 'And then came the bloody peace,' he observed to his doctor as a very old man, referring to 1918.

When, at the age of seventy-two, he decided to lead the Opposition a year after the end of the Second World War, he announced the fact to his doctor as follows: 'A short time ago I was ready to retire and die gracefully. Now I'm going to stay and have them [the Socialists] out. I'll tear their bleeding entrails out of them. I'm in pretty fine fettle.' Eight years later, after surviving no less than three strokes, he was back in office. Writing of the eighty-year-old prime minister after a debate in the Lower House, his doctor commented: 'Even now, at the end of his life, when the nation, regardless of party, insists on looking to him as the sagacious world statesman ... his tastes lie in the rough and tumble of the House of Commons. He loves a fight ... enjoying every minute of the back-chat. In short, he is still at heart the red-haired urchin, cocking a snook at anybody who gets in his way.'

The first of the war-winning ruses devised by Churchill during the six months when Britain plumbed the depths of military weakness – and scaled the heights of moral strength – did not spill a drop of British blood. After France was occupied and the British Expeditionary Force had unpredictably escaped from the Continent, it misled Hitler and his equally purblind generals into believing that the British were ripe for surrender – that they would merely save face by allowing a decent interval of a few weeks to elapse between their flight from the beaches of Dunkirk and the opening of peace talks. Churchill systematically fed Hitler with this rumour – ostensibly Britain's most closely guarded state secret – via his embassies in neutral countries such as the USA, Sweden, Spain and Switzerland. Hitler swallowed it whole. He *wanted* to believe it because his plans had never allowed for an invasion of Britain – because the inferiority of the small German navy, which had been badly mauled during the invasion of Norway in April, made any such venture seem too hazardous.

And so the island that had never for an instant meant to sue for peace obtained precisely what it needed more urgently than bread: time to gird itself against a Nazi invasion.

The 224,585 men of the British Expeditionary Force who embarked on their flight to England from Dunkirk early in June 1940 brought only 100,000 allies home with them – Frenchmen, Poles, Belgians, Dutch – and no equipment at all. Britain owned the world's most powerful navy, but it could not do battle in the Channel until Hitler's air force had been neutralized, and that, too, was the most powerful in the world. The British army was almost defenceless. Most of the fighters whose task it would have been to shoot down German transport planes during an invasion had themselves been destroyed during the French campaign, either in the air or on the ground. Only three anti-tank guns were strung out along nearly five miles of coastline at Dover, and each of them had a mere six rounds of ammunition.

Britain had never been weaker in the whole of her long history. Just how Churchill stalled Hitler until this moment of weakness had passed was revealed in 1967, two years after Churchill's death, by Laurence Thompson's succinctly entitled book *1940*. Weizsäcker's and Goebbel's still unpublished diaries for the year 1940 bear witness to what Thompson himself did not know, even in 1967: that Hitler snapped avidly at Churchill's doctored bait. There were two reasons why the Austrian ex-corporal never had a moment's misgiving. In the first place, like anyone whom no one dares to contradict, he had a perfectly developed capacity for believing what he *wanted* to believe; in the second, Churchill's ruse was not only brilliant in its simplicity but, having no material foundation, absolutely undetectable.

Hitler said more than once that, apart from the occupation of the Rhineland, the invasion of Norway was the operation he had feared most. This was because, like almost every commander of large land forces, he found naval warfare alien. Even at the end of April 1940 he told Goebbels that the severe losses sustained by his battle fleet in Norwegian waters could be written off because the navy had no further tasks of importance to perform in the present war. Ergo, he never counted on having to land in Britain. The swift defeat of France surprised him as much as it did the rest of the world. On reaching the Channel coast in June he 'discovered' that he did not even possess any blueprints for landing craft, so all his hopes now rested on the delusion that Britain would knuckle under without a fight – an astonishing miscalculation. Just how much at a loss he was to find work for his millions of 'unemployed' soldiers can be gauged from his irrational decision of 31 July 1940 to march on Moscow, a plan conceived less in hubris than from fear of his inability to deal with Britain, too, by any other means.

But he had already spent eight irrevocable weeks in idleness since the start of the British evacuation from France on 2 June, thanks to the false reports with which Churchill plied him through diplomatic channels. The first of these came on 7 June, when the Under-Secretary of State for Foreign Affairs, R. A. Butler, told Ambassador Prytz of Sweden that Downing Street's attitude would be governed by 'common sense and not bravado'. Some days later, the possibility of peace talks was broached by a representative of the British consul-general in Geneva to one of his German opposite numbers. In Madrid, the British ambassador personally told Franco's brother-in-law and foreign minister, a notorious pro-Nazi, that Britain was ready for peace (the whole matter was described as strictly confidential) in the certain knowledge that every word would be retailed to Hitler, which it was. The British ambassador in Washington, Lord Lothian, went so far as to state that his country had lost the war and must pay the price, and the British ambassador in Berne was instructed to hold secret peace talks with a German prince who was in close touch, not only with his foreign office but with the SS authorities. Hitler positively thirsted for the fulfilment of his life's dream, a blank cheque from Britain which would permit him to turn Eastern Europe into a German penal colony. This being so, he believed every one of these pseudo-indiscretions on the part of British diplomats whose manner tended to imply that not even Downing Street must get wind of how far they personally thought it reasonable to go in appeasing the Germans. Churchill had not miscalculated: six whole weeks went by before Hitler finally steeled himself to abandon his long-standing desire for a bloodless negotiated settlement with Britain. On 16 July 1940 he gave orders 'to prepare a landing operation against Britain...' The date and wording of this directive are as remarkable as anything in the entire war, because they make it clear that no invasion had yet been 'prepared'. Hitler's bafflement and lack of method are also exemplified on the same day by his remark to Halder, the Army Chief of Staff, who noted it in his diary:

'Something has happened in London. The British were completely down [he used the English word]. Now they are up again.'

But he still nursed the futile hope that Britain was in process of collapse. It was not until 19 July that 'the long-planned session of the Reichstag finally took place', noted Weizsäcker, Hitler's state secretary at the German foreign office, on 23 August. 'It had been repeatedly postponed to allow time for internal developments in Britain. The Führer, who would genuinely like to come to terms with Britain, keeps wondering what Churchill is really counting on by continuing the war ... Churchill's resistance is, in fact, a psychological problem, not a logical one. Churchill has committed himself and cannot do otherwise ... He has yet to speak out. All we have is one curious peace-feeler from the British ambassador in Washington ...'

Churchill poured cold water on these speculations. So far from replying in person to Hitler's arrogantly worded offer of peace, he saw to it that the Germans received 'an extremely sanctimonious but quite definite refusal', as Weizsäcker puts it, from the very member of his cabinet whom they thought most amenable to a peace settlement: the Foreign Secretary, Lord Halifax, or 'Holyfox', to use Churchill's nickname for him. The dreamers in Berlin – and they were all that, whether Nazis or not – pinned their 'best-founded' hopes of a British collapse on Halifax, who had probably been selected for just that reason to titillate them with informal peace 'offers' via neutral intermediaries since the beginning of June.

Though master of Poland, Scandinavia and France, Hitler was quite as disconcerted by Britain's new attitude as he had been on 3 September 1939, when his response to her unexpected declaration of war was to ask his foreign minister 'What now?' All that occurred to him this time was to attack his friend Stalin, an insane proceeding which he clothed in a semblance of logic, for his own and other people's benefit, by remarking to General Halder a fortnight later that 'Russia [is] the factor Britain counts on most ... If Russia is smashed, Britain's last hope will be destroyed.'

Incomprehensible, the degree to which he succeeded in repressing his awareness of the USA's continued existence – nor, incidentally, did his remarks on 31 July 1940 embody even a pretence that he felt threatened by Stalin, who had carried out his treaty obligations to the letter ...

Churchill's second ruse, the enticement of German war-planes away from Britain's fighter bases and their diversion to London, cost lives – civilian lives. To maintain the air superiority which alone could thwart a German invasion, he baited his trap with a capital city susceptible to damage but not to total destruction by the level of aerial bombardment attainable in 1940. Churchill not only knew this but said so out loud in the Lower House. Needless to say, Hitler's generals were ignorant of this fact too. They must have confused a city of eight millions with the small Spanish township of Guernica, where Germany's Condor Legion had bombed ninety-eight people to death – an act which horrified the civilized world but satisfied the British that combat aircraft of the type built by the Germans, who had eschewed long-range bombers in the belief that all they needed was a tactical air force to support their army, were incapable of 'wiping out' a metropolis.

In luring Göring's planes away from Air Marshal Dowding's fighter stations and offering them London instead, Churchill did something which may one day be compared to the sacrifice of Moscow in 1812. Stendhal, who had marched with Napoleon to the Kremlin, called the Russians' decision to burn their own city and deprive the *Grande Armée* of shelter the most significant moral act of the nineteenth century. Churchill's decision to make London 'the Verdun of the German Air Force', as Colonel Wodarg described it to Goebbels on 4 October 1940, will be similarly assessed because it was, in all probability, the only thing that preserved Britain's fighters, radar stations and aircraft factories – in other words, her means of repelling an invasion.

Churchill's ruse demonstrates that a great warlord must also be a considerable psychologist. As he himself wrote in his masterpiece, *The World Crisis 1911–18*: 'Moreover, these same Germans were, of all the enemies in the world, the most to be dreaded when pursuing their own plans; the most easily disconcerted when forced to conform to the plans of their antagonist. To leave a German leisure to evolve his vast, patient, accurate designs, to make his slow, thorough, infinitely far-seeing preparations, was to court a terrible danger. To throw him out of his stride, to baffle his studious mind, to break his self-confidence, to cow his spirit, to rupture his schemes by unexpected action, was surely the path not only of glory but of prudence.'

This was the mentality and this was the policy which had, by 9 September 1914, robbed the Germans of victory at the Marne, the most numerous land battle of all time.

But Hitler had never read Churchill's personal account of the First World War, nor had he deemed it necessary, despite all the lessons it still held in 1940, to have his adversary's ABC of war translated for purposes of study. *Habent sua fata libelli* ... But destinies are also *made* by books, not least by those that remain unread. Until 1943, the infuriated German dictator had no conception of the military genius who faced him across the Channel. It never occurred to him that Churchill's only motive in launching seven air raids on Berlin between 25 August and 7 September – provocative little pin-pricks so technically inadequate that they scarcely damaged a building or claimed a life – was to achieve something other than that which he was so patently *unable* to achieve in 1940: the widespread devastation of Berlin.

(Between March 1943 and the end of the war, Churchill proceeded to make Berlin the most-bombed city in history. In the course of 363 air raids, over 45,000 tons of bombs – six-and-a-half times the weight of the Eiffel Tower – were transported to Berlin by 18,468 British and American bombers. These figures are based on estimates supplied by General Rumpf, war-time head of the German fire service, and by Werner Girbig, the historian of the US Eighth Air Force, which lost nearly 44,000 men during the war in Europe. The same two sources accept that 50,000 Berliners lost their lives under aerial attack, but this has been cut to less than 30,000 by Olaf Groehler's discovery of extant damage and casualty reports in the Berlin city archives. Groehler further estimates the number of people killed in only four days' raids on Hamburg at the end of July and the beginning of August 1943 at between 35,000 and 41,800. Routine Order No. 47 dated 22 March 1945 and issued by Colonel Grosse of Dresden's regular constabulary seems to imply that 250,000 of the city's inhabitants were killed in February 1945. Although most authorities now consider this a forgery, Frau Eva Grosse insisted that her late husband's total was correct when David Irving interviewed her in Munich on 10 July 1965. We shall never know exactly how many people died in Dresden. An ex-mayor of the post-war period, Weidauer, spoke of 'only' 35,000, a figure endorsed in 1977 by another chronicler of the tragedy, Götz Bergander, who was serving as a schoolboy anti-aircraft auxiliary when the city underwent its ordeal by fire. Equally, we shall never discover how many Berliners were missing after raids.)

Churchill had written long before, in 1935, that every enemy aircraft lured on to an open city would be grudgingly withdrawn from the fighting fronts. He not only thought this essential but was brutally honest enough to tell the nation so in advance. Virginia Woolf noted in her diary on 20 May 1940: 'Last night Churchill asked us to reflect, when being bombed, that we were at least drawing fire from the soldiers, for once.' And so it came to pass. As late as March 1943, Churchill stated in a letter to Stalin that he was emboldened by the Londoners' fortitude in 1940 to relieve the pressure on his invasion forces before dispatching them to France by once more tempting the Germans to divert aircraft to London. Hitler had no inkling of this. He blathered about the Geneva Convention and 'open' cities, meaning open to his tanks, open to his summary execution squads and the Jew-gassing teams that followed in the wake of his combat troops. Churchill was not disposed to give these deep-laid plans a chance to mature. Even before the war, he had consistently spoken out against Britain's adherence to any international law for the protection of cities from aerial attack – a scheme supported by Hitler among others – because he realized that an island devoid of substantial ground forces could only oppose the German army by air and sea. Although Churchill had assured Ambassador Ribbentrop in 1936 that Britain would again mobilize the entire world against Germany if she pushed eastwards, Hitler not only failed to allow for Britain's active hostility but persisted until war broke out in believing that the British would give him a free hand in Eastern Europe. He duly bowed to the advice of Ernst Udet, a playboy flyer in general's uniform, who persuaded him to neglect the construction of bombers in favour of a tactical ground support air force consisting of planes like the Stuka dive-bomber. (The Stuka had to be withdrawn from the Battle of Britain after a week because it was too slow, even though it made up one-third of the bomber force available to Hitler at the start of this decisive confrontation.)

But Britain would never have survived this air battle without Churchill's cunning, for heroically though her fighter pilots fought – inspiring Churchill's famous pronouncement at the height of the duel that never in the field of human conflict had so much been owed by so many to so few – Göring's numerical superiority was too great. Between 24 August and 6 September he was able to launch a daily average of one thousand aircraft at the British Isles. Being under strict instructions to bomb military targets, they shot down or seriously damaged 466 British fighters for the loss of 'only' 385 planes, 214 of them fighters. Churchill saw that 'the scales had tilted against Fighter Command'. Although he knew, unlike Hitler, that the Battle of Britain was becoming crucially significant, not only to the war but to western civilization as a whole, he had the unequalled nerve to wait until his opponent gave him a chance to play the card that would save his country. Churchill's physician once likened him to a bull elephant trampling everything in his path, but he could also, when necessary, play the cool and calculating hunter. What was he waiting for, day after day, while his fighter squadrons sustained such terrible losses? So as to brand Hitler in the eyes of the world as the man who attacked London before he attacked Berlin, he was waiting for the inevitable: the moment when a German aircraft strayed from a military to a civilian target. The Germans were already bombing industrial installations, fuel dumps and airfields on the outskirts of London but had only killed fourteen hundred people in fifty days' raids – in other words, they had confined their attacks to targets of definite military value. At last, however, a few of their aircraft (it may only have been one) strayed off course and *inadvertently* killed nine Londoners – nine. This was Churchill's long-awaited moment. The following night he dropped twenty-two tons of bombs on Berlin – a mere fleabite if his object had been to cause the devastation of which he was still incapable, but it was not. Accurately gauging the character of an opponent bloated with delusions of victory, Churchill intended the raid as a challenge (though one extremely important by-product of the 1940 raids on Berlin was that both the Russians and the neutral Spaniards abandoned their belief that Germany had already won the war).

Churchill only managed to kill ten Berliners during his first raid, but that was quite enough to pique Hitler, who had not long driven back to the Chancellery along flower-strewn streets after his triumphal entry into Paris, and to destroy the equanimity of the capital's inhabitants, who had never set eyes on an enemy since Napoleon rode through the Brandenburg Gate in 1806. Churchill's ruse had succeeded to an extent which became clear to him next day, when Goebbels's newspapers broke out in a rash of headlines like 'Dastardly British Attack!' and 'British Air Pirates over Berlin!'

It took seven night attacks on Berlin before Churchill finally, on 7 September, got his enemy where he wanted him: over London and away from Dowding's fighter stations. Spluttering with rage, Hitler had on 4 September promised an ecstatic and expectant audience at the Sportpalast that unless Mr Churchill promptly abandoned his 'brainchild, the night air raid' – a form of 'nuisance' to which he had resorted only 'because his air force cannot fly over German soil by day' – he, Hitler, would raze Britain's cities to the ground ...

Never for a moment, any more than in the case of the third ruse that lured him to Belgrade, did the exasperated dictator suspect that Churchill was outwitting him. Göring was also taken in. He not only failed to grasp the truth but yielded with ironclad consistency to the vanity that was his most prominent characteristic: he managed to persuade himself and Hitler that the new strategy 'forced' on them by the enemy – the bombing of London – would only hasten the attainment of their objective, the surrender of Britain; indeed, that night attacks would so terrorize the population of London as to render an invasion quite unnecessary. After all, blazing cities photographed at night look far more spectacular and make an incomparably bigger propaganda impact than raids on fighter stations, which are difficult to film ... Göring and his air force generals never guessed that Churchill's raids on Berlin had any purpose other than the devastation they so signally failed to inflict, even though the capital underwent another twenty-nine attacks during 1940. Eager for revenge, Göring blindly hurled all his strength at London and killed 824 people in two nights.

Thanks to their acquisition of Germany's Enigma cipher machine from the Poles, the British were able to eavesdrop on nearly every important German radio message from autumn 1940 onwards. This was first revealed in 1974 by Group Captain F. W. Winterbotham of the air department of the Secret Intelligence Service (MI6), who submitted these decrypted intercepts to the prime minister daily until 1945. Recalling the events of September 1940 in his war memoirs, *The Ultra Secret*, he says: 'Then ... Göring made his biggest mistake of the war. Had he kept up his blows at the aerodromes in southern England for another fortnight, he might well have grounded our remaining fighters, but at 11 a.m. on September the fifth Göring sent out an order ... for a three-hundred bomber raid on the London docks ... Was the raid simply in revenge for a raid that the RAF had made on Berlin, which had given the lie to Göring's boast that it could never happen? ... Strategically, his change of course was entirely wrong ... The switch of bombing to the docks had saved the remaining RAF fighters from being grounded ...

'On September the seventh ... German bombers struck again at London itself, the first of the real blitzes, purely against the civilian population. On September the ninth we got Göring's orders ... for an early evening raid by two hundred-plus bombers, again on London.' Göring's 'switch of attack away from our aerodromes' strengthened the impression that Hitler had dropped the idea of an invasion: 9 September – the date of the Marne 'miracle' in 1914 – had coincided with an epoch-making German defeat in the Second World War as well. With very few exceptions, Göring's bombers were contained by the British fighter screen, which had been alerted in good time, and failed to reach London. That night they returned and a few more got through. Then, for a week, the sky remained overcast. Sunday 15 September was when all German hopes of an invasion finally perished. With the onset of autumn gales in the Channel, the British realized that this day – for Göring chose to attack in daylight – would bring the ultimate test of whether the Germans could carry out a sea-borne invasion in 1940 by eliminating the RAF fighters which Air Chief Marshal Dowding had thus far deployed so shrewdly and husbanded so secretively. Dowding made sparing use of his planes, never committing them all – never allowing them to attack German fighters, only bombers ... Today, however, he flung every last one at the Germans, and Göring's airmen, who were flying without fighter escort, were startled and appalled. Winterbotham writes: 'Göring must obviously have been getting frantic by this time. He promptly ordered a second raid ... His signal was duly picked up and ... the speed of the Ultra operation ... made history ... Once again the raiders dropped their bombs wherever they could and fled.'

Two days later the British deciphered a tell-tale order from Berlin to air transport and supply units in Holland: they were to dismantle the loading equipment that had been installed for the air-lift to Britain. 'Churchill read out the signal, his face beaming ... This marked the end of Sea Lion, at least for this year.' Sea Lion was Hitler's code name for the invasion of Britain ...

Now for Churchill's third ruse during these crucial six months. By December 1940, decoded German signals had satisfied him that 'that man' would attack Russia early in May. Having promptly but vainly warned Stalin (who dismissed the report as a provocative British hoax), Churchill was more perturbed than relieved by Hitler's digression because, if his forthcoming blitz-krieg in Russia proved as successful as the one in France the previous summer, Germany might well win the war. It thus became necessary to upset the dictator's timetable and delay his invasion until summer was so far advanced that his armies would still be locked in battle when winter engulfed them as it had engulfed Napoleon's, which had also set out late in June.

Well over a year before the USA entered the Second World War, Churchill telephoned Roosevelt. The two leaders quickly agreed that only 'a mess in the Balkans' – which they themselves would have to engineer – might tempt Hitler to break his schedule: if the Balkans caught fire on his right flank, he would have to quench the flames before marching on Moscow.

Nothing Churchill did throughout the war incurred fiercer derision than the crass failure, so called, of the Balkan 'escapade' whose underlying purpose he was not, of course, at liberty to disclose.

Not until 1976, or eleven years after Churchill's death, was it revealed that the Canadian millionaire businessman William Stephenson and Colonel (later General) William J. Donovan, founder of the agency that spawned the CIA, had ignited the Balkan conflagration, their object being to goad Hitler into running amuck in Belgrade and Athens and so compel him to delay his attack on Russia by six precious weeks.

Who was Stephenson?

Even before the newly appointed prime minister found time to move from the Admiralty to Downing Street on 10 May 1940, he granted Stephenson an interview prior to the Canadian's departure for New York. His mission: to supervise 'co-ordinated secret intelligence and special operations in the American theatre'. When the war ended, Stephenson was the first (and only?) foreigner to be awarded America's highest civil decoration, The Medal of Freedom. The head of the FBI wrote: 'When the full story can be told, I am quite certain that your contribution will be among the foremost in having brought victory finally to the united nations' cause.' As for Churchill, he recommended Stephenson for a knighthood with the words 'This one is dear to my heart' but never mentioned him once in his six-volume history of the war. Generals and statesmen have too often owed their own achievements to those of their secret servicemen for them willingly to advertise the fact.

This is why, particularly in Britain, restrictions on the disclosure of official secrets remain in force, often to no practical purpose, for a generation or more, if not *ad infinitum*. In the British Isles as elsewhere, members of the military establishment are loath to share their glory with the 'lower orders' ... Once in a while, secret servicemen have been known to hit back. Group Captain Winterbotham is scathing in his references to Field Marshal Montgomery, who owed *all* his successes in North Africa and Normandy to the decipherment of German signals by Winterbotham's codebreakers (and the Poles!). Field Marshal Lord Alanbrooke, Britain's senior soldier and the man to whom he daily submitted German intercepts for five long years, receives no mention at all in *The Ultra Secret* ... Kim Philby, Russia's master-spy in Whitehall, is another who points up the role of the secret service in his memoirs, *My Secret War*. He confirms, albeit in a sarcastic vein because he rightly refuses to credit the instigators of a popular revolt with more importance than the people who take to the streets, that the SOE (Special Operations Executive, or branch of the secret service to which he belonged in 1940–41) was on hand in Belgrade: 'The Jugoslav revolution of April, for which SOE claimed some credit (our people had been there and *post hoc*, *propter hoc*), was followed by the prompt invasion of Jugoslavia and occupation of Greece.'

It is inordinately interesting to observe the effects of this Allied *ruse de guerre*, the first historic product of Roosevelt's friendship with Churchill, on an unsuspecting Hitler and his generals. We can trace this process, day by day, in the diaries of Joseph Goebbels, which were not available to William Stevenson when he recorded the war-time exploits of his friend and near-namesake, Sir William Stephenson, some thirty-five years after the events in question. Although they may have saved Moscow from capture by Guderian's tanks, the said events cost the lives of more than ten thousand Yugoslav civilians, namely, the Belgrade citizens who were bombed to death on Hitler's orders at Easter 1941, without any declaration of war ...

The British had landed at Piraeus on 7 March 1941 in response to intercepted German reports that Hitler meant to invade Greece so as to relieve the pressure on his Italian allies, first in North Africa and secondly in Greece itself, where they had suffered an almost unbroken string of defeats since invading the country against Hitler's wishes on 28 October 1940. Hitler, whose lack of oil precluded the abandonment of Romania, which he had bullied into submission like Bulgaria, had to expel the British from Greece in advance of his march on Moscow rather than risk fighting with his southern flank exposed and losing one source of oil before seizing another in the Caucasus. In view of the Germans' numerical strength, however, Churchill did not think the Greek bait sufficient by itself to guarantee the post-ponement of their scheduled attack on Russia. He duly enlisted Yugoslavia, which had just joined the Tripartite Pact and been requested by Hitler to grant elements of the German Second Army (commanded by General von Weichs) right of access to Greece. This was because Britain's chances of defending Greece against the Germans would be nil if the country were invaded from Yugoslavia as well as from Romania and Bulgaria (by Field Marshal List's Twelfth Army). Few people in England grasped why Churchill tried to defend Greece at all now that a pact had been concluded between Berlin and Prince Regent Paul's Yugoslav government, headed by Premier Cvetković. Despite this, Eden and Donovan persuaded General Simović of the Yugoslav Air Force to demonstrate public opposition to the Berlin pact by overthrowing the government, proclaiming Crown Prince Peter of age and unleashing a full-scale insurrection in Belgrade. The Yugoslavs had thereby broken their alliance with Hitler, who characteristically christened his act of vengeance – aerial bombardment plus occupation – 'Operation Punish-ment' ...

The brutality of this 'punishment' laid the emotional founda-tions of a partisan campaign, soon to be led by Tito, which tied up more German divisions for more years than any guerrilla war outside Russia. So brilliantly was it conducted that Hitler several times told his generals that he wished just one of them could measure up to Tito, whom he called 'a hell of a fellow' – an accolade usually reserved for Stalin.

By now, Goebbels was spending every day at Hitler's side. Of all the facts that emerge from his diary, none is more fascinating than Hitler's full awareness that Roosevelt and Churchill had engineered the Belgrade *coup* to bar his path to Greece, coupled with his total failure to recognize that the insurrection was only a means, not an end in itself: a means of upsetting his timetable for the attack on Russia and inducing him to blunder into Churchill's most disastrous trap of the entire war. He delayed the start of his most hazardous campaign *although he knew*, and had often stressed, that he must not cross swords with the Russian winter. Though much preoccupied with Napoleon's defeat by the elements, he still set off on 22 June, the very date on which Napoleon had issued his 1812 proclamation, likewise to the largest invasion force ever deployed in Europe – a truly ominous and spine-chilling coincidence.

Hitler also knew full well, and daily discussed the matter with Goebbels, that Donovan and the British foreign secretary had been roaming the Balkans for weeks with the aim of starting a conflagration there. Determined that no one should provoke him unscathed, he launched his 'Operation Punishment' without the least inkling of who would be its ultimate victim – yet another illustration of the terrible fact that reason is powerless when emotion gains the upper hand. Yugoslavia's signing of the Tripartite Pact in Vienna was violently opposed, not only by student demonstrators but by a broad cross-section of Belgrade's inhabitants. Emotion told Hitler that he, the master of Europe, must not take this insult lying down. Goebbels noted: 'The Führer looks rather tired. The Yugoslav business annoys him intensely ... It is now officially admitted in the USA that Roosevelt lent the Belgrade comic opera revolution something of a helping hand ... Churchill exultant in his speech about Yugoslavia. The Führer is indignant.'

Goebbels again, on 29 March: 'Large-scale demonstrations against us in Belgrade. London and Washington proclaim their solidarity.'

Or, on 1 April: 'There are Britons and Jews behind it ... Eden back in Athens. The itinerant warmonger.' Or, on 2 April: 'Eden in Belgrade. He naturally wants war ... Belgrade denies Eden's presence, adds that he wasn't invited ... Jew-boy's funk.'

One of Hitler's commanders-in-chief came out with a topical 'bon' mot at this period:

Question: 'If Yugoslavia offers no resistance, Field Marshal, how long will you take to occupy it?'

Answer: 'Twenty-four hours.'

Question: 'And if the Yugoslavs resist?'

Answer: 'Twelve hours.'

Question: 'Why?'

Answer: 'Because there won't be any speeches of welcome.'

The fish stank from every fin, every scale. Megalomania had become the German epidemic. Not for the space of a minute's silent reflection did it occur to this field marshal – any more than it did to a single one of the ultra-intelligent German generals who all tried, after the war, to saddle the 'Bohemian corporal' with sole responsibility for 'squandered victories' – that each of these Anglo-American challenges was attuned with brilliant psychological precision to the mind of the infuriated man in the Berlin Chancellery.

None of this dawned on the Germans. Goebbels again succumbed to the St Vitus's dance of insanity as soon as he was able to record that on the Saturday morning of the Orthodox Easter festival, without any declaration of war, the people of Belgrade had been murdered in their beds by German airmen under the command of General Löhr, the only Second World War bomber pilot to be hanged at the scene of his crime.

On 3 April Weizsäcker noted: 'A pity, having to squander our strength on the Balkans ... The south-east front in Europe is a boon to Britain.' On 5 April: 'The Yugoslav ambassador made three attempts to confer with me in the course of 4 April and the morning of 5 April. As instructed by the Foreign Minister, I was always out to him.' The Yugoslav military attaché, Colonel Vauhnik, nonetheless indicates in his memoirs, published at Buenos Aires in 1967, that Weizsäcker was humane enough to have him warned. Weizsäcker himself had not been told until 29 March that Hitler intended to bomb Belgrade, which had been proclaimed an open city, without declaring war.

'This part-time country,' gloated Goebbels, 'will forfeit its existence for having defied the Reich.' On 5 April he noted: 'The attack on Yugoslavia and Greece is now timed to start bright and early on Saturday morning ... Yugoslavia will be dismembered. The coast will go to Italy, Macedonia to Bulgaria, and the former Austrian provinces to our own Austrian administrative districts ... Belgrade is desperately trying to appease us and indulging in tearful protestations of loyalty.'

Hitler, being considerably more intelligent, was nonetheless forced to make the following admission – likewise recorded by Goebbels – five days before his attack on Russia: 'The campaign in Greece has severely depleted our equipment, so the affair will take somewhat longer.' The affair in question: 'Our deployment against Russia.' Hitler stifled the thought that the lost months were gone beyond recall, and that he was now being *compelled* to do what prudence had counselled him to avoid doing; in other words, cross the Russian border as late in the summer as Napoleon. His faithful scribe, of course, never once realized that Hitler had abandoned his own timetable and was conforming to Churchill's by marching into the jaws of winter.

Three *ruses de guerre*, three battles. Modern school textbooks deny Churchill's assertion, made in 1935, that 'Battles are the principal milestones in secular history.' They do so in the most laudable and humane belief that nothing as loathsome as war should have first say in civilization, which ends whenever and wherever war begins. The more we detest war, the more natural it seems to deny its claim to have changed the face of the world, of mankind, even of our maps, more profoundly than any other phenomenon. Yet it is true: 'Great battles, won or lost, change the entire course of events, create new standards of values, new moods, new atmospheres, in armies and in nations, to which all must conform.' Anyone who doubts the truth of what Churchill says here in his life of the Duke of Marlborough, and what Plato knew before him when he declared that even artistic systems can only change in tune with their political counterparts, should ask himself what standards, moods, views and national boundaries might now exist in Europe had the Second World War resulted in London's occupation by Hitler rather than Berlin's capture by the Red Army.

The stars of home

Poor Erich Knauf! I'd known him twenty years. A compositor with the *Plauener Volkszeitung* ... before he became an editor, publisher and writer. A man of the people ... I also recall another man ... the swine who kept a nice neat record, night after night, of what Knauf and the artist E.O. Plauen had been saying. The one who then went and turned them both in. The one who, before either of them knew anything about it, was disposing of their rooms – 'after all, they'll soon be vacant anyway.' What is he doing now, this Herr Schulz, then a captain of the reserve with the Armed Forces High Command – this publisher of periodicals whose devotion to 'physical culture' was a licence to reproduce photographic nudes on art paper. Did the worthy captain survive the last year of the war, hale and hearty?

Erich Kästner, 1946.

'She's given the Polack a shirt,' said Maria, '*and* a tie!' Her doll's-house of an apartment, ever so tidy but drab and comfortless, was in the same small block as Pauline's miniature vegetable and flower shop, kitchen and sleeping quarters. In other words, within earshot.

'So she gave him a shirt,' her husband retorted curtly. 'What does that prove? The Melchiors gave him a whole suit.' Maria qualified this. 'Only an old one. Anyway, you can't compare the Melchiors with our lady-friend next door. The Pole works for them. He lives with them – he even sits down to meals with them at the kitchen table.' She repeated the words with relish. 'At the kitchen table, even though it's strictly forbidden to let a prisoner of war eat with the family!' Maria's interest in all that was forbidden when others had the audacity to do it was as old as herself. Always poking and prying, thought her husband, remembering all the stories Maria had already inflicted on him about her female friends and neighbours. Anger began to oust the boredom he usually felt. He said, 'If they eat in the kitchen themselves, where's their foreigner supposed to eat – in the pigsty? Or maybe you'd sooner they waited on him in the front parlour?'

His tone counselled caution. 'I'm only telling you,' she replied, 'and it *is* forbidden.'

It was typical of her to repeat this. He said, speaking with un-disguised contempt now, 'There ought to be a law against some of the laws they make these days, hasn't that ever occurred to you?'

She didn't reply, but he could tell from her face that the thought had never crossed her mind. How strange, he reflected, without saying so, that anyone can combine so much cunning with such a doglike urge to obey. As a child I couldn't stand cats and liked dogs. Now I feel just the opposite because cats defy discipline whereas every so-called 'compatriot' comes to heel like a well-trained dog. He would have liked to say this to Maria but thought better of it. No use getting into deep water now, during a couple of days' leave.

Not that he had ever dictated the topics for discussion in their marriage. Although Maria was lying quiescent beneath his touch, as appeased as she only ever was for a few hours after sex, the furrow above the bridge of her nose indicated that she had started brooding again. And because her obstinacy was proof against any male vigour – and his was reserved for his work – she never for a moment felt inclined to grant his plea and drop the subject that sickened him. Her sole concession was to revert by a round-about route to the neighbour whose shop she coveted and would soon acquire, just as she had always got what she wanted. 'It's going from strength to strength,' she said. 'That's because fruit and vegetables are pretty well all you can buy these days without a ration card. She sells flowers too, now, though it's ten to one she isn't licensed to – they don't allow every greengrocer to sell flowers as well, and the price of flowers isn't fixed by the authori-ties the way it is with potatoes or apples. There's money in flowers.'

Without knowing why he bothered to get involved, he said, 'Who buys flowers in this place? Everyone grows their own.'

Her laugh was unamused. '*You* never buy *me* any, that goes without saying, but some people do.' Then she kissed him on the eyelids and said – softly, because his hand was still resting on the place which alone determined how sweet or sour Maria was at any one time, 'Forget it, you don't have to buy me any flowers – you brought me ever so many things, not to mention yourself and *him*!' She stressed the word with affectionate irony and even held her tongue for a few moments, raising his hopes that she had forgotten about the shop. During this silence his mind returned bitterly to the day before yesterday. He had hardly been home an hour before she was complaining how careless they'd been and that she'd probably 'copped it'. She talks about conceiv-ing the way other people talk about stopping a bullet, he thought. It never occurs to her that *I* might want a child for the very reason that I'm likely to be feeding the fish in the Channel before long, if I don't roast to death in my cockpit or draw a dud chute and ram my skull into my rib-cage against a London rooftop. She said, 'That woman sold ten hundredweight of peaches the other day – ten hundredweight in a single day, and she was dumb enough to brag about it – told me so herself, she did. And guess who helped her with the crates? The Pole! He carted all the full ones inside and all the empty ones out the same evening, late.'

Her husband was relieved to hear this, because it gave him a chance to say, 'What are you accusing her of? That makes it all right with the authorities. The woman keeps a store and her husband's been called up. Why shouldn't she get a prisoner of war to help her out?'

'Nights,' she sneered, 'help her out *nights*! Oh yes, we heard him helping her out at three o'clock this morning, when we could have used some sleep ourselves! And her husband's such a decent sort. He sends her a parcel every week, half the size of a grand piano – I've seen them. That whore would never have got the shop at all if it wasn't for that nice husband of hers – they let the place to him, not her. I'm going to find out whose name they put the lease in.'

He removed his hand, took some cigarettes from the bedside table and said in a bleak voice, 'What's it to you whether the shop ...' Mechanically, he switched on the little 'national receiver', one of the radio sets which had been ballyhooed for years and sold at a state-subsidized 'bargain price' because all citizens of the Third Reich were expected to welcome the Führer – or, still more important, the Führer's carefully chosen background music – into their kitchens or front parlours. This set had stood on the kitchen dresser until Maria's husband was called up. Now she shared her bedroom with it. 'Oh yes,' she snarled, 'that's you all over! You want a child, fine, but first ask yourself what I'm supposed to live on if something happens to you – after all, it *might*. The kitchen's right behind the shop and I could earn money without setting foot outside the door – it would be ideal, even if I had a baby.'

He smoked, staring at the ceiling. It was some time before he could bring himself to say, 'I've nothing against you opening a shop if we can find one to rent, but I don't fancy being married to someone who owes her living to murder. They'd kill the Pole if we reported him, you know that as well as I do, and as for the woman ... The least she'd get is a dose of concentration camp, just for doing the same as her husband, most likely. Nine out of ten servicemen end up in bed with foreign girls.'

That stung her. 'You should know! I suppose you've been sleeping around yourself, in France.' But she didn't wait for an answer to this well-founded reproach. It was all the same to her – her sights were set on one thing only. He sidestepped by reverting to her fears – and they were far from groundless – that he mightn't survive. 'If I'm killed,' he said soberly, 'you'll get a pension which'll guarantee you a better living than any damned shop. Whatever you made in that ridiculous little store would be deducted from your widow's allowance. And as far as the child's concerned, I don't think we – I mean, two days ago ...'

She cut him short. 'You want one, though. Fair enough, but I want a shop. Women without families are being drafted into that munitions factory in Wehrethal, and that wouldn't suit me one bit. I'd have to get up at five and cycle all the way – they start at six, and there's a night shift too.'

The same thought recurred to him throughout her spate of words: she makes me sick ... He ... no, *it* – something nameless in the depths of his being – rebelled against the fact of his marriage, rebelled against this naked woman beside him and her determination to prevail at any price, murder not excluded. When Maria had met him at the station on Tuesday and told him during the short walk home of her nocturnal eavesdropping on the couple next door, he had ascribed the glint in her eye to malice born of frustration. They had dived into bed and seldom left it since, except on the few occasions when she'd bullied him into his best uniform because she delighted in showing him off to the neighbourhood. Now that her grass widow's envy was assuaged by the repletion which should have mollified anyone, however spiteful, he had managed to persuade himself that she would stop hounding the woman next door. How stupid of him! Unless he could concoct some plausible argument and bring it to bear on his wife's acquisitive urges, the unsuspecting greengrocer and her Polish boy-friend would fuck themselves into a lethal predicament. But the thought had hardly taken shape when he realized that Maria would still spread the story round the village even if her sole object were to visit tragedy on the couple beyond the bedroom wall. She had lain there in silence for a remarkable length of time, chewing some marzipan from Brest. Now she said, 'You always pour cold water on everything, sweetheart, but can *you* come up with a better idea than a shop like that? We won't get rich on what you send home from France. Besides, every patriotic housewife ought to take a job – they're always saying so on the radio. I tell you, if I can't get hold of a shop they'll draft me into that munitions factory!'

He simply couldn't remain lying next to this – this ... He debated what he would have called someone whose mind worked like Maria's but who wasn't his wife. Throwing off the bedclothes, he got out of bed and stood, still smoking, at the window. 'They'll see you from the street,' she said, 'the net curtain's so thin.' He stepped back, and she melted with satisfaction at having him there with her. She enjoyed looking at him – he still had the small, firm, lean buttocks of a boy. Even after their wedding she had taken ages to banish the fear of losing such a handsome husband, but it had passed. It had, in fact, been a long time before she grasped that she, who was less than averagely attractive, had hooked a boy who aroused universal envy in girls as far afield as Lörrach. And now they had made him a sergeant pilot, and this early promotion was attributable to the fact – which Maria effortlessly dismissed from her mind – that he sometimes had to fly no less than three missions to London in twenty-four hours because the British – this Maria didn't know – were shooting down so many German planes ...

Controlling himself with an effort, he now unveiled an idea calculated to repel her designs on the shop. Relieved that his back was towards her because lying wasn't his forte, he said, 'Look, darling, about the shop – it isn't a good plan from any angle. I'm thinking of putting in for officers' school.'

She stopped munching and propped herself swiftly on one elbow. 'Thinking about it?' she exclaimed. 'What's there to think about? Of course you should be an officer! When I tell Erika' – her sister – 'she'll go green with envy!'

'Oh, sure,' he said drily, 'that's one argument in favour.'

Maria couldn't contain her delight. She was out of bed in a trice, hugging and kissing him. Then a thought struck her. 'But ... is it on? I mean, you never went to college. Can you really become an officer when you've only ...'

He cut her off in mid-sentence. 'How can I explain if you keep interrupting?' he said with unconcealed irritation. 'Get back under the covers ... It's all to do with combat missions. If you fly enough of them – twenty-five, I think, and I chalked up twenty-five a long time ago – you can get into officers' school without taking a preliminary exam. But if you rent a shop or your wife runs a greengrocer's – well, I don't know for sure, but I doubt if it's the right social qualification for an officer's wife.' He had no idea if this still applied. He only knew that his father and his uncle had once complained of getting nowhere in the army in the '14–'18 war because one was a shop assistant and the other a tradesman. 'Mind you,' he went on, thinking aloud now, 'the Führer isn't out of the top drawer himself, and we don't have half as many blue-blooded officers in the air force as they do in the army. I'd like to apply, anyway, but not because I want to go places. I need a few months' rest, that's all.' That was the crux of the matter. He knew enough about statistics to estimate that he'd already used up a bigger ration of luck than the RAF generally allowed. He lapsed into a brooding silence. Only his career, not the war, could have moved Maria to such geniune curiosity. She said, 'That'd be wonderful. Nothing could happen to you at the school and I could come and visit you ... You never tell me anything – I'd no idea you were going to be an officer.'

His irritation grew. 'I never said I was "going to be" one – I may be, that's all.'

Maria laughed. 'Trust you to look on the bright side! You'll pass the exams on your head.'

He laughed too, but brusquely. 'If I don't land on it somewhere else first. I'm not out of the shit yet.'

'Come on back to bed,' she urged, as much in love with him as if she were already entitled to be addressed as *Frau Leutnant*. 'It's time you told me what it's really like over there. You never talk about it, just scare me by coming out with words like "shit" all of a sudden. Is it very much worse than you let on? Hey, come back ...' But he didn't. He paced back and forth on the tawdry strip of jam-red carpet in front of the double bed, cursing the long-regretted stupidity that had made him listen to the BBC in her presence because her rapacity over the shop was yet another proof of just how dangerous she'd always been. 'You listened in yourself three times, what more can I tell you?'

Childlike, she asked, 'You mean the English tell the truth? I thought ...'

'They tell at least half the truth where losses are concerned, that's why I tuned in to London in the first place. You've got to understand, Maria – while I'm out of it for a few days, the least I can do is hear how many of our boys they've shot down. If the English say twenty-one and we say seven I split the difference and call it fourteen. Fourteen planes are a lot.'

'Do they always end up dead, the ones who get shot down?'

'No – no, sometimes you stand a better chance bailing out than trying to crash-land back at base. That can be riskier because a lot of the planes catch fire.' He fell silent. So did she, but her new-found fear for his safety got the better of her. 'This transfer to officers' school – can't you speed it up?' Her question stirred the embers of his own fear, which was so strong and so near the surface of his mind that he altogether failed to register the background music oozing quite loudly into the little room from the national receiver, which should really have been called a national deceiver but was not, here and now, doing its job as a state-administered analgesic against the cares of the contemporary world.

He hurriedly sought distraction by climbing back into bed. Although she moved closer at once and kissed him, they were talking for once, and there was no greater passion-killer than conversation. He said, 'There's a shortage of air crews. Some nights they send us over at eight, eleven and two, that's why I doubt if any of us will be transferred for training in the middle of a battle.'

'How long do these battles go on for? I always thought they lasted three or four days – that sort of thing ...' She gazed at him with such sudden apprehension that he put his arm round her neck and, rather than see her eyes, pillowed her head against his chest. He said, 'Nobody knows how long it'll last, darling. London's a big city. We've only ever tackled one before, and that was Paris in 1871 – and then it took a damned sight longer than Bismarck expected. One of our boys pointed that out recently, not that it did him much good.'

She raised her head and looked into his face. Although he had tried to sound like a man discussing the weather, something in his tone revived her fears. He even felt a trace of satisfaction at her obvious misgivings on his behalf. She said, 'What do you mean, it didn't do him much good?'

'They shot him, of course.' She was dumbfounded by the startling simplicity of this reply, so he added, as if to justify the shooting, 'He didn't only compare London to Paris, which we captured in 'seventy-one the way we did this time – he said it was turning into the Luftwaffe's Verdun. Verdun was a fortress in the last war. Both sides lost more men there than anywhere else, and we never even took the place.' It seemed a good time to let her know what denunciations could lead to. 'One member of the squadron reported him and another ten were privileged to shoot him – they volunteered for the job. You always get more volunteers than you need when it comes to shooting a member of your own outfit.'

She made no comment, but his revelation must have sunk in because she got up and said, 'Lucky you remembered to bring a drop of the hard stuff.' He stared after her as she went into the next room. Maria's back was definitely her most attractive feature – she was skinny as a cat in front and her bottom looked funny sideways on. It was a relief when she finally reappeared after opening the cognac in the kitchen. Any distraction was welcome – anything that could help him forget Dieter Bracke, whom they had shot, but not just for calling London the Luftwaffe's Verdun. Dieter had also done an imitation of the air fleet commander chatting to Goebbels, monocle screwed in and buttock-like cheeks distended with caviare canapés. 'Another fortnight,' he had proclaimed, almost braying with triumph, 'and life will be extinct in London – completely extinct. They'll choke to death in their own shit!'

Goebbels, his big brown eyes radiating enthusiasm, listened

to this forecast with a marked scepticism which had favourably impressed all who were detailed to act as mess waiters during his ministerial visit to Sperrle's sumptuous headquarters in Deauville. Though also in uniform, Goebbels looked far less pretentious than Sperrle – 'the monocled Swabian', as Dieter Bracke had christened him – who was four times as broad and had just been made a field marshal. As expertly as he had caught Sperrle's rich Swabian, so Bracke imitated Goebbels too, with his Rhineland accent and stridently nasal delivery. He also demonstrated with a lavatory brush how Sperrle had removed the Sunday-best edition of his marshal's baton from its lacquered silk-lined case – he didn't carry it as a rule – before meeting the plane from which Göring and Goebbels descended. Goebbels had said, 'But Herr Sperrle, we really must keep a sense of proportion. These raids are quite awful, I'm sure, but the British Empire won't collapse because a few titled ladies relieve themselves in Hyde Park.' Before they had been called on to hand round caviare and champagne, the marshal had displayed some aerial photographs and quoted an agent's report to the effect that London's sewers and water mains had been so badly hit that people were already manuring the parks. While Maria was half filling two tumblers with cognac and he was holding up the covers so that she could get back into bed, she asked, 'When was that – and ... do you often have to shoot your own people?'

He drained his glass. While she was refilling it, already back in bed, he said bitterly, 'Give it a rest. I told you, it isn't a question of having to, there are always plenty of pals ready to do the job – more than they can use.' Although he had asked her not to pursue the subject he did so himself. 'It was just after I sent you those photos from Berlin, the ones of Goebbels's visit. I'd been detailed to escort his plane there on the return flight – sixty planes to shepherd the little chap home, but I reckon he's more than just a bigmouth ... Maybe it's his limp that stops him marching through life all bright and breezy like our generals and Fatso.' She knew he meant Göring. He had sent home some photos of Göring's visits too. 'To think of all the people you're seeing with your own eyes!' she had written admiringly, but this rapturous exclamation struck no answering chord in her husband. Göring had, for the first time, been wearing the Lohengrin-white leather uniform of a Reich Marshal, the rank created for him after the fall of France. Sperrle, his bulbous belly echoing the curve of Göring's, was always at the Reich Marshal's side, whether inspecting guards of honour or taking dips in the Atlantic: two overweight and outwardly bonhomous men who were really engaged in a savage contest for personal prestige at the expense of the air crews – 'their' air crews – who were being so cruelly decimated over the British Isles. Göring's triumphal attire – white cape, boots of burgundy leather – went ill with the scowl of annoyance that accompanied his pep-talk: he knew all about the worries of 'his' air crews because he himself had flown so-and-so many missions in the first war and fought the British man to man. He was right, except that this time it wasn't a question of fighting man to man – this time it was like being ordered to fire the Atlantic with a cigarette-lighter. Nobody who had flown over London and seen how little of that urban ocean had so far been burnt could be in any doubt that it was turning into an aerial Verdun. And Dieter now lay in some nameless grave without a headstone, without a wooden cross ... His parents! What did they think, the parents of someone shot for telling the truth? Were they ashamed of him? An appalling thought. They were probably ashamed of him – appalling! He could picture them slinking along the street with their heads down, reluctantly explaining to other worthy citizens why they hadn't been able to insert an obituary notice in the local paper – the reward due to all who died for their country. Dieter had been in the right, but they'd shovelled him into an unmarked grave like someone caught stealing from a comrade ...

But what had affected him still more deeply was something he had already found it impossible to digest on three separate occasions: that the execution of a comrade always produced more volunteers than were needed. 'Ah well, it'll be a new experience,' one of them had explained. 'You've got to try everything once.' And he had held his tongue but secretly wondered why this stupid sod, a cabinet-maker in civilian life, should be so keen to sample the 'new experience' of shooting a room-mate.

'People are like that,' his grandfather used to say...

Just outside the window in Lörracher Strasse he could see from the bed that women were emerging with shopping bags full of fruit and vegetables from the shop Maria had made up her mind to rent although – no, because – she knew that she would have to sacrifice at least one life to get it.

'People are like that ...' For the first time in ages, he recalled precisely when his grandfather had applied that phrase to Maria. The old railwayman had asked him to help pick some runner-beans during a spell of leave. They were alone in the garden, and he had confided to the old man what he would never have admitted to his brothers and sisters or parents – a thing he had long ceased admitting to himself: that Maria had coerced him into marrying her. He would have done so anyway, but she had thought it safer to tell him that her parents were away – which they were. Then, one night as he was sneaking out of the house, Maria's brother had 'happened' to arrive home on leave in his SS uniform and caught him red-handed. 'Oho,' he jeered in a menacing voice, 'so you've been upstairs with my sister already, eh?' – and they were married quicker than you could turn a potato patch.

"Yes, my lad, people are like that ...' He dwelt on the words as though they could resurrect the old man whose only bequest to him had been a warning, for Grandad was dead and his SS brother-in-law feeding the worms on the banks of the Meuse – just as I'll soon be feeding the fish, he thought again, plunged in melancholy. Bed's fun while you're at it, but you're apt to get moody afterwards. Moody and something else – but he was too tired to pursue the thought. He meant his tendency, which had always been excessive but was now irresistible, to appease, to behave with a compliance verging on imbecility and defer over-much to this woman who was now sucking a crystallized fruit from Antwerp. She had presented her smooth, shapely back to him. Now, before he could clamp his eyes shut, she abruptly turned round and beamed at him. 'Oh, you're awake – I thought you'd dozed off.' At once she reached for him, and he, docile as ever, was glad to be distracted by her warmth, by the hair and skin that smelt so good, from her face and the ominous thoughts that roused his hostility towards her; towards himself, too, because he despised himself for the way her firm smooth body – and, without a doubt, his fear of death and yearning for exemption from the need to think – were once more turning him into her obedient servant. 'What, there again already!' She laughed approvingly, and because his self-contempt was becoming too much to bear, he put himself out of his misery by helping her to climb on top of him. But, stronger even than her presence, the end of his leave loomed up – a vision of such Damoclean menace that he muttered defensively, 'We still have to go and see my parents. I'll be gone by this time tomorrow.'

'Is that any reason to get up' – she meant 'off' – 'right away?' Smiling, she dominated him as a horsewoman masters her mount, and he could only think with impotent fury – though he obeyed as usual – that this same woman, this gentlest and tenderest, most melting and solicitous of bedmates, would be literally bent on murder as soon as she collected her small store of wits and regained her capacity for singleminded concentration. And to think that he, wet fish that he was, always gave in to her ... At that moment he became aware that, for the first time since their frenzied and precipitate lovemaking on his return, Maria was taking no precautions. Because she already saw him as an officer, that was the only reason – *now* he could give her a child! The realization made him bristle. 'Promise me,' he said, 'promise me you won't report those two next door, do you hear?' All at once, he felt a positive dread of making a child with this woman.

'Don't talk,' she sighed, self-absorbed, 'go on, go on!' But he was still in command of his senses. He pushed her roughly off and left her in a tumbled heap, and she shouted, 'What's the matter with you, are you crazy!' – and he shouted back, 'I've just told you what can happen when someone informs on a comrade. First promise me...'

She hated him, incensed as never before, and he quailed under her verbal onslaught. 'And that's why you left off half way through? "Comrade"! Is that what you call a filthy Pole who's stealing the wife of a German serviceman? Anyway, do you think

I'd be dumb enough to go running to the police and report them myself, so *my* name goes down in the books? Ha!' Her laugh was like a hyena's bark. 'I'll only have to tell Frieda König what's going on there at night and leave the rest to her!'

Shuddering inwardly, he reflected that a rabid woman's resolve could crush rock. Except that this one wasn't rabid at all – she was infinitely cool and unerringly calculating. She now lay curled up like a hedgehog on the defensive, speechless with hatred. He, too, remained silent until the light began to fade outside. Then he said, without conviction, 'Frieda König's Melchior's sister. He told me himself how glad he was to have such a reliable, hard-working prisoner – *and* one who understands German. The König woman won't give a damn whether or not the Pole sleeps alone at night as long as he delivers her brother's coal in the day-time. Besides, she isn't the type to inform on anyone.'

Maria swung round, and the look in her eye convinced him that any row was worth it, provided he didn't have a child by her. She'd taken him in the belief that he'd soon be a lieutenant, if not something even more exalted, so her love had burned more fiercely than ever. The mere thought of being an officer's wife had made her melt inside with an almost sexual deliquescence. That was the only reason why she'd deliberately omitted to take precautions for the first time. And then he'd gone and mentioned the Polack ... Well, it was done now. She was white round the nose, so deeply had he wounded her and so much did she hate him: or rather, so much did she hate the thing that had come between them, not for the first time but while they were actually having each other. And that, in turn, was why she now said, with a dispassionate air which made him wonder why the Devil was always portrayed as a man, 'Frieda König's head of the Women's League – that makes her the Party's number one woman round here. You honestly think she'd dare to ignore something like that if I reported it? Not on your life! – Hey, have you gone to sleep?'

He had moved away from her long ago and was lying with his head on his forearm, hoping she would think just that. Sure enough, she got up, put on her bathrobe and went off to make supper. He knew it now: she was still the extortioner she had always been, just as he was still a weak-kneed fool who could actually forget while screwing her how dangerous she was – and he'd committed the capital offence of listening to the BBC in her presence. She'd inform on Pauline Krop and the Pole anyway, even if she weren't so set on the shop. He wondered why he'd come home instead of spending his four days' leave in Antwerp, and had a vision of the Belgian prisoner of war's wife – blonde, corpulent and not in the first flush of youth but still extremely handsome – getting out of the bath. He shared her with one other flyer – well, maybe more than one – on short leaves. She had her price, but still, what a decent sort she was compared to his wife ... He wondered whether to warn the woman next door. The radio was now churning out one of the most popular songs of the period, *Heimat, deine Sterne*. Even he found the tune agreeable. Legitimate as nostalgia is, however, the lyric's reference to the stars of home now struck him as a mockery. 'Who do you have to be,' he thought with wry contempt, 'to make up that sort of slush?'

What would he have said, though only to himself and certainly not to his wife, had he known that the writer of the song, Erich Knauf, would soon be denounced in just the same way as Dieter Bracke and Stasiek Zasada? Bracke they had shot; Knauf they would behead for having remarked that Germany was losing the war; E.O. Plauen, the artist who was jointly denounced with Knauf, hanged himself in his cell to escape the guillotine. And Zasada the Pole...

But then Maria called, 'Are you still asleep?' Although he wanted to pretend so, marital and military training evoked an obedient response: 'I was, darling – is it supper-time already?' Her voice again: 'Almost!' She had barely said it when he heard a hissing and a sizzling from the gas-stove, and he couldn't help grinning and wondering if there was a woman in the world who didn't finish up cracking eggs into a pan after doing it in the day-time.

Always travel solo on a research trip when you have to interview a woman because you'll get nothing out of her if you turn up with a female companion. Interview a man or a family, on the other hand, and you must never travel without a woman in tow – better still, your wife and children, who are prime aids to ease of access. Turn up with a child and you'll never, repeat never, have the door slammed in your face like an unwelcome travelling salesman before you can get your questions out. Using a child as a door-opener is almost as reprehensible as shoving a woman along in front of you to stop a sniper's bullet, but Balzac wasn't being flippant when he conceded that an author should acquire his copy like a thief in the night. If the immortal Frenchman could be less than gentlemanly at times, how else could the likes of me hope to turn up at this farm, alone and unannounced, and make even a start on the preliminary conversation which, though devious in the extreme, was absolutely essential?

We were calling on a horse-breeder and riding-stable owner because his father Arthur Stackmann – an ex-policeman and war-time commander of the village SA, or Stormtroopers – now lived in retirement at this farm on the edge of the forest. A child can ask questions which will secure you admission even when the object of your quest is genuinely or ostensibly not at home. This is important because relatives of the person you need to interview may reveal far more about him than he would himself – unless, of course, they simply go and warn him of your presence! When that happens, as it sometimes does, direct access to your reluctant witness is barred. You then open up an indirect route by interviewing his friends – fellow-creatures whose tongues you can loosen are always to be found – and, having sewn him up tight, telephone him as though eager merely to verify what his confederates have told you. This is a sure-fire oral laxative because it never, ever, happens that one accomplice makes a statement about another which the latter can forbear to amplify, embellish or dispute – or avenge. He will always disclose more in the heat of self-vindication than he intended – more, too, about himself and his doings ...

'You've dropped me in it good and proper, Thuri!' Thus, from the dock of a French court in Freiburg, spake Joseph Zinngruber to the departing witness Arthur Stackmann, who, having begun by painting the former district director a paragon of all the anti-fascist virtues, heard the presiding judge read out a deposition signed by himself, ex-Sergeant Stackmann, while imprisoned by the French immediately after the war. This cited numerous incidents in the everyday life of Brombach village which proved that the said Joseph Zinngruber had been an ardent Nazi throughout the war years ...

It was evening when we drove there. Built into a lovely Black Forest mountainside above Brombach, the farm was an imposing establishment with a big new indoor riding school for the twenty-plus horses which the Stackmanns stabled but did not, for the most part, own. A stupefying scent rose from the lush pastures, which looked damson-blue in the early evening light, like the sky and the fields below. The forest was already black: it would be invisible on the return trip, like the quarry we had seen just now ... The nestling mountain meadows were female in conformation and femininely fresh in the cool of the evening – indeed, the colours of a broad field of forage maize, seen against a chill white limestone rock face, together with the fading light filtering through the leaves of an already dark and sombre copper beech, were enough to arouse my recurrent regret: that it was insufficient to paint or at least sketch such a landscape in words, and that we exiles from Nature – which is only another word for paradise – could no longer set eyes on that quarry down there, almost overgrown with elder, without recalling what human beings had once done there to another of their kind. Earlier writers have not only regretted this as keenly but have even expressed their regret, as I do now, in mid-story – for instance, in *The Charterhouse of Parma*: 'Politics in a work of literature are like a pistol-shot in the middle of a concert – something crude but impossible to ignore. We are about to speak of very ugly matters which, for more than one reason, we should prefer to leave unsaid. We are, however, compelled to turn to happenings which come within our province because their theatre is the heart of our characters.'

We turned up as late as we did because farmers are easier to buttonhole in the evening than during the day.

Once we had satisfied ourselves that the grumpy dog, an ailing St Bernard, was securely chained, my youngest boy darted into the stable as if he were at home on the premises, evidently creating the impression that we had come to fix him up with some riding lessons. Conversation soon languished, of course, because we knew even less about horses than the week-end riders to whom most of the inmates belonged. I wondered how the policeman's two sons had acquired such an impressively manorial farm because neither of them could have married into the property or they wouldn't have owned it jointly. I soon discovered the predictable truth: although 'Father State' doesn't cover all farmers' expenses, it extends them wellnigh interest-free loans with a generosity denied any other occupational category. Every German government has made a point of doing this, both before and since the Nazis, hence the fact that so few agriculturalists were immune from Hitleritis. He who pays the piper has always called the tune…

Nice to hear that riding has become a popular sport and is far from confined to 'the gentry'. Nurses and secretaries, some of whom pool expenses, keep their own horses at Stackmanns' so they can ride for an hour in the evenings or longer on Saturdays and Sundays. 'I'm here,' I said abruptly, 'to ask your father about the Pole – you too, of course. You must have been there.' I gestured in the direction of the quarry.

'I was only twelve at the time,' said the man. He knew instantly what I was talking about, even though thirty-six years had gone by. 'Children weren't allowed to watch. Ah yes, it was a bad business – a rotten business,' he amended, using a form of words which he later repeated several times. 'Thanks to that, our old man was locked up by the French for three years, even though he didn't have a thing to do with it. All he did was parade the prisoners from the local PoW camps or the farms where they worked and march them to the quarry so they could see it. The body, I mean, not the execution.'

This checked, because one of the Poles escorted there by Stackmann had married the daughter of his German employers after the war and stayed on in Brombach instead of going home to Poland. He had told me the previous day that Stackmann did not march the prisoners past the gallows until their fellow-Pole had already been hanged.

We couldn't question 'the old man' till next morning because he retired to bed early, being in poor health. I suggested that he could hardly have been jailed on account of the Pole but was automatically detained by the occupying power like every SA commander and police sergeant. His son agreed. 'Yes, that's right, they carted all the police away – the old man was only a witness when the French put District Director Zinngruber on trial.' I had gathered as much from Zinngruber himself and from the documents he had lent me. Because the policeman was detained without pay for three years after the war, and because his wife and sons couldn't scrape a living from his then very meagre agricultural holding, better described as a few poor fields, the two boys had been compelled to earn a little food and money by working for other farmers – 'and my health's been poor ever since,' said the son in question, who really did look alarmingly ill and many years older than his age ... You have to give people a chance to introduce their own destinies into your research for a story of this kind; otherwise, being reluctant to discuss it in the first place, they will never open up at all. It is pointless to rebut or correct, pointless to impose standards when people not only have fixed and immutable standards of their own but are determined to splice them into the conversation. If I'd objected that these two brothers – I didn't see the other at this stage – had been deprived of their father for only three years instead of mourning his loss for thirty, like other Germans of their age-group, because, being a keen Nazi, the elder Stackmann was privileged to remain at home rather than leave his bones on one of Hitler's battlefields, I should only have destroyed all chance of pursuing the conversation further. Very circuitously, I once more steered the farmer back – we were still in his tan-scented riding school – to the story whose details I was compiling. He finally pronounced the whole affair 'a rotten business', and not just the fact that his 'old man' had been taken away by the French. 'What about the people in the village?' I asked. 'Did they think it reasonable to hang someone for adultery?' No, he replied, repeatedly and with great conviction, the bulk of them had been opposed to hanging the Pole. Although it was forbidden to discuss the matter, everyone had done so heatedly for a long time afterwards. I was relieved to hear this, but my relief was precipitate. Stackmann junior's over-large eyes – eyes set in a prematurely sunken, almost skeletal face – lit up with an inner fire as he added, 'If you ask me, *both* of them deserved to be strung up. Why not the woman as well? She was more to blame than him, being older. Besides, she was married.'

By noon next day I was back at the horse-breeders' farm to 'pump' their father, as they defensively termed it. A short, bent, hesitant little man in his mid-seventies, wary but not forbidding, he trudged towards me across the well-tended stable yard in dungarees and gumboots. I was in luck: it had been too late last night for the son to forewarn his father, nor had he spoken to him that morning. It therefore came as a surprise to the old man that I was able to quote my previous evening's lengthy talk with his son about 'the Pole down there'. The old man, too, knew at once which Pole I meant. His cold glass-grey eyes narrowed, but he could hardly elude me now. Rather brazenly, I kept introducing his son into the conversation so he couldn't wriggle off the hook – only correct, amplify or deny what the son and Zinngruber, the 'District Director', had already told me. He pricked up his ears on hearing that I had been referred to him by a confederate and superior of the Hitler vintage. Was I, he asked, 'from the newspapers'? He appeared to believe me when I told him I was a German, but the question exercised him greatly because the companion who had brought me on the pillion seat of his Vespa looked nothing like one. He was a Basle medical student, but he didn't look Swiss either. 'Are you from Poland?' Stackmann demanded. One could physically sense the uneasiness aroused in him by this dark-haired giant, who looked like one of Tito's partisan lieutenants in his combat jacket and who now, as so often, sought to disguise his congenital good nature behind a louring expression as he put the finishing touches to Stackmann's bewilderment by answering him in the purest Swiss German. 'No, I'm Swiss. I've lived in Basle for the past fifteen years – before that I lived in Zurich.'

Stackmann was so taken aback he removed the pipe from his mouth. From the look he gave me, I could accurately gauge the thought that was lurking in the head beneath his grubby felt hat: 'Some times we live in, when even a spy can jabber away in Alemannic!' It occurred to me that my wife, too, had been disapprovingly quizzed about her origins by his son the evening before. If I wanted to get anywhere with the old man I would have to elaborate. 'He's my brother-in-law,' I said. 'His parents came from Yugoslavia.'

Although the retired policeman found this a lame excuse, it dispelled his fear that someone from Poland had turned up to ask questions. (I realized, yet again, how unfathomably deep is the lower-middle-class aversion to all who come from abroad. Quite recently, when the Swiss held their second Sunday referendum on whether to kick out an annual twelve per cent of the imported drudges who have been working in their country for years, they confirmed the fact which Marxists find so unpalatable: that it is the workers, not the wealthy, who feel no scintilla of compassion, sympathy or international solidarity for luckless foreigners. Although Switzerland is fortunate in having almost no unemployment, ninety or more per cent of the electorate in working-class areas voted to kick the foreigners out. Some – though far from all – were permitted to remain for the simple reason that no more than fifteen per cent of voters in middle-class and, more especially, affluent districts marked their ballot papers in favour of packing them off home. It is the wealthy, not the workers, who make money out of foreign labour; true, but it is the workers who owe foreigners a debt of gratitude for doing the dirty jobs they no longer have to do themselves!)

Stackmann's reaction to the Slav who had given me a lift disclosed the depth of the universal gulf – indeed, the antipathy – which even today, in the age of mass tourism, divides native from foreigner. How effectively must this antipathy have been whipped into a ferment of brutality and tyranny during the war, when every Stackmann, provided he was a German but not necessarily a Nazi, was legally invested with authority over dispossessed human jetsam from countries prostrate under Hitler's heel!

The fact that my brother-in-law couched all his questions in the Basle–Wiesenthal dialect turned out to be helpful because even Stackmann deigned to converse with him, which he did in such a farrago of peasant dialect and standard German that I, who can only speak rural Hessian, was sometimes hard put to it to understand him.

It seemed that Stasiek Zasada's tragedy still upset the retired Nazi policeman because – and only because – it called to mind a violent altercation between himself and Karl Mayer, head of the Lörrach Gestapo. Mayer, whom I couldn't question because he and a Gestapo colleague had reportedly shot themselves in Lörrach cemetery when the town was occupied by French troops, had arrested the Pole at noon on 30 April 1941 and taken him to Lörrach. However, he had promptly driven back to Brombach to reprimand Stackmann, in menacing tones, for having neglected to obtain a signed declaration from Zasada that he, like all Polish prisoners released for work on individual farmsteads, had been warned that he would be hanged if he slept with a German female.

'You could find yourself in trouble!' Mayer had threatened. Stackmann underwent a transformation as he recalled this. All his reticence disappeared in a flash: he spoke heatedly, with a resurgence of anger. It riled him even now, almost forty years later, that Karl Mayer – 'I told him, I said, how dare you speak to me like that, you aren't my superior officer!' – had given even a moment's credence to Zasada's statement and entertained the possibility that he, Stackmann, had omitted to obtain written confirmation from this Pole, as from all the rest, that he had been formally threatened with the death penalty if he slept with a German woman. Stackmann not only told us this, he re-enacted the scene in Brombach's mayoral offices and demonstrated how he had slammed the folder down on the desk in front of Mayer so that the Gestapo man could pick out Zasada's signature from those of his compatriots, all of whom had acknowledged receipt of an official warning. It was some time before Stackmann dropped the subject, the more so because he had to admit that Karl Mayer had usually shown himself a reasonable and efficient colleague. That he, of all people, could have thought Stackmann capable of the most heinous offence of all: slipshod paperwork! As if he hadn't kept the signature of every last Pole neatly filed away! He had lectured the Poles in advance, standing on the steps of Brombach town hall with the prisoners drawn up below him, and informed them that it was a hanging matter. 'And would you credit it, some of them laughed. There's no cause to laugh, I told them – and there wasn't. A year later they were all back on the same spot – all except one – waiting for me to escort them to where the missing Pole was hanging. And he'd probably laughed himself, a twelvemonth before ...'

There was no mistaking Stackmann's satisfaction on two scores, first that his police records were in order, and secondly that Polish deriders of a German regulation had been taught such a fearsome lesson about the perils of laughing at a policeman. 'They didn't laugh that time,' he summed up, profoundly content that this mirth at his expense had not been left unexpiated by the natural scheme of things. In other respects, he'd done a lot for the Poles. He'd always seen to it – and argued the point with the authorities in Lörrach – that they were 'decently shod' – 'decently clothed', too, because they had the run of the village till nine at night, when they were confined to camp or their farmhouse billets, so it was only proper for them to look 'neat and tidy' ...

The three of us were standing in the sons' stable yard. At this point, a red-faced roly-poly woman ran up, shouting – almost shrieking – as she came, 'Stop spying on our Grandad!' It was the daughter-in-law, who had spotted us from the stable and was 'fed to the back teeth' with 'all that old garbage' and the people who kept pestering the family about it. 'It was bad enough in those days!' I said she was surely far too young to know anything about it, and she laughed: she wasn't *that* young – just how old did I think she was! Her husband, the chronic invalid, had never recovered from those years when Grandad was in a French jail. Anyway, 'Why rake it all up – I mean, he knew what he was letting himself in for, so why did he get mixed up with that woman? She was even worse than him, being older.'

As for what happened, 'What's the use of raking it up? Why not worry about what's going on today, with those terrorists? *They* deserve to be topped and strung up ...'

My brother-in-law pointed out the difficulty of hanging someone when his head was already off, but the vernacular isn't that fussy. Stackmann curbed his daughter-in-law's vehemence because he had been talking to us for quite some time with reminiscent satisfaction. We were, after all, recalling his heyday – the golden age when most people clicked their heels and shot out their right arms at the very sight of him. Although it had no bearing on the Zasada affair, he frequently mentioned that, quite apart from being Brombach's senior policeman, he had also commanded its Stormtroop detachment ...

To expect young men to work for ten or more hours a day in close association with women whose husbands had been conscripted into the army, to shut them up for years in these women's homes but hang them if they touched or were touched by them – Stackmann fully recognized this problem when we put it to him. He also said, with undoubted sincerity, that no one could root out human nature with a pitchfork. Yet it would never have occurred to him, even if he had been wholly unconnected with the state and not one of its conscientious instruments, that the state was in the wrong. No, the prisoners were to blame because the state had 'told them beforehand what would happen if they broke a regulation like that'. The threat of execution having been duly delivered, it was legal to carry it out, and how could anything legal be wrong? That the laws of those days were framed *by* criminals, not against them, was an idea which this man, with his lifelong public servant's training, could never even have entertained had we voiced it in his presence.

His daughter-in-law, too, calmed down when she heard that the former mayor and district director had advised us to consult

Stackmann because, unlike Zinngruber himself, he had *not* – as I was quick to emphasize – had a hand in Zasada's execution. 'But you ought to mention that too, if it gets into the papers. Our Grandad didn't have a thing to do with it, he only had to cordon off the quarry ...'

He firmly denied this. 'No, I didn't, I had more important things to do that day. My job was to ...'

And he told us again how all the Poles from far and wide, together with the French prisoners billeted in the district, had been marched to Brombach early that morning so that he could shepherd them past the man on the gallows.

I said, as though morally justifying the presence of hundreds of sightseers on the surrounding slopes and ridges, 'There wasn't a hope of cordoning off the quarry – you can see into it from all four sides.' This had a soothing effect, much as if I had produced some vital piece of exonerating evidence. The time of the execution, about nine in the morning, had been announced to the village one or more days in advance – I never found out. My first informant, a woman, told me that Zasada died crying 'Mother!' Stackmann denied having heard this, either then or afterwards, but other women confirmed the statement. 'There weren't any women there,' Stackmann insisted.

He sounded very sure for someone who wasn't there himself.

Anyway, he asked, why had I picked on Brombach? 'The same sort of thing happened all over the place – Grenzach, for instance, and Wehrethal ...' I admitted having heard that there was an arms factory there, one in which Russians and Poles were employed, and that some of them had also been hanged for sleeping with German women. This I had learned from eyewitnesses, as well as from a historian, Olaf Groehler, who has compiled some figures which indicate that not even terror could wean many Germans from their penchant for consorting with 'inferior' members of the human race. In 1940, a mere 1,216 German citizens were convicted of 'illicit association' with prisoners of war and conscripted foreign workers. The number of convictions rose to 4,345 in the following year and to 7,974 in 1942, while 4,530 were recorded in the first six months of 1943 alone. The number of arrests was higher still. The Germans detained 2,031 of their compatriots on similar grounds between June and end-December 1941 and 4,962 between May and August 1942. Gestapo and Ministry of Justice files relating to this 'complex' are missing for the last two years of the war, but during the first nine months of 1943 no less than 15,410 German citizens were locked up for having personal dealings with members of the foreign labour force.

There is something peculiarly soothing about statistics which prove that other people in other places have done the same thing at the same time as oneself. The Brombach episode might never have occurred at all, so greatly was Stackmann reassured by his own allusion to the neighbouring villages which had duplicated it. Nothing that had happened 'all over the place', and was therefore the norm, could have been reprehensible in a normal conformist who hunted with the pack (or sometimes took a short lead) because it was a normal thing to do ... And so the old man sent us on our way with a handshake, as if he'd sold us a basket of cherries. But, seeing him stand there as we walked back to our scooter, I abruptly discerned a strong resemblance to the policeman who had threatened the Poles almost forty years earlier: anyone who averted his eyes, anyone bold enough to shun the sight of a compatriot on the gallows, would be hanged alongside him!

Hitler's war was less than a month old – though lone Blenheim bombers were already raiding German soil by night – when a conference on improving night fighter tactics was held at the Berlin Air Ministry. Among those summoned to attend was Johannes Steinhoff, then twenty-five and commanding a night fighter squadron, later highly decorated and severely wounded, still later one of West Germany's post-war service chiefs in Bonn. In 1969 General Steinhoff recalled how Göring, Hitler's air force supremo, conducted this meeting. Steinhoff was the youngest participant and had been invited because he alone could contribute up-to-date combat experience. The other men present – all generals or general staff officers with the exception of the stenographer – had fought, if fought they ever had, in the First World War. 'The conference chamber ... bore witness to the Marshal's predilection for oak, heavy leather and furniture of imposing dimensions,' writes Steinhoff. 'The pale wooden panelling extended to the ceiling, from which hung a massive chandelier shaped like a wagon-wheel. The long oak table was flanked by chairs whose seats and backs were upholstered in pale cowhide, and at the head of the table towered a special variety of chair distinguished by its truly Germanic proportions. This was Göring's place. A panel in the wainscoting opened and he strode in. He was wearing a white uniform, and while he settled himself in the vast armchair he lit a long Virginia cigar of the kind they smoke in Austria. Then he began to speak. He spoke ... of the failure of our night fighters and anti-aircraft defences. There were still no radar instruments available at that stage, neither to us nor the anti-aircraft guns ... It was, he said, a disgrace that the Blenheims should be making undisturbed joy-rides over the Reich. He worked himself up into a real fury, and all at once he was back to the dogfights in Flanders [1917] and the great days ... under Baron von Richthofen. He raised his hands and demonstrated the tactics of attacking from below ... His language was graphic ... Gradually, however, a feeling of bitter disillusionment stole over me ... This man has no comprehension of modern aerial warfare, it ran through my mind. He lives in the past and doesn't know his own air force.'

Perhaps because Göring himself wasn't old – a mere forty-six – and also, perhaps, because Steinhoff imagined that he had been summoned to Berlin, despite his extreme youth, on the strength of his unique claim to combat experience in the present war, he felt called upon to add a word of correction – inject a note of realism. That was his final illusion. 'The urge to interrupt him and say something based on practical experience became overwhelming,' he recalls. 'When he paused for a moment to relight his Virginia, I raised my finger. Simultaneously, I quailed because the generals' faces, which turned towards me as though at a given command, plainly conveyed their disapproval of my audacity ... Göring levelled his Virginia at me, signifying that I had permission to speak. I stood up and began to describe ... how difficult it was to detect the enemy, who flew over with good navigational aids in poor weather and at high altitudes ... We, on the other hand, had no way of navigating in bad weather and could not, therefore, do our job. What we needed were better navigational aids in our aircraft and new methods of locating the enemy in darkness from the outset. I spoke concisely and, to my mind, convincingly. The whole thing was quite obvious, anyway, and if anyone knew how to conduct night fighter attacks in those days, I did.

'There was no sign of anger on Göring's face when he removed the Virginia from his mouth to interrupt the well-ordered flow of my remarks. He looked more amused than anything else. "Sit down," he said, as though addressing a sixth-former, "sit down on your little backside, young man. You'll have to chalk up a lot more experience before you rate a hearing in this company."

'With that, he turned to one of the generals on his operational staff and took no more notice of me.'

This anecdote is as sad as it is German. It demonstrates that, even in 1939, the German citizens who bore prime responsibility for Hitler's European massacre – the generals – were appalled when a fighting man dared to criticize one of the senior Nazis whom those same generals tried to saddle with all the blame, even in the military sphere, when Hitler's war had been lost. Even Udet was among young Steinhoff's listeners – Udet, who bore the resounding title 'Master-General of Air Ordnance' and was soon to shoot himself because of the deficiencies in his ill-conceived aircraft construction programme, notably a lack of bombers ...

Maria's husband, the bomber pilot, caught two more glimpses of Reich Marshal Göring on the Channel coast before a Spitfire shot him down. On the last occasion he remarked to a fellow-flyer, 'Fatso doesn't come to France to visit the front, he –' His friend, who was even more pugnacious, broke in. 'The front? The front isn't in France. The most Göring does is visit us when we get *back* from the front – those of us that do ...'

Maria's husband completed his original sentence. 'He comes to filch paintings and antiques. It sounds incredible, but I know for a fact there's a so-called operations team specially designed to handle them.'

They both needed to let off steam before they could go to sleep that night in the early autumn of 1940. For the first time ever, nearly fifty German planes had failed to return from London – fifty out of the first or late afternoon run.

Exactly how many were missing not even the air crews could discover because missions were jointly flown from several bases at once ... Göring was standing a hundred yards away beside Sperrle, who, with monocle-distorted features, was yelling something in his ear above the roar and whine of the stragglers who were still coming in to land. Looking at him, Maria's husband said, 'Does he really have to wear wine-red boots and gold spurs with blue breeches, just to pick out paintings?'

His friend didn't laugh. He said, 'Oh, go on, don't begrudge him the gold spurs – he can't hang any gongs on his boots.' Maria's husband laughed, but ruefully. 'Spurs on an air marshal ... I wouldn't like to be the horse that has to carry *him*!'

While they were strolling back to their quarters – there seemed an element of protest in their departure, at least to them, because the majority had lingered to enjoy this unwonted close-up of their lords and masters – the friend said, 'Don't speak too soon. We're two of the horses that'll have to carry the man or haul his coach in the victory parade, all the way to Trafalgar Square.'

'You really think we'll get there?' said Maria's husband. Unsmiling now, he quickened his step and added, 'I'm going to take a shower – sluice off all that cold sweat and grab some sleep.'

Only when he was overwhelmed by his own exhaustion, but unaware that what underlay it was disillusionment as opposed to physical strain, did he reflect on the purpose of the self-sacrificial raids which were incapable – that much was obvious to him and all who took part in them – of altering the course of the war. Britain had a formidable navy, it was true. The Danes and Norwegians hadn't possessed one worthy of the name, but what good would it have done to bomb Copenhagen and Oslo? You had to land in a country to take it, and if they couldn't land in England – and it was beginning to look that way – they ought to dream up something else. Anything rather than these thrice daily, nightly attempts to drop bombs into a sea of bricks and mortar inhabited by two-and-a-half times the population of Berlin. What was the point?

Even when fear and necessity drove him to ponder such things, he could only fasten his thoughts on details which directly affected his existence. He not only knew nothing of the general picture but refused to dwell on it because he was too much of a stolid, down-to-earth craftsman even to gossip about matters beyond his ken. But he could only afford this lack of involvement as long as he trusted those who were thinking for him. So what *were* they thinking, those two tubby men on the edge of the runway, Göring and Sperrle? To judge by their language when they delivered harangues and blared out orders of the day, their studious optimism was based, not on ignorance, but on turning a blind eye... Were they what Goebbels called 'men who make history', he wondered helplessly, or just the stuff of which history is made? He had never, not since his schooldays, read a book which even touched on history. Coming from a family of railwaymen – both his grandfathers had been drivers – he suddenly found it impossible to suppress an unutterably heretical thought: locomen had to know their job; as a fitter, he too had been obliged to learn how to make a living in peace-time, so where did the politicians, the strategists, learn their trade? Of the two men standing on the runway with their ludicrous marshals' batons, one had been a fighter pilot twenty years ago and the other an army officer. Where could *they* have acquired a knowledge of how to enforce surrender on a city with eight or ten million inhabitants? Where did politicians in general learn about the specialized fields they headed in a ministerial capacity? Minister ... That was the only job you didn't have to train for, but say so out loud and they'd lop off your head! He knew, roughly at any rate, how high aircraft losses were and how meagre was the flow of replacements, not of planes but of trained air crews. If only for that reason, he also knew that the air offensive against London *couldn't* achieve its object. And because he knew this like all his fellow-flyers, Göring too must have known it for weeks – and they surely wouldn't shoot *him* for telling the Führer. But would they shoot *anyone* – Sperrle, for instance – who asked Göring why he didn't tell Hitler the truth? Of course not, so would Sperrle literally be running no risk at all if he recommended breaking off a battle which could never be won?

He stared up at the ceiling. Then, so as to sleep, he strove to think of his girl-friend in Antwerp. He *had* to get some sleep because he was due for another trip to London in six hours' time.

Poor man! Only two days later, fish were nibbling his half-charred remains in the Channel ... He was fortunate enough to die before the full absurdity of his sacrificial role dawned on him, though an inkling of it had already infected his mind. He had never, of course, heard of Hegel. That much at least he was spared, for this devotee of the state – 'philosopher' means lover of wisdom, but Hegel was only in love with power – burdened the anonymous masses with the demeaning realization that only the foremost representatives of an age enlighten their inferiors on what that age demands of those who inhabit it and – herein lies the ultimate horror – on what the majority, swept along by their own momentum, do in fact end by wanting. Another Hegelian insight: that the masses revel in their love of obedience as if doing of their own free will what they are only and unwittingly doing for the sake of another, who will destroy them in the process. To think, since it cannot alas be denied, that millions of

German soldiers perished in an attempt to get somewhere purely because it was Hitler's chosen destination! To think, too, that many of these men would have had no personal will but for Hitler, who imbued them with his own, and that the transmission of his will was effected in the vast majority of cases – many isolated exceptions apart – not under duress but by simple appeals to love of obedience! Malignly but with perfect truth, Hegel put it this way: 'He who *thinks* what others merely *are* is their power.'

Let no one suppose that the educated, or even those well versed in history, are any less prone to the orgasms of the political St Vitus's dance. They differ from mindless conformists only in their desire to furnish themselves with an intellectual pretext for conformism. Hegel and Beethoven, in their giddy enthusiasm for Napoleon, are cogent evidence that fellow-travelling is not peculiar to any one class or level of education. Hölderlin didn't balk at referring to Napoleon on paper as 'Most Glorious', and even Heine's divine irony deserted him altogether when he extolled Napoleon *knowing* what he had done to his soldiers in Russia. Being a Jew, Heine was dazzled by his gratitude for Napoleon's emancipation of the Jews. What diminishes his stature is that someone so alive to the plight of Silesian weavers could deny the conscripts of the *Grande Armée* the sympathy he extended in verse to their murderer. Heine knew, for example, that Munich had only fifty thousand inhabitants in 1812, when 'the finest army Bavaria ever had filed past the king's window' there, bound for total annihilation. The king, a prince-elector who owed his brand-new throne to Napoleon, looked on as 27,500 men marched or rode past him on their way to the corpse-strewn battlefields of Russia. They were followed by 5,200 reinforcements. Of the troops who set out from Munich, 28,700 never returned, not counting the Danzigers of the Bavarian garrison – an infantry regiment and a battery of artillery – who likewise perished in Russia, almost to a man. The historian Hummert somewhat sarcastically notes that the death rate among the officers whom the Russians captured, fed and later released was only in the region of thirty per cent. As if reassured by some presentiment of this, the officers marched off delirious with enthusiasm even though Bavaria's sole interest in the campaign was the compulsion felt by her new 'royal' house to render thanks for its elevation in rank – disproportionate thanks. Bavaria, which had never been in conflict with Russia, contributed the whole of her regular army to Napoleon's Russian venture and only kept a national guard at home. The little country, whose pre-war prosperity was such that it had started building a national theatre in 1811, supplied the Corsican dictator with only 1,300 fewer troops than Austria, a great power ruled by an emperor who was also Napoleon's father-in-law. The Prussians sent a mere 20,000 – and they deserted the French under Yorck at the first opportunity. Prince Baryatinsky, Russian minister plenipotentiary at the Bavarian court, predicted the tragedy with great accuracy, thereby proving – incidentally – that the plan to annihilate the invading armies was not Kutuzov's brainchild alone. The Russian minister's warning is recorded in the memoirs of Christian Mannlich, Bavaria's national director of art galleries, who died in 1822. I reproduce it here because it tallies almost word for word with what Hitler's ambassador in Moscow, Count von der Schulenburg, was just as unsuccessful in impressing on the man whose fears of a Napoleonic winter did not deter him from marching into its jaws 120 years later.

Baryatinsky to Mannlich, over dinner in 1811: 'I am sincerely sorry for your son Karl and for you, my dear Mannlich. The whole of Europe is girding itself for war against us. Everywhere, alliances are being made in order to coerce us into a humiliating treaty. We are facing the storm steadfastly and without arrogance. We shall, however, show our enemies what can be achieved by a nation which is beginning its gradual ascent from the wild state to civilization, which still has religion and morals, which is still a stranger to luxury, which loves its native land and will make any sacrifice in order to preserve its most hallowed possessions. If the enemy succeeds in penetrating our territory, we shall reduce everything in his path to ashes, thereby depriving him of spoils and preventing him from looting and burning in his accustomed fashion. He will find our towns and villages laid waste, will want for assistance and guides and be harassed unceasingly by our innumerable bands of cavalry, who will cut off his supplies of food. We have some invincible allies on our side: Napoleon's absurd presumption, hunger and cold. Of the army that sets forth against us, many thousands strong, few will see their native land again without some enduring reminder of ambition's most senseless undertaking.'

Mannlich adds that, although he himself was troubled by dark forebodings, neither his son nor his son's comrades could wait to be off: 'They had a burning desire to see Russia.' Confirmation of this can be found in the history of the Bavarian army printed by the War Records Office: 'The Army, and the officer corps in particular, were far from reluctant to embark on the new war, from which, as during its predecessor, they expected a fulfilment of their military ambitions and thirst for action. On 25 February, therefore, when Munich received Napoleon's request that immediate preparations be made to march, the consequent beginning of mobilization was hailed by the Army with rejoicing and delight.' The same could be said of all the belligerents in 1914, but not in 1939: memories of Verdun and the Somme were too green.

In this respect, Hegel's adage that 'governments are the sails and the people the wind' is as dated as any other. Before the defeat of France in 1940, which was accomplished in six short weeks, the people of Germany generated no wind to fill the sails of Hitler and his clique. They did after that, but only until disillusionment set in with the fall of Stalingrad.

Maria's husband, the bomber pilot, had been missing for two years by then. Fortunately for him, he too had been temporarily numbered among the millions who delighted in their obedience as if doing of their own free will what was merely the will of Hitler and, thus, of Göring and, thus, of their countless subjects. Why fortunately? Because it would have done the man no good to grasp whose folly it was that drove him across the Channel, only to die after killing who knows how many Londoners with his bombs. More than that, this realization would only have blighted the little that remained of his swiftly extinguished life.

How could he have climbed into his cockpit – as he had to, or be shot – in the knowledge that Hitler's hopes of an invasion had been buried for all of four weeks, since 17 September 1940, and that German airmen were still being sacrificed on missions to England only to mask the Wehrmacht's eastward withdrawal from France and its regrouping in readiness for the invasion of Russia? And what did this pilot know of Göring, whose gruesome popularity moved even the sardonic Berliners to affectionate applause as late as 1943, on the last occasion when he dared to board an open car and tour the bomb-blasted streets for which he himself bore the blame? Many there were who also shouted 'Meyer!' without being arrested – without even causing offence – because the cry betokened their lingering sense of solidarity with a beaten gangster. (Göring had announced when war broke out that he would change his name to Meyer if a single enemy bomber succeeded in raiding a single German town.) What makes people applaud those who have sent at least one member of every family in the land to his death – not to mention the families in neighbouring lands termed 'enemy'? 'Reviewing the history of the European peoples, I can discover no instance in which the sincere and devoted cultivation of their peaceful prosperity has exerted a stronger attraction on their sentiments than martial glory, the winning of battles and the conquest even of recalcitrant territories,' wrote someone who himself waged three wars and provoked two. Semi-contemptuously but with some surprise, Bismarck went on: 'Charles XII of Sweden wilfully led his country into national decline, yet Swedish farmhouses more often display his portrait than that of Gustavus Adolphus as a symbol of Swedish renown ... Louis XIV and Napoleon, whose wars ruined the nation and ended in scant success, have remained the pride of the French.'

Hegel welcomed what Bismarck grudgingly conceded, though he was naturally aware that 'since 1793 (i.e. up to 1812) more than three million Frenchmen have been called to the colours and most of them killed in battle.' He also knew that French conscripts had latterly been forced to march chained in file until they left French soil. The unfortunate men were then released and 'allowed' on to the chopping-block – the battlefield – because they were so detested abroad, purely for their nationality's sake, that no foreigner would have given refuge to a French deserter. Here is Hegel rhapsodizing in a letter written during 1806, in ignorance that Napoleon would leave his *Grande Armée* to perish in the snows of Russia six years later: 'I saw the Emperor, that universal spirit, ride out of the city to reconnoitre. It is indeed a wondrous sensation to see such an individual, who, centred on this one spot, seated on a horse, reaches out across the world and dominates it.'

Which, just because it really was so, seemed 'reasonable' to a self-styled philosopher. It was typical of Hegel, who never – needless to say – heard a shot fired in anger, that he should compensate for the absence of the word 'manpower', which had yet to be coined, by disdainfully enclosing the word 'people' in quotation marks: 'The "people" is that part of the state which does not know what it wants.'

Hitler, who thought likewise, treated this 'part' of the state as if Hegel had tutored him in what could be done with it.

The barely articulated fear that Göring had no idea how to defeat Britain because he had 'never learnt it anywhere', as Maria's husband was warned by his craftsman's sound common sense, revives the question of how Göring ever managed to rule the destiny of millions and issue orders to hundreds of thousands of fighting men who claimed innumerable lives. Five years after RAF fighters shot the air out of Hitler's grandiloquent human balloon, aided by the guile and tenacity of Winston Churchill, whose 1940 speeches had – *à la* Hegel – voiced what the Londoners *ought* to want and what, in consequence, they actually *did* want like everyone outside the fascist penitentiary, namely, all-out resistance to Hitler – five years afterwards, two American psychiatrists paid independent visits to Göring in his cell at Nuremberg. Both of them asked what had made him join the Nazi Party, rather than another, in 1922. The answer was disconcertingly simple. Göring hadn't even been motivated by the banality of evil, merely by the urge for self-advancement which is everyone's birthright. Before he joined forces with Hitler,

Göring was one of the very few surviving First World War pilots to have won the Kaiser's highest military award, the Pour le Mérite. He was also renowned as the last commander of the legendary Richthofen fighter group. Under the Weimar Republic his status brought him a very meagre pension, nor did it exempt a man of twenty-five from the duty to earn his own living. But this, at a time of widespread unemployment, was difficult for an ex-serviceman who had learnt nothing but the arts of war. One is therefore inclined to accept what Göring told the American psychiatrist Douglas M. Kelly (who incidentally rated him the most intelligent of those who had been detained for complicity in genocide) was his reason for backing Hitler: 'I wanted to help destroy the Republic and to be, perhaps, the ruler of the new Reich ... You see, it was this way. There were at that time about fifty organizations – call them parties – of World War veterans in Germany. They didn't like the government. They didn't like the Versailles Treaty. They didn't like the peace – a peace in which there were no jobs, no food, no shoes. I knew that the overthrow of the Republic would be brought about by these dissatisfied men. So I looked over the parties to see which ones showed promise. After studying each one, I decided to join the National Socialist Party. It was small – that meant I could soon be a big man in it.' Göring told the other psychiatrist, Gilbert, that only the merest chance – a date – had prevented him from fulfilling his plan to join a freemason's lodge in 1919. 'I wouldn't be here today!' he added (he was in the condemned cell by this time). It was true: no former freemasons were ever admitted to Hitler's ranks ... And yet, apart from Hitler himself, Göring became the most culpable mass murderer in the Third Reich. It was he who, on 31 July 1941, gave Heydrich the 'final solution' order which resulted in the wholesale deportation of Jews from Central and Western Europe to 'classified destinations' in the east. Why the east? Because the extermination of the insane, a process begun and then discontinued in response to protests from the Churches and the general public, had taught the Nazis that their murder-machine could not function with sufficient secrecy in densely populated Western Europe. It could do so only if they consigned families and communities to limbo *en bloc,* leaving no relatives behind who might try to trace them ... The killing of Russian-born Jews had been inaugurated a month before by the SS and Security Police task forces attached to German army groups as specially constituted murder squads.

The horrifyingly *casual* way in which Göring teamed up with Hitler and tackled so many 'special assignments' which were beyond him, being unqualified for anything but the work he had performed so well as a fighter pilot in the First World War, is equally characteristic of this, the most frightful of all his edicts. For Göring was *not* an anti-Semite. His mother, as he well knew, had been the mistress of a Jew for many years. Even in 1934, when a Jewess whose appearance on the stage of the Berliner Schauspielhaus was greeted – because of her race – with catcalls, Göring applauded so ostentatiously from his box that the playwright Wedekind's widow, who was present, wrote: 'Göring was not an anti-Semite at that stage.' No, but he was second only to Hitler in his lack of scruple.

But Hitler – this is a statement, not an excuse – was a sick man. He differed from Göring in having 'motives', albeit demented ones, for his hatred of Jews. The Göring who ordered Jews killed in deference to his leader – and Hitler doubtless had this order passed to Heydrich via Göring because he *knew* that Göring wasn't an anti-Semite – had no hatred of Jews; he merely had an urge, first to impress Hitler with his all-round versatility, and secondly to 'Aryanize' as many Jewish-owned works of art as possible into his personal possession. He did not even regard certain individual Jews with the spurned suitor's hatred which Goebbels felt for Jewish publishers who had rejected his manuscripts – the hatred that later moved him to condemn Jewish publishing houses as 'rotary synagogues' ...

Being the vainest of all the Nazis apart from Goebbels, Göring wasn't man enough to admit to his ministerial visitor, if to no one else, that he had lost the Battle of Britain – and this although it seems probable that by 20 October, or four weeks after Hitler had taken its loss for granted and framed his orders accordingly, Göring must himself have realized that victory had eluded him.

It is not, of course, certain that he was capable of admitting such a thing to himself. What is proven, on the other hand, is that he gave no hint of it to Goebbels when escorting him to Sperrle's headquarters on 20 October. The top Nazis' passion for lying, even among themselves, was only surpassed by their flatulent and ceaseless braggadocio, for they themselves were the first to succumb to their own talk of victory. Goebbels's unclouded optimism when he flew to see Göring on 20 October is yet another almost incredible proof of his capacity for seeing only what he chose to see and giving priority to the elimination of his own misgivings. Goebbels had, in fact, already been briefed on the true position. His diary testifies that a fortnight earlier, on 4 October, an air force liaison officer had told him the whole grim truth to his face. Still drunk with victory, Goebbels failed to perceive its full gravity and finality even though the officer in question, Colonel Wodarg, had gone so far as to compare London to Verdun, the soldier's inferno of the First World War: 'Wodarg reported to me ... a decline in the strength of the air force units operating against London. They feel as if they are tackling Verdun. Too many demands are being made on the men. They get little rest. Although they are inflicting terrible damage on the enemy, we ourselves are not escaping wholly unscathed. We must do something for those boys. Morale in the country is patchy. People are still hoping for a speedy end to the war. It is hard to persuade the public otherwise ...'

We ourselves are not escaping wholly unscathed ... Goebbels didn't blush at such euphemistic turns of phrase although Wodarg, whose current appointment was 'General Staff Officer (Intelligence), Luftwaffe Operations Staff', and who had been bold enough to compare London to Verdun in the minister's presence, must also have reported that Göring's air fleets were being badly mauled. But Goebbels only wanted to hear what would reinforce his 'blind faith' in the Reich Chancellery's gangster-in-chief, with whom he spent many hours a day at this period. The craven courtier in Goebbels would never have dared to discuss this latter-day Verdun with his master; it was as if Wodarg had never broached the subject. A fortnight later, after he himself had

had an opportunity to question some of the pilots whom Göring – in full awareness that the battle was lost – was still chivvying across the Channel, he noted: '20 October ... Yesterday, ate with Göring ... Flew to Deauville. Opposite, the English coast. Superb weather. Fighters and fighter-bombers roared overhead. Sperrle expecting us. Lengthy situation report on the war in the air. An extremely intricate piece of clockwork, but designed with German attention to detail. One can only commend it. Sperrle is a hell of a fellow. As for his men – simply fantastic. Flew back to Paris after a three-hour visit. Said goodbye to Göring. He was particularly nice. We parted friends ... That evening to a little restaurant where they sang French *chansons*. All very nice and charming. This city is a big danger, especially to unpolitical Germans.'

Not a syllable of what Goebbels later claimed to 'recall' in July 1944, when he intimated to his desk chief Wilfred von Oven that Reich Marshal Göring was principally to blame for losing the war: 'I flew at that period to our operational air bases in France. I sat with commanding officers and pilots, conversing at length in their messes ... The flames of the open fire danced and flickered over faces so earnest and mature that one would never have thought they belonged to twenty-year-olds. No one there spoke in the brazen tones of Herr Sperrle ... They were all thinking of the fallen comrades who had, perhaps, been sitting there among them only yesterday or the day before ... The mood that possessed them was Hölderlinesque. They spoke of sacrifices made for the Fatherland and pondered the purpose of a hero's death ... I flew back to Berlin, filled with concern and misgiving.'

Served up for his own and his subordinate's edification in 1944, this moving tale is typical because it contains no word of truth: Goebbels never paid a second visit to the Battle of Britain front. What makes it still more typical is that Goebbels obviously believed it himself – yet another proof that mood has the power to transmute facts in the human memory. One is forced to conclude that witnesses are even less to be trusted than (all too easily manufacturable) evidence, and that what exposes the complete futility of hoping to report or clarify bygone events is the undeni-able subjective *sincerity* of witnesses' statements. Goebbels wasn't alone in believing his story at the time of its telling. Four years' disappointment with Göring's Luftwaffe had imbued him with the certainty that he had four years earlier seen and said what he took for granted in 1944: that Sperrle and Göring were a pair of bumptious braggarts whose personal incompetence had lost Germany the Battle of Britain. Still 'reminiscing' in 1944, Goebbels went on: 'Sperrle had moved into the most palatial establishment in the fashionable international resort and sur-rounded himself with every kind of luxury ... I returned to Berlin after this visit to Deauville with the worst possible impressions. The canker of good living and arrogance had already bitten deep into the body of our air force ... At about this time, Colonel Wodarg came ... to see me. His face was drawn and worried. He had lost the jaunty nonchalance habitual to our air force officers. "Minister," he said, "London is becoming our aerial Verdun."'

It is interesting to note how, in the minister's memory, Colonel Wodarg's words of warning are inserted *after* the trip to Sperrle's headquarters. His diary proves that he first heard the Verdun ana-logy a fortnight *before* he visited Sperrle but that, with his wonted capacity for enthusiasm, he had been so unthinkingly carried away by Göring's and Sperrle's talk of victory that he forgot the colonel's warning because he *wanted* to forget it. Until only a few days before he killed his six children with poisoned blanc-mange and lethal injections and then got the SS to shoot him and his wife, Goebbels was the most easily swayed of all Germans. He believed what he wished to believe – though only when it came from his own lips – to an extent that almost precludes one from calling him a liar, yet he was the most adroit of all the Nazi confidence tricksters apart from Hitler. So adroit that his adroitness completely baffled his own intelligence.

Night talk

Attacks on the Führer and other prominent figures assume such a discreet form that one can never pin them down. I myself have heard from my bedroom passers-by make the following remarks: '... but how can a corporal command an army millions strong?' From his voice I recognized the speaker as an intellectual of my acquaintance, but I could not see because it was dark, nor could I go after him because I was already undressed and in bed. Another night, I heard: 'Here we go again – he keeps all his promises, work and bread.' That was after the announcement of a cut in the meat ration. I thought I recognized this voice, too, as belonging to a former official of the Red Front.

From 'Ideological Report by the Director of Training, Feucht Branch, Nuremberg District,' 11 June 1943.

'Herbert was awake just now!' whispered Pauline. Zasada's heart almost missed a beat because he only caught sight of her as she spoke. Despite her pale nightdress and the moon, which had a bruised, battered look, the yard was so dark that her figure was barely distinguishable against the white surround of the doorway where she had intercepted him, shivering and still half asleep. She had never come to meet him before, simply left the yard door open. She had never heard him coming, either, and it always took so long – not for him to kiss her awake but for her to be 'there' – that he had once playfully asked her whether all women slept as soundly as bears in winter-time.

'You're the bear,' she had murmured when she could finally do so. 'You've got great big paws like a bear and you're just as quiet and quick and strong when you grab hold of someone. You're as heavy as a bear, too.'

Perturbed, he had whispered back, 'I too heavy for you?' And she had had to hold him tight with all fours to keep him lying there on top of her, the way she liked, because he was so diffident and considerate. He could never give her a present, and he knew that he was almost powerless to help her suppress the qualms she felt about deceiving her husband. A parcel arrived every week, and these parcels were their bone of contention. She thought nothing of sharing some of the food her husband sent from Holland, which was so much more tasty than anything that could be bought at home. Pauline found it quite natural, but he wouldn't accept it and that hurt her. With a brusque and un-wonted sarcasm which reduced him to silence for a long time, she had said, 'Oh yes, his wife you can take, but not a few crumbs of Delft gingerbread.'

He squatted down in front of her and helped her on with his shoes because her feet were bare. He could not offer her the warmth of a jacket because he never wore anything but a shirt, trousers and shoes when he stole over to see her, but she didn't need a jacket. She wasn't shivering because it was damp and misty at one in the morning but because she was almost asleep on her feet. 'The child must have been dreaming,' she explained in a whisper. 'He woke me up with his crying, but he was off again in no time.' So they could have retired to bed as usual, but he could sense that she was reluctant to go back into the house. As though reproaching herself – and who knew whether she wasn't to blame? – she said, 'What could he have been dreaming about, to cry like that?' Zasada smiled and shrugged. 'I more afraid of horses than witches when I boy. I remember my father – he come upstairs one time because some horses scare me in my dreams, and now I drive coal cart! Come...' He had enveloped almost the whole of her back in his big strong arms while they were speaking, to warm it, but she was still warm from bed. Now he picked her up with one arm under her knees and the other encircling her shoulders and carried her for seven paces – all that were needed to traverse the entire yard – to the only tree that stood there, a spindly pear-tree hemmed in by a stretch of concrete, and sat down with her on a garden chair and massaged her calves because they were cold and so ready to hand.

'It's no use, Stani,' she said, feebly and very softly, but lay with her open mouth against his short sturdy neck as if she meant to stay there for ever. He said nothing – after all, he knew what was coming. Though not a cause of dissension between them, it depressed him whenever he thought of her: she made him sense that she didn't want him to come – that she was simply too weak to say no because his loneliness and sexual torment made her feel sorry for him. This dejection only left him during the fifty or sixty minutes devoted to the reason for his coming, and it happened in a way that absolved him from any self-reproachful notion that she might be mothering him – giving herself to him out of pity. His one uncertainty during this hour was whether walls had ears. The scrawny neighbour with eyes round as buttons and hard and black as gun-muzzles – her husband, too, was stationed abroad in the air force – lived right next door to Pauline, with only a partition wall between them. And Pauline, who took so long to wake, waxed loud in passion and was deaf to her own cries. And despite the pillow he made her moan into, when she didn't stifle her exultation in the hair on his chest, this was nothing short of deadly dangerous. Even so, his chief delight was the assurance that she enjoyed him quite as fiercely as he did her –

that she was not just indulging a boy young enough to be her son. But now, sounding more disconsolate than ever before, Pauline whispered, 'That woman from next door – she was back in the shop again last night, even though she'd bought everything she needed in the morning. She only came to pry . . .' Zasada said, 'I know, I see her.' Pauline retorted impatiently, 'That's what I'm saying, she only came back around six because she wanted to see you and me together. And the way she looked at you, with smoke coming out of her ears! She'd jump into bed with you like a shot – she's *drooling* for a man. And you're so strong, she can tell that a mile off.' Pauline clung to him as she spoke, as though prising him away from the woman next door.

'Let her see – let her see me, I allowed to carry things for you. How you carry sacks of potatoes and . . .'

Pauline broke in. 'But she said something too. Must be nice for you having company at night, she said, does the Pole speak good German? He's locked in at nine, I told her, over at Melchior's, but she didn't give up. You don't say, she said, I'd no idea the Melchiors were so strict with those Polacks of theirs. They aren't strict, I said, it's regulations, that's all. Believe me, Stani, she's heard us!' Infected by her fear, he didn't reply. Then he said, 'But I never speak you Polish, I . . .'

Pauline smiled faintly. 'How would you know – how would either of us know what we say when we're at it?'

He smiled too, now, but there was little conviction in his voice. 'Perhaps she . . . Perhaps she hear you with man – all right, yes, but she not know who.'

'Who else would it be?' she said. 'There isn't another man in the place it *could* be . . . I feel safer out here than I do in the house because there's the outside wall between us and that poisonous bitch, but we mustn't do more than whisper.'

She was still sitting across his thighs. 'Cold?' he asked, and she said, 'Not yet.' He rose, still holding her, and put her down on the chair. Barefoot, he padded round the yard beyond her range of vision, checking, and went back to the wall he had to scale when climbing across from Melchior's yard to satisfy himself that there was no one lurking on the far side – not that he really feared there would be. She had taken off his shoes when he returned and was sitting with her feet tucked up on the chair, hugging her knees because she was cold. He removed his shirt and trousers. 'Stand up,' he told her, bundling them into a cushion for the chair. And he thrust his hands, big and warm as slices of farmhouse bread, beneath her buttocks, which were as cold as the calves that now, as he knelt down before her and took her with his mouth, lay draped across his shoulders. She only had his hair to occupy her hands, which yearned for the whole of his stalwart young body because she needed the full weight and length of it, more than anything else to ward off a fast-growing temptation to retreat into the lonely legitimacy of her married state. His lust, transmuted into love by gratitude for what she gave him and risked by so doing, carried her away, but only when he had her 'where horse sense goes a-grazing', as the local saying went.

But tonight he failed completely – in fact his tongue-play only made her more edgy, magnifying her qualms into an irritation she had never shown before. Fear lay on her like a dead weight. 'Stop it,' she whispered impatiently, 'I can't, not tonight. I can't, Stani – get up, I haven't told you the worst part.' She got up herself, and he sat down and took her on his lap. With her lips close to his ear, she said, 'When you went back for supper I could tell Elsbeth wanted to say something – something bad about you. You can feel these things. She was only waiting for you to go.'

Zasada frowned. 'Tonight?'

'Of course, she turned up before you left. Well, she said I ought to visit my husband right away, preferably this Sunday. I told you they'd transferred him to Germany, remember? He's stationed in Bavaria, guarding – I don't know – an aircraft factory, I think, where prisoners work. But then it came out: Elsbeth looked at me as if I'd put a snake in her bed and said, "Make sure you go and see your husband so the rest of the village gets rid of the idea you're gone on Stani, because that's what they're saying!"

'And then I told her the truth. It was crazy of me, I know.'

Silence engulfed them both.

At last she said plaintively, 'She'd never give us away, not Elsbeth. I'd only have made her angrier if I'd lied to her.'

'Angry?' he said. 'Not her business. Why angry?'

She laughed, but wrily, as if someone had ripped a plaster off her cheek. 'Women – you don't understand, they're like that. It's because she doesn't have what I have ... And there's something else, Stani. I don't like to say this, but – well, I know nothing can happen tonight, but I can't be sure it didn't a fortnight ago. It's a real stroke of luck, I suppose, being able to see my husband again. I'm that scared I'd go tomorrow if I could, but I can't just leave the shop and...'

He cradled her face against his neck and whispered, 'You not be frightened of baby, I sure nothing wrong.'

And now they returned to the subject they had so often discussed in the past three nights, he as calmly and she as impatiently as she had rejected his soothing words of the night before. 'It's all right for you – you could make a run for it, but what about me? How could I run out on two children because I've started another? The other day in the shop I saw Rosi Lindner hanging from a beam as plain as anything, and it was broad daylight – I even had a customer. It shook me, don't you understand?'

He said, 'I understand very well, but perhaps it is a sign – you say me yourself, only yesterday. Nervous tonight, nervous last night – no reason. Perhaps it mean your period come soon. You say me yourself you always so – so touchy then.'

'No reason?' she repeated. 'What do you mean, no reason – didn't I just tell you I confessed to Elsbeth? I told her it only happened twice, weeks ago. It's all over and done with, I told her, but she didn't believe a word of it, I was so – oh, I don't know! I *knew* she was going to say something, but when it came – well, all of a sudden I was sitting there opposite her with my face all bare. I never knew a person could feel that way, as if their face was naked – like an open book. What on earth gives you that idea, I meant to say, but I just couldn't do it. I was so flummoxed when she said the whole village was talking about us...'

Zasada said, 'Not true! If village talking, why Herr Melchior not lock my door? Why not take yard key out at night? And Frau Melchior, why she not speak me about you? Poor Pauline!' He said 'poor' to disguise the fact that he meant silly, foolish Pauline. 'Elsbeth only sus – suspicious, nothing more, only try, only try to find out truth. And you – oh, why you fall into trap? She only *try*, not *know*!' How stupid she is, he thought bitterly.

She sensed what she had done to him. Till now she had only been conscious of her own predicament. She fondled and kissed what she liked to kiss most, the place where his neck and shoulders merged. Seeking to distract him, she said lightly, 'When you're sitting with a man he always uses his right hand to pet you, the way you're doing now. Never when you're lying down – never. Why is that?' She laughed softly. He hadn't understood, so she repeated what she'd said. Then he smiled too, in puzzled concurrence, unable to advance a reason. 'Why men always lie and make love on left, always with left hand?'

They laughed. He, in turn, sought to distract her by asking, as he had already done once before, 'Breast – that word I know, but why you never use words for – here and here, me and...'

She said, 'Do you say those things in Poland? We don't – they sound so crude in German, the words for them, so we don't use them. Women don't, at least, though men do.' She smiled, then spoke in his ear. 'You don't have to put everything into *words* – touching is better than talking.' And she guided his hand there with hers. And soon she slid down him, brushing his body with her lips, wanting to console him as a means of forgetting, at least for a few minutes, what she had done to him and herself by her idiotic confession, which was a truly terrible thing, a still immeasurable threat for which there was only one remedy, if any: never to meet again, always to remember that they could never again feel safe for a moment. But this line of retreat was denied them – beyond their power to pursue. For now Pauline began to do as he had done: now, his hands entwined themselves in the kneeling woman's hair until he gripped her by the shoulders and raised her up. And when he reached for a contraceptive and she whispered, 'There's no need, not tonight – it's the only thing we're safe from ...' they both knew they would never be able to live so close without possessing each other as they had done till now. And just as a fugitive leaps in the dark because he cannot do otherwise, so now, Pauline took him and, as she impaled herself, pulled up her nightdress and thrust her right breast into his mouth. 'Slow, nice and slow,' was all she managed to say, but the effect of fear was such as to transport her instantly into a frenzy intensified, perhaps, by mortal terror. He had to exert the full strength of his arms as she arched her body and clasp her round the shoulders and the nape of her neck so as to imprison her face and mouth against his throat, smothering her cries. This he almost neglected to do because the certainty that he could not make her pregnant, tonight at least, had drugged his senses, too, more potently than usual – and who knows whether the fear of retribution was not impelling him, too, more blindly towards her so as to blot out the awareness that this same impulse would *inevitably* spell his death? She stormed home so quickly and so often that he could barely support her limp and exhausted body astride him by the time he came himself. She seemed to have plunged headlong into an abyss of withdrawal, of sleep itself, when the unheralded chill of dawn made him carry her indoors.

The doorway was so low and narrow that he had to set her on her feet; they would not have negotiated it otherwise. 'Look Herbert!' he whispered, but went to see for himself when she slumped on the kitchen couch and lay as though felled. Picking his way carefully through the gloom, he peered into the bedroom and saw that both children were fast asleep. Then he took Pauline's bedspread and rejoined her. 'I warm you,' he said. 'You get warm quicker without that.' He stripped the nightdress off her huddled form with difficulty before covering her twice over, first with himself, forehead to forehead and toe to toe, and then with the bedspread, which was too short for the pair of them. He desired her fiercely as she lay there half dead beneath his ever warm, never cooling flesh, more dormant than returning his desire, no part of her more thoroughly chilled than the winter-cold buttocks cupped in his hands – he desired and gently revived against her...

'Making a sandwich,' she had called it once – an expression

of her husband's. 'Spoons' was when they lay like spoons in a canteen, she with her back against his chest so as to warm those parts of her, as of all women, which are slowest to lose their chill: the cheeks which now, as she settled into a sleeping position, compressed themselves against his rekindled loins. Abruptly she sat up, assailed by a sudden and far from groundless fear. 'Mind you don't drop off too – I'm nearly asleep!' She subsided again, but he pleaded in a whisper, 'Not yet!' And although she was genuinely near sleep she guided him in as he lay behind her, at first indifferently and for his sake alone because she was once more overcome with anxiety at his having stayed at all. But his joy, his breath on her neck, his hands round her breasts from behind – all were so arousing, like the pulsing regularity of his controlled, protracted, ever deeper and more lingering thrusts, that she outstripped him again, first in her frenzied surge of excitement and then in her utter release.

And then, with unpardonable ineptitude, he fell asleep immediately after her, and it was already light enough to be seen had anyone on the yard side looked. An object lesson, this belated but timely awakening at four! Another half-hour and it would have been impossible to get back without being seen by one or both of the Melchiors.

Case History No. 2: Heinrich Müller's priority directive

Krawiec, Stanislaw, Special Court, Posen, 10 October 1942.
To be executed on 23 October 1942.

The convicted person sabotaged the management of the farm formerly owned by his evicted parents and now belonging to a woman settler, where he was working as a hired hand. He stole grain, allowed the farm machinery to deteriorate, and threatened the local farmers' leader when reprimanded by him.

Volksgenosse – 'compatriot' – was the Nazi equivalent of the Communist 'comrade', just as 'Heil Hitler!' was the cry with which all Germans who bore this official designation were 'in honour bound' to greet others of their kind for as long as Hitler ruled the roost. The words were delivered with the right arm extended – 'with right hand held on high,' mocked satirist Werner Finck – in what was termed the 'German salute'. Once in the war, when Munich's leading psychiatrist, Oswald Bumke, was ironically hailed in this manner by his son, his weary response was, 'You think it's that simple, my boy?'

Bumke wrote that Hitler had been far too smart ever to allow a psychiatrist near him, and his colleague Ernst Kretschmer, the constitutional typologist from Tübingen, went on record as follows: 'The strange thing about psychopaths is, in normal times we treat them, in times of political ferment they govern us.' They govern us (shouldn't we draw this further inference?) until the times, which are never normal but merely mad in various ways – many of them innocuous, thank God – become politically turbulent and ultimately murderous...

Isn't the sole difference between one age and another that its spirit, which never comes without an attendant sickness of the soul, inhabits 'lords and masters' who differ in their morals and ideas? (These rulers may naturally be women such as Cleopatra, Joan of Arc, Catherine the Great or Mesdames Perón, Mao and Gandhi.)

What they and a minuscule proportion of their confederates think, whether 'by nature' or because it has been preconceived by a handful of publications as obscure as the gospels of anti-Semitism or significant as the Communist Manifesto, turns into collective 'thought', irrespective of quality, purely because it inhabits the minds of those powerful enough to disseminate it – and eradicate the thinking of others. A modern dictator has no need to abolish parliament as Hitler, who was rather old-fashioned, deemed it necessary to do. Today he has only to compel parliamentarians to read newspapers because his first step, obviously, will be to pocket the press tycoons and television commentators. The constitutional lawyers, who are on his payroll anyway, will be entirely won over if he tells the most illustrious of them that they are philosophers as well.

Thanks to the power they wield, the 'spirit of the masters' becomes the spirit of the age. From this it has wrongly been concluded, not only that what the masters think becomes the 'concern', objective and desire of the bulk of the nation – which it unhappily does – but that thinking itself is an activity pursued by the many, by society at large. The masses are flattered by this notion as long as fortune smiles and things go well – indeed, nobody will win their allegiance faster than he who can persuade them that his ideas and aspirations are identical with those of all who are urged to elect him. But in time of misfortune, amid the ruins of their native land or an entire continent, that same notion is represented as the foulest slander on those same masses, who were never asked whether they wanted to assist in doing what they actually helped to do during the march into the abyss. Anyone who disputes this would have to contend that the criminal coterie in the dock at Nuremberg were no guiltier than the millions who had to march at their behest or face a firing squad. (The undoubted fact that many more of them marched voluntarily for Hitler than under duress is only one more proof of the epidemic virulence inherent in the thinking of those whose exclusive power it is to spread their ideas; for power, when allied with success, has the same capacity to enslave as sex appeal – and enslave the one as well as the many. Besides, anyone who pours scorn on 'the masses' should always bear in mind that each of us is more a part of them than he imagines!)

It is probable, though not provable, that all historical epochs are *quantitatively* deranged to the same degree. *Qualitatively*, however, worldwide differences prevail. Murderous mental illnesses like fascism and the Counter-Reformation, both of which wrought torture and death on dissenters or racial outsiders, may be succeeded by comparatively inoffensive mental aberrations which mould and dominate the ensuing period. One such delusion, current less than forty years after Hitler's demise, is that pensioning off a healthy man of fifty-five enhances his 'quality of life', whereas any doctor knows that it generally kills him.

Another mania: that there is some useful purpose to be served, apart from creating jobs more cheaply obtainable in other ways, by probing space with rockets which can do no more than penetrate our own solar system and make wholly futile landings on planets where nothing grows for lack of oxygen.

There is no solving the *moral* problem posed by the depressing realization that fascism and 'space' travel are mental illnesses of epochal significance and epidemic proportions, just like the colonialism and fervid naval propaganda of Imperial Germany a century ago, or, half a century later, the Nazis' war-mongering talk of *Lebensraum*. If, however, we accept the view that ideas which have mobilized whole generations, first for rallies, then for parades and finally for death, are mental *illnesses*, why should not those who collaborate with the trumpeters of such ideas be guilty as well as sick? Are they, or doesn't this realization necessarily and unconditionally acquit the individual of complicity when even his children's generation can tell that he was not of sound mind at the time, but jointly infected with the prevailing mental illness of his age and, like the bulk of his contemporaries, incapacitated by that epidemic disease? 'Thou shalt not follow a multitude to do evil' is the Bible's most topical advice to us denizens of the twentieth century, all of whom are media-impaired, but what if the multitude, like the individuals comprising it, can no longer discern the beginnings of evil or its nature?

The doctors, lawyers, municipal employees and policemen of Brombach, near Lörrach, not to mention the woodmen who built a gallows for someone 'guilty' of sexual intercourse – could they still, eight years after their hearts and minds were first steeped in Hitler's laws, have preserved those insights into good and evil which had once been implanted in them by their parents, teachers and priests, or simply by nature? Even if they had, would they have withstood the spirit of the age? How could they have earned a living and supported their families when the mildest penalty for resistance would have been forfeiture of the right to pursue their profession – when they would probably have been imprisoned, if not executed? How could *anyone* exist in those days without becoming a confederate of the criminals who were identical with the state? These criminals' responsibility for the cataclysm that rent an age asunder becomes no less if we concede that they were not only the leading germ-carriers of their time but the earliest and most gravely infected victims of their own disease. In short, they too were deranged – idea-blind and idea-deficient – just as the rabble-rousers of earlier centuries showed themselves abnormal when they persuaded their contemporaries (doubtless because they believed it themselves) that witch-hunts were essential or child labour in mines was natural...

On 5 July 1941 Heinrich Himmler, 'Reichsführer-SS and Chief of the German Police at the Reich Ministry of the Interior', transmitted a new set of guidelines through his Gestapo chief, Heinrich Müller. Embodied in a circular headed 'Priority Directive SIV D2c – 4883/40g – 196', they offered even Poles a first slender chance of survival if they were caught making love to German women. 'Reference special treatment of Polish civilian workers and prisoners of war employed in the Reich,' Müller began. (Special treatment, it will be remembered, invariably meant death, so prisoners of war were not alone in being hanged for sleeping with German women; the same rule applied to foreign civilians who had come to work in the Reich.) The Gestapo chief went on: 'It has in many cases been found that Polish civilian workers recommended for special treatment on grounds of illicit sexual intercourse display an infusion of Nordic blood, are of good appearance and rate an extremely favourable character assessment. Under certain circumstances, such persons lend themselves to Germanization. The Reichsführer-SS has therefore laid it down, in his conjoint capacity as Reich Commissioner for the Consolidation of German Nationhood, that Polish civilian workers and prisoners of war who have had sexual intercourse or other improper relations with German women and girls shall in future be examined as to their fitness for Germanization before being recommended for special treatment ... So as to ensure uniform treatment, racial assessments which could ultimately lead to special treatment shall in future, and on principle, be conducted by heads of Race and Resettlement Bureaux subordinate to Senior SS and Police Commanders or by subsection heads of the SS Central Office for Race and Resettlement at Waffen-SS Reserve Centres. As a rule, therefore, racial certificates will no longer be obtained from medical officers of health (for exceptions see following paragraph). Instead, regional State Police headquarters shall, after concluding their investigations, promptly forward such cases complete with all requisite documents (photographs comprising head full-face, head in profile and full-length picture, also character assessment) to the Senior SS and Police Commander, who will, being the local representative of the Reich Commissioner for the Consolidation of German Nationhood, ensure that the subject is racially examined and tested as to his fitness for Germanization.

'To avoid lengthy delays in the processing of cases when the Race and Resettlement head or subsection head at a Waffen-SS Reserve Centre is absent for an appreciable period, the following procedure will come into effect. The Senior SS and Police Commander shall advise all the regional State Police headquarters in his area that, during the absence of the racial assessor responsible for special treatment cases, racial assessments will – in accordance with existing practice – be obtained from the relevant medical officer of health. Medical officers' certificates must contain:
1. Racial designation
2. Details of height (without shoes)
3. Details of physical type
4. Description of most salient features
5. Details of colour of skin, eyes and hair

'State Police headquarters shall promptly submit all medical officers' racial assessments, together with the remaining documents, to the Senior SS and Police Commander. The latter will then, enclosing racial certificate and photographs, seek a final ruling from the Central Office for Race and Resettlement.

'Where fitness for Germanization is confirmed, State Police headquarters shall, enclosing the usual documents (but excluding photographs of the place of execution), notify the Central State Security Bureau, which will decide on further treatment. In most cases, a shortish spell of Category I detention in a concentration camp will be deemed a sufficient penalty.

'Where Germanization is precluded, a special treatment recommendation will as usual be submitted together with the appropriate documents, including the racial certificate prepared by the Race and Resettlement officer.

'In dealing with special treatment cases, State Police headquarters should additionally bear the following points in mind:

1. Recommendations for special treatment shall always state whether and, where appropriate, when the Pole concerned was formally instructed that Polish civilian workers are forbidden to have sexual intercourse with German women and girls *on pain of death.*

2. The Reichsführer-SS further reserves the right of final decision in those cases of sexual intercourse or improper conduct between Polish civilian workers and German women and girls which seem unlikely to result in special treatment (uninformed Poles, persons whose nationality is in doubt, Poles under eighteen years of age who have had intercourse with considerably older German women and were obviously seduced by them).

In these cases too, therefore, the views of the Senior SS and Police Commander must be sought and the usual documents submitted.

3. Photographs of the German women involved must be submitted in every case, that is to say, even when no blame attaches to them (rape).

4. The completion report to be submitted to the Reichsführer-SS immediately after an execution has taken place (See General Directive SIV D2a–3382/40 dated 10 December 1940 on Para. 3f of the Implementation Orders) must in future contain the following details:

(a) Offender's name, place and date of birth.

(b) Date and place of execution.

(c) Whether carried out by Polish civilian workers or by Poles held in custody.

(d) Details of the manner in which Polish civilians employed in the vicinity were conducted past the place of execution.

(e) Notes on how the execution was publicly received. (Information under (d) and (e) only in the case of executions outside camp.)

5. Objects left by executed Poles, articles of clothing and the like, will be allocated to Polish civilian workers of proven diligence without any intimation of their source, whereas sums of money and valuables must be forwarded to the National Socialist Welfare Organization or the German Red Cross.

'I would again point out, in conclusion, that all investigations in special treatment cases are to be conducted with the utmost possible dispatch. Signed: p.p. Müller. Witnessed: Bambowsky, Secretary.'

Gestapo chief Heinrich Müller, who has never, incidentally, been traced (his 'grave' in a West Berlin cemetery, surmounted by a marble slab dedicated to 'our beloved Dad and Grandad' by his children and grandchildren, proved to be empty when finally opened), could only write such a missive because the nation was already sick and in the throes of racial mania. Remembering that a fish's head is the first to stink, we should not be surprised to learn that 'scholars' such as lawyers and doctors were no less affected by this mania – indeed, smitten far earlier and more lastingly – than the coalmen and carters who, though unable to disguise from themselves that they performed the same work as Stasiek Zasada the Pole, were privileged (and officially *obliged*) to be conscious that they did so as Germans; not merely, like the Pole, as members of an 'inferior race'...

Overnight, however, Müller's directive of 5 July 1941 presented Zasada with a chance of acquiring full German citizenship because he had illicitly slept with a German woman, whereas until 4 July 1941 the *invariable* penalty for doing precisely what now afforded him this sole chance of naturalization – having intercourse with a German woman – was the noose. There was nothing else a Pole could do to become German. He could not, for instance, apply for naturalization; he could only, if he aspired to rise to membership of the master race, commit an act which had hitherto been automatically punishable – and was usually

143

but no longer invariably so punishable from 5 July onwards – by hanging. In future, doctors decided whether he should be reclassified or hanged. The decision was essentially but not solely theirs. What also governed it – and this alone spelt the end of Zasada, a fair-haired 'Aryan' – was whether a Pole had been formally advised that he would be hanged if he slept with a German woman, and whether – red tape, red tape *über alles*! – he had acknowledged this information in writing. If so he was doomed, however Nordic and Aryan his appearance and however impeccable his conduct in other respects. 'Germanization' – the greatest boon which Germany's supreme leader could bestow, according to his own lights, on a Pole who had until yesterday been scorned as a subhuman Slav – was then replaced by the stigma of public strangulation. What was more, his path to the gallows was smoothed by senior army officers, for no prisoner of war could be hanged until he had been 'dismissed the service' – that is to say, discharged from his camp – and handed over to the Gestapo...

This officially prescribed procedure, which was followed during the war by tens or, more probably, hundreds of thousands of German physicians, officers, lawyers, registrars, town hall thumb-twiddlers, secretaries, doctors' assistants, Party officials and policemen, none of whom appeared clinically abnormal to his or her compatriots, was not recognized as a mental illness because it was carried out by substantial groups of people, not by one person or a few individuals. That alone was why it seemed normal to all concerned. Had an individual asked them to do such things they would have laughed him to scorn or locked him up like the madman he was – unless, of course, the request emanated from the Führer. And it did. The request came essentially from him, though its details were worked out by Himmler, Heydrich and a handful of other individuals.

Whatever takes root in the mind of a sick, powerful and unbridled man, or of three such whose 'mental' affinity has made them his closest confederates, has only to be enforced on a wide circle of people in the form of an order. In the first place no one will dispute it; in the second, it will soon be esteemed sane and sensible – indeed, expedient. It will then be transmitted by the said wide circle to their countless underlings and duly put into effect. The inference is that while psychopaths *may* not be the strongest of personalities – though they usually are that *too* – they have a pre-eminent ability to gain power in times of political crisis. From this all else follows, resistible only by murder. (Count Münster's definition of Tsarism, 'Absolutism tempered by assassination', won fame and even social acceptance during the nineteenth century.)

Thus only two preconditions are required to make insanity seem the norm: first, that it be practised by a collective and not merely by the individual who decrees it; and, secondly, that it be *officially* decreed and confer pension rights on those who act as its instruments. Then everyone will 'think' the same insanity. Once legally entrenched as the norm it becomes a collective phenomenon – and sometimes vice versa: having once gained collective acceptance, it becomes legally entrenched.

Heinrich Müller's priority directive confirms the accuracy of the Nietzschean proposition from which we embarked and to which, willy-nilly, we keep on returning: that insanity is rare in individuals but habitual to nations and ages. Enemies take on each other's attributes, albeit to a limited extent, because wars create similarities between them – for example in their choice of weapons, given that defence would otherwise be impossible. It was only logical, therefore, that the mental illness which Hitler's war carried to extremes so infinitely much more brutal than its precursor should have spread to his opponent's camp. In London it declared itself, not in racial mania but in the delusion that no large land armies would figure in the current war, as Churchill assured Harry Hopkins, Roosevelt's special envoy, on 10 January 1941. (To cite only one consequence of this belief, Churchill then proceeded to kill over two hundred and fifty children in a single night, all of them being the registered patients of a single doctor, Dr Paul Melchior, in a single German city, Kassel. Of the children resident in the old quarter of Kassel up to October 1943, nearly *all* were burnt alive, crushed by falling debris or asphyxiated.) The prime minister had added during his conversation with

Hopkins in 1940 that, should Britain gain air superiority with American aid, Germany and all her armies would be done for.

Churchill was humane by nature. This makes it doubly hard to understand why he should have continued to bomb Germany with mounting fury and intensity for years after he himself had not only built up large ground forces but seen that *they*, not the bombing of residential areas, were the key to victory – a policy which sacrificed his own airmen in droves and did little to the Nazis but absolve them from having to issue ration cards to non-combatant members of the population. It seems equally incomprehensible that a genius whose own large land armies were to march from the brink of annihilation in Africa to the Elbe a few years later should then, in the winter of his deepest discontent, have contrived to believe such nonsense. He did so because it represented his only store of strength during the months when Britain stood alone, with nothing to pit against Hitler's huge land forces but the hopes she pinned on a strong bomber arm. On 9 July 1941, A.O.C.-in-C. Bomber Command received a directive from Air Vice-Marshal N.H. Bottomley, Deputy Chief of the Air Staff, which exhibited the same measure of insanity as Heinrich Müller's directive, sent two days earlier: 'I am directed to inform you that a comprehensive review of the enemy's present political, economic and military situation discloses that the weakest points in his armour lie in the morale of the civil population and in his inland transportation system.'

The prime minister had been sold on this by Professor Lindemann, later Lord Cherwell. By producing 'scientific' appraisals which strengthened Churchill in his last remaining hope at this period, Lindemann ensured, first, that Churchill henceforth listened to him alone in his capacity as the government's scientific adviser and, secondly, that he dismissed scientific advisers as eminent as Henry Tizard, who had materially contributed to Britain's aerial defence and salvation in 1940, because they strove to resist Lindemann's mania for bombing civilians. C. P. Snow's account of this feud is based on an intimate knowledge of Whitehall. He recalls how the 'faint but just perceptible smell of a witch hunt' created an atmosphere in Whitehall and the British press which was 'more hysterical than is usual in English official life'. Lindemann managed to convince Churchill that within the space of eighteen months, or between March 1942 and mid-1943, one-third of the entire German population could be rendered homeless and bombed into submission provided their city centres, not German industry, were made the focus of attack. The result: 56,000 British and over 40,000 American airmen lost their lives in pursuit of a strategic mirage.

Air Chief Marshal 'Bomber' Harris, also known to his aircrews as 'Butcher', deserves his place in history as the world's greatest incinerator of towns and townsfolk even if we dispute that his ill fame reposes on the corpses of three-quarters of a million European civilians (his residential targets were far from exclusively German) and credit him with 'only' half a million victims. We shall never know the exact number, any more than we shall know for certain whether Colonel Grosse's report of a quarter of a million dead in Dresden was true or false ... Churchill's pilots cannot be likened to SS killers even then, in February 1945, because they risked their own lives while burning noncombatants to death whereas SS men escaped combat duty for that very reason. But Churchill himself, with victory already in his grasp, chose this moment – this one moment – to stoop to Hitler's level. When the plight of German refugees from the east became known in London, he called on the RAF to 'tan the hides' of the fugitives trekking westwards from Breslau, and his private secretary noted that the horrific reports of the Dresden fire-storm left him quite unmoved ... It still seems irrational that Lindemann and, through him, Churchill should ever have yielded to the erroneous belief that bombing demoralizes any civilians it fails to kill – and this four years earlier, when Hitler's raids on Britain had just made it plain to both men that, on the contrary, civilians become fanatics under indiscriminate attack. Quite apart from that, of course, no one German civilian could have determined whether or not Hitler would fight on. Like Hitler's, Churchill's terror raids did nothing but prolong the war for an appreciable

Lörrach Hospital

Secret State Police,
Regional Headquarters, Stettin.
Letter No. IIE 1 – 3015/41

> Stettin, 16 January 1942.
>
> To: Commissioner of Police,
> Stettin.

Re execution of the Pole Stanislaus Krawczyk,
born Posen 25 July 1921.

Documentation: None   Enclosures: None

By order of the Reichsführer-SS and Chief of the
German Police, the Pole Stanislaus Krawczyk
is to be hanged for having sexual intercourse
with a German national, the worker Käte
Link. The execution will take place at 8.30
a.m. on Monday, 19 January 1942, at the rifle
range in the Bredower Schiesspark, Stettin
(now a Polish camp). I hereby give notice
thereof.

> p.p. Dr. Nedwed

Melchior's telephone rang. The busy coal merchant, thankfully just too old for military service, though it could still catch up with him, called to his wife.

'You take it!'

He was snowed under with work, but not only because he was a farmer and part-time village hearse driver as well as a coal and wood merchant whose teams had to haul wood from the forest to the village and coal from the station to the yard. It was his additional bad luck that one of his two Polish workers had been in Lörrach Hospital for nearly a fortnight – and it *would* be Zasada, who spoke German. Popilarczek, the other Pole, spoke no German – in fact he hardly spoke at all and hadn't for months, not since his mother wrote and told him that his wife was sleeping with a German soldier back in Lublin ... But what made it so much more of a nuisance that Zasada had been admitted to hospital with suppurative tonsillitis – possibly because Frau Melchior couldn't heat the room he shared with Popilarczek, there being no stove up there – was that Zasada, when he delivered coal to the villagers' homes and toted it into their cellars, could not only take their money on the spot but collect their coupons and bring them back to the yard. There had been coupons for coal and even firewood since last winter, the second of the war, just as there had been coupons for food since war broke out. And Zasada, because he spoke German, knew just how many coupons to clip for people's half-hundredweights or hundredweights of coal – or more, when he was delivering to stores, offices and workshops ... Where on earth could he have caught such a heavy feverish cold, considering how well clad he was whenever he sat on the driver's box or worked in the forest?

Hunched at the table with some sheets of old newspaper spread out in front of him, gumming cut-out coupons on them as regulations prescribed – an odious and unprofitable pastime which he usually left to his wife or Zasada – Melchior heard his wife say, 'You'd better tell him yourself, Doctor. One moment please, I'll get him. Here!' The last word was fired at her husband, so fiercely that he jumped to his feet in alarm. Looking worried, she held out the receiver and said in an undertone, 'It's Doctor Griesbrecht

– there's trouble at the hospital.' Melchior said, 'Melchior here. Heil Hitler, Herr Doctor.'

Without giving him good day or even paying a ritual tribute to the Führer, the doctor snapped, 'That Pole of yours has really put me on the spot, Herr Melchior.' Melchior started to ask how Zasada was, but the medical superintendent brusquely cut him short. 'How is he, how is he! What about the state of *my* health if people outside this hospital start broadcasting what everybody in here already knows? I should never have put a Polack in with a wardful of our own people – it's against regulations, I could be hauled in front of the People's Court for that – and now he gets a visit from some German woman who kisses and cuddles him in front of all and sundry! What's that? How should I know who the creature was? Anyway, she's hardly out of the gates – carrying a bag she dumped at the porter's lodge, incidentally – when a couple of patients complain to one of my nurses. Why? Because they've been obliged to watch this woman canoodling with your Pole in the bed next door, that's why. I ask you, the bare-faced cheek of it! Well, the nurse reports it to the sister, naturally, and the sister reports it to the matron and the matron comes running to me. All right, so tell me – who is this woman? Eh? You don't know? What's that? Nonsense, the Pole won't say. Claims he doesn't even know her name, says he delivered some coal to her once – how should I know? Anyway, I've informed you now, officially. You're the Pole's employer, Melchior. As such you've a duty to see he behaves himself, so don't try and laugh it off. What do you mean, the man can't help it if somebody visits him in hospital? It isn't a question of the visit itself, though you must know as well as I do that German citizens are forbidden to have personal dealings with prisoners and civilian workers – but you know all that, as I say … All right, so he's ill, but that's neither here nor there. I'm not inhuman and I can't spare the staff to stand guard over sick foreigners – I mean to say! – but those two were at it like a couple in a bedroom. Yes yes, Melchior, very funny, a ward *is* a bedroom, but listen – we're both in a jam, not to mention the Pole, who seems a nice enough lad on the whole. My nuns – most of the staff are state nurses, but we do have one or two nuns – they all dote on him because he keeps a rosary over his bed. At least, that's *their* story. The simple fact is, we've finally got a young man in bed here who hasn't been shot to pieces. He's popular, like all forbidden fruit, which is precisely why there's such a commotion now. Jealousy comes into it. All my nuns had managed to convince themselves that the Polish boy was *their* secret bridegroom, like the Lord above, when in walks this determined madam, suitcase, presents and all, just like his lawful wedded wife. It's causing bad blood, Melchior, and that I can do without ... He'll be discharged by Easter anyway, the Pole, but I've told you the whole damned story in front of witnesses now – it's no concern of mine what you do about it. What? No, I'm not interested in knowing whether you lock him in at night, there are plenty of frustrated grass widows around in the day-time. A strapping young fellow like that – maybe coal isn't all he delivers, who's to say? Still, she must have been crazy, mauling him around in a public ward with ten other men looking on – and *they* aren't all lucky enough to have female visitors ... Well, Herr Melchior, duty calls. Goodbye, Heil Hitler, and do me a favour: give the man a roasting – talk some sense into him. I can't do it here, not with a dozen people listening. Anyway, I'm not responsible for him – you are, being his employer, so Heil Hitler.'

Melchior glanced at his wife. Her opening conversation had put her in the picture and his few interjections had amplified it – few because the doctor had talked without drawing breath. All he said now was, 'Well, fancy that! A suitcase – he said it was a woman with a suitcase.'

Startled but without a moment's hesitation, Frau Melchior jerked a thumb in the direction of Pauline's shop. 'Then it was her from over the way. She was carrying a suitcase when she left this morning – she's gone to Bavaria to visit her husband. So she kissed him, did she? I'd never have thought it of her, not with a decent husband like hers.'

Melchior, who viewed the matter less seriously by now, brushed this aside. 'Just a goodbye kiss. Personally, I think she

152

was right to go and see how he was getting on. We could have done that ourselves.'

She rounded on him. 'You want me to go there and kiss him too?' Still playing it down, he retorted, 'Kiss him? It can't be much fun kissing a man with septic tonsils...'

His wife took a harder line, but more towards her neighbour than the Pole. 'If she kisses him in a public ward, what does she get up to when she's got him alone over there in the evenings?'

This exasperated him, and he vented his annoyance on her. 'Rubbish! What do you mean, alone? She's never been alone with him in her life – there's always someone there till he comes back here for his supper. There's the Schnittgens woman for a start, the one who keeps her books for her. And what about the children? They're both awake at seven and the boy's in and out like a yo-yo. You think he turns down the bed for them?'

She stared at him. 'You were a whole lot smarter and more resourceful when you were running after me!' her expression seemed to say, but she didn't speak again until he had gone back to sticking coal coupons on newspaper with the foul-smelling brown glue they sold these days. Then she said, 'Why did you tell Doctor Griesbrecht you lock Stani in at nights? I know we lock the outside door, but you've never taken the key out or shut him in his room.'

He swivelled irritably in his chair. 'Shut him in his room – how could I? What are they supposed to do up there when they have to get out in the night, pee against the wall? Leave off, woman, I've had enough. The man's an A-1 worker and a wizard with horses. You think I want to lose him because of some idiotic tittle-tattle? You can see for yourself how pushed we are without him – and have been for the past ten days.'

She poured him a schnapps to go with his slice of bread and dripping – something she seldom did at this hour – and said soothingly, 'The way you talk, anyone'd think I wanted us to lose the boy. It's just that ... Well, she's playing with fire as it is, so why does she have to go and kiss him in front of everybody? She must be out of her mind.'

He raised his hand, playing the subject down again. 'Yes, if it's true.' Then, abashed by the transparent foolishness of this remark, he added, 'Of course it's true – those people in the ward wouldn't have made it up, the bit about the woman with the suitcase. If you say she went off to visit her husband with a suitcase, that settles it. I'll have a word with my sister and get her to ask the Schnittgens woman if she's heard anything.'

'Her?' said Frau Melchior, with a touch of malice. 'She lives too far away to *hear* anything. I'll ask Maria Buschel – she'll have *heard* something if anyone has. Anyway, he'd better watch himself, had Stani. If people start talking it'll end in tears – for us as well as him. Like the doctor said, he's your responsibility.'

Though not unimpressed, Melchior shrugged his shoulders. 'My responsibility – at night? What am I supposed to do, keep the man chained up when he's been slogging away from half-past five in the morning till seven at night? As far as the nights are concerned, the Party can get stuffed. I joined it so they'd leave me in peace, not expect me to spy on my men!'

Whom God
would destroy...

The Führer says, 'Once we've won, who's going to ask us how we did it? We already have so many black marks against us that we must win, otherwise our entire nation, with us at the head and all we hold dear, will be wiped out. And so, down to work!'

Goebbels, diary extract dated 16 June 1941.

Socially, Maria Buschel belonged to the lower middle class; sociologically and in the original sense of the word, she was a proletarian – a person who owns nothing. Her craving for a neighbour's rented shop illustrates, at the bottom of the social scale, the exemplary effect of the acquisitive urge which, at its summit, rendered the Nazi dictator as witless after his unexpectedly swift defeat of France as the fisherman's wife after her first wish had been granted...

Hitler had found France invincible during his four years as a front-line soldier in the First World War. When he himself decided to attack the country a quarter of a century later, he reckoned on losing a million men but added, in Weizsäcker's hearing, 'So will the other side, and they can't afford to.'

As it turned out, his losses during the brief six-week campaign amounted to only five per cent of the casualties he had allowed for (27,074 dead, 18,384 missing). He confided to his inner circle that Burgundy would never be restored to the French. As for Belgium and Holland, he had resolved to Germanize them in perpetuity. On 7 July 1940 Goebbels noted in his diary: 'The Führer has permitted the French fleet to remain under arms. We could now win over the French entirely if we wanted to, but we don't. We want to inherit them and we must.' Goebbels, who was the most humbly devoted of all Party members, was here reproducing his master's opinion, not his own. He also shared the Führer's fear lest Britain evince a readiness to compromise before she too had been 'inherited'. 'Let's hope Churchill doesn't crack at the last moment,' he had written on 23 June. Before six months were up, there was nothing he and his master desired more eagerly – and vainly – than the submission of the man who had already won the decisive battle: the Battle of Britain.

Logically enough, Hitler's lack of moderation during summer 1940 also manifested itself in that most salient of his characteristics, his ferocity. Four weeks after his moment of supreme outward triumph, the day of his return from Paris to Berlin, he issued a decree which Reinhard Heydrich, Chief of the Security Police and Security Service, was obliged to transmit to ten different categories of police, SS and SD authorities in his 'Priority Letter No.

3642/40g – IVA1c' dated 5 August 1940: 'I would draw particular attention to the fact that, by order of the Führer, French, British and Belgian prisoners of war who have sexual intercourse with German women and girls are to be punished with death in exactly the same way as Polish prisoners of war.'

Hitler had thus extended his sexual persecution to prisoners of war from Western Europe although he repeatedly – and doubtless sincerely – insisted how tragic he found it to be waging war on 'racial equals' like the Germans' so-called British brothers. This makes it fair to assume that his actions really were prompted by 'the insane compulsion of a vengeful and impotent man', as Carl J. Burckhardt, author of *Richelieu* and last League of Nations Commissioner for Danzig, phrased it in his sidelight on Göring. Hitler's hatred of things sexual found further expression in his order that homosexual SS men were to be executed rather than sent to concentration camps. It was his almost invariable habit, when posing for the camera, to fold his hands over his pudenda as if they stood in need of concealment. This gave rise to a potentially lethal joke which enjoyed special currency among the opposite sex, who were disturbed by the sight: 'Our beloved Leader is hiding the last member of the unemployed!' Be that as it may, Hitler was by 1940 eager to ensure that even Britons, Belgians and Frenchmen were hanged for having sexual intercourse – and for that 'crime' alone – whereas countless 'offences' committed by those he called subhuman Slavs had carried an almost automatic death penalty from the first. However long it may have slumbered within him as an ultimate desire, his urge to persecute was triggered by the intoxication of victory. His propaganda minister's diaries – Goebbels kept them in longhand until 8 July 1941, which made for brevity, and then started dictating up to thirty pages of typescript a day – attest that Hitler did not throw off his inhibitions until he entered Paris in triumph.

Blind and insensate homicidal mania, a fundamental impulse common to Hitler and a handful of his closest henchmen, came to fulfilment in Germany only because the country possesses such a long tradition of contempt for intellectuals, for reason and the things of the mind. The Germans have never lost a war waged by intellectuals. Frederick the Great and all who played a decisive part in the Napoleonic War of Liberation, Blücher excepted, were brilliant intellectuals like Bismarck and Moltke, whereas Ludendorff and Hindenburg, who lost the First World War, were not; they were distinguished but militarily blinkered strategists like the generals whose presence Hitler tolerated. One has only to read Jodl's brutal and foolish recommendations that Churchill be induced to surrender by terrorizing the Londoners with Göring's bombers... By contrast, Hitler never suffered the proximity of the one outstanding intellectual among his military commanders, Manstein, for more than a few hours at a time. Goebbels was the only intellectual he could stand, with the exception of his architect, Speer, but only, one presumes, because Goebbels was the most utterly spineless intellectual in the Party. Nowhere in his diaries, which run to tens of thousands of pages, is there a single indication that this truly abject form of life at Hitler's side *ever* took a firm line with him, however often he may have inclined to a different, more moderate and shrewder point of view...

It is doubtful if any historical figure of passing eminence has better exemplified the depressing conversion of an intellectual into an advocate of all he thought wrong, ridiculous, dangerous and nonsensical – for instance Hitler's anti-Semitism, his two-front war or war in general – than Goebbels, the diarist with the servile soul. Whether in his first diary or his last, in his novel or his innumerable conversations and articles, he constantly referred to intellect and intellectuals with the sort of loathing which only self-hatred can engender. In just the same way, the truly murderous anti-Semites were those who suspected themselves, rightly or wrongly, of having Jewish blood: Hitler, Heydrich and Hans Frank, the Governor-General of rump Poland. It is also recorded that Adolf Eichmann's SS colleagues sometimes twitted him on his 'Jewish' appearance. In the case of Goebbels, who had no such grounds for misgiving, *gratitude* served to boost his hatred to boiling-point. He and his wife owed more to Jews than to anyone except Hitler. (Magda Goebbels was saved from having to grow up as the illegitimate daughter of a maidservant by a wealthy Jewish businessman named Friedländer, who married her mother, adopted Magda herself – although he hadn't fathered her – and gave her an education fit for a princess. Another Jew assisted Goebbels financially while he was studying; his doctoral supervisor was an aristocrat of Jewish extraction; and Friedrich Gundolf – yet another Jew – was the university teacher he most admired. Finally, and until the very eve of his departure for Berlin, where Hitler had appointed him Gauleiter, Goebbels was for years engaged to a half-Jewess who also lent him regular financial support.) It was not the Jews whom Goebbels hated in his heart of hearts, but the intellect which had so often prevented him from yielding to the Church-instilled desire for 'blind faith' that dated from his days as an altar-boy. His intellect told him that war was an appalling risk, but Hitler gave the order to march – and so, much as he enjoyed his minis-terial existence as a protector of beautiful actresses and collector of country mansions, Goebbels duly preached war. His intellect warned him against the gassing of Jewish deportees, but Hitler decreed it (and resisted his two recorded attempts at dissuasion) – and so, while discussing the matter in private with Göring, who shared his qualms, he contrived to talk himself round: 'We are so firmly committed,' he wrote on 2 March 1943, 'particularly on the Jewish question, that there can be no escape for us. This is all to the good. Experience shows that movements or nations which have burnt their boats will fight more wholeheartedly than those that still possess a means of retreat.' His intellect warned him against a war on two fronts, and he thankfully recorded more than once that the Führer had congratulated himself on not hav-ing to wage one. Yet when Hitler dropped his plan to invade the British Isles for fear of getting his feet wet, Goebbels too favoured a surprise attack on the Soviet Union and ostentatiously bought up red flags to mask the Wehrmacht's preparations and persuade the world that Berlin was getting ready for a state visit by Stalin ...

Look where you get by denouncing intellect: 'Everything in me rebels against the intelligentsia,' wrote Goebbels. Or again: 'There is a deep yearning in the German soul for deliverance from things of the mind.' Or again: 'Intellect is a threat to character-building.' Or again: 'We Germans think too much; this has robbed us of an instinct for politics. Intellect has poisoned our nation.'

The moment Goebbels began to equate Jews with intellectuals his hatred of them became homicidal. He had lost touch with the Christian faith in adolescence and decided against taking holy orders. He had suffered terrible spiritual and material isolation in his parental home, the little terrace house where he skulked for years after completing his studies, poverty-stricken and chronically unemployed. It was understandable, therefore, that his strongest desire should have been for human contact, for stability, status and a regular income, yet his intellect threatened to prevent him from forging close links with a rabble of predominantly bird-brained, pin-headed Nazis who equated 'intellect' with 'Jewish intellect' to the extent that they lacked it themselves. Goebbels hated the brains and verbal dexterity that crippled him worse in the eyes of Hitler's henchmen than his club foot. As for his intellect and the malign quirk of fate that made him the only one out of many millions who was unable to play follow-my-leader in boots like all the rest, he only gradually and laboriously forgave himself for these un-Nazi attributes when Hitler rehabilitated him by warmly declaring that Goebbels was the only public speaker he could listen to without falling asleep...

Hatred of intellect is as old as German intellectual history.

The Nazis had to provoke the most shameful defeat in the annals of Germany, if not of the world, in order to bequeath the lesson (which may already have been forgotten) that those who scorn intellect lose wars in addition to all else. Few Germans can fail to be depressed by the frequency of this hatred for reason, which could prompt even a left-wing thinker like Franz Mehring, the Social Democrats' most noted intellectual, to declare in 1917 that Lessing, like Voltaire before him, had been handicapped as a writer by his intellect just as Zola and Gutzkow had been hampered by their passion for politics ... It was not until the effects of this attitude became evident in a practical, computable form on the battlefield – for instance, when it transpired that the builders of the atomic bomb, most of whom were based in Berlin and Göttingen before 1933, had been driven into the enemy camp by hatred of intellect – that a suspicion arose, even in Germany, that people ought not to be gassed for having more brains than the police thought fit ... In West Germany, ill will towards writers is still the most German of all party-political symptoms. Just as Dr Goebbels called the Jews 'fleas' in 1941, so, in 1978, Dr (*honoris causa*) Franz Josef Strauss referred to certain editors and an author who were defending themselves against legal proceedings instituted by Premier Filbinger of Baden-Württemberg as 'rats and bluebottles'.

Among the Nazi leaders, contempt for reality whenever it imposed restraints on their megalomania was *the* attitude which governed or gave rise to every other. Because their spectacular successes early in the war had proved them right despite their own misgivings, and because they beheaded doubt-ridden nonconformists for 'defeatism', their delusions of victory released acquisitive urges in the humblest members of the national community. Just as the farm-hand assured that the Führer would reward him with a vast estate in the Ukraine when the war was over, so the waiter could already picture himself as a prosperous canteen concessionaire in a German military installation somewhere between Narvik and Cairo. The fish's fins had begun to smell quite as repulsive as its head...

Preserved and documented in countless newsreels, the chauvinistic orgasms unleashed by Hitler whenever he showed himself to 'his' people furnish unmistakable evidence that Hitleritis had developed into a mental illness from which very few were exempt.

Hitler's mania for aggrandizement always attained a special pitch of absurdity just before he launched his most momentous military operations, or before and during the early weeks of his campaigns in Poland, Norway, France, Yugoslavia and Russia. Goebbels was his all-recording scribe, by now a pathetic puppet who had destroyed his own innate intelligence rather than feel bound to gainsay the man at whose feet he sat and with whom he now spoke daily, for Hitler set off each of these historic avalanches from the Chancellery in Berlin. More characteristic than many similar entries in Goebbels's diary, because of their generalized nature, are the following extracts dated 9 July 1940: 'The Führer has great plans for Norway. Near Trondheim a big German city, probably [to be called] Nordstern...From there a motorway down to Klagenfurt. A road link right across the Germanic Empire. The kings will have no further say. The Norwegian king, the Dutch queen and the Belgian king, too, will not get their thrones back...The Führer has instructed that Frank's domain, Poland, will simply and solely be called "the Government-General" from now on. We must coin a new term or a new name for every dependent or incorporated country. We shall leave the smaller nations free to differentiate themselves by name. It will be a Germanic Empire without frontiers ... In France they are toying with an authoritarian system...That country is obviously doomed to destruction as a great power, which is only as it should be. We must have room...'

A few weeks earlier he had noted: 'Norway and Denmark occupied at five-fifteen this morning ... If the kings behave themselves they can stay on, but we shall never hand either country back.'

Next day, when the surprise attack had succeeded and the British Home Fleet, alerted too late and thoroughly outwitted, had foolishly let Hitler's navy steam past unscathed, Goebbels noted, just once and never again: 'I tremble at the envy of the gods.'

By the time France had been steamrollered by Hitler's tanks, Goebbels had lost his fear of the gods and was well on the way to total blindness. None of his misgivings ever survived a conversation with Hitler, who talked him out of them, and never did his intelligence curb his faith in the Führer; on the contrary, he detested intellect and intellectuals precisely because they diluted faith with doubt. It was only logical that he sent people to the guillotine for casting doubt on final victory just as his most authoritative teacher, the Church which he himself called the one true source of salvation, had burnt heretics while it still possessed the power to do so. Shrewd as he was by nature, Goebbels was less an intellectual than a believer – one who thought what he wished to believe rather than believed what he thought. He admitted this himself, innumerable times. 'We have learnt,' he said, brazenly disputing Bismarck's commonsense maxim, 'that politics have ceased to be the art of the possible. We believe in miracles, in the impossible and unattainable. For us, politics are the miracle of the impossible. We don't give a damn for the art of given possibilities!'

A few months earlier, Goebbels exultantly noted in his diary that the Führer had no need to emulate the Kaiser by waging a war on two fronts because Stalin was such an obliging purveyor of raw materials. As soon as he heard that Hitler intended to overturn his previous calculations and attack the Russians after all, the Führer's plans and prophecies instantly whipped him into a mindless lather of enthusiasm and wild expansionist dreams. He became a demented Rumpelstiltskin hobbling with glad cries round the Russian holocaust which Hitler had already kindled in his mind's eye. This was the moment when Goebbels – for once, but never again – voiced an opinion that differed from his Führer's. Hitler predicted that Russia would withstand the German onslaught for four months; not so, retorted Goebbels, Russian resistance would crumble in a mere eight weeks! Only five days before the Wehrmacht set out, Hitler told him: 'Moscow means to steer clear of the war until Europe is exhausted and bled white. That's when Stalin would prefer to act.' As soon as Hitler saw during the winter that victory had eluded him, he propagated the assertion that he had merely forestalled a surprise attack by Stalin. In conversation with Goebbels on 16 June, however, he declared: 'Our operation has been mounted in such a way ... that failure is completely out of the question.' He also observed on the same day that the Russians had 'some 180–200 divisions at their disposal, or perhaps a few less, but at any rate roughly as many as we do'. Goebbels added in his diary: 'I put the Russians' combat strength very low, even lower than the Führer. If ever there were a sure-fire operation, this is it. We have to attack Russia anyway, to release men. Undefeated, Russia permanently compels us to maintain 150 divisions whose personnel we badly need for our war economy...'

He went on to speak, with probable accuracy, of 'the biggest deployment in the history of the world ... 160 complete divisions, a front 3,000 kilometres long' and added, though with rather less accuracy: 'Bolshevism will collapse like a house of cards. We are on the threshold of an unprecedented victory.'

In the foregoing weeks and months, Goebbels and Hitler had often poked fun at Stalin's unremitting efforts to satisfy Berlin of his good faith. In his diary, Goebbels portrays Stalin as a tragic figure desperately anxious to keep the peace with Hitler, whose defeat of France had persuaded the entire world that he was invincible. Weizsäcker, who shared Hitler's firm belief that Stalin would never take the field against Germany, paints a similar picture. Four days before the beginning of the end (Germany's end), he wrote: 'I'd still think the Russians had no interest in this war even if Stalin hadn't publicly embraced our ambassador on the station platform yesterday and told him "We must remain friends."' More appalling still is Weizsäcker's entry four days later – his last before German troops crossed the Russian border: 'The only worry here now is that Stalin may wreck our plans at the last minute by some conciliatory gesture. The Russian ambassador called on me today. A sigh of relief went up in high places when I was able to report that Dekanozov had only discussed minor items of current business in a relaxed and cheerful mood. Otherwise, they'd all have set off in their heated special trains.'

It transfixes one to read how this senior member of the foreign office, who had steadfastly opposed the Russian venture in a number of memorandums, caved in as soon as he convinced himself that 'Nemesis is at work, expiating the twenty-five-year-old sin of rabid Communism'. He was just as proof as Goebbels against any presentiment that Nemesis had swung into action against Germany. All his well-founded misgivings were dispelled by the second day of the invasion. As besotted as any Nazi, he countered Churchill's promise of the previous day – to destroy Hitler – with the very argument he had rightly dismissed as untenable for months beforehand: 'Our extremely rapid and manifest successes against the Russians will diminish this extremism in

Britain. Our next objective must remain a settlement with Britain when the war in Russia is over.'

Everyone in Berlin, whether in thrall to Hitler or brainwashed by him, whether German or foreigner, felt utterly convinced that the Red Army's end was imminent. This is drastically illustrated by the Papal Nuncio's remark to Weizsäcker in August – 'Anyone who talks of peace now is a Stalinist ...' – though Weizsäcker also recorded in the same month that there were 'officers who call the Russians' escape from the Dnieper Bend a second Dunkirk'.

Only hours before his dawn attack on Russia, Hitler told Goebbels that he had been 'working on it since July of last year' – a remark which retains its topicality because would-be defenders of Hitler's invasion persist in claiming that it was forced on him by the need to forestall Stalin. There are countless indications, some of them supplied by Goebbels himself, that this thesis is absurd. Hitler never believed in the imminence of a Soviet attack but made play with this spurious threat as soon as he realized that he was done for and needed to justify his senseless decision. Indeed, he ruefully remarked that Stalin was too shrewd a strategist ever to do him the favour of taking offensive action against the Reich. Even on 16 June Hitler and Goebbels still found it amusing to reflect that every Kremlin communiqué was 'born of fear' and that Stalin was 'quaking at the shape of things to come'.

This may also explain why Stalin repeatedly and brusquely rejected every British warning of a German attack even though Churchill accurately notified him of its timing on three separate occasions. Reviewing the Russians' attitude in spring 1941, Churchill called them 'the most completely outwitted bunglers' of the war because they had averted their gaze rather than see Hitler coming. But this is unfair. Stalin knew that it was in the Red Army's interest to keep Hitler at bay, if nothing more. He naturally had his suspicions – in fact even the Germans sometimes got wind of Churchill's advice to the Kremlin. Hill, the editor of Weizsäcker's diaries, states that the British and Americans tipped off the Russians no less than eighty-four times, and a more detailed account of these warnings may be found in Weinberg and Whaley. On 13 March 1941, for example, Weizsäcker noted: 'The British ambassador in Moscow, Cripps, has in recent days ... told the Russian foreign ministry that Hitler plans to attack Russia so as to reach a settlement with Britain in the west by surrendering the occupied Channel territories while recouping in the east...'

What makes Weizsäcker's diary so much more depressing to read than the journal kept by Hitler's infatuated minister of propaganda is that Weizsäcker had wisely opposed war in general and the Russian campaign in particular. Then, carried away by success like all around him, he temporarily changed his mind: 'an instrument of Nemesis' was his serious description of the very man whose war he had equated with *finis Germaniae* (and forecast for 1938). Weizsäcker's diary is a disturbing document because it illustrates how Hitler's successes on the battlefield induced a change of mind and heart in him and all the Berlin intelligentsia – a conversion devoid of moral standards and blind to the Führer's unexampled crimes and breaches of good faith. One has to read the diary kept by Ambassador von Hassell, who was dismissed and hanged after the 20 July bomb plot, to preserve one's faith in the ability of at least *some* few people – if only those destined for murder – to retain their intellectual and moral integrity in times of political crisis ... While Weizsäcker himself was still engaged in a stubborn and subtle war of words against Hitler's plan to smash Russia, he recorded his failure to immunize the dictator's senior military commanders. Weizsäcker, who had warned in a memorandum that 'beating Britain in Russia is not a programme', thought it expedient to make an ally of Stalin in his capacity as a supplier of raw materials. His diary proves that even the non-Nazi generals whose acumen he most admired, Halder and Geyer, considered the march on Moscow 'attractive' and easy enough to be accomplished in a few weeks by the temporarily idle German forces. Weizsäcker's tireless jeremiads against the attack on Russia are a measure of the delusions that reigned in Berlin, even among the military experts of his acquaintance: 'The German officer [H. Geyer] whose opinion I value more than any other tells me he would favour making war on Russia in the spring, preferably in June ... To carry the war to Moscow would be easy, he says, but to the Urals pretty difficult. He thinks this war essential, however, because other methods have failed. We won't finish Britain off in the air or at sea.' Weizsäcker stuck to his guns: 'Britain would construe this change of tack as a loss of confidence in the successful outcome of the Anglo-German duel ... Last autumn the Russians ... formally notified us of their aspirations to the trans-Caucasian oil-fields and their designs on the Dardanelles ... For the first time, they referred to political and military measures against Turkey ... This is an offer of an offensive alliance. To take it up and bring Russian pressure to bear on the Straits as well as on the areas south of Batum/Baku, in the direction of the Persian Gulf, would hit Britain harder than any attempt to incorporate Russian territory in our war machine by force.'

Common sense had fled the Third Reich, not to mention morality. The ingrained, traditional hatred of intellect – a sentiment that had even left its impress on the literary history of the romantic German people and was destined to outlive Hitler – now reigned supreme. What was more, unreason *revelled* in what it was doing. On the morning of Sunday, 21 June 1941, when the war was several hours old, Joseph Goebbels exultantly noted what Hitler had told him the day before: 'Molotov requested a visit to Berlin but was given the brush-off. Naive impertinence!'

And then Goebbels recorded how the night of decision ran its course: 'It is half-past two in the morning. The Führer is very grave. He plans to sleep for an hour or two, which is the best thing he can do at this juncture. I go over to the office ... My assistants put in the picture. Utter amazement all round.' So the gentlemen in Berlin can't have been as scared of a Russian attack as they claimed after the war! Their ministerial chief goes on: 'Now the guns are thundering. God's blessing on our arms! Outside in Wilhelmsplatz all is silent and deserted. Berlin sleeps, the Reich sleeps ...' Unable to sleep himself, Goebbels continued to write, and one of the passages in his diary echoes Herodotus' account of the oracle that foretold the destruction of a great empire if Xerxes invaded Greece. Bedazzled by grandiose dreams, the Persian king failed to grasp that the empire was his own. Goebbels wrote: 'The breath of history is audible. A wondrous time – one in which a new empire is being born.'

He never stopped to think that his diary ran counter to the oldest parables found in world literature, in Herodotus, in the Old Testament and the Greek tragedies. God having chosen to blind him, Goebbels was unable to discern that his accurate presentiment of the genesis of a new empire bore the same significance as the oracle granted to King Xerxes before he invaded Greece. All the admonitions to mankind contained in these earliest statute books of civilization – that they who sow the wind shall reap the whirlwind, that God blinds those whom He means to destroy, that no man should account himself fortunate until he dies, and that the day of victory harbours the seeds of the victor's destruction – Joseph Goebbels made a special habit of casting these warnings to the winds whenever Germany was about to attack a neighbouring country. Nearly every last entry in his journal brushes them aside in a manner so ludicrously inept, so contemptuous of God and man, that the gruesome death of the diarist and his six innocent children (and his far from innocent wife) has a terrible logic which almost inspires religious awe.

It was taking longer than expected to transfer Pauline from the Gestapo jail at Lörrach to the women's concentration camp at Ravensbrück. In the first place, a batch of prisoners sent by rail under escort had to comprise enough women to make it worthwhile. Secondly, it had still to be decided how long Pauline would spend in the camp and what 'grade' she would be assigned. The severest form of punishment was 'destruction by labour', but the odds were that she would be sentenced to the mildest, or road-building. Her case was, after all, so simple and straight-forward that she had not been brought before a judge – nor, of course, had she needed a defence counsel. She could be grateful that she had not been shipped off to Ravensbrück long ago – if grateful is the word, for the longer the delay in transferring her the more distant her date of release. This was because Gestapo chief Müller's Priority Directive SIV D2c–4883/40g–196 had recently, or since 5 July 1941, afforded her Polish lover a chance of being Germanized rather than hanged. In the former event, Zasada himself would serve only six months in a con-centration camp in the lowest penal category, while Pauline would not go to a concentration camp at all but spend six months in prison.

It was true that Himmler's secret edict, duly drawn up and signed by Müller, applied to Polish civilian workers, whereas Pauline's lover had been a prisoner of war. On the other hand, Hitler's total dissolution of the Polish state had 'reclassified' all captured Polish servicemen as civilian workers, so Herr Karl Mayer estimated that Zasada had a good chance of 'coming within the scope' of the new directive – officialese for escaping the gallows. Mayer was positively delighted to be able to convey this hope, which he himself shared, to Pauline and Zasada. Although he never even privately debated the merits of the order to hang 'sexual offenders', he was genuinely repelled by the idea of carrying out such an execution in public, as instructed, because he felt in his bones that its 'popularity rating' would be extremely low ...

Mayer could not even be sure, if he conducted a race-law offender to the gallows in his native land, that his own family would refrain from branding him a hangman when next they clashed over the supper table. In his overpowering desire to avoid such a contingency, he never for a moment doubted that Zasada's 'Aryan' appearance and good character would save him, the more so because the fair-haired Pole was fighting for his life: it was hard to verify but almost impossible to disprove Zasada's claim that his mother in Lodz, now renamed Leitzmannstadt, came of German stock ...

The Gestapo man had therefore been quick to get the prisoner photographed – clothed and unclothed, front, back and sides – and send the prints off to Freiburg with a glowing certificate of good conduct which also mentioned that the Melchior family were supremely well-satisfied with their Polish carter and coalman. That done, he knew that the decision between hanging Zasada and letting him live now rested with Reichsführer Himmler and a handful of doctors.

He said as much to Pauline, whom he felt sorry for, when he informed her of the directive in the prison yard. He also had another piece of good news for her. Her husband had been granted compassionate leave immediately after her arrest. Having collected the children from her parents and entrusted them to the care of his sister in Lörrach, he was now writing letters and petitions aimed solely at securing her release ...

Mayer was not to know that, two years later, Security Service reports on the 'internal situation' would be compelled to record that most wronged husbands were being tolerant to the point of endangering national security. One such report dated 15 November 1943 stated: 'In conclusion, it is also characteristic that most *husbands* of accused or convicted women vigorously *defend their wives*. They forgive them for having sexual intercourse on the grounds that this is an inevitable result of their long absence. They have, they say, lived happily with their wives and will do so again. They further state that their farms, businesses, shops and children cannot afford to lose a wife and mother. Thus, husbands regularly petition the State Police, public prosecutors, courts, welfare officers and other authorities, asking them to refrain from punishing their wives or to grant them a pardon. In such cases, this is also frequently effected through the Ministry of Justice.'

'You won't be released,' Mayer told Pauline. 'That's right out, of course. You'll naturally have to pay for what you did, which means a spell in a concentration camp – or in prison if Zasada's Germanized. Still, your husband's given you a very good chit. That and the fact that he forgave you straight away – or so he keeps saying in letters addressed to all kinds of people he isn't really entitled to write to – well, it'll all help to get you out in three or four years' time ... Maybe even sooner.'

Pauline, with tears in her eyes, said she wanted to apply to have the children returned to her parents. 'My sister-in-law hates me,' she said. 'How could she ever love my children?' Mayer counselled patience. He pondered, then told her, 'Your husband has put in a request for permission to visit you. Speak to him when he comes. The application for the children's transfer from his sister's custody to your parents' should come from him, not you. They own a farm, don't they? In the interests of a healthier and politically irreproachable upbringing on a German family farm, that's the best way of putting it.'

This kind of phraseology was as much in vogue at the time as one-inch haircuts for men – after all, every generation favours fads and phrases incomprehensible to the next. Mayer reeled off the words by rote, meaning well, but quickly saw they were lost on Pauline, who found them bizarre. He went on, 'Look, tell your old man to come and see me in my office before he drafts his request. I'll help him strike the right official note – I may even add an endorsement of my own ...'

Mayer had accosted Pauline in the prison yard while she and some other female inmates were circling it in their daily 'bear-dance'. Being a meticulous custodian of the law, he was determined never to have it rumoured by his subordinates that he spent time alone with young women in their cells – 'Just so I'm covered,' he told himself, employing yet another of the prefabricated, predigested phrases that ruled his whole existence, not only as a Gestapo officer but as a family man. He knew that somewhere in the east a brother officer had been posted to a

Wehrmacht punishment battalion – which meant, in eight cases out of ten, condemned to death – for having taken advantage of a female prisoner on remand. That the sight of Pauline should in any way have reminded Mayer of this doomed conscript was attributable to two reasons. First, there was nothing he feared more – or brooded on more constantly – than the possibility of a transfer from the Gestapo to the army or an SS combat unit. Much as he loved the Führer, his love owed much to the circumstance that, unlike those members of his age-group whose loyalty to the régime was less conspicuous, he had not been drafted into the armed forces. In Lörrach, as opposed to Russia, Mayer could rest assured that anyone he drew a gun on would be unarmed. Better to detain a person like this woman here than be forced to 'smoke out' enemy snipers! But the other reason why Pauline so often put him in mind of his ill-starred Gestapo colleague was that this thirty-six-year-old greengrocer had crept beneath the bedclothes of his imagination. So potent was her erotic aura and so strong her sexual attraction that not even the sacklike prison smock which was meant to standardize her figure, not accentuate it, could deprive her of something that Mayer, with petty bourgeois bravado, euphemistically described as 'worth a trip to the confessional'. He could never have explained why Pauline stimulated him to such an extent that indifference overcame him in the bedroom at nights. Sympathy for this 'dishonoured' woman who had violated 'wholesome public sentiment', as the official definition ran, was sapping his conception of duty. More than that, he paradoxically extended that sympathy to the man under provisional sentence of death who had 'had', or taken, what his jailer could only dream of. Ever since Berlin had issued the directive that offered a means of escaping the noose, not to Slavs but to Germanic-looking males from non-Russian countries who had engaged in 'GV' with German females (the edict didn't apply to Russians), Pauline's lapse had seemed almost as venial as adultery with a compatriot. Once, while arguing that 'GV' with foreigners was penalized too harshly, he had told his wife, 'A good hiding from her husband would do the trick just as well.' He spoke with himself in mind, even though – alas – he had no grounds for self-reproach. He would never have said such a thing at the office, nor did he tell himself that the sight of the handsome young Pole, who had merely seemed 'quite a man' until his perusal of the latest directive but now looked 'almost German', played such havoc with his imagination that he envied the prisoner's audacity in sneaking across to his mistress, night after night, with the death penalty looming before his eyes ...

Mayer spoke to Pauline more often than circumstances warranted – in fact he sought her out so assiduously that he several times admitted to himself that it would be a good thing when she finally disappeared into a concentration camp. It was less what he could see that made such a deep impression on him, for that he could define. Other Badenese women, hill-farmers' daughters like Pauline, arrived in the Wiesenthal with the same natural endowments: not only the dark brown hazel-nut complexion which was celebrated in song, but, above all, a certain statuesqueness. The squat and neckless Mayer, whom his colleagues sometimes credited with a strong resemblance to the Führer's right-hand man, Reichsleiter Martin Bormann (the comparison was respectful but ironic), had been exceptionally impressed by this quality ever since his own lack of it was officially brought home to him. Mayer's physique was no more imposing than a rubber stamp. That was his personal cross, but at least it helped to safeguard him against conscription into the Waffen-SS, who declined to employ racial and physical misfits like Mayer even as rear-echelon personnel. He was bewitched by Pauline's movements; by her sturdy peasant haunches and the broad shoulders whose masculinity was tempered by breasts so firmly palpable that not even a prison smock could belie them; by her rounded tobacco-brown arms and legs, inured to hard work and as bare as the nape of her strong neck; even – or especially – by the smell of her, for prisoners were allowed just two showers a week. (Regulations prescribed only one, but Mayer was a stickler for personal hygiene and had actually submitted written grounds for this, his wilful contravention of a standing order issued by higher authority – an act of moral courage which had gone undisputed and filled him with pride.) Pauline's body disturbed him enough in itself – yes, but less so than the tragic tension that now enhanced and refined her looks. Mayer could not have found words to describe this quality had he sought them, but he dismissed the impulse, in any case, as 'exaggerated'. Although Pauline often wept in her cell when she thought of Zasada, grief had not inflamed her eyes or destroyed the bloom on her skin. Any mention of the Pole reduced her to an apprehensive silence which told the Gestapo man that she didn't want to break down in his presence, as she would have done if she herself had breathed a single word about him. Her self-reproachful sense of 'having the boy on my conscience' – she told herself that daily but above all nightly – was wellnigh killing her despite the hope to which she clung as all prisoners do, even when there is little or nothing to hope for. Mayer had assured her that the Pole was temporarily safe. 'My application's in the pipeline,' he told her in his best officialese, meaning his request that a fair-haired Pole be Germanized, not strangled.

That was why Mayer felt as if he had been kicked in the crotch when, out of the blue, the post brought a one-and-a-half line 'confirmation of sentence' instructing him to hang Zasada at the earliest possible date, meaning tomorrow, because the Pole had been advised that 'GV' was a capital offence ...

Mayer read the stark words three times over, then jumped up, almost overturning his chair, and scuttled off with uncharacteristic speed to see the most senior of his underlings. 'Take a look at this crap, Gustl!' he said. He was so outraged he didn't even bellow – and bellowing in cold blood was his normal practice, simply on account of the long corridors, spacious prison yard and lofty stairs. The news had dealt such a blow to his best-developed feature, an orderly mind, that he became almost philosophical about it. 'What's the object of this whole Germanization scheme if we don't have a single Pole who *hasn't* been advised of the consequences of "GV", can you tell me that, Gustl?'

In fact, *every* Pole had not only been 'formally instructed' what would happen to him if he were caught committing 'GV' but had signed a statement to that effect. 'This order – I tell you, it's beginning to make me wonder if the top brass know what they're doing.'

This was a fearsomely critical remark. Mayer flinched as soon as it escaped his lips. He glanced round and saw that he had left Gustl's office door open in his agitation, but they were alone. 'Himmler's right – the Pole was duly informed – but he was just as right when he said that anyone fit for Germanization ought to be usefully employed, not strung up.'

Gustl said, 'On the face of it, we won't be hanging the man for "GV" – we'll be hanging him for ignoring instructions.' He grinned. 'But how can anyone commit "GV" *without* ignoring them?' Mayer said nothing because he was already preoccupied with the now ineluctable necessity of ordering an execution, so Gustl went on, 'That means the old rule still applies. Ex-prisoners of war will continue to be hanged for "GV", every last one of them, because they've all been warned. The only possible exceptions are civilian workers who've arrived here so recently there hasn't been time to put them in the picture. It's a foul-up, Karl. You'd better phone Berlin and point it out.'

Mayer glared at him. 'What are you trying to do, giving me a piece of cock-eyed advice like that, get rid of me? *I'm* not daft enough to suggest that our two Heinrichs up there, Müller and Himmler, don't know what they're doing. It really does seem crazy, though. The Poles who came here as POWs two years back, *they* get sent to the gallows even though they've been pulling their weight the whole time, like our man, whereas a Pole who turned up yesterday can screw the first woman in sight and get a German passport for his trouble. I ask you, Gustl – if that isn't crazy, what is?'

Gustl made no immediate reply because he was less irate than Mayer and capable of clearer thought – capable, too, of drawing the ultimate inference from this interpretation of Himmler's clemency. 'It's even crazier than that, Karl. It isn't just that a Pole who's been working here for years gets hanged while another earns himself a passport for doing the same thing because he only arrived here yesterday. Don't you see? The new Pole can *only* earn a passport by doing what the old one has to swing for. That's worse than crazy – it's an unholy mess!'

The deranged but almighty Reichsführer-SS and Chief of the German Police had ordained that non-compliance with an instruction should be punishable by hanging, whereas the offence which that instruction was designed to prevent should be *rewarded* by making it the sole grounds on which a Pole could obtain a German passport. Even to these two men, whose duties formed a context which they thought normal, this seemed so abnormal that they treated themselves to an unauthorized mid-morning schnapps from the office bottle.

Three cigarettes

Hanging is to be carried out by detainees; wherever possible, in the case of foreign workers, by members of the same ethnic group. Detainees will each receive three cigarettes per execution.

The Reichsführer-SS and Chief of the German Police, Communication No. SIV D2 – 450/42g – 81 dated 6 January 1943.

Karl Mayer, head of the Lörrach Gestapo, ordered the guard to unlock the door of Victorowicz's cell. The Pole had admitted wearing a pair of shoes which the local authorities at Steinen had issued to a fellow-Pole eleven days before his escape, and on which several payments were still outstanding. It was five weeks since Mayer had arrested Victorowicz in the field he was manuring and detained him with a view to proving his complicity in the other Pole's escape. But Victorowicz had defied all efforts to nail him. He merely admitted that his workmate, with whom he had shared a room on the same farm, had once, while hauling timber in the forest, taken a close look at the German–Swiss frontier to satisfy himself that both sides were closely guarded. According to Victorowicz, the runaway had probably headed for Poland, overcome with homesickness. He might even have thrown himself into the Rhine at Weil, for why else should he have left his only serviceable pair of shoes behind? From Victorowicz's manner, which fluctuated between timidity and incomprehension, and from his habit of repeating questions as though uncertain of their exact meaning, Mayer sensed that the Pole was better informed and more intelligent than he let on ... The shoes had been Jewish-owned before the state acquired them and sold them to the vanished Pole. Mayer confiscated them but couldn't hold Victorowicz any longer because no penal offence could be proved against him.

Berlin had issued frequent reminders that Poles stationed in the Reich were there to work, not rot in jail. On the other hand, Mayer's orderly mind was such that he jibbed at discharging a man, albeit on a leash, who had been detained because of an undispelled suspicion that he had criminally abetted plans for an escape; a man who had arbitrarily donned some shoes which the German Reich had expropriated from Jews destined for special treatment and issued to another Pole for use at work – shoes, moreover, which had yet to be paid for in full ...

Mayer reflected that the return of these shoes to the German Reich's possession would entail an appreciable amount of paperwork. They couldn't simply be stored in the Gestapo offices at Lörrach but would require inspection before resale to another foreign worker, and a report would have to be filed stating their provenance from the fugitive and containing a recommendation as to what should be done with them. Ever a worried man, Mayer was still preoccupied with these problems when Victorowicz stiffened to attention in his cell – prison regulations prescribed a military stance – because he had heard the key in the lock.

Mayer was so wrapt in thought that he greeted the prisoner's rigid form with a 'Heil Hitler!' – a wholly improper proceeding. The use of the German salute on foreigners was banned, needless to say, just as foreigners themselves were forbidden to use the greeting 'Heil Hitler!' Directing it at a detainee was worse than absurd – it was an insult to the Führer. 'Good morning, Herr Kommissar,' Victorowicz replied humbly. Mayer was gratified. The man's deportment was good – almost German – and his cell was impeccably tidy despite the wood-carver's tools and shavings. There being no risk of suicide in view of the prisoner's status, Mayer had let him have a couple of chisels and some lime-wood in his cell. Victorowicz, whose hobby was wood-carving, had gratefully volunteered to make Frau Mayer a hand-mirror adorned with roses and leaf-work. It lay there now, almost finished. Mayer picked it up, said 'At ease!' and, when Victorowicz remained at attention, translated: 'Relax, man, take it easy.' Then, holding up the empty wooden frame as if he could already see his reflection, he said admiringly, 'This is coming along fine, Victorowicz. Will you finish it off if I let you go tomorrow? There'll be a bottle of schnapps in it for you.' Although Mayer knew he wasn't supposed to give schnapps to a foreigner, the man was a genuine artist in wood. Besides, Mayer's scrupulous approach to subordinates – and still more so to prisoners – forbade him to accept the mirror as a gift. As for the schnapps, which he legally acquired from Party stocks, at least it wouldn't help the man to escape as money might have done ...

Mayer drank no spirits at home, only on duty and when standing orders permitted. As, for instance, when evidence had to be beaten out of a prisoner – 'rigorous interrogation' was the official term – or at executions like the one tomorrow morning. This official schnapps was paid for by the department and subject to special regulations.

The Pole's eyes lit up. Imprisonment was preying on his nerves, so he gazed at Mayer deferentially, awaiting further instructions, and hastened to assure him that he would finish carving the mirror even when he was 'free' – he actually used the word, but nobody would have detected the latent sarcasm. Victorowicz, who had given his occupation as 'teacher', never spoke German with anything like the fluency he could muster and feigned a passion for agricultural labour because he had heard that all Polish secondary schools had been closed since the fighting ended, like the universities, and because he knew that university teachers had been the first to be carted off to unknown destinations by the occupying power. There was no doubt that, by rounding up university teachers first and Jews second, the Germans had established an order of precedence which clearly identified the group they regarded as their mortal enemies – 'which we are,' Victorowicz reflected with grim satisfaction. Not yet a university lecturer, he had taught at a grammar school while working on his thesis before being drafted. His subject: 'The Final Year, 11 November 1917 to 11 November 1918.' At Mons, one year to the day before Imperial Germany surrendered, Ludendorff had evolved his plan for the offensive that led to the collapse of the German front in France. And Imperial Germany's last day had been Republican Poland's first – the day of Poland's foundation ...

But Victorowicz, who had also studied in Berlin for eighteen months until autumn 1938 and was almost as proficient in German as French, would have bitten his tongue off rather than reveal that he had an almost sexual craving for something to read, so he had only asked for wood-carving tools. Mayer must think him, at best, as educated as he was himself. The Pole was only awaiting his chance to steal a civilian suit and head for Strasbourg. He already had the fare, and from Strasbourg he planned to sneak through into the part of France which Hitler had so far left unoccupied ...

Mayer picked up the mirror again, steeling himself to say what had to be said. He spoke very slowly because he assumed that the Pole would otherwise fail to understand him. 'You'll be out of here – out and free – by midday tomorrow. But before that you've got to do something for your fellow-prisoner and fellow-countryman, Zasada. A last favour...' He hesitated. Victorowicz stared at him, spellbound but genuinely uncomprehending. As casually as he could, because he was anxious to conceal how disturbing he found it to say what must be said, Mayer went on, 'You're going to hang Zasada in the morning.'

Avoiding the Pole's eye, he replaced the carving on the table and braced himself for the inevitable. It came a moment or two later, almost inaudibly. 'Me? Why me, Herr Kommissar? Please! Hang *me*, but don't ask me to ...' So dispassionately that the underlying threat was lost, Mayer said, 'You've got a nerve, Victorowicz – Germans don't hang Poles. One of your people seduces a German soldier's wife, and you expect *us* to do the dirty work? I'm not authorized to hang a Pole – or a Frenchman or an Englishman for that matter. Foreigners have to be dealt with by their own kind – that's an order from the very top.'

Because Mayer had spoken to him at such length and with growing familiarity, indeed, quite amiably, Victorowicz succumbed to the hope that he would be able to talk him round. 'Please not me, Herr Kommissar – I'll die if I have to do it.' His voice rose to a near shout. 'I *can't* do it, I won't – I'm ...' He was stammering now. He found it inexpressibly humiliating to say what he had to say but sensed that, humiliating or not, no other line of argument could ward off this monstrous thing that Mayer had asked of him. 'I'm a religious man, I – I know God would never forgive me for this murder. I'm weak, too – I'd faint if I had to hang someone who ...'

Mayer changed tack. He said curtly, 'You were in the army, didn't you ever pull the trigger on a German? Why should you go weak at the knees if...' The Pole was bold enough to interrupt him. 'Yes,' he blurted out, 'I fired at enemies with guns, but never – never – at unarmed men. Never! Hang *me*, I won't hang anyone!' He turned away. He had spoken firmly and with finality, not tearfully. His obstinacy touched off a similar emotion in Mayer, who matched his tone. 'I can't hang you for refusing to obey my order,' he said, 'I'd have to send you to a concentration camp. You'd be hanged all right, but not by a German – by a Pole. Go on, then, refuse – you'll only be saddling two more of your Polish comrades with a job you don't have the guts to handle yourself. Very decent of you, I'm sure! One'll hang Zasada tomorrow and the other'll have to do the same for you in a few days' time. Where's the sense in that?'

Victorowicz shrugged. Mayer pointed to his stool and the Pole, whose horror had begun to sap his strength, sat down. Mayer's ascendancy was further enhanced because he remained standing. He found it hard to tell how serious Victorowicz was in his refusal. 'It's quite normal,' he went on. 'Soldiers often have to execute their comrades – every army in the world does it. Haven't you ever been assigned to a firing squad?' He had to rephrase the question. Victorowicz, his pale face moist and growing paler every moment, hadn't understood. At last he replied, 'I was never there when they shot a comrade.'

Mayer said, 'If you Poles had stood a few more Poles against a wall you'd have held out longer than eighteen days, that's for sure.' He spoke so contemptuously that Victorowicz felt emboldened to reply in kind. 'We Poles weren't beaten because our courage failed us. We had to fight without tanks and Stukas – and allies who had promised to attack you from the west!'

Mayer had given him a cigarette and was smoking himself, perched on the edge of the table. He said affably, 'Zasada's a big fellow but you're a head taller. You're kind-hearted too, that's why I picked you – you won't hurt him. If you're shorter than a man when you put the rope round his neck it sometimes goes adrift. The noose, I mean. It works round under his chin, and then he dies slowly. I don't want that.'

Victorowicz stared hard at his cigarette to avoid seeing what Mayer had removed from his tunic pocket: a rope which was more like a length of thick cord and a black sack no bigger than

183

a shopping-bag. 'You slip it over his head – like this!' He said it so quickly that Victorowicz had no time to duck. Mayer slipped the hood on and off in a single movement, then put it on the table and started to fashion a noose – deftly, like a shop assistant tying a parcel. 'Come on, look!' he snapped, because the Pole had ostentatiously turned his head away. 'No, I won't do it!'

Mayer rose and said, as if the matter were settled, 'You won't have to tie the noose – that'll be hanging there by the time you and Zasada get on the cart. All that happens then is, they drive it away from the gallows as soon as you've got the noose in place – here ...' And he indicated the spot that mattered on his own neck before doing the same to Victorowicz, who was still seated. 'I won't do it,' the Pole said in a muffled voice. He repeated the words twice more and, to underline his refusal, boldly shook off the hand that was fumbling with his collar, Adam's apple and neck – not that he followed the point of Mayer's instructions in the least. Then he stood up and, greedily though he had been smoking it, stubbed out his cigarette.

Mayer, who was locked in with Victorowicz, banged the cell door three times with his fist. It opened at once, but he didn't go yet. 'You're an artist with a chisel and I'm a patient man,' he said, 'but you'll do the necessary. You'll do it because Zasada will ask you to. You've talked to him now and again – I let you, even though it was against the rules – and it's my guess you get on well together. That sullen, dirty runt of a chicken-thief in the cell opposite, the one who only speaks Polish and smells of cat-shit and looks like a child rapist – he'd be only too happy to hang Zasada, but he's two heads shorter and he'd hurt him. You do it, Victorowicz – nobody could wish for a kinder hangman than you. I'll let you talk to Zasada.'

So saying he went out. Victorowicz, who had leant against the wall beneath the barred window, thought he was going to be sick. He bent quickly over the slop-pail but nothing came – he only retched and gagged. It was hysteria, panic. Before he could hit on the idea of putting himself out of his misery with a chisel, or at least of injuring himself so badly his hands would be useless next morning, Mayer got there first. He had the cell door reopened and the two chisels removed. He also had Zasada, manacled and wearing convict's uniform, pushed roughly inside.

Behind bars

In the pre-eminently Catholic districts covered by this Section (Upper Palatinate, Lower Bavaria, part of Upper Franconia) the fact that the majority of Russians are also Catholic has the effect of blurring the distinctions between German and foreign blood ... The extent to which Catholics lack discrimination in regard to Russians is illustrated by an incident which occurred in Bamberg on 7 June 1942. Approximately forty Russian civilian workers of both sexes took part in the Corpus Christi procession there, led by the camp overseer in person. The Russians accompanied the procession for about a hundred yards with a view to attending Mass in the cathedral. The Russians were then expelled from the procession and the camp overseer was taken into custody, but not until the police stepped in. None of the townsfolk taking part in the procession lifted a finger to get rid of the Russians ... As ... already stated, the Catholic population find it sufficient that a Russian is likewise Catholic and devout for them to regard him as a 'fellow-man'.

Security Service internal affairs report dated 20 July 1942, Bayreuth Section.

The *Föhn*, that warm Alpine wind that deepens and strengthens colours but renders them even more diaphanous than they already are in the grape-picking month of October, made it seem to the inmates of Lörrach's eighty-year-old jail that the Tüllinger Hügel vineyard was closer than ever – that the grapes were within smelling distance, like their foliage and the blue damson-trees and the yellow-stippled birch-leaves and the smooth swift poplar-silver river in which, exactly one year ago, Pauline had first glimpsed her lover as he watered Melchior's horses, riding bareback and stripped to the waist. She had been smitten even then, unconsciously, by the sight of that handsome bare-chested young horseman. Today she saw the hill, already half harvested of grapes, just as she had seen it a year before, and felt – without being able to think it – that the earth was unmoved by mortals like herself. They meant nothing to it and could derive no comfort from it unless they were at least able to touch it. Otherwise, its splendid indifference became a torment – as it now was to her because Nature was beyond her reach in any form, in any thing or person. She could not touch it in her children, nor in a man, nor even in a forest track or patch of grass behind the house. The very sight of it only intensified her sense of deprivation. And she remembered a woman telling her, when her husband was cremated after nearly sixty years of marriage, 'Not dying too, that's the worst part...'

The fact that Pauline herself was imprisoned while waiting to be transferred to a concentration camp, though she could not conceive what such places were like, afforded her great spiritual consolation in the agony of self-reproach that racked her for having brought Stani to 'this' – 'this' being the cautious euphemism she needed to quell the dread that was beginning, nonetheless, to assail her for minutes on end...

On the other hand, this was a traditional-looking old-fashioned prison. Pauline's imagination, which was limited at the best of times, ran little risk of being driven by its appearance to conclude that people were done to death there – except in the heat of the moment. From all she had heard, there seemed a strong possibility that prisoners were sometimes beaten to death during interrogations. But executed? It cheered her to be able to cling to the belief that Mayer had promised to tell her when Stani was no longer 'there', which she took to mean somewhere far away in another wing of the same building. When a person has nothing more to hope for – though this she didn't know – there is almost nothing to which hope will not cling. She didn't know that either.

It might well have been possible to smuggle a message to her lover, but she took care not to. She would never have done anything to risk making his sentence 'worse', as she phrased it to herself. The thought of the gallows was so inconceivable that she genuinely feared she might prolong his term of imprisonment – the only penalty she could bring herself to contemplate – if she tried to re-establish contact with him. She also refrained because all that had sentenced him to death were the letters she had sent him from Bavaria via Elsbeth Schnittgens – the only evidence to have fallen into the hands of his judicial murderers...

Thus her sole recourse was to tell herself 'They just can't do it!' – meaning hang the boy, for it was the boy, not the man, who was causing her such agonies of self-reproach. She had given in to the boy – she told herself that too. It wasn't true, but that was how she now saw what had 'happened'. She found it impossible to admit that it was the man who had swept her off her feet after the boy, admittedly, had claimed her maternal compassion. It was too hard, shamed as she was by her husband's spontaneous readiness to forgive her and resume their life together. But that a *boy* should stand in the shadow of the gallows on her account ... That was what sometimes drove her from her plank bed in the middle of the night, sent her pacing round the cell for hours, made her beat the wall with her fists – even made her beat her head against it. 'My heart is breaking ...' A foolish turn of phrase which she would have dismissed – had it ever crossed her mind before – as merely what it was: a turn of phrase. Now, however, the shooting pains and cramps below her left breast convinced her that these words had a real physical basis – one that constricted her breathing and filled her with mortal terror. She felt as if a clenched fist were pounding her heart to pieces

– and wished it really were so. Her husband was behaving so decently ... She was sure, if her death-wish came true, that he would take the children to her parents as he had already promised to do by letter. But he must make good his promise before leaving for Russia! The campaign had already been raging for nearly four months. It was the longest ever – longer than the campaigns in Poland, in Denmark and Norway, in France, in the Balkans. Pauline could not conceive that Hitler would lose the war, and although she wished him in hell, him and the whole of his Party, who knew whether they mightn't really murder Stani if disaster overtook them on the battlefield? Who knew, either, whether her husband wouldn't have to share their fate?

How little the individual knows, far less foresees, of what eventually befalls the juggernaut that is crushing him to death, and how little it would avail him if he did! If Pauline had guessed the truth, what good would it have done her? How would it have consoled her to *know*, as she half suspected, that her husband was among those foredoomed to vanish for ever during the Russian campaign? And when her 'boy' was led to the gallows next morning – of this she still had no presentiment – would it have comforted her at all to know what would happen on 16 October 1946, five years later to the day? Would it have allayed her grief to know that at least a handful of the bandits-in-chief who had Zasada and another six million Poles on the debit side of their account – not, of course, on their unused consciences, which were clean and in mint condition – would go to the gallows at Nuremberg?

Ten days before, on 5 October 1941, a medical corps colonel named Benn attached to the Armed Forces High Command in Bendlerstrasse, Berlin, wrote a personal letter to a friend – risky enough in itself – predicting the Napoleonic disaster in store for the German armies in Russia. He did so unaided by the knowledge that those balmy October days were a bright and banefully seductive mirage heralding the coldest Russian winter for a century. So devilish was the delusion that lured them into the maw of winter, with its sudden onset of death-dealing cold, that Hitler's generals, who were in no way wiser than their master, actually forgot to protect their soldier-victims by providing them with winter clothing. These 'strategists' had been intoxicated by the unwonted waves of mellow autumn light and warm autumn air. Not so Benn, who wrote: 'Where the East is concerned, nothing has been achieved despite our major victories which is likely to bring peace nearer. On the contrary, it isn't so important that we'll be lucky to gain our strategic objective – the Petersburg–Moscow–Rostov line – after five months instead of four weeks, as the General Staff thought. What matters is that we haven't achieved any kind of political outcome and that our losses are almost irreparable ... If the Russians had twelve million men to start with, they still have seven million left even if our figures are correct. Of our own three million on 22 June 1941, *one* must have been put out of action complete with equipment. There are virtually no replacements to be had ... 1942: the year of decision. In Spengler's sense, I presume. The third volume of his magnum opus won't appear in book form but as an operational and General Staff map...'

That a German officer could write such a letter, which would have been quite enough, if read by the censor, to send him to the guillotine, is heartening proof that there were plenty of minds immune from the national paranoia. Benn, too, found an evocation of melancholy in this warm and cornucopian time of year: 'How are things with you this lovely autumn? Plenty of apples on the trees, I'll bet, and plenty of dahlias in the gardens.'

Lörrach was radiant with October light, clear as white wine, but the nights had turned chilly. 'The sun's deceptive,' Pauline told a fellow-inmate – they both wore convicts' stripes – who was helping her scrub the stone stairway leading to the suite of prison offices on the first floor. They were unguarded, but where could they have run to if they had escaped? Each woman knew why the other was there and both were awaiting their 'transfer', as it was officially termed, to a concentration camp. Unlike Pauline, the other woman had been tried by a special court in Freiburg. She had cheated the guillotine by an unexpected stroke of luck because the neighbour who had denounced her, and whom she, too, had mistakenly regarded as her best friend, persuaded the court that the accused had listened to BBC broadcasts but failed to establish that she had transmitted their contagion to others. Only the spreading of reports from the enemy camp was punishable by decapitation; the penalty for merely listening to them was indefinite confinement in a concentration camp. It could also happen – if the judge was not an out-and-out Nazi, though most such judges had been posted to the front – that an accused person was lucky enough to be delivered from the clutches of the SS by receiving a long term of penal servitude...

This woman was poised and composed – happy to be alive, in fact, because her court-appointed attorney had held out little hope before her trial that she would end up anywhere but on a slab in the dissecting-room at Freiburg University. Besides, she had no idea what went on in concentration camps ... 'Did you manage to get a bit of sleep?' She had just asked this question when she dropped her scrubbing-brush, gripped Pauline by the arm and drew her to the window. 'The men!' she exclaimed. 'Is yours down there?'

Pauline couldn't speak. But while she was mutely, tremulously, clumsily wrenching at the yard window, which refused to budge, her companion in misfortune confirmed that the Pole was down there too, being marched round and round. For the last time. Tomorrow at this hour – not that he knew it – Professor Dr. So-and-So of Freiburg would be pulling on his rubber gloves and preparing to remove Zasada's vital organs, the routine procedure before a gutted cadaver was deposited in a bath of formalin...

Pauline called, 'Stani!' It was her first glimpse of him for six months. Tears welled into her eyes, but they were not the reason why she failed to see that the catch of the barred landing window had been permanently secured. While she was banging on the pane – vainly, because the yard was as big as a parade ground and Zasada was on the far side – her companion scrambled on to the sill without a word and, by reaching through the bars, managed to half-open the narrow window above the transom. Throwing caution to the winds, unafraid for him or herself – unthinkingly – Pauline called his name twice more. Then he had heard her, seen her! He broke ranks and sprinted across the gravel, burst through the near side of the shuffling procession and came to a stop below the window. That was when Pauline saw his handcuffs. She didn't know that men under sentence of death were permanently manacled, and not just when marched round the yard, nor did she notice at that moment, for a moment was all they had left, that Zasada was the *only* man in handcuffs ... She tried to speak. So did he, but neither of them could. At last she called down, 'Forgive me – please forgive me, Stani ...' That was all she could manage.

Whether because he couldn't hear or or didn't know the word, her meaning eluded him, but she saw through a veil of tears that his face had lit up from within. 'Forgive...' She had never said that to anyone, not even the God she sometimes prayed to, being a Catholic. But now, involuntarily, this impassioned word had escaped her lips because it was the only one that could approximately convey her abysmal sense of guilt – a feeling stronger than any she had ever experienced before.

The warder in his cardboard-grey uniform, a noncombatant with ulcers, had already gone in pursuit of the man who had broken ranks. He had also drawn attention to Pauline's indiscipline by gesticulating at the onlookers watching from the office windows on the first floor. His rather underpowered voice could be heard shouting, as he panted up behind the Pole, 'Back, back – get back in line, Zasada!'

Zasada barely turned to glance at the mouthing figure. He beamed at Pauline as though some definite decision had been reached. Then the inner light that had transfigured his face went out. He lifted his captive hands to his uptilted chin and called, 'I must – hang!'

'They can't do that!' she called back, torn between hope and despair.

Then the warder was on him. He gave a futile tug at Zasada's sleeve. Pale, hollow-eyed and gaunt with hunger but still steady on his feet, the Pole didn't even look round. He shook rather than pushed the man off and shouted, 'For you, I happy to die!'

He continued to gaze up at her, but Pauline went limp. If her friend hadn't caught her she would have fallen from the sill. By now two prison officers had darted out of different doors, alerted by the cries of the yard supervisor, and were converging on the head of the stairs. And while the two myrmidons, one in uniform, reassured themselves in the upstairs corridor by automatically giving vent to the usual stream of professional invective, the ageless and ineradicable jailers' jargon of every time and place, with its not alloweds and strictly forbiddens, its threats of harsher penalties and solitary confinement, Pauline half leant, half lay against the window surround. And her friend supported her as they both looked down into the yard and watched the Pole being led away, flanked by two warders who gripped him by the elbows, not back into line but down some steps to a basement door in the building opposite. Zasada did not look round. The prisoners circling the yard stared up at the women until one of the men who had hurried to the scene stepped between the women and the window and bawled at them 'You two, get back to work!'

Strangely, though, Pauline was left in peace when she walked back to the stairs and, ignoring her brush and bucket, sat down on the top step with her face clamped hard against her right forearm.

She had no idea, even now, why Mayer's pair of dutiful minions should have been so undutifully lax with her on this of all days.

No farewell letter

Notification of relatives will on principle be delayed until sentence has been carried out ... Should the relatives of an executed person not be resident in Reich teritory, or should they be Poles resident in the incorporated eastern territories, the Central State Security Bureau will assume responsibility for any notification required. In the case of workers from the east, the relevant regional headquarters of the State Police will notify the Labour Office, intimating that relatives should not be apprised of the cause of death.

The Reichsführer-SS and Chief of the German Police, Communication No. SIV D2 – 450/42g – 81 dated 6 January 1943.

On the strength of the mirror he had promised to carve for Frau Mayer, Victorowicz had been granted a special privilege. He had asked Mayer for permission to wear his watch while in custody, and the Gestapo chief, after eyeing him warily, had agreed. Ten minutes later the watch was withdrawn from the personal effects store and irregularly returned to the prisoner on remand, who had to sign a receipt in duplicate. Yesterday afternoon, when Zasada was thrust into his hangman's cell, this watch had proved a boon of the first order, but the more night yielded to the misty white embrace of day the faster the hands seemed to turn. And although there were moments when Zasada wished the second hand were the hour hand, other moments brought a sudden heart-stopping suspicion that it really was so – that the hours were speeding past like seconds. For the first time in his life, and consequently the last, it hurt him to breathe. The tightness in his chest was a physical manifestation of fear...

It was four a.m. The hangman and the man to be hanged had now shared the same cell for thirteen hours. Both had managed to sleep for quite some time. Zasada was only granted this most precious of all gifts, oblivion, because his older and less resilient companion resorted to a simple device: he pretended to sleep himself – doggedly, until he actually did so. And this, in turn, had enabled Zasada to think himself as unobserved as he very soon was, unobserved and at liberty to do, quite naturally, the thing that ended by reducing even him to soporific exhaustion and was all that could banish the paralysing, panic fear of death; at liberty to ejaculate and wing his way beyond the confines of his cell to the girl at home whose body he had been privileged to enjoy, and to the woman in Germany who now lay in a cell like his because he had made love to her. Pauline was a prisoner because he had made love to her – that was the version he clung to so desperately, though it would have been truer to say: because she had stupidly written to him. If it hadn't been for those letters ... But why pursue the thought? Wasn't pursuing things to the bitter end the sole source of all human tribulation? It was a pointless exercise.

Esther in Lodz ... Why speculate on the possibility, or even the probability, that she was sleeping with German soldiers? After all, she was working at a German headquarters in return for enough to eat and a chance of smuggling food home to her parents – and anyway, why shouldn't she, when he had slept with a German himself? Nationality was no sort of criterion on the threshold of death, not to any decent person, considering the havoc it had wrought on nations and countries – on whole eras ... The Germans were going to murder him, but it was a German who had tipped him off about escaping to Switzerland, a German who had loved him ... Nationality was the most pernicious, depersonalizing, homogenizing label that could ever be attached to the human individual. Why bother with it, now least of all?

Yet it was the dementia of nationalism that had brought him, first into the war, then into captivity and ultimately to this cell, so the thought of it was quite inescapable. To dismiss it as irrelevant would only accentuate the horror of his situation, for who wanted to think himself the victim of something utterly senseless? On the contrary, he would have – because he didn't believe in God – to rebuild his sense of nationality into a last supreme arbiter, into the sea-anchor which would, if only for a few hours, steady his existence as it drifted into death. To have to tell himself that he was dying for no good reason would be the bitter end, precisely because it was true!

But Zasada, like anyone in his position, had no further interest in persuading himself of what was true, only of what was expedient. He found it helpful, for instance, to remain on his feet until ... until they dangled in mid air. Instinct told him to do this, not conscious deliberation, just as instinct unerringly told him that only a great *idea*, transcendent of self and charged with emotion, could impart the steadfastness he needed if he weren't to gratify his murderers by cutting a pitiful figure in the morning. Because religion had no hold on him – nor ideology, ever since his schoolboyish flirtation with Communism had been blighted in 1939 by the traumatic news that Stalin and Hitler had concocted a plan to share out Poland between them – this transcendent idea could only be patriotism.

So only love of country could distract his thoughts from what awaited him in the morning and fill the unendurable emotional vacuum with meaning, with a feeling bigger than the individual who would be snuffed out a few hours hence. *Vengefulness* was the emotion he felt. It flooded over him, bearing him up and away with a force intensified by the knowledge that he himself would never assuage it – that others, fellow-countrymen and allies, would have to do so in his stead. Thinking of this, he felt as if he were with them, and their companionship blunted his agonizing sense of isolation ... Hatred focused on an object is vindictiveness, and the hatred he felt, dull and debilitating at first but now fierce and purposeful, had been aroused by yesterday's news that he wasn't entitled to write a farewell letter. He hadn't believed it at first. He would never have thought it, even of the Germans – in fact he had seen, *seen* from the sheepish way in which Mayer twice turned down his request for permission to write one last letter to his parents, how incomprehensible even a German policeman found this ban. But there it was: Himmler had ordained, not only that 'aliens' from the east should be forbidden to write farewell letters, but that their relatives were to be told nothing – not even that the victim had been put to death. They might or might not come to hear of it, though friends of the dead man would almost certainly convey the news sooner or later. (Nobody here knew, for example, that the Krupp works at Essen generally burnt the incoming and outgoing mail of their 'alien' Slav labour force for simplicity's sake.)

In Zasada, rage at the denial of his request gained the upper hand so quickly and completely that it mitigated his despair. It may only have been Mayer's realization that not even Germans ought to show such inhumanity, however victoriously they were now storming eastwards, which prompted his clemency in allowing the condemned man a sympathetic cell-mate during his last night on earth. That it should be Victorowicz who was to hang Zasada in the morning seemed far less important to the pair who owed their enforced intimacy to such gruesome circumstances than the calming effect of the hangman's promise that he would write to Zasada's parents.

Zasada had expended a lot of strength – born of necessity alone

– in trying to console his executioner, for yesterday and until well after nightfall Victorowicz had been by far the more desperate of the two. 'I can't go on living unless you do it yourself,' he had pleaded with the light of madness in his eyes, and there was no doubting his sincerity when he sketched out a means of personal salvation: not being manacled like Zasada, he would wait until they were standing on the cart, and then, just as it was about to be driven away from under them, put on the noose destined for Zasada and jump ... Zasada had pointed out how childish this was. 'They'd only keep me standing there, maybe for an hour, while they found another Pole to do what you shirked doing.'

'Shirked?' cried Victorowicz. 'You call it shirking if I die with you?'

'Yes,' said Zasada, 'that's all it would be. Anyway, even if I wanted to save you the trouble by doing it myself, how could I? It's ten to one they'll handcuff me with my arms behind my back, the way they've often done before.'

They stared mournfully at each other and avoided each other's gaze by turns until Zasada removed one of his wooden-soled sandals – a condemned man's only footwear – and said, as he tapped the floor with it, 'You can't avenge me unless you stay alive, so run for it. France is on the doorstep and you're bound to get to England from there – oh God, why didn't I try it myself!' These words put new life into Victorowicz. Zasada was unaware how closely they accorded with the plan that had long been a secret reality to his companion in death ... Victorowicz had told him there was no need to bang the stone floor with a wooden sandal: the bare concrete walls of the cell couldn't possibly conceal a listening device – he had checked them innumerable times. And Victorowicz was right. Monitoring techniques were far less sophisticated in 1941 than they became a few years later, when no wall was proof against them and there was no need, as there still was then, to install microphones in a room under surveillance ...

Zasada's anger at being forbidden to write to his parents and his request that Victorowicz do so for him had sown the seeds of conversation and distracted them from the thought of what Victorowicz would have to do before writing the letter ... And with the realization that he could still do something for this doomed man – no, a great deal – Victorowicz became infused with the 'Holy Spirit of resistance', as he called it, and rekindled with the defiance that had always burned within him until it was quenched by Mayer's order to hang a fellow-countryman.

Night is the mother of ideas – the cruel and unnatural mother, for the ideas that visit us in darkness are not of the best. Most nightmarish of all, however, are those that loom in the shroud-white mists of dawn ... Victorowicz had once been told, he couldn't recall by whom, that the early hours of the morning bring a physical and psychical crisis. Once satisfied of his ability to sleep after all, he felt it would be irresponsible to do so and leave his friend alone in the possible or probable event of his being unable to follow suit. Although Zasada might ask questions he couldn't answer because he himself knew nothing of the language of priests, he felt it his duty to talk to him. He longed to be able to send him on his way with at least one placebo, but he didn't have even the makings of a spiritual confidence trick. It was a betrayal of ignorance. All he knew was this: that since we know nothing of the so-called *last* things, we cannot dismiss the possibility that they are *first* things. We knew nothing of life before living, yet it proved to be a reality nonetheless, so we cannot logically deny the possibility that death, of which we know just as little before dying, may be just as much of a *beginning* as life itself turned out to be.

He said this when Zasada suddenly asked, out of the blue, though Victorowicz had seen the question germinating inside him, 'Tell me, is there anything left after death?'

Because he could do so in all honesty, Victorowicz promptly told Zasada what had just been running through his mind. He went on, 'We don't know what death is any more than we knew what life was before we existed, but that doesn't rule out the idea that it offers us a new form of existence. If anything, it's an argument in favour. Being there one day and gone the next are just earthly, localized aspects of our existence. The fact that they aren't alike doesn't mean they don't exist.'

Zasada was inclined to reject this as cheap consolation. 'Maybe, maybe not,' he said. 'What you've been saying – how do you know it isn't a myth?'

Victorowicz replied quietly, without any missionary fervour. This he felt sure of – *this* at least. 'Because it's based on an inviolable law, the conservation of energy. The mind – the soul, if you like – is the strongest conveyor of energy there is. Even matter changes but doesn't cease to exist – that's been proved beyond all doubt – so the soul just *can't* be destroyed.'

Zasada said nothing. He had intended his question about survival in a different, more personal way. But even while Victorowicz was speaking he felt abashed at having asked it, because it immediately raised another: why should *he* be so presumptuous as to hope that something of *him* would survive when a European war had been in progress for two whole years, claiming hundreds and sometimes tens of thousands of lives in a single day? By tomorrow he would be just another of its victims, so it seemed more honest to play down what Victorowicz had said about the mind as a supreme conveyor of energy. 'But isn't sex our strongest impulse? That's quite inseparable from the body, so it's bound to die too.'

Victorowicz echoed his question. 'Sex? Certainly not. What about children who are too young to be motivated by it – what about people who are so old that sex plays little or no part in governing their actions? They develop vast amounts of energy, and its source is the mind.'

Victorowicz had noticed that his companion became calmer in spirit if he could be induced to listen. He had been careful not to ask more about Zasada's background than he needed to know in order to write to his parents. From then on his prime concern was to prevent conversation from straying back to the doomed man's home and family. Strangely enough it was a fairy-tale, albeit a highly realistic and wholly topical one, that gave him his fullest opportunity to satisfy Zasada's most powerful emotion apart from the fear of death – revenge – and imbued both men with a strength that was almost as elemental as their anger at the despicable way in which Zasada had been denied a farewell letter. It was the tale of the fisherman and his wife ...

Instruments of the Führer

It was National Socialism which first created the mental climate essential to an effective reconstruction of German law. The Reich Penal Code is, by descent, a typical child of the nineteenth century and was decisively influenced by the ideas of that period. The legislator was primarily at pains to fulfil that (not exclusively) liberal ideal, certainty of the law ... The new penal law will put an end to this state of affairs and bring about a radical change in the one prevailing hitherto.

Hans Karl Filbinger, 1935.

The convicted person's act (absence without leave) would normally have been punishable by death or a long term of penal servitude. Six months' imprisonment should be regarded as an exceptionally lenient sentence.

Filbinger on 6 September 1945, in a British POW camp.

I interview the ex-mayor and former district director of the Brombach branch of the National Socialist Party, Herr Josef Zinngruber, who looks appreciably younger than his eighty years, in the living-room of the two-storeyed modern concrete house which his architect son built for him in Schopfheimerstrasse during the 'sixties. He gives me a warm welcome – in fact he even says he hopes my story will gain him the acquittal he was denied by two French courts, once at his original hearing and again on appeal. They sentenced him to five years' imprisonment for denouncing Pauline and her Pole, though the term was commuted by twelve months ... Zinngruber lends me the court findings and some (hand-picked) documents for photocopying. I leave him my gold watch as a guarantee of their safe return.

Zinngruber's wife, paralysed by a stroke, is suspicious and promptly inquires where my wife comes from. My wife, who is dark and looks like a native of eastern Switzerland, quickly reassures her by speaking Basle dialect. Frau Zinngruber sheds a tear nonetheless – stroke victims cry easily – and laments the fact that this 'business' (evidently the local vogue-word for Zasada's execution) should be raked up yet again.

Zinngruber is the one person who doesn't deny, because he *can't*, that he was present at the execution. His comments on it merely disclose the way his mind still works today. 'It was a rotten business, and I ...' He becomes even sprightlier now that he has broached the subject anyway, and he speaks with remarkable verve for an octogenarian. Burning to justify himself, he goes on, 'I flatly refused to wear uniform for the occasion. I mean, you can't go disgracing a uniform, can you? That's why I told Mayer, straight out, I don't intend to soil the thing by wearing it. *I'm* coming in civvies!' To object that Nazi uniform was a fancy-dress costume designed for criminal buffoons, not an honourable form of attire, would have destroyed all hope of extracting further information, so I lamely confine myself to saying, 'But Mayer was in the Gestapo, Herr Zinngruber. He wasn't your superior – you could have worn what you liked, being the senior Party official present.' Not so, he replies: the senior official there was Regional Director Rudolf Allgeier from Lörrach.

He adds that Allgeier had submitted an appeal for clemency which Himmler personally rejected. (The district director won't have a word said against his regional director, who vainly tried to get him off the hook during his trial by the French!)

Apparently, Zinngruber and Mayer also argued about the place of execution. Mayer had proposed to hang the Pole in the village itself, from one of the three splendid lime-trees that still stand today beside the *Waldhorn*, a venerable old inn with a sign depicting the hunting horn from which it takes its name. 'Think of it,' exclaimed Zinngruber, 'plumb in the middle of the village, from one of the very trees where our schoolkids hold their singsongs! Who knows, they might have put up a plaque by now – for the Pole, I mean. Then everybody could read what went on here. No, I said to Mayer, that's out, I forbid it, hang him somewhere else, not there – and I got my way!'

The thought still rejoices him. Cautiously, I say, 'But there weren't any trees in the quarry. You must have had a gallows built specially.'

His face darkens at the implied question. 'Not me,' he says quickly, 'I had nothing to do with it.' (Those words – 'I had nothing to do with it' – are the most overworked of any uttered in German since Hitler's death.) Not wishing to alienate the old man, I spare us both the embarrassment of asking how he contrives to look so artless while lying in his teeth. As mayor, he himself ordered the construction of a gallows made of timber from Brombach's communally owned forest. This I have already learned from the chief recipient of his order, Forester Klages, whose story is corroborated by the man chosen to assist him, Farmer Matzke. With a thrill of horror which other war-time incidents don't seem to give them, many Brombachers still recall the evening when these same two men made their way through the shocked and silent village – an announcement of the morrow's execution had already been posted – and went to the quarry to build a gallows for the morning. After all, it isn't often people hear a gallows being built (it was done within earshot of many inhabitants) by two normally sane and reputable fellow-citizens! Matzke and his sons now run a sizeable modern state-financed farm while Klages lives on his forester's pension (his son has succeeded him in the job). When I ask Klages if it wasn't 'difficult' for him to build a gallows, the retired forester seems puzzled by the obtuseness of my question. 'Difficult? It was child's play. Two posts, one here, one there, and a cross-bar on top.' And he uses his left and right hand in turn to demonstrate just how easy it was, as if accustomed to building a gallows every day of the week. No problem, no regrets – he was a Nazi, according to some of the locals. His wife adds, 'Perhaps it was a mercy you spent so long in that Russian POW camp, otherwise the French might have pulled you in too when the war ended, on account of that Pole!' He agrees. I put another question, sensing that it is the very most I can ask if conversation is to continue at all: 'Couldn't you have told Zinngruber it wasn't part of a forester's job, building a gallows?' Klages again looks mystified. He shrugs, then says, *Somebody* had to do it.'

Plenty of 'dirty work' went on in France too, he argues. By all accounts, many Frenchwomen were murdered after the war for sleeping with Germans – murdered or dragged through the streets with their heads shaved and then locked up. 'Quite so,' I reply. 'I'm not interested in what happened to the Pole because I'm deluded enough to think it couldn't have happened in France too – it's up to everyone to put his own house in order.'

According to François Mitterand, then Minister for Ex-Servicemen, who published the figures on 16 June 1946, the French took advantage of the Liberation to make away with 133,000 of their compatriots for actually or allegedly collaborating with the Germans. That the vast majority were slaughtered without trial emerges from the phrasing of this statistical analysis of war victims: 'Civilian casualties (sundry causes) and civilian fatalities (documentation still incomplete).' By comparison, 'only' 92,233 Frenchmen were killed in action during 1939–40. On 1 January 1946, *Le Figaro* put the number of detainees at roughly one million, or 'one-tenth of those members of the French population who are in the prime of life.' The ecstasy of liberation had been transmuted into blood-lust. (Quoted from Paul Sérant's *Les purges politiques en Europe occidentale*.)

'Purge' is a word to be approached – or better, shunned – with extreme care and mournful irony, if only because it was one of Nazi Germany's favourite terms. The fact, bewailed by one of the world's earliest historians, that 'enemies exchange attributes' was here confirmed in a novel but equally horrific fashion. The number of those killed affords no clue to the unofficial estimates of missing persons or those who were 'merely' tortured, some of whom survived. Sérant writes: 'Victims were sometimes led through the streets, where the mob struck and spat at them. These street scenes were intended by those in charge to impress the population. Women suspected of having had relations with Germans had their hair shorn in public; sometimes, too, they were stripped completely naked and had swastikas daubed on them in tar or red lead. There were even instances where unfortunate women were raped by self-styled "patriots". So outrageous were these incidents that the poet Paul Eluard, himself a Communist and advocate of a relentless purge, fiercely inveighed against them in *Lettres Françaises*.

'Those responsible for these atrocities knew that they would go unpunished. Public authority had completely broken down. From prefect to ordinary policeman, every public servant was in danger of arrest. Power belonged only to those who appropriated it. They could, without risk to themselves, arbitrarily arrest anyone they thought fit. In order to survive this phase, the authorities were obliged to concede that might was right because they themselves were under the closest surveillance. Members of the Maquis formed their own police forces, set up prisons and established internment camps to which no one dared object.'

Twenty years later, in 1964, the frenzied excesses of the Liberation were analysed more soberly – perhaps unduly so. 'La Répression de la Collaboration et l'Éruption,' a research report by Marcel Baudot in *La Libération de la France*, states that only 126,000 Frenchmen and Frenchwomen were arrested for collaboration by 28 April 1945. But the arrests continued, of course, and Baudot's claim that only 9,000 genuine or alleged collaborators were summarily killed by members of the Resistance leaves us no wiser about the ones who were dispatched by 'regular' courts ...

Brombach's ex-mayor and ex-district director, Josef Zinngruber, now insists that he declined to recruit terrorists on behalf of Lörrach's Gestapo chief, Mayer, who had proposed that volunteers should march Pauline through the village with her hair shorn – and Mayer himself dropped the idea. The French found Zinngruber guilty of denouncing Pauline and her Pole although he claimed – and still claims today – that he wasn't in Brombach at all, but attending a refresher course for junior Nazi officials, when tragedy overtook the couple at Easter 1941. He insisted in evidence that the course lasted several days longer than the court found proven, and that the charge sheet could not, therefore, have been forwarded to Lörrach by *him*. Bad luck caught up with him years later in the person of someone who had been heaped with post-war abuse and driven into a neo-Nazi corner: Colonel Remer, the man who used his Grossdeutschland Guard Battalion to eject the conspirators from their Bendlerstrasse headquarters on 20 July 1944, after the attempt on Hitler's life had failed. It was Remer, of all people, who exposed the falsity of Zinngruber's evidence and completely demolished his case in the process. The ex-colonel, who happened to be a post-war political associate of the son of one of the women whom Zinngruber had tried to saddle with responsibility for his own conviction, went to work on the ex-instructor whose false statements about the timing of the course had provided the basis of Zinngruber's defence. He finally induced him to admit the truth: that Brombach's district director had already returned to his official domain when Pauline and Zasada were reported to the Gestapo in Lörrach...

Zinngruber's term of imprisonment would have expired on 30 June 1952 if the French hadn't granted him a year's remission on 13 July 1951. By 1 May 1952 he had approached the director of public prosecutions in Lörrach and laid complaints against the persons whose allegedly perjurious statements – he still calls them perjurers to this day – had helped to convict him. He wrote: 'The indictment brought against me ran: "Denunciation of a Polish worker and a German woman to the Gestapo ..." I consider myself not guilty as charged and regard the verdict returned against me as unjust because it relied on prosecution witnesses who, being German nationals, did knowingly and wilfully make false statements under oath.'

After listing five persons by name, Zinngruber went on: 'Of these witnesses, Frau König and Frau Schnittgens were co-defendants before the court of primary jurisdiction but were acquitted by that court and likewise gave evidence under oath at the appeal hearing ... Since all the witnesses are German nationals, and since their course of action, which resulted in my imprisonment and financial detriment, does, to the best of my knowledge, constitute a crime against humanity under German justice and law, I request that the German Directorate of Public Prosecutions institute criminal proceedings.'

But the Baden-Württemberg Ministry of Justice, acting on instructions from the French authorities, replied on 9 February 1953 that 'German judicial competence in this matter is not conceded ...'

Zinngruber now claims, with unflagging vehemence, that perjury alone put him behind bars. Not so much as a sigh escapes him at the fact – to which he never refers – that both courts found it proven that he *was* the person who denounced the Pole and his mistress to the Gestapo in Lörrach. He also makes no mention of having dismissed the head of Brombach's Women's League in May 1941 'on the grounds that Frau König had ceased to be worthy of her post because of her conduct in respect of the Pole Stanislaus and Frau Krop, in that she knew of the affair but neglected to render him an adequate report. The fact is that Frau König was dismissed as head of the Women's League and that Headmistress Rösch succeeded her.' This passage occurs in a statutory declaration made to a French court on 6 January 1949 by Gottlieb Wagner, a retired headmaster, his purpose being to exonerate Frau König, whom Zinngruber – to further his own defence – had described as chiefly responsible, with two other women, for denouncing the Pole to the Lörrach Gestapo. The court, which based its 'suspicion ... that the accused is, in whole or part, trying to *conceal the truth*' on 'other denunciations attested by witnesses', cited the testimony of one Pastor Fetzner, 'who himself fell prey to a denunciation'. (The Melchior and

König families were related by marriage and occupied the same house. Just how they treated their Polish workers is evident from the fact that Popilarczek, Zasada's old room-mate, asked the French for permission to remain in Brombach when the war ended. Instead of returning to Poland, he stayed on of his own free will and continued to work for the Melchiors and Königs until his death from cancer thirty years later.)

It must be said in Zinngruber's favour that Pauline's imprudent visit to her lover in hospital, while it did not make disaster inevitable, certainly caused talk in the village. Many people came to know of the affair, and their knowledge of it was at once pleasurable and perturbing. It was fear that prompted one of Zinngruber's co-defendants, the Frau König whom he dismissed as head of the Women's League a month later, to discuss with a village policeman named Regenhardt what could be done to rebut Zinngruber's charge that she had failed to report Zasada's affair with Pauline. Regenhardt conferred with her but kept mum about their conversation until the Pole had been arrested.

Zinngruber himself would unquestionably have run something of a risk by ignoring the village gossip instead of reporting it to Lörrach. But then, Zinngruber was a man who could order a woman out of his office – a fellow-villager and childhood friend who had bidden him good day on entering – and instruct her to shut the door, knock again and enter with a regulation 'Heil Hitler!' You have to know a minor detail like that before you can gauge what a pathological Nazi he used to be. It is idle, therefore, to speculate whether the Pole would still be alive and whether Pauline would have been spared two years' hard labour in Ravensbrück concentration camp had Zinngruber merely threatened to report them unless they ended their relationship. There *were* local Party bosses in Germany who tossed denunciations into the wastepaper basket and cautioned those who had been denounced, but Zinngruber wasn't among them. Not all who wore Hitler's brown livery were Nazis, just as many Party members were far more decently inclined and politically inoffensive than many who never joined the Party but played the Nazi in industry or the armed forces, in medicine and the law, in trade associations and labour organizations...

Frau König's son Max, who was then fourteen, advised Zasada to run for cover after Pauline's visit to the hospital had caused such a flurry of rumours. 'Take it from me,' he says today, 'Zinngruber could have saved Stani.'

Precisely because of his status as a dreaded village despot, Zinngruber could doubtless have flung his uniformed weight around – which he did in any case and on every possible occasion – and claimed to be competent (which he wasn't) to deal with Pauline's violation of the ban on informal contacts with foreigners. None of the scandal-mongers could prove that she had actually slept with Zasada; the sole proof was supplied by letters which came to light because Zinngruber summoned Mayer from Lörrach by phone. It was to Mayer that Pauline's helper in the shop, the woman she naïvely considered her friend as well as her book-keeper, handed one or two letters which Pauline had sent her from Bavaria with a request that she pass them on to Zasada, who was 'naturally' forbidden to receive mail from a German woman. Zinngruber's counsel made the following comment on Point 31 of the court's findings: 'By turning over correspondence to the Gestapo, as has been confirmed, Frau Schnittgens presented the latter with proof positive of an actual relationship. Even if Zinngruber did submit a report to the Gestapo on 28 April, the evidence required for a conviction was solely and exclusively surrendered to the Gestapo by Frau Schnittgens.' According to a submission from Frau Schnittgens's landlady, however, it was Zinngruber who sent the Gestapo to her to collect the letters. On the other hand, Frau Schnittgens told people in the village that Pauline had asked her to act as a go-between – in other words, she publicly complained of the fact.

The findings of the 'Tribunal de Première Instance du Pays de Bade à Fribourg', published on 29 March 1949, stated 'that Zasada was on 12 April 1941 admitted to a hospital where he received a visit from Frau Krop, and that this visit occasioned rumours in the village; that Frau Krop went away for some days on 15 April ... and instructed Frau Schnittgens to hand Zasada a letter she had left on the sideboard, and, furthermore, to give Zasada the letters she proposed to send him during her absence ... that Frau Schnittgens admits to having passed on one or two letters to Zasada as well as having turned over one letter, which was still in her possession, to the Gestapo officer; that Frau Krop was thereupon questioned by Mayer, who produced three of the letters written by her.' The court eventually found 'that it is proven in respect of Frau Schnittgens that she entrusted to Frau W. letters which she had received from Frau Krop for forwarding to Zasada; that she handed the Gestapo one or more letters which were then shown to Frau Krop by the Gestapo officer; that these statements exhibit discrepancies in regard to certain points which give rise to doubts about their candour; but, nevertheless, that the sole fact admitted by Frau Schnittgens, to wit, that she surrendered at least one letter to the Gestapo officer while he was interrogating her, is insufficient to invest her action with the quality of spontaneity which constitutes judicial substantiation of the offence or crime of denunciation. In consequence, there are grounds for acquitting her.'

Frau Schnittgens, who is now a quite exceptionally well-preserved and self-possessed woman in her mid-sixties, seemed almost surprised when I mentioned having come to see her from Brombach (I was visiting her in Lörrach Hospital). 'From Brombach?' she said. 'No point in asking questions over there – they're all Nazis.'

She told me with understandable uneasiness that she had given Mayer the letters entrusted to her – she thought there were two of them (this was in 1977), which was what she had testified to the French tribunal in 1949 – but she twice stressed something which Pauline had likewise told me, word for word: 'Mayer was a decent sort.' (Pauline went so far as to say that it had reassured her whenever Mayer spoke to her in prison because he obviously, and to the very last, shared her belief that Zasada would never be executed.) Frau Schnittgens made no reference, any more than Pauline had, to the fact that she, Frau Schnittgens, had been asked to take the enclosures addressed to Zasada and drop them in the nearest mailbox. This would, admittedly, have been foolish because Pauline might just as well have mailed them to him from Bavaria direct, and everyone in Brombach was naturally aware that Poles were forbidden to receive mail from sources inside Germany. The truth is that there was nothing to prevent Frau Schnittgens from adopting the safest course of all: she could have handed the letters to Zasada in person, since he likewise helped out at the greengrocer's shop and was often in her company...

Love being as blind as Pauline so obviously was, it is equally true that Frau Schnittgens was quicker to recognize the danger Pauline and her lover were in, and that she urged Pauline to visit her husband, who was guarding prisoners of war in Bavaria...

When the first proofs of this book appeared (they resulted in my being sued by Premier Filbinger, then still in office), Frau Schnittgens instructed her lawyer to send me a corrective declaration which is printed in full below. Any memory is overtaxed by a lapse of nearly four decades; four days are enough! On 12 July 1978 her lawyer wrote: 'You will undertake, either to suppress all reference to my client's involvement in the said affair, or to reproduce the following, which accords with the above corrigendum and thus with the facts...

1. Frau Schnittgens was not a friend of Frau Krop's. My client's relations with Frau Krop were purely of a business nature in that she kept the books for her retail store (groceries), Frau Schnittgens being a book-keeper by profession. No personal relations existed...

Frau Schnittgens learned of Frau Krop's unfortunate affair because the whole village was talking about it. She at once realized what a dangerous predicament the Pole and his mistress were in. My client therefore urged Frau Krop to visit her husband in Bavaria, hoping in this way to avert disaster. When Frau Krop actually left, Frau Schnittgens wound up her business.

2. Frau Schnittgens came into possession of only one letter written by Frau Krop to her lover. This she received by commercial post, sealed and franked. Frau Krop requested her in a covering note to drop it in the nearest mailbox.

My client did not, however, comply because she thought

it dangerous to forward the letter. She accordingly kept it, intending to return it to the sender on her return.

3. While it is true that Frau Schnittgens surrendered the letter to a Gestapo officer, she did not do so voluntarily. As bad luck would have it, Frau Schnittgens mentioned the letter to a small circle of acquaintances. By some means which cannot now be ascertained, this information must have been conveyed to the Gestapo. The latter were already alive to the affair in any case, however, because Brombach and Lörrach were buzzing with it and everyone was talking. All the authorities needed, quite clearly, was solid evidence. Frau Schnittgens was duly summoned for questioning. When she failed to appear, Herr Mayer went straight to my client and compelled her to hand over the letter, which she had secreted in a cupboard. Frau Schnittgens would never have surrendered the letter voluntarily...

Frau Schnittgens has already suffered considerably in the past as a result of this deplorable war-time incident. The French military authorities investigated my client's involvement in the Pole's case after the war ended, Frau Schnittgens having been indicted for denunciation. At the third main hearing on 29 March 1949, the military tribunal at Freiburg finally acquitted my client of the charge brought against her...'

It is interesting to note how all the versions of this story, even – or especially – when they strive to be as objective as Frau Schnittgens's lawyer, inevitably produce shifts in stress and emphasis. Take the words 'Frau Schnittgens was duly summoned for questioning. When she failed to appear...'

Anyone reading the above could be forgiven for concluding that this witness had the audacity to obstruct no less a person than the head of the Lörrach Gestapo in the execution of his duty. In fact, everyone in the village knew that Frau Schnittgens was in an advanced state of pregnancy, so the mayor's office telephoned to ask whether she could come over or would prefer Mayer to visit her instead. Only this telephone call later enabled the landlady – Frau Schnittgens had no telephone of her own – to recollect and testify that it was Zinngruber who called Frau

Schnittgens to advise her that Mayer was coming to pick up Pauline's letters. Just why Frau Schnittgens didn't burn the letters (or *the* letter, if there was only one) so as to be able to tell Mayer that she had done so long ago because she knew, as every German did, that no 'compatriot' was permitted to correspond with a Pole, is a question which may sometimes haunt her today...

Alfred Betting, a local carpenter and war-time sergeant, hailed his call-up papers as a blessed release from the Nazis because he had been largely unemployed since 1933. It is only fair to record that this man, who as former chairman of the Brombach Communist Party was forbidden to pursue his trade, periodically imprisoned and occasionally beaten up, tells a story about Zinngruber which amounts to an accolade. Apparently, the Party boss saved Betting's daughter from having to leave grammar school when her father became unable to meet the fees because of his punitive and almost permanent unemployment. Zinngruber not only ordered the fees to be paid out of public funds but declared that the child oughtn't to suffer because her father was a Communist. Mayer, on the other hand, who 'didn't speak like us' (that is to say, wasn't a Lörracher), had struck Betting in the face when he was dragged off to Lörrach jail between two mounted policemen, stumbling along with his wrists manacled to those of his captors. Referring to the Gestapo thugs 'responsible' for Brombach, Betting also says, 'Nobody knew them, the bastards!' They were outsiders transferred there from another part of the country.

Zinngruber looks as amiable now as he used to look grim, if not downright menacing, when photographed in Party uniform. Watching the old man's face as one sits at his table today, can one detect literally *nothing* of his attitude forty years ago? Was it his background that accounted for his callousness?

It certainly explains his allegiance to his late lord and master, for thirty-six years of his life would have passed in vain but for Hitler. The French court defined his antecedents as 'Born Basle, 7 January 1897, father's name unknown, mother's name Zinngruber, Crescentia'. A mere warehouseman when Hitler seized power, this impoverished son of a maidservant was transformed overnight into a mayor and Party official with immediate pension rights.

Hitherto imprisoned in a thoroughly menial class of society from which he had no hope of escape, Zinngruber now assumed a dual role which made him *the* local bigwig. Let him who could have resisted such a temptation cast the first stone! Even in post-war Germany, careerism is undoubtedly the consideration that governs a person's choice of the party he joins. The blame for this rests, not with the individual, but with a republic that has tolerated the growth of a situation in which its plum jobs are beyond the reach of any candidate who declines to wear the invisible cloak of political allegiance – even when his one desire after a day's work is to water his flowers. Enforced politicization, even of citizens who don't really want it, is a form of state-ordained hypocrisy for which the state alone stands liable, not the hypocrite. When the morgue attendant, medical superintendent and accountant of a hospital are all made dependent for their livelihood on acquiring the 'right' party membership card, no party or state can demand loyalty from those who are dragooned into a political belief. If this applies in largely liberal and democratic times, how much harder it becomes for the younger generation to pass judgement on the motives and compulsions that turned people into fellow-travellers, or even pacemakers, under a dictatorship of Hitlerian perfection! Anyone too young to have lived and toiled in the cold dank shadow of those penitentiary walls, 'minded' by informers and eavesdroppers, can only recount such a tale from the days of dictatorship by omitting the names of all those involved who are still alive today. The names of the dead, like Stasiek Zasada the Pole, have here been left unchanged. It would, however, be tantamount to 'visiting the sins of the fathers' to reproduce the name of the district director, let alone the name of the woman in whom Pauline confided because she was ingenuous enough to regard her as a friend ... A change of name is the only form of amnesty which later generations, who have so far been spared the politico-moral tensile tests to which their parents and grandparents were subjected, can grant the surviving casualties of yesteryear ...

But an amnesty – from the ancient Greek for oblivion – is inappropriate in the case of practising politicians such as Hans Karl Filbinger, who still thought it 'proper' in 1978, while premier of Baden-Württemberg, to have treated German servicemen as he did while serving Hitler as a naval judge-advocate – even while detained in a British prisoner-of-war camp. This was the man who as late as September 1945, or over five months after Hitler killed himself, repeatedly insisted in writing that a sailor's action in going home to his Norwegian wife two days after Hitler's suicide 'would normally have been punishable by death or a long term of penal servitude' and that six months' imprisonment was 'an exceptionally lenient sentence'. Filbinger (who omitted to mention that the said petty officer had additionally been stripped of his rank) is one of those people whose ideas never change and who probably confuse their inability to learn from historical events with conservatism. Bismarck said, 'Anyone who holds the same opinion at sixty as he did at thirty must be an ass.' Filbinger, who already equated right with right-wing as a law student, wanted the Bismarck era's liberal penal code of 1871 subjected to 'radical change' because 'National Socialism ... first created the mental climate essential to an effective reconstruction of German law'. By 1935 he was demanding that penalties be imposed for 'lapses in political commitment' as well as subversive acts proper. During the war this offence became known as 'undermining the war effort' or 'defeatism' and cost many thousands of German servicemen their lives. But that wasn't enough for Filbinger. Even when the war finally ended – though not for the Germans at Filbinger's mercy in British POW camps – he cited a 'lapse in political commitment' as grounds for awarding six months' imprisonment to a sergeant probationer who had ripped the swastika off his uniform and refused to be ordered around any longer. The sergeant probationer, a former Hitler Youth leader who had never once been disciplined in several years' service, had shouted 'Nazi swine' at his company commander. Filbinger refrained from mentioning in his 'judgement' that the company commander had held a pistol to the man's temple and threatened to shoot him like a dog. He thus sided with the 'Nazi swine' who had threatened, even in captivity, to murder a German serviceman with an unblemished record.

It was consistent that three decades later, in his small Baden-Württemberg domain, Filbinger should have seen to it that radical left-wing students were subjected to the 'ban on professional employment' whose incorporation in the Nazi penal code he himself had publicly espoused as a radical student of another hue. But even that form of intimidation failed to satisfy him. In the end, young people in 'his' part of West Germany were debarred not only from professional *employment* but also from vocational *training* if their political views seemed unconstitutional to Filbinger and his underlings ...

Aren't people Nazi by nature far more than by party or law? Isn't the Nazi the abject creature lurking in each and every one of us, everywhere and at all times? Isn't it released or repressed, variously and in varying degrees, by virtue of personal and social standards alone? Isn't it the ever-recurrent, sometimes rampant, sometimes latent monster from the deep? Reflect how many people were Nazi extremists long before Hitler saw the light, and how many more have remained or become so since his death! They are back with us again today – worldwide – in homes and offices, schoolrooms and factories, courtrooms and operating theatres, in prison cells and at large ... Such people had no need to join Hitler's party – though they sometimes did – in order to unleash their pernicious Nazi instincts. Of the German judge-advocates who killed at least sixteen thousand German servicemen for Hitler's sake, most were *not* members of the Nazi Party. The majority of Party members were harmless non-activists compared with the rabid Nazi industrialists, soldiers and concentration camp guards who never held a Party card. Only *one* of the twenty-odd field marshals who, although they were the only group in Germany capable of eliminating Hitler, ravaged Europe at his behest and probably degraded it for ever into a plaything of the superpowers – only *one* of them, Reichenau, was a Party member. All the rest posed as anti-Nazis while simultaneously immolating the men and boys in their charge on the Nazis' behalf.

'The concentration camps only survived for as long as the fighting fronts held.' The author of this remark was a Christian Democrat politician, Blüm, who made it during the debate on Filbinger's career as a judge-advocate in Hitler's navy. Construed in the light of what has been said above, it was perfectly objective, and the public outcry it provoked showed just how near the mark it was. 'To my mind, there is only a difference of degree between whether a person served Hitler in a concentration camp or at the front.' This remark, also by Blüm, was unobjective and offensive, not that he meant it to be. The difference was not only qualitative but infinite. The killer in the concentration camp was primarily there to dodge combat duty, save his own skin and prove his mettle – by Hitler's lights – in a place where he only needed to murder defenceless people. It is equally mistaken to put Allied bomber pilots who killed defenceless civilians morally on a par with concentration camp goons. Bomber pilots, too, risked their lives – and risked them in an arm of the service which lost more men, relatively speaking, than almost any other. By contrast, the German judge-advocates who helped Hitler to kill sixteen thousand German soldiers, sailors and airmen – not counting a similar number condemned to imminent death in penal battalions – are wide open to a charge of having killed defenceless men. In the vast majority of cases, these men owed their trial by court martial to the fortunes of war, not personal guilt. They were so utterly at the mercy of their military judges that their execution amounted in many instances to murder. It was a crime committed exclusively by Germans who killed without risk to themselves – indeed, whose exercise of their judicial functions was all that stood between them and combat duty, between them and the fate of the Germans they condemned.

The howl of fury provoked by Blüm, which conveyed the self-delusion of an entire generation – conveyed but did not articulate, a howl being inarticulate by definition – had a by-product. This took the form of an open letter from a lieutenant in the Federal Armed Forces who distinguished himself by tackling that most sacrosanct of all problems, Hitler's war, with a moral courage almost unique in post-war Germany: 'This (Blüm's statement) makes it clear that all who served the National Socialist state during the war of 1939–45 were supporting an unjust state. This realization ... must stand at the outset of our new and better road.'

To non-Germans, all that seems surprising is that someone thirty-three years after Hitler's death can apply the word 'realization' to what is merely a barbarous banality: that no one could serve the 'criminal state' (Jaspers) without complicity; and that no one could defend it without prolonging its existence – and, thus, the existence of concentration camps and the 'work' of guillotines and firing squads. The accuracy of Blüm's contention is underlined by a passage from the minutes of the Wannsee Conference chaired by Heydrich on 20 January 1942, when guidelines were issued to Adolf Eichmann, the gas chambers' forwarding agent: 'Europe will be combed from west to east as the practical fulfilment of the final solution proceeds ... The start of each major evacuation scheme will depend largely on military developments.'

Precisely. As long as Narvik and Crete remained unoccupied by German forces, nobody there could be rounded up for consignment to the gas chambers. Similarly, when the Wehrmacht could no longer 'defend' Sofia and Marseilles (defend them for Hitler, nobody else!) no more of their inhabitants could be transported to Auschwitz, whose crematoria were blown up when – and only when – the Red Army had advanced to within earshot. No one who disputes this can escape a charge of wilful mendacity unless he is, in the clinical sense, an idiot.

While serving a twenty-year sentence as a prisoner of the Allies, Hitler's former armaments minister, Albert Speer, confided to his diary: 'I could, perhaps, excuse myself for everything. To have been his architect is defensible. I could justify having acted as his minister of armaments. One can also conceive of a position from which to defend the industrial employment of prisoners of war or conscripted labour ... But I stand there utterly defenceless at the mention of a name like Eichmann's. I shall never get over the fact that I served a régime, and served it in a senior capacity, whose real efforts were directed towards the extermination of human beings.'

The great divide was between Nazis and decent people, not between Party members and other Germans. Even among the 'special judges' who presided over the 'special courts' which earned such a dreadful and well-merited reputation for condemning political offenders, some were so humane and un-Nazi that defence counsel would ask them to sentence the 'guilty' to terms of penal servitude long enough to guarantee them against committal to a concentration camp! These banalities – for even quintessential evil becomes banal when legalized – must be borne in mind by anyone proposing to tell this tale to those who have just turned twenty. They are ignorant of such things, just as many things now defy recall by the narrator himself – or even by those who witnessed and were jointly affected by them. Which brings us back to the problem fundamental to all narration.

Anyone who seeks a personal insight into the dramatis personae of the Nazi era should realize that joining Hitler's party in order to become a student, pursue a profession, shovel dirt in a road gang, sell door-to-door or ride a horse, no more made a person a Nazi than his subsequent conscription into the armed forces made him a war criminal. Nobody can expect the ordinary citizen to possess the makings of a martyr. If Lloyd George, the man who led Britain to victory in 1918, could visit Hitler in his Obersalzberg eyrie and come away publicly extolling him, who can blame Farmer Schulze for gullibly cheering Hitler to the echo? How was he supposed to know that faith in politicians is invariably foolish?

Little thieves hang, big ones go scot free ... This adage didn't apply. Even Zinngruber got his full pension straight away, though imprisonment hit him hard. Filbinger's activities as one of Hitler's naval judge-advocates were not investigated, any more than those of the other military judges who can collectively pride themselves on a 'bag' of sixteen thousand German servicemen, before he became premier of the province in which Brombach is situated.

But woe to those who were wanted by the Allies for crimes against Allied nationals! (The occupying powers, who had enough on their plate as it was, were virtually uninterested in crimes against Germans.) *They* could fare as Josef Zinngruber fared – sometimes even worse ... Reviewing four decades of Filbinger's career, isn't it possible to discern a thread of continuity in his way of thinking and conception of the law? Back in 1935 he called for the penalization of 'lapses in political commitment'; latterly, in 1978, he was one of the busiest radical-hunters and political inquisitors in the wretched remains of a country dismembered by Hitler's war. There is a widespread pretence and self-delusion in West Germany that everyone simply did his duty, however zealously he may have co-operated in the destruction of his native land. This was the attitude that not only granted all the Zinngrubers a pension denied to most of their victims but – grotesquely enough – gave it to them *sooner* than they would have received it had they not been such out-and-out Nazis that the Allies expelled them from their jobs. Instead of receiving an annuity or pension from the age of sixty-five, which few would have begrudged him, Zinngruber received it many years earlier than other people who are obliged to work until they reach that age or fall sick ...

But this goes without saying in a country which calls itself a 'liberal-democratic constitutional state' but which *by law*, not by chance, awards far smaller pensions to victims of the Nazis than to those who victimized them. In very many cases the former get no pension at all – like Pauline, who has never received a sou although her years in a concentration camp deprived her of her living as a shopkeeper as well as her liberty. Filbinger took particular exception to one chapter of this book, which formed the basis of his suit against me. Its publication brought me a letter from a Baden-Baden lawyer who was wrily amused by my naivety. 'I could give you the name of a German woman,' he wrote, 'who spent two-and-a-half years in Auschwitz for having an affair with a Polish academic. I represented her all the way up to the Federal Supreme Court, but you can read in every commentary on the Reparation Law that the "Aryan" women involved in such cases are not entitled to the smallest compensation ... One final comment on the so-called concentration camp hearings. It was the grossest mistake ... to believe that it would be possible, despite all the snares and pitfalls present in German criminal procedure, to assist in the triumph of truth when German judges are presiding ... Would you believe me if I told you that thousands of concentration camp survivors have it trenchantly demonstrated to them that their physical and mental disabilities are *not* attributable to their sojourn in a concentration camp?'

Franz Schlegelberger was one of Hitler's ministers of justice at the height of the Nazi reign of terror, or during the war. Although the Allies sentenced him to life imprisonment in 1947, it is entirely consistent with what has just been said that by 1951 he was at liberty and in receipt of a monthly pension of DM 2894.08 – a sum equivalent to a top-level salary of that period. Having been released on compassionate grounds, ostensibly because he was too ill to withstand further imprisonment, Schlegelberger died nearly twenty years later at the ripe old age of ninety-four! On 22 June 1941 he had a conversation with Himmler. The following is an extract from his notes:

'The Reichsführer pronounced it unwarrantable that a Pole should be deprived of his civil rights, though he quite understood that the courts may in certain circumstances be driven to such a decision under the law as it stands. He was nonetheless bound to object to such a decision because of its implicit acknowledgement that Poles do, in principle, possess civil rights. I replied that I considered his misgivings justified, but that this was essentially a question of wording. It should not, I said, be difficult to take remedial measures in this respect. The Reichsführer concluded our discussion by stating that his one desire was to work in concert with the judiciary towards the attainment of our common goal. I replied that the judiciary, for its part, fully reciprocated this desire, and I requested the Reichsführer, in this connection, to inform me if ever he deemed the courts' findings unsatisfactory from his own point of view.'

The fisherman and his wife

The spiritual person is almost as intent on realities that distress him as dolts thirst for realities that flatter them.

Thomas Mann.

Victorowicz could tell that nothing sapped Zasada's strength and drove him to tears more easily than talking about home, so he carefully eschewed the subject in favour of something that would preoccupy the condemned man's emotions and take him outside himself. That something could only be their homeland and its liberation from the Germans, but he avoided the very word homeland because it seemed too emotive. 'Mother country,' too, struck him as embarrassingly high-flown. Poland – that was the most appropriate word ...

Zasada's outburst of hatred when he told Victorowicz that the Germans had denied his request for permission to write a farewell letter was almost volcanic in intensity. It had to be channelled in a direction that was purposeful, or at least seemingly so ... Victorowicz realized, as he watched his cell-mate, that hatred breeds apathy whereas hope of its fulfilment acts like a shot in the arm. Having himself been condemned to weeks of silence, he now argued with passionate conviction that their common thirst for revenge would be assuaged as surely as the tale of the fisherman and his wife was true.

'Don't you see, Stasiek?' said Victorowicz. 'There's only one reason why a parable like that gets handed down from generation to generation. It's because the political set-up always echoes it in some way – because the pattern of events is inbuilt, like the watermark in a banknote. And there's another strange thing about the story – something just as timeless: the people who behave like the fisherman and his wife back in ancient times – they're blinder than anyone else to the parallels between themselves and the way the story turns out. Does it bother you, listening?'

Zasada gave a weary smile. 'Do I have any choice?' Victorowicz smiled too, but in a different way. He went on quickly, 'You'll be avenged – you and Poland will be apocalyptically avenged, just as surely as the history of Germany in the past forty years is a perfect reflection of the tale of the fisherman and his wife. Believe me, this is my pet subject – I'm not making it up. I know the Germans well. I lived in Berlin for eighteen months before the war, working for a place on the staff at Cracow

University. I was writing a thesis on the 365 days between 11 November 1917 and 11 November 1918 ...'

Zasada interrupted him. 'Because 11 November's our national day?'

Victorowicz smiled again. 'That among other things.' With a trace of melancholy, he added, 'No school, remember? It also happens to be the first day of carnival in a lot of countries, but it marked the end of the German Empire as well as the founding of the Polish Republic. That's when the Germans surrendered, 11 November 1918. I spent years studying those last twelve months, so I often discussed them with the Germans I had to interview. All kinds of people – retired generals, sailors who'd mutinied at the end of the war, double-dyed Nazis, ex-Republicans who'd been hounded out of office by Hitler ... And do you know what? Whenever I made a sly allusion to the fisherman and his wife, none of them got the point! None of them, even though a blind man could see what the Germans achieved by transferring fifty divisions to the east for their triumphal march through Russia in 1918, when Russia had already stopped fighting. If it didn't rob them of victory in France, it certainly led to a peace settlement that cost them dear. Ironical, isn't it?'

He fell silent. Zasada said, 'How does your theory apply to other periods of history?'

Relieved at this chance to distract the doomed man with his realistic parable, if only for ten or fifteen minutes, Victorowicz became more animated. 'Well, you must be as familiar with the history of nineteenth-century France as you are with our own – all Poles are. The Germans are living out the fisherman's story for the second time this century – the second and last, believe me, *and* the bloodiest – but turn back the page and what do you see? What about Napoleon I, didn't he share the same fate?' Victorowicz warmed to his subject. He might almost have been reading aloud from his thesis. 'Bonaparte's last abode on St Helena corresponds exactly – with the force of a Biblical revelation – to the hut where the fisherman and his wife ended their days because they'd done themselves out of their palace by asking to become gods. As for Napoleon III, who declared war on

Bismarck after twenty glorious success-sated years on the throne, there's an equally perfect analogy between him and the fisherman's wife, with her impudent and sacrilegious request for divinity.

'Napoleon III was an ageing man who squandered his waning energies on a surfeit of mistresses and suffered excruciatingly from gallstones – they killed him within three years, in point of fact. He was terrified of taking such an irrevocable step, but the Empress, who'd once been a very discerning woman, was blinded by her Spanish pride. It was the same story all over again: she browbeat her husband till he meekly acted against his better judgement and declared war for no good reason, dashing himself and his empire to destruction like a lemming jumping off a cliff. When she was regent, Eugénie joined in the cry "*A Berlin!*" Instead of dying in the Tuileries, she died in exile at the age of ninety-four. That gave her fifty years to mourn her own downfall, which she'd brought on herself just as senselessly as the fisherman's wife.'

Victorowicz laughed aloud. 'The Germans pride themselves on being more thorough than other people, as you know. Slower to learn would be a better way of putting it. Only fools learn from personal experience. Wise men learn from the experience of others, but the Germans not only learnt nothing from what happened to the two Napoleons – they learnt nothing from their own experiences in the First World War, and this one's a carbon copy when you study the sequence of events in detail. It's amazing! A year ago they lost the Battle of Britain but refused to accept that it clinched the war in the west. The same thing happened on 9 September 1914. The Battle of the Marne forced them to abandon the plan that underlay the whole of their strategy, but they either didn't notice or wouldn't admit it to themselves.'

Zasada said, 'It talked about the Miracle of the Marne in one of our schoolbooks. Is that what you mean?'

Thankfully, Victorowicz nodded. Zasada even remembered something else. 'Paris taxis – it said they won the battle, or is that just an old wives' tale?'

Victorowicz pounced on the point. 'Well, it's true the military governor of Paris was the first to grasp what a vital opportunity the French would be missing if they didn't make a stand at the Marne. He launched a counter-attack and rushed six thousand men to the front in fifteen hundred taxis. The taxis clinched nothing, of course, but they *are* a reminder of something important – something almost unbelievable but true. Although they'd been polishing their plan of campaign for a decade, the Germans simply forgot – forgot! – to motorize at least one of their armies. I'm talking about the one that had to make the biggest detour so as to cross the whole of Belgium and take the French in the rear. The Germans were dead beat by the time they reached the scene of the battle – a lot of their horses actually died of exhaustion – and why? Because they never hit on the simplest idea of all: transporting their troops across Belgium in trucks to save time as well as manpower and horseflesh – and trucks had existed for years!'

Zasada disputed this so firmly that his story-teller could sense how involved he was and how dissociated, at least temporarily, from himself and what lay in store for him. 'But that *can't* be true. Surely they must have known what it would do to infantrymen and horses, flogging them through Belgium like that?'

'I told you,' said Victorowicz, 'it's incredible but true. For all their mental gymnastics, they never even *thought* of trucks. Mind you, the fact that they didn't had less to do with brains than character. Nature equipped the Germans to see things as they want them to be, not as they are.

'Ever since 1905, they'd wanted the Belgians to guarantee them right of way in the event of war – in fact they even wanted the Belgian railways to transport their illustrious armies round behind the French flank. And because the Germans *wanted* the Belgians to give them the run of their railways and based their war-games on that fanciful assumption, they not only thought it feasible but took it for granted. Just to show you how far self-delusion can go: the last German emperor, Wilhelm II, was so good at mistaking pipedreams for reality that he actually unveiled his army's deployment plans to the King of the Belgians several years before the war. The Kaiser drew a blunt refusal, together with a categorical assurance that Belgium would *not* stand idly by while Germany used her as a back door to France, but his generals persisted in believing that the Belgians would let them through just the same.

'When war came, the Belgians' first act was to demolish their rail network so effectively that it couldn't transport a single German division to the Marne. The Germans prefer to base their plans on wishful thinking, not facts, take it from me – and I'm not just talking about individuals. It's a national character defect. That's why, a quarter of a century later, they promptly acted as if they'd never paid for their blunder in 1914 by losing a world war. They only attacked us in 1939 because they refused to believe what the British had told them and the world at large – in writing, what's more: that they'd declare war on Germany if Hitler marched on Warsaw. The Germans didn't *want* to believe that, so they didn't. It was the same in 1914. Britain's declaration of war took them completely by surprise because it didn't suit their current plans to believe what they'd been told so many times: that Britain would come in without question if Germany violated Belgian neutrality. The world had known that the British would join forces with the French since 1907. The Germans knew it too, but because it conflicted with their wishes they "reckoned" until two days after declaring war on Russia and France that the British would, after all, leave the French and the Russians in the lurch.'

Victorowicz regarded Zasada in silence. Then, before a lull could develop, he went on, 'The second of their miscalculations indirectly lost them the Battle of the Marne, and it was largely a product of megalomania: they made a deliberate decision *not* to stop the British landing in France if they did come in after all. Although they owned the second most powerful navy in the world by 1914, their commander-in-chief expressly stated before war broke out that no attempt should be made to attack British troop transports crossing the Channel. Britain's contribution would be 164,000 men at most, he argued, so why not kill two birds with one stone – why not floor them with the same right hook that was meant to catch the French off guard and put them down for the count? As things turned out, it was the British who clinched the greatest battle of all without having to over-exert themselves – they only lost two thousand men. They did it by driving a wedge between the German First and Second Armies. This threw the Kaiser's headquarters into a panic and triggered off the order to withdraw.

'But there's something else worth remembering – a lot of books hardly mention it, which is pretty damn mean. Even at that stage, it was the *Russians* whose self-sacrifice at Tannenberg did most to save Europe from German domination. They kept their word against their better judgement. They only took the field because they were bound by treaty to relieve the pressure on their French allies, and they sent two armies marching into East Prussia sooner than they should have, considering how long their armed forces were taking to mobilize. If it hadn't been for the Russians, France would have been beaten in 1914. Churchill's one of the few western historians to acknowledge this, and certainly the most appreciative.

'But now, Stasiek – now comes another solid crumb of comfort and pointer to the future. Although their failure at the Marne had lost them the war, the Germans didn't see it that way. The Kaiser's chief of staff actually told him the truth – with tears in his eyes, so they say – but he got sent home for his trouble. And on 9 September itself, the day when Germany suffered her greatest military reverse, the Chancellor – who was reputed to be easily the most moderate political figure in the country – drafted a secret memorandum listing the bare bones of Germany's war aims. She planned to incorporate the whole of Belgium, the French iron-ore basin round Longwy and Briey, and substantial stretches of the French Atlantic coast which the Germans never even penetrated throughout the war!

'If you think these territorial demands were cut down to size by the Marne, you're wrong. The Chancellor's ideas were the same in 1916 as they'd been in 1914, and some of his compatriots wanted to carve even bigger slices off their western enemies when victory was won. For all that, the Kaiser did realize that things "hadn't gone well" at the Marne. As far the annexed areas of Belgium and France were concerned, he abandoned the scheme to "clear them of people" – meaning expel and resettle their native inhabitants and colonize them with German veterans' families. But two years later, in 1916, secret talks with the neutral authorities in Washington about helping to negotiate a compromise peace settlement were completely knocked on the head by the Germans' refusal to give up Belgium and their insistence on wresting Poland away from Russia and converting it into a kingdom ruled by a German prince. It wasn't the exhilaration of victory that made them megalomaniacs – victory does that to everyone. For four whole years, while two million of their soldiers died, four hundred thousand German civilians starved to death as a result of the British blockade and all their colonies were captured by the enemy, they refused even to discuss a peace settlement based on their pre-war frontiers because they still hoped to annex an area almost as big as their empire had been at the outbreak of war. They refused, when they were already beaten!'

Victorowicz gazed at Zasada, and the fire in his eyes stemmed from utter conviction. 'Crazy, wasn't it, Stasiek, but don't you see how much hope it holds out for the future? And here's the most remarkable thing of all. Even after their total defeat in 1918, the Germans failed to see that nothing in the history of the twentieth century could be more perfectly, photographically reminiscent of the fisherman and his wife and their relegation to a wretched little hut than what happened to the last of the Kaisers and his empress. They were confined to the Huis te Doorn and its grounds – a plot of Dutch soil as small in relation to their lost empire as an eggcupful of water to the North Sea! No German recognized the royal exiles as a reincarnation of the figures in the fable, even though their fate provided another perfect parallel: it was greed, straightforward land-grabbing greed, that cost the Kaiser his throne – greed of such grotesque dimensions that its very exorbitance proves the Germans were as crazy in 1918 as they are today. Except – and this is crucial – that they weren't mass murderers then. All wars lead to crime, I know, but there's a difference between war making criminals and criminals making war. Territorial greed is another matter. The Germans were just as deranged in that way twenty-five or thirty years ago as they are now. They were so blind to practicalities even then – and even though Bismarck himself had warned them that politics are the art of the possible – that their defective sense of proportion *guaranteed* the Allies they couldn't win in 1917 just as surely as it tells us the same thing today ... They're insane, believe me!'

Zasada looked at him with lingering doubt. 'Perhaps,' he said quietly, 'but it doesn't stop them being dangerous.' Victorowicz said reassuringly, 'Not when they're so crazy they don't even notice the men in white coats standing by with a straitjacket at the ready. That's what it came to in 1918, when they sent Lenin from Zurich to St Petersburg in a sealed train so he could preach Red revolution – the Tsar had already fallen by then. The idea was to end Russia's alliance with the western powers and take her out of the war against Germany for good. But as soon as the Kaiser saw the Russians on their knees his lust for land flared up again, worse than ever. The French and the British had also lost nearly two million dead, but they fought on grimly in the knowledge that the Americans had also declared war and would soon be coming to their aid in France. For three months the Germans launched a series of desperate offensives aimed at winning total victory in the west as well, yet those were the months when they also carved a vast eastern empire out of Russia, which was hamstrung by war and civil war and had ceased to offer any resistance. It was easily the largest slice of territory a European ruler had ever lopped off one of his neighbours – Napoleon took as much, but not from a single source. As late as spring 1918 the Germans planned to strip the Russians of six major assets: access to the Baltic, access to the Black Sea, the whole of the Ukraine, Russian Poland, Finland, and the Baltic provinces – statistically speaking, over seventy per cent of Russia's coal and heavy industry and more than a quarter of her pre-war territory. Just to make a bad joke even worse, I should tell you that the Germans weren't actually in possession of this empire on 3 March 1918, when they bullied the Russians into ceding it to them under the so-called Treaty of Brest-Litovsk, which was virtually an ultimatum. They didn't hold these defenceless territories, but they needed more than a million men to trick them into submission. And it was this same trickery that finished the Germans only eight months later by leading to their total collapse in France. Even their legendary courage was no match for their stupidity. Just think: on 3 March they entertained the crazy notion of marching down to the Crimea, which they proceeded to do, not having any enemies left in the east. But during precisely the same period, the five weeks from 21 March to 30 April, they lost fourteen per cent of their strength in the west, or 350,000 men, in a last desperate offensive against the British and French. The British lost 300,000 men and found themselves fighting with their backs to the sea, as the current saying went – in fact the French commander sarcastically predicted that his British opposite number would soon be surrendering on the field of battle. The British commander said later that, since the Americans had yet to reach France, another half-dozen divisions might have won Germany the war. But the Germans didn't have half a dozen divisions to spare because they were simultaneously wasting *fifty* whole divisions in the east – for instance on occupying Rostov and the Crimea, not to mention Finland, where they were getting ready to install a Hessian prince on the throne at Helsinki – Hesse was one of the smaller German states. I tell you, Stasiek, they just aren't normal. That's why they'll lose again this time, never fear ...'

Zasada couldn't hold his doubts at bay. Wearily, he said, 'I believe all you say but I don't understand it. The ordinary folk round here, the ones I used to work with – they're no more irrational than my parents are. Why should their leaders be any different?' Victorowicz thought for a moment. 'The ordinary folk? What can they do against the Berlin land-grabbers and murderers who are killing off their sons, husbands and brothers? As for understanding what I've told you, I wouldn't expect them to – I don't understand it myself. Reason goes by the board when emotion gains the upper hand. You won't find a loser – and precious few winners – whose thought-processes aren't ruled by emotion.'

Zasada said, still dubiously, 'What about educated people – people like you? Are they all heart and no head?'

Victorowicz nodded without hesitation. 'Of course. It's just that intellectuals concoct smarter and more dangerous arguments to convince themselves and other people of the rational necessity of acting and even thinking as their emotions dictate. It was emotion that prevented the Germans – all of them, I suspect – from admitting the truth about 1918 to themselves and those who'd beaten them: that after defying the entire world for four epic years – which was fabulous enough in itself – they'd finally been defeated in battle. And because this defeat was contradicted by emotion, by national pride, reason supplied emotion with an excuse. The Germans persuaded themselves they hadn't been defeated at all – not in battle, anyway – but stabbed in the back by an internal enemy who never existed, or by the Jews, although twelve thousand of them died for Imperial Germany in 1914–18. Oh yes, they discovered any number of "reasons"! After ten years they believed every word of it and completely dismissed the possibility that they'd been beaten in 1918. They were going to try again – we all sensed that too ... The Germans *do* have an irrational streak, but that's what's going to save us all, just as it did in 1918, when they sent a million men marching through Russia, all the way to the Caucasus, while simultaneously trying to hurl the British into the sea and take Paris before the Americans arrived – simultaneously, mark you: that shows how deluded they were. And that, Stasiek, is why they're going to lose the way they lost in 1918. The Kaiser ended his days chopping down trees in Holland, thanks to their megalomania, but this time they're going to lose their dictator, their army, their country – everything, just like the fisherman and his wife ...'

We still have one cigarette, thought Victorowicz. He reached for it, then left it in his jacket pocket. Zasada's attention was still engaged; he didn't need the last cigarette now – he wouldn't need it till they came to fetch him. Zasada had, in fact, been impressed by the certainty with which Victorowicz had predicted the downfall of their mortal enemy, but he remained unconvinced that the course of the second war could be foretold from that of the first, and he said so. Intrigued by a point of detail, he asked, 'That bit about the Kaiser becoming a lumberjack – was it just a figure of speech?'

Victorowicz's eyes flashed with sudden amusement. 'No, only real life could invent a thing like that. He used to chop down trees in a wood near the house where he lived for a quarter of a century, just to get some exercise. He had such itchy feet in the old days the Berliners made up a joke about the initials after his name. I.R. didn't stand for *Imperator Rex*, they said – it stood for *Immer auf Reisen*, always on the move ... Trust fate to find his Achilles' heel! The only moving around he did in exile was swinging an axe – he didn't even have enough room to ride a horse ... He died four months ago, incidentally. I read it in a Nazi paper – they dismissed him in half a dozen lines. Wilhelm invited Churchill to watch the imperial manœuvres twice before 1914, and Churchill wrote an essay about him just before I became a student. He described his host in all his imperial splendour – more sympathetically than sarcastically – and ended up by saying that none of the millions of disabled ex-servicemen came off worse in 1918 than this onetime supreme warlord, who'd had to sit in a gilded cage for twenty years, gnawed by self-reproach and chopping wood for relaxation ... The Kaiser's uncle – Edward VII of England, who died in 1910 – he saw the whole thing coming. "The most brilliant failure in history" – that's what he called his German nephew. Even the Kaiser's beginnings are a reminder of the fisherman in the fable. He inherited his "hut" from Bismarck, and Bismarck warned him over and over again not to enlarge it at his neighbours' expense – above all, never to build a big navy. In the first place Germany didn't need one, being the owner of the biggest land army since Napoleon, and secondly it would provoke England, Germany's next of kin and long-time ally against France during the eighteenth and nineteenth centuries ...

'In 1938 Churchill's son paid the Kaiser a last visit in his Dutch open prison and wrote a piece about him for *The Times*. The old man was eighty by then. He said he'd spent twenty years reading every history book he could lay hands on, and there was only one eternal truth: anyone who steals land he wasn't born on is doomed!

'So rest assured, Stasiek,' Victorowicz concluded. 'The Germans aren't secret realists who only miscalculated the *first* time they made a bid for absolute supremacy in Europe – far from it. They never do their sums at all. That's proved by their attitude in September 1918, only two months before the Kaiser fled to Holland. Even at that late stage they still planned to annex vast tracts of territory – from the western powers as well as Russia. After all, it was the Germans who declared war on the French, not vice versa. Having conquered an eastern empire the size of France itself, they even begrudged the French the territory that had belonged to them when war broke out. No, nothing had changed since 1914. Just as if they'd never been forced to withdraw from the Marne, the Germans coveted French canal basins and iron ore deposits, insisted on keeping Belgium and discussed in writing whether to restrict their demands on the British Empire to substantial slices of Central Africa or claim a share of Egypt as well. To put it in a nutshell, they were crazy! And that, Stasiek, is why they're going to lose this war as sure as two and two make four. Look at Hitler's decision to march on Moscow with two arch-enemies, Churchill and Roosevelt, breathing down his neck. His lines of communication are frayed and overstretched, strung out from Narvik to Tripoli and Crete to the Pyrenees. His armies have become diluted – they're seeping away like those buckets of water we sluice the prison yard with ... Men as sick as that can never win a war, Stasiek – never! Plenty of nonsensical things have happened in the course of history – that's an established fact – but never on this scale, believe me. That's why Poland will emerge from this war bigger than she entered it. That's why Germany will remain occupied until she ceases to be what she is and can never become again – or until she loses her national identity altogether.'

Reflections of a medical officer

The Führer's speech on the 15th inst. has left a deep impression. Special importance is being attached to the unbounded faith in victory communicated by every word ... One statement which went down particularly well was that the Bolshevists will never defeat us after failing to do so this winter, and that they themselves will be defeated in the coming months ... 'The Führer never says these things unless he's sure,' declared a local judge, and a farmer observed, 'Have you heard? He told them again yesterday, the Führer did – now you'll soon be beaten.' It is clear from many similar remarks that this was the passage that attracted most attention. Women, too, were struck by the same passage.

Report dated 31 March 1942,
Security Service Outstation, Berchtesgaden.

Zasada preserved his taut composure until he caught sight of the coffin, unaware that he would never be buried at all. The coffin, made of thin unvarnished deal, was not delivered to the prison yard until three minutes past the appointed hour of eight, by which time the execution convoy should already have 'marched off' (it was characteristic of German officialdom to cling to this archaism in the age of the internal combustion engine).

Karl Mayer's nerves unwound and his spirits rose at this opportunity to tongue-lash the limping war-wounded carpenter's mate who had just delivered the coffin on a horse-drawn cart. 'You can tell your boss I'll buy my coffins somewhere else in future, unless ...' He refrained from completing the sentence. It had occurred to him that he wouldn't have to buy another coffin because Zasada's would be ready for re-use as soon as it came back empty from the university dissecting-room at Freiburg this afternoon ... Where mass hangings were concerned, wastage of coffins was prohibited in any case: if the persons executed numbered more than three, they were either buried unboxed or cremated ... While an auxiliary policeman – a civilian drafted into the force for the duration of the war – was helping the carpenter to unload the coffin from the cart and transfer it to the truck, Mayer called across the yard, 'Bring out the prisoner!' He glanced at his watch: scandalous, this lack of punctuality. Like all staunch supporters of totalitarian régimes, Mayer lived according to Goethe's maxim – its authorship was unknown to him – that injustice was easier to tolerate than disorder.

Zasada, handcuffed to two policemen, was waiting at the foot of the stairs inside the door to the yard, which had been left ajar. Now they set off ... Mayer kept his eyes averted and engrossed himself in the question of how to enter the charge for the coffin in his accounts. This being the heaviest single expense incurred by today's proceedings, his original intention had been to include it, quite simply, in the cost of Zasada's execution. Now, however, a problem had arisen because the coffin could not be written off like other expenses but would pass into the possession of Gestapo headquarters at Lörrach and remain available for indefinite use – a capital asset with a negligible depreciation factor. From that point of view, it would be incorrect to write it off completely once today's execution had taken place. Mayer knew enough about his subordinates' shortcomings to realize that they wouldn't produce any bright ideas on how to resolve this ticklish problem of accountancy, which meant that he would be obliged to refer it to higher authority. He decided to dictate the letter after lunch. A faint cough, testy rather than chesty, drew his attention to the man beside him, the district medical officer of health.

The doctor felt as if he hadn't eaten for two days. 'Who's the fourth man,' he asked irritably, 'the one in convict's uniform?' Mayer replied without looking. 'That's the hangman, another Pole. I had a hard time talking him round.' He forbore to describe how he had browbeaten Victorowicz into acquiescence. They could already hear the crunch of feet on gravel. From beyond the walls came a rattle of milk-churns as a horse and cart sped past. The doctor felt so annoyed with himself for failing to think up a reason why somebody else should have been sent in his place that he took it out on Mayer. 'Poles are Catholic,' he said, almost peremptorily. 'I don't see a priest around.'

Mayer edged closer to the doctor and looked him in the eye to avoid the sight of his victim, who was almost within earshot. 'We don't have any Polish priests and our own aren't allowed to officiate. Orders from up top.' The doctor said, 'Up there, you mean?' and glanced at the sky. The feeble joke had only slipped out because he was feeling as sick as a dog. Mayer, too, felt the need for some kind of emotional outlet. He wasn't a cynical man, but cynicism now came to his rescue from a realm of the mind which usually lay fallow. 'He bedded his German girl-friend without the blessing of the Church, so he'll have to die the same way.'

The sixty-year-old doctor winced with distaste and said nothing. Zasada was led towards the truck amid the sort of silence that descends when a corpse is carried out of a house. That was when he saw the coffin. The boy – he still looked like a teenager – had displayed nothing more than prison pallor until now. Instantly, his face turned white as paper because the coffin had made his death seem truly conceivable for the first time. The two helmeted constables halted, pointlessly but automatically, in front of Mayer and the doctor. The Gestapo chief, who had also been robbed of speech by Zasada's spellbound look at the coffin, gave them an impatient nod. It was a tacit order to board the truck quickly, which presented problems because they were manacled together, and also, perhaps, though this was not apparent, because the man to be murdered had buckled at the knees. Once on board, the policemen sat down on the coffin. The nonchalance with which they did so, as if it were a bench in a normal army truck, made it clear that the psyches of these two public servants were no more sensitive than the beefy buttocks in their breeches, which were tucked into jackboots. They stared up at their victim, not exactly tugging at the handcuffs but puzzled by Zasada's reluctance to join them on his own coffin. Never mind, their faces said, he'll soon sit down when the truck moves off.

The auxiliary policeman closed the tailboard. Now invisible in the gloom beneath the tarpaulin cover, Victorowicz lit the last of the three cigarettes which Mayer, in humane defiance of regulations, had ordered him to be given before his work was done, and tried to insert it between Zasada's lips. Zasada stood with his calves brushing the coffin but stubbornly remained erect, even though this self-imposed strain was eating up the little strength he had left. He stared into the darkness of the truck's interior, away from Mayer and the doctor, away from his two captors, ashamed at his overpowering need to weep. He didn't know how much they helped him, these silent tears, or guess that they would soon enable him to feign composure in the presence of spectators – for a while . . .

'Doctor,' Mayer said quickly, relieved that the condemned man was hidden from view, 'we don't need two cars. Why not save petrol and come in mine?' The doctor, who had been wrestling with an unasked question for some minutes, now put it to the man who was striding off to his car dressed in a combination of civilian jacket, riding breeches and boots – every inch a popular edition of Reichsleiter Bormann. 'Tell me, Herr Mayer, I know you don't wear uniform as a rule, but . . .' He halted, as did

Mayer, who turned to face him. 'I hope you're carrying a gun all the same.' Mayer couldn't have looked more baffled if the doctor had asked whether he'd remembered to bring his eyebrows along. 'Never go anywhere without one – never,' he said, baring a fat gold tooth. 'Why do you ask?' Eventually, after climbing into the car, the doctor replied, 'In case you have to finish him off.'

Mayer stared at him in dismay. He hadn't thought of that. Uncertainty made him say, more crisply than usual, 'He'll just have to hang there till he's dead.' The doctor frowned. 'When they shoot a deserter in the armed forces the officer in charge of the firing squad has to give him the *coup de grâce*. Besides, I strongly doubt if the other prisoner knows his job – he looks like a limp rag already.' Mayer had taken the wheel himself. Behind them, the heavy truck could be heard starting up. Mayer was feeling thoroughly unsettled by the doctor's remarks. At last he said, 'I'm not authorized to finish him off. My orders are absolutely clear: special treatment will be effected by means of hanging.'

Carried away by his mounting uneasiness, the doctor shrugged and said curtly, 'Hanging, yes, but you've got to know how.' Mayer gave him a look of understanding. It never crossed his mind that the doctor's objections might be motivated by lax and illicit compassion for the Pole: he was just a tidy-minded German who wanted everything to go off 'properly'. The more perplexed Mayer became, the more grimly he clung to his orders. He said, 'I'm also bound by instructions when it comes to picking a hangman. I *can't* do it myself, though I'd find it easier than watching an amateur strangle the man instead of breaking his neck. Reichsführer Himmler has expressly forbidden acts of brutality during special treatment, but a German simply isn't allowed to do it.'

To the doctor, this seemed to offer a way out. 'If Herr Himmler has forbidden acts of brutality, Obersturmführer, that means you're entitled to administer the *coup de grâce*.' Mayer was driving quite slowly so as not to leave the truck behind. They had almost reached Brombach when a column of marching figures came into view. The prisoners and foreign civilians employed in Lörrach were being conducted to the place of execution, not to witness the execution itself – that was forbidden, clearly because the authorities feared that condemned men might incite their compatriots to rebellion – but for an enforced and deterrent look at the body ... Before the doctor or the Gestapo chief could remark on the column or had even caught it up, Mayer said, 'You're putting me on the spot, Doctor. What makes you think I'm entitled to finish him off? If my orders say special treatment is to be effected by hanging, it can't be successfully terminated by a bullet. I've absolutely no authority to do it.' Successfully terminated ... He spoke the words without a hint of irony and strove to dismiss the subject because it was getting on his nerves, but the doctor persisted. 'And I', he said in a firm voice, 'have absolutely no obligation to witness an act of brutality. For the record, my sole duty is to certify the man's death, not attend his execution. If the knot works round beneath his chin – I couldn't help looking at his neck back there, and he's strong, that boy, with a neck like a stallion – if that happens, he'll go on kicking for ages ...' Mayer answered quickly, 'Thanks for pointing that out – I'll have to lash his ankles together when he's up on the cart ...' The doctor said no more. If all that perturbed the man beside him was the prospect of a pair of flailing legs, he might as well give up. But the doctor's words had reawakened the book-keeper in Mayer. Smart of me, he thought – smart of me to leave instructions for the Polack to wear his own gear this morning. That means I won't have to deal with the filth – they always let fly when they're hanged, but the people in Freiburg can worry about that. What they do with his shitty pants in the dissecting-room will be their pigeon, not mine. I'll send them the regulation covering letter – garments of executed person to be issued to other foreign workers free of charge and without any indication of source – and that'll let me off the hook. If I'd left the man in his prison gear, which he really ought to be wearing now, I'd have been racking my brains about how to get it back from the dissecting-room. Prison pants and tunics are entered in our cloth-ing inventory, whereas the Pole's civilian clothes aren't registered in Lörrach at all, so no departmental inspector will try and trace them ...

He was driving past the long column of prisoners and foreign workers, who were marching along in semi-military fashion. There were two hundred of them on their way to inspect the body, and a good three hundred more would now be converging on Brombach from other villages and factories. The majority were Poles. The doctor asked, 'Any Russians among them? There seem to be plenty of French – or are they Belgians?' Mayer said, 'Both – plus seven Britishers, but we don't have any Russians yet. Let's hope our boys take Moscow soon, it's getting cold out there.' The doctor, who was still seething, capped the last remark with spiteful satisfaction. 'They could still find themselves out in the cold when they've taken it. The Russians have been known to burn Moscow down as soon as an enemy moves in.' Mayer thought it tactless of the doctor to compare the greatest military leader of all time, albeit indirectly and on a day which marked the Germans' capture of Odessa, with one who had died a beaten man. To get his own back, he said, politely but inflexibly, 'By the way, Doctor, I'm afraid I must correct you: you *are* obliged to attend the execution because I don't have an SS doctor on tap. All the local SS medics are serving in field hospitals or concentration camps.'

'I see.' The doctor bowed his grizzled head. He sounded half resigned, half appeasing. 'Well, here I am – I'm not trying to back out. But tell me, you say there are some Englishmen among the prisoners. What happens to them if they do what the Pole did?' Mayer hesitated, then set his own mind at rest by saying, 'The order was never made public, but it isn't classified. Last August, just after we'd wound up the French campaign, Heydrich sent us a priority directive expressly stating that British, French and Belgian prisoners who have intercourse with German women are also to be executed in accordance with the Führer's personal wish. The odd thing about that directive ...' He paused before quickly producing the information from his card index of a brain. 'That's right, it was dated 5.8.40. The odd thing is, it didn't mention Dutchmen. Was it just an oversight? I hope *I* don't get landed with a Dutchman, that's all. You never know how they'll react up top if you pussyfoot around and check with higher authority.'

So that's his only worry, thought the doctor. Aloud, he asked, 'This Pole – was he tried by the special court at Freiburg, or what?' Mayer's tone became didactic. 'The special courts have let us down too often in the past. The younger judges are away on active service and the older ones tend to hang on to their sloppy middle-class ideas, even when they're veteran Party members and do a first-class job in other respects. That's why the Reichsführer got the Führer's permission to bypass the courts in sex cases, at least as a general rule. The women don't have to be brought to trial anyway, even on the less serious charge – exchanging caresses without engaging in sexual intercourse, I mean. That's been subject to a minimum sentence of twelve months' concentration camp since 'thirty-nine.'

He braked to a halt. As officer in charge, Mayer was greeted on the village outskirts by the notables of Brombach – far from all Party members – under their mayor and district director, Josef Zinngruber. Zinngruber, likewise in civilian dress but also wearing riding boots, raised his right arm in salute. 'Heil Hitler, Obersturmführer! I beg to report Brombach District Branch ready for execution.'

Mayer acknowledged the salute. 'Heil Hitler, District Director.' He had climbed out, leaving the doctor in the car. Zinngruber's preposterous announcement that he and his cronies were ready for execution – after all, the village itself wasn't under sentence – unearthed another item in Mayer's well-kept mental filing system. It concerned a Jewish village in Poland which really had been executed – males over fourteen shot, women and children deported, houses burnt to the ground – but this gruesome recollection faded as he quickly shook hands all round with Zinngruber's underlings, who had frozen to attention. He shot out his right arm after each handshake, marionette-like, and stepped back briskly because the heel-clicking recipients of his salutes shot out their right arms too. The exceptional nature of the proceedings had imbued all present with a sense of occasion, if not drama, and this in turn reinforced the German tendency to seal every social exchange (and solve every social dilemma) with a handshake. Even the men who hadn't turned out in uniform sported riding breeches and boots or, in two cases, puttees. All wore modest hunting outfits of semi-military cut, almost all wore peaked caps rather than hats, and two were carrying stout walking-sticks. They could have been beaters or the tenants of a small shoot – and that was what the occasion really amounted to, the culmination of a game-drive. Whether this thought presented itself to their individual minds, for they all had minds, cannot be ascertained, but the broad smirk of pleasure with which a policeman from the next village later described the doomed man's death-throes on the gallows (he even mimed them) was probably unrepresentative. Being a shrewd customer – if anyone can be called shrewd who put his shirt on Hitler, though the Hitler of 1941 wasn't the Hitler whose ranks he had joined in the late 'twenties – Zinngruber may well have sensed, even then, that his poster announcing Zasada's execution had not been well received by the village. Zasada was popular with the womenfolk, who fondly remembered him as a handsome and helpful purveyor of coal. It was also rumoured that he came of 'good family', as the saying went. Why, only that March he had got his family firm in Lodz to send a set of cycle tyres as a Confirmation present for fourteen-year-old Max König, son of the head of the Women's League and nephew of Melchior the coal merchant! This had caused a great stir in Brombach, where no one could purchase cycle tyres without coupons – and where everyone, of course, knew everything about everyone else. Some women later recalled (or persuaded themselves, whichever) that they wept on the day of his execution. It is, however, an attested fact that the Franciscan nuns of Lörrach Hospital, who had nursed the Pole for ten days during his bout of tonsillitis, did not tend their patients on the morning of 16 October because they were down on their knees in the hospital chapel, praying for a fellow-Catholic in the shadow of the gallows ...

Mayer, who was noticeably on edge now, addressed himself to the reception committee. 'A cord,' he said in a low, urgent voice. 'I must have a short length of cord with a slip-knot ready tied.' Zinngruber didn't understand. The proximity of the truck was making him nervous too, and apprehensive. 'Short – how do you mean, short? It's long, the rope. It's been hanging from the gallows since last night.' Jerkily, hurriedly, Mayer prefaced his reply by gesturing with his hands as though trying to illustrate something, but his movements conveyed nothing. 'Not for his neck, not that sort of rope – for his ankles.' He switched syntax and elaborated: 'To tie his feet together.' But nothing could have been harder to come by at this particular place and time. Zinngruber stared helplessly at Mayer, then at the others. The man who broke the silence spoke impatiently, because he was already ashen-cheeked at the prospect of the enormity he had yesterday clamoured to attend but was now attending only because he couldn't wriggle out of it – an attitude typical of many Nazis in respect of much of what they did. 'Who'd have a cord on him out here?' he snapped. 'Take this, I don't need it.'

He was already pulling the leather thong from the waistband of his field-grey shooting jacket. Mayer shouted, 'All right, everybody, carry on!' He took the belt and got back into his car. The rest followed suit. Someone yelled, 'Rendezvous in the square!' and they all set off. And all of them doubtless regarded their presence as a patriotic duty of the same order as the one that fell to their lot a few months later, when, here in Baden as elsewhere in the Reich, Jewish families who had already been deprived of their rights for years were herded off by them to meet a still more horrible death . . .

'For his ankles,' Mayer said as he started the car again, depositing his accomplice's belt on the medical officer's lap. The doctor refused to give up. He had no reason to fear Mayer. Being a Party member and an official of the local Medical Chamber, not to mention the owner of a thriving practice and a racially flawless family tree, he had nothing to fear from the Nazis but the destruction they ultimately visited on all their fellow-countrymen. 'Look,' he urged, 'the state takes a very poor view of cruelty to animals thanks to Göring and his game laws – in fact every animal in this country is officially entitled to a *coup de grâce*.' His latent sarcasm was lost on Mayer, who glanced at him anxiously. 'You're absolutely right, Doctor, but still . . . I just hope our hangman doesn't bungle it, that's all, because I'm not empowered to finish him off. There's a total ban on snaring game in this country – it's punishable by imprisonment with hard labour. That means there aren't any precedents, so to speak, not for killing animals with a noose. If the Pole was going to be shot like a stag instead of snared like a rabbit in the old days, there'd be no problem – we could go on blazing away till he was dead, as it were. But in this case? They'd think I was stark staring mad if I phoned Berlin about a minor detail like that!' He had spoken fast, thoroughly unsettled by this line of argument. Now, in the absence of any word of approval from the doctor, he added more hesitantly, 'I'm not saying it's a minor detail to the Pole, mark you. It's damned hard luck on the youngster. He's a splendid specimen, properly speaking – just the type of new blood they're always wanting in the SS Guards. And there's another thing: he claims his mother's German, or has done ever since he thought there was a genuine possibility he'd go to the gallows ...'

Quickly, as if still hoping to save something from the wreck, the doctor cut in. 'In that case, Mayer, you can't hang him for sleeping with a German!'

Mayer was quite touched by the omission of his rank and 'Herr' – it lent the conversation a note of father-and-son intimacy. '*I'm* not hanging the boy,' he said in passionate self-justification. 'I even told Freiburg he claimed to be of German descent on his mother's side, but they said it made no difference – as an ethnic German, he should have been strung up ages ago for fighting in the Polish army! It wouldn't have mattered what I did, his goose was cooked the moment I got those letters from the woman who was running his girl-friend's shop. If only she'd chucked them in the fire ...'

The doctor asked, 'Do I know her?'

'Elsbeth Schnittgens,' said Mayer. 'A decent enough sort.'

They had to pull up. The square in front of the mayor's office was filled to overflowing with prisoners of war from Brombach and other villages. Prisoners lose their nerve, thought the doctor. Two hundred here and another two hundred on the way ... They could spring their friend and make a dash for it, through the woods and into Switzerland. There'd be casualties, naturally, but – who knows? – maybe all on our side if the whole four hundred piled into them and took their guns away – there can't be more than seven or eight with guns: this fellow here beside me, and Zinngruber – possibly – and, of course, the policemen, but there are only five of them – nobody else is armed. And if they commandeered the cars as well, how long would it take them to get across the frontier? Ten minutes at the most. They work all over the shop, so they must know perfectly well there isn't a garrison for miles around, and once they were across, well ... They do deport lone individuals and German deserters, the Swiss, but whether they'd risk provoking an international outcry by handing back three or four hundred men ... I don't think they'd do it, frankly, not our friends the cuckoo-clocks! Filled with fierce but numbing rage at himself and his involvement in the morning's work, the doctor had never felt such impotent fury since he stopped wearing knee-pants. With the inward knowledge that robs a person of speech, he stared at the figures lining the village street and their mournful, soulful, bovine eyes. He could detect no malice or desire to see murder done, only a mute sorrow suggestive of beasts being led to the slaughter. Its lack of human dignity revolted him. No handcuffs, he thought – no handcuffs on any of the four hundred except the boy to be hanged. No guards around either, but I don't see one of these well-fed cattle who isn't looking on meekly like the villagers – or like me, the man who plays God every spring and autumn when he gives the eighteen-year-olds their physical and sternly certifies them fit for combat duty – writes them off as cannon-fodder ... What swine we human beings are, and how lucky we are there's nothing to choose between us! And now keep your trap shut and get out like the others or you'll go crazy ... Fresh air's the thing – fresh air and a faint hope that something may happen to remind me, even vaguely, that human beings and cattle aren't identical ... How sure, how frighteningly sure we Germans are that prisoners don't need guarding two miles from the Swiss border, even when we have the gall to parade them for the murder of one of their people! If this tide never turns – if it never turns

Enigma means riddle in ancient Greek, and Enigma was the name given by the Germans to their cipher machine, which went into mass production in 1938. With its intricate system of electrically driven rotating drums, each bearing a complete alphabet, it was used throughout the Second World War to encrypt the signals sent by Hitler and his commanders to their forces in the field and at sea, who signalled back in the same manner. Writing thirty years later, Hitler's former armaments minister, Albert Speer, recalled in 1976 that the Führer 'often told his field marshals and me, in didactic terms, that in this war we possessed the finest secret code the wit of man could devise'. Hitler was, of course, as ignorant as any other German that two *Poles* working for their own and Britain's secret services had by 1938 purloined an Enigma from the German factory where it was being made, and that Polish and British mathematicians had almost solved the riddle of the 'riddle'-machine by the end of February 1940. Although the Germans improved its permutation capacity between 1940 and 1942, this secret, too, was fathomed by the British cryptanalyst 'Dilly' Knox. After Hitler's invasion of Norway the British succeeded in salvaging another Enigma machine, complete with operational keys, from a German aircraft shot down off the Norwegian coast. They soon acquired some equally valuable information from a German armoured signals unit which had ventured too far ahead during the Battle of France. On 8 May 1941 a British escort vessel depth-charged U110, which had been attacking a convoy south of Greenland, and forced it to the surface. The British then boarded the abandoned submarine and 'recovered, intact and undamaged, its cipher machine with all its accompanying material and many other secret documents'. Suppressed until 1958, this incident is described by Patrick Beesly, who was serving in the Admiralty's Operational Intelligence Centre and has chronicled its war-time activities. Of 39,000 German submariners, 27,212 failed to survive largely because Dönitz, their commander-in-chief, relied so heavily on Enigma that his faith in it remained undimmed thirty years after the war ended. 'Even as recently as 1973,' writes Beesly, 'Dönitz ... was apparently still loath to accept that most of his ciphers had been consistently and thoroughly penetrated for four years of the war.' The same blind faith inspired his order that every U-boat should radio him an exact daily position report. Similarly, it was Admiral Lütjens's breach of radio silence that helped the British to sink his command, the battleship *Bismarck*, when she had already given her pursuers the slip. Beesly relates what happened: 'Peter Kemp (head of the direction-finding plotters) began to take down the bearings of a German signal on the big ship frequency. Just under one hour later a further long signal was intercepted. The German admiral cannot have realized that he had at long last shaken off his pursuers, and thinking that his position, course and speed must be known to his opponents, decided he would report details of the engagement with *Hood* ... his now critical shortage of oil and his determination to make straight for France. None of this, of course, could be known to us. To Denning (subsequently Director of Naval Intelligence) and Kemp, who had by now returned to the Admiralty, it was inexplicable. What emergency could be causing the Germans to reveal their position in this way? Surely they must realize that we had lost them and had no idea in which direction they were moving? ... It was OIC's skilled interpretation of the D/F bearings of her long signals which, at the eleventh hour, provided the clue which led to her second interception and destruction.'

Secret servicemen may create openings for victory or defeat, but destruction itself must always be endured or inflicted by the men on the ground – the anonymous rank and file in every armed service and theatre of war. This knowledge should temper the amusement of those too young to bear the scars of history when they read how Hitler's code was broken by the Poles and the British. The earliest source of the belated Enigma revelation, Group Captain Winterbotham, was also the first to raise this point in 1974. Why, he asked, did the Allies take five years to storm Hitler's 'Fortress Europe' when they had eavesdropped on his most vital military secrets throughout that time? His answer: because the Germans were a strong and courageous enemy. No foreknowledge of an attack can repel it, just as no attack is assured of success even when the enemy's decoded signals have revealed the exact location and strength of his defences. In each case, the anonymous fighting man must do the job himself. Montgomery, who had been accurately informed by Ultra of Rommel's minefields and dispositions before the Battle of El Alamein, illustrates this point in one brief but graphic passage: '9 Armoured Brigade was to pass through the infantry ... and form a bridgehead ... As it became light 9 Armoured Brigade ran into a formidable anti-tank gun screen and during the day suffered over 75 per cent casualties.' (Its 132 armoured vehicles had, in fact, dwindled to 19.)

The biggest armoured engagement of the war took place at Kursk. Here, Hitler's last attempt to regain the initiative was transformed into a decisive Russian breakthrough, but how many of the Red Army men riding in or on their tanks had to purchase this victory with their lives, although the British, thanks to Ultra, had been able to give the Kremlin precise information about the timing, strength and direction of the German assault? The historian Olaf Groehler has warned against 'creating a new stab-in-the-back legend, as though the dark forces of the secret service decided the outcome of the war'. They certainly *helped* to do so, but the following point has been stressed not only by Groehler but by Beesly (*Very Special Intelligence*), Lewin (*Ultra goes to War*) and numerous German military men who, like the bad losers they are, felt deeply affronted by Winterbotham's book. Rohwer, the German naval historian, sums it up: 'Anyone even moderately well acquainted with an army's communications system knows that the bulk of signals are sent by teleprinter and cannot, unlike radio traffic, be broken. Experience of the Second World War confirms that no army succeeded in preserving the complete integrity of every code it used. In North Africa, for example, the Germans were able to eavesdrop continuously on the tactical radio traffic of the British Eighth Army or the US military attaché's reports from Cairo to Washington.' This is quite as indisputable as Beesly's detailed account of the security precautions observed by the German Navy, whose system was 'superior to those of its sister services, and also to that of the

Royal Navy. Every power, including some of the neutrals like the Swedes, managed, at one time or another, to decrypt some of the signals of other nations.' By tapping a transatlantic cable, the German Post Office was sometimes able to present Hitler with verbatim transcripts of telephone conversations between Churchill and Roosevelt. The German Navy differed from the other two services in using an Enigma machine with seven rotors instead of four. The far more frequent changes of setting made possible by this system posed new problems of decipherment so laborious that they were often solved too late to assist British naval units in destroying U-boats at sea.

It remains a war-winning *Polish* achievement of the first magnitude that 'from the end of May 1941 onwards not a day passed without the receipt by OIC (Operational Intelligence Centre), sometimes in small quantities, sometimes in a large mass, of teleprinted English translations of German W/T signals of one variety or another'. The other British armed services benefited similarly. Beesly also summarizes what Winterbotham was still forbidden to divulge in 1974: 'It seems to have been the Polish Intelligence Service who first realized what the Germans were doing, and by sometime in the late twenties or very early thirties they had reconstructed the German Army machine and may have been decrypting at least some of the Wehrmacht's W/T traffic. The French too, with the help of an agent employed for a time in the German General Staff's Cryptographic Department, had made some progress. How far, if at all, the British had progressed is not known, but there seems to be little doubt that their first real step forward occurred when Commander Alistair Denniston, the Head of the GC & CS and his French opposite number, Colonel Braquenie, met the chief Polish cryptanalyst Colonel Langer in Warsaw on 24–25 July 1939. From this meeting they brought back, in the very nick of time, two of the Polish Enigma machines, a gift quite as valuable as the *Magdeburg*'s signal book had been in 1914, and one for which Britain owes the Poles an immense debt of gratitude. If Chamberlain's guarantee to Poland did little for that unfortunate country, it certainly produced a priceless asset for Great Britain. Possession of the machine did not, of course, mean that the British or the French were immediately able to read German W/T signals. In order to do that they had to know the current keys or settings, and these were changed at increasingly frequent intervals. Nor was there, in peacetime, a sufficient volume of traffic for the cryptanalysts to work on. However, after the collapse of Poland in September 1939, some of the Polish cryptanalysts escaped to France and by the end of October they and the French had made a partial break-in, and were decrypting, though often with a considerable time lag, a certain amount of German Air Force traffic ...'

The slow but steady flow of information continued until early 1942, by which time the decoding machines in England, which were ultimately maintained and operated by ten thousand personnel (mostly women), had gained complete mastery over German radio traffic. (The department continues to operate in peacetime. According to *The Times* of 17 March 1977: '1856 officials engaged in code-breaking' were still employed at the government communications centre in Cheltenham.)

Thanks to the code-breakers, Hitler's orders were very often read within the hour by Churchill, Roosevelt and the Allied chiefs of staff. The theft of Enigma was Poland's war-time revenge for all that Hitler's Germany did to her, which was a great deal. One can say without exaggeration that it offset the Allies' appalling inferiority until Hitler, after being worsted on the outskirts of Moscow, declared war on the USA as well – mysteriously enough, without securing Japan's agreement to attack the Soviet Union in return.

Poland lost more lives in Hitler's war than any other country, a fact which can never be recalled too often. That loss has not been made good – for lives mean more than land – by her compensation with German provinces for the territories she was forced to cede to Russia because the Red Army was chiefly responsible for reducing the Wehrmacht to scrap and expelling it from her soil. This chapter merits a place in our story because it was the *Poles*, too, whose contribution to the grand alliance – the discovery and theft of Hitler's cipher machine – represented the most bloodless and momentous victory of the Second World

War. Countless people – mathematicians, generals and statesmen, but above all their human charges on the battlefield and in residential areas – became beneficiaries of this machine. Indeed, large numbers of them owed their survival to it alone.

Poland's bequest to Britain may not have clinched the outcome of the war, as was said by many Allied generals including Eisenhower, but it very probably enabled Britain to carry on the struggle between summer 1940 and summer 1941, the year when she stood alone.

Thus Poland's contribution to the crucial engagement of that period, the Battle of Britain, was as great as that of the British themselves – who have conceded this since 1974 – not only because so many Polish pilots fought and died in Dowding's fighter squadrons, but because the Polish *coup* gave London prior warning of every major German order to attack.

Thanks to British censorship, this feat was suppressed until 1974. Not even Churchill breathed a word about it in his six-volume history of the Second World War.

Vanquished nations cast around for scapegoats. The Germans, with whom the British had played a brilliant game of blind man's buff for five whole years by courtesy of Poland, subsequently imagined that an arch-traitor must have been lurking at headquarters. The British had established a staging-post in Lucerne to process selected Enigma information for forwarding to Moscow (they never confided the source of their haul to the Russians). The Swiss proudly claimed this, after the war, as a national achievement which had substantially helped to decide its outcome. In reality, every item of 'Swiss' intelligence was solely attributable to the fact that two mathematicians of the Polish secret service had located Dr Arthur Scherbius's Enigma machine at the premises of Chiffriermaschinen AG, 2 Steglitzer Strasse, Berlin SW35, and handed it over to the British – two Poles who have never been named to this day although their influence on world events was incalculable.

The theft must have been staged so skilfully that it passed unnoticed by its victims, for why else would they have neglected to draw the obvious conclusion? It is possible, on the other hand, that the Germans in charge of plant security dared not report their loss for fear of draconian punishment ...

Whatever the truth, the first chronicler of the Enigma machine and its evaluation by the Allies, Group Captain Winterbotham, had to wage a thirty-year campaign for government permission to report on the activities of the secret intelligence department which he headed throughout the Second World War – and even then he was denied access to the government archives in which his own war-time records are stored. Few foreigners realize that every Briton writing about political or military matters covered by the Official Secrets Act is obliged, even after a lapse of thirty or more years, to submit his manuscript to official bodies who often delete its most valuable passages and cause the writing of history to verge on historical falsification. Many British intellectuals seem to find this quite unexceptionable. This is apparent from the eagerness – inexplicable to any foreigner – with which they seize on every opportunity to emphasize how obediently their books have complied with the demands of state censorship at the expense of the truth – like Patrick Beesly, whose standard work contains no less than three invalidating references to tons of earlier literature on maritime warfare. Beesly, who blithely says of Roskill's *War at Sea* 'but Roskill could not refer to this at the time he was writing', piously points out that he can only write about the government's war-time Code and Cipher School 'having regard to ... continuing security restrictions' and concludes his foreword with the virtuous assurance that: 'The entire manuscript of this book has been submitted to the Ministry of Defence to ensure that there has been no breach of the Official Secrets Act.'

Well, there are genuine security precautions and ostensible ones. Where Operation Ultra is concerned, they must surely be spurious and outdated. The true reason for suppression is a chauvinistic excess of national pride that flatly refuses to acknowledge how far Poland's Enigma conquest was responsible for the Allies' defeat of Nazi Germany. (Winterbotham mentions hundreds of Britons, Americans and Frenchmen in his book, but not a single Pole!) But this may have been only one of the authorities' reasons for bowdlerizing Winterbotham's account. The other is that the whole truth about Enigma would disclose how much the Allied military commanders owed to their own strategy and how much to a cipher machine. It would also answer the crucial question – to which Winterbotham cannot devote so much as a syllable – of how much Enigma information the British transmitted to their Russian comrades-in-arms via Lucerne and how much they kept to themselves – too delicate a subject ever to be aired in public. Any overt admission that London confined itself to passing on hand-picked German secrets while suppressing the rest might well cause so much resentment that the Russians would forget what a great debt of gratitude they *do*, nonetheless, owe the British.

It distresses Winterbotham, as he himself said in spring 1978, that his account had to confine itself to mentioning the beneficiaries of Poland's greatest contribution to victory – the generals and statesmen of the Western Allies – and say nothing about the Poles, most of whom are elderly gentlemen who cannot open their mouths except to graze on the lean pastures allotted them as pensioners of the British government ...

Little is known in general about the numerous Poles who served with the British armed forces, not only as fighter pilots in the Battle of Britain but in Africa and at Monte Cassino and in Bomber Command, which alone lost one thousand Polish airmen over Germany. By giving Enigma to the British, the Poles repaid them in full for what they did towards the preservation and re-establishment of a Polish state. No Polish balladeer should omit to point out what Winterbotham so cogently demonstrates: that only Poland's theft of this machine made it possible for the Allies – outside the Soviet Union, at least – to direct every major battle in full cognizance of their German adversaries' plans. If any further proof of this be needed, we should reflect that Hitler's last offensive in the Ardennes, whose *surprise* effect on the Allies was disastrous, took them unawares *only* because he did not have his orders encrypted by Enigma before transmission but sent them to all units in the good old-fashioned way, by messenger and dispatch-rider ...

The quarry

The relevant head of department shall decide, after due consideration, whether the remains are to be conveyed to the nearest crematorium for cremation or made available to the nearest university hospital (dissecting-room). If the transportation of the remains to the nearest crematorium or dissecting-room will consume a large quantity of petrol, there is no objection to their being interred in a Jewish graveyard or in the suicides' corner of a large cemetery. All costs incurred will be borne by the Secret State Police.

The Reichsführer-SS and Chief of the German Police, Communication No. SIV D2 – 450/42g – 81 dated 6 January 1943.

For the fifth time at least, Zasada asked his executioner, 'You won't forget the address? Say it again!'

Victorowicz repeated it, then took the cigarette out of Zasada's mouth. And Zasada, whose silent tears at the shock of seeing his coffin had calmed him considerably, blew out the smoke, and Victorowicz replaced the cigarette between his lips; and the two constables, whose wrists were still manacled to Zasada's, tolerated this irregularity by looking the other way. And Zasada asked what he had already asked so often before: that Victorowicz should write that very day in case his parents heard the news from another quarter. 'Tell them how sad I was, not being allowed to write to them myself,' he added – but that brought him back to the verge of tears, so he relapsed into silence even though he had thought of something else to put in the letter Victorowicz was going to write for him. They had agreed that Victorowicz should tell his parents that their son had been shot for falling in love with a German girl. He had died instantly, and he asked them to console themselves with the thought from which he himself had tried to draw some consolation: that unlike so many of the fellow-conscripts who accompanied him straight from the schoolroom to the front, he at least had known love – a really great love – before his death. 'And don't forget,' he said urgently, 'tell them they mustn't reply on any account – not on any account. Anything my parents wrote about these murdering swine would only get them hanged as well – and you!' He paused for a moment, then broke into another agitated plea. 'No, that's nonsense – you mustn't even write your name legibly. Tell them you'll go and see them as soon as the war's over, but for God's sake don't put your name. My mother'll be bound to want to know more – she won't be able to stop herself writing, and then you'll all be in trouble...'

Victorowicz gripped him soothingly by the arm – he had often done that in the past hour – and Zasada blurted out, 'I'm so grateful to you – more grateful than anyone ever was to his ...' He couldn't bring himself to say the word. 'Think how I'd be feeling now, cooped up alone in here with these two dumb bastards in uniform!' Victorowicz sensed that talking kept Zasada's fear at bay. 'Grateful – to *me*? If only I could tell you a fraction of the things a priest could, but I wouldn't know where to start.' Zasada was genuinely distracted by this. 'A priest?' he said defiantly. 'I'd only welcome a priest because we could talk the same language, not for any other reason. What could he say to me? I know I'm paying for all those nights I spent with Pauline, but they're my only consolation. A priest wouldn't even leave me that. No, I'm glad they didn't let me have one. The power they represent, if they really do – priests, I mean – what does it do to help us where we need it, here on earth? Life's unfair – that's what struck me as soon as I could think about anything but escaping, and by then it was too late. It'd be laughable if it wasn't so sad, the way I've been blinded by fate, or whatever you like to call it – prodded into making the wrong decisions, carefully and consistently, ever since the first time they questioned me. And for what? Just so they can hang me for having something ...' He thought, then smiled and said, 'Something other men get a lot more cheaply – a nice-looking woman.' Dully, he repeated, 'Life's unfair.' No awkward silences, not now, thought his friendly executioner, so he leapt into the breach. 'Stop reproaching yourself,' he said, quickly and with utter conviction. 'If you think you're "paying" for something, forget it. Paying for *what*, damn it all?'

Zasada said, 'I've landed Pauline in a concentration camp.'

'What about *her*?' Victorowicz retorted, close to fury. 'Where's she landed *you* with her idiotic letter-writing? You're quits – the Germans don't kill their womenfolk for sleeping with prisoners. She'll survive!' Zasada said, 'They can. The Germans can murder anyone they like. There isn't a Jew left in Lodz ghetto – my mother said so last time she wrote. You think they've been *resettled*? Not taking any of these bastard Germans with me – that's what riles me even more than...' He broke off. To bridge the dangerous gap, Victorowicz said, 'More than what?' Zasada looked tormented. 'Than my own stupidity! The way I've made a hash of things ever since they came to take me in for questioning. I wasn't handcuffed then – I could have sprinted across Melchior's yard and into the barn, up the ladder and out of the window into the place next door. I knew every nook and cranny, not like those flatfeet from Lörrach. They'd have used their guns, naturally, but so what? Even if they'd hit me – not that I think they would have ...' Victorowicz shook his head. 'Look, we've been over that scores of times and it doesn't – well, it doesn't add up. You did the right thing. In the first place, you thought you'd hurt the woman's chances if you ran for it ...' Zasada laughed. 'Yes, *that* was wrong for a start. A fat lot of good I did Pauline by staying!' Victorowicz said, 'You know that now but you didn't know it then. Besides, the Swiss would have handed you back.'

They were skirting the column of prisoners now. Seeing them, Victorowicz was even more transfixed by the sight than by the thought of what he had to do. Suppressor mechanisms had begun to operate inside him too: he had stopped thinking about the final abomination. 'Man, look at that! The Germans are making a bigger mistake than you ever did.' As if to reassure himself that the policemen on the coffin really didn't understand a word, he glanced at the stolid helmeted figures before continuing. 'They're taking our boys to see the show, the Teutonic twits, but they've forgotten to put a proper guard on them – so near the frontier, too ... Look, count them! Well over a hundred – no, two hundred, and only a pair of pathetic old policemen. *They'll* help you run the gauntlet, Stasiek – *they'll* get you away from these murderers!'

They had left the marching men behind. Zasada stared at him, breathing faster. He smiled and said, without meaning it, 'That only happens in films, not in real life.' But even as he spoke Victorowicz could sense the hope that welled up inside him, potent and proliferating. Victorowicz had never been in contact with anyone whose predicament was as hopeless as theirs. Neither of them knew that, in condemned men as in cancer victims, hope flees the confines of reality the more certain the end becomes. Even had they known, however, the hopelessness of their position would have inhibited them from relating this knowledge to themselves. Victorowicz was already discussing details. 'First they'll have to get you away from these two ... After that – well, there are plenty of cars around.'

Zasada struggled with the hope that was beginning to over-whelm him. 'I don't want anyone killed on my account – anyway, it mightn't work. You can't expect it of them.'

'You think they'll take a vote on it first?' said Victorowicz. 'Look, there are some more of our boys lining the street – as many again. There must be five hundred of them counting the first batch. You don't imagine they'll stand there goggling like sheep while I put the rope round your neck ...'

Words failed *him* now. The truck came to a standstill. They had passed Pauline's shuttered store without seeing it, thanks to the tarpaulin, any more than they had seen Melchior's coal yard. Now they were in the middle of the village and had stopped, perhaps – they thought – because the crowd was blocking the road. 'Where's it to be?' asked Zasada. All the blood had drained from his face when the truck pulled up, as it had when he first set eyes on the coffin. Victorowicz, who also knew every building in Brombach, said, 'Not here – it wouldn't be in the middle of the village. Besides, what about the prisoners who are meant to be watching? They aren't all here yet.'

He had voiced their final illusion. The two constables didn't budge from the coffin, just chatted more briskly as they peered over the tailboard. This was another indication that they hadn't reached the gallows, but Zasada, who could see nothing of what was happening ahead of the tarpaulin-covered truck, was so un-nerved by the lack of movement that sweat erupted on his fore-head. He suspected, as he had so often done in recent weeks, that they might be going to hang him from one of the big trees outside the inn – and the trees were only a few yards off. He tried to forget about himself and listen to the policemen's conversation, straining his ears to fight back the fear that they had already reached the place of execution. Although the constables spoke broader and cruder dialect than Pauline had ever done, even when she lost her temper, his self-imposed concentration on their words bore fruit. 'You don't get a removal allowance if they transfer you to the occupied territories,' one was saying, 'nor a coal allowance neither, but you do get plenty of perks, that's for sure!'

The other man agreed. He had also heard what colleagues serving in Holland were able to send home in the way of luxuries, and he avidly enumerated them. Fur coats and gold watches came top of his personal scale of values, it seemed, because he alluded to them three times. His friend had some stories of occupied Poland to contribute. You could rustle up fur coats there too – he didn't know about gold watches, but the food made up for it. 'The thing is to know somebody on the railways, then you can send home as much stuff as you like – whole sides of pork, even! Mind you, this thing we're on this morning – in Poland they have to do it every week, nights too, and it isn't only men they execute, though old Fritz Jacob didn't say anything about stringing 'em up, not in Poland – I reckon they shoot most of them. All he told me was, never a week goes by without an execution, and raids every other night ...'

The other man pronounced this 'no picnic' but added, 'It pays off, mind you. They say anyone who does five years in the east gets given a fair-sized farm, free gratis and for nothing, and the Pole it belonged to before has to work for the German who takes it over ... Jesus, what's taking them so long?' He rose and looked out. Zasada had to follow him because of the handcuff, and the second constable, who was also compelled to stand up, started grousing. 'It *would* be today, when my Erna's at the dentist. She asked me to fetch the sausages from the butcher and put them on to boil – we always have them Thursdays. You never know how long Selzer'll keep her waiting, and her with pus coming out of her jaw – it's down at the bottom on the left ...' They both returned to the coffin, and the first man said, 'Added to which, they could cut our lunch break because of this lousy job we're on ... Take a look at people's faces, Karl – it isn't popular, what we're doing. The woman deserves to be hanged along with him, if you ask me – that or neither one of them.'

Karl mellowed at this. 'I knew her,' he said. 'Lucky *I* wasn't shut up next door to her without any skirt like this Pole here, seeing her all the time and helping her out in the evenings.' He whistled through his teeth to underline the point, 'I'd have risked it myself – she was hot stuff, that woman!'

Having worked and shared his meals with Alemannic-speakers for eighteen months, Zasada could follow their dialect even if he couldn't imitate it. It had helped him to concentrate on his captors' gossip, much of which he had understood. He retained enough self-possession and detachment to know that all he had to do was keep his feet for another few minutes or a quarter of an hour – not collapse or exhibit the sort of weakness that would bring a satisfied smirk to his murderers' faces. But although the doomed man perceived this with utter clarity, his mind again became shrouded in the irrational hope of rescue by his compatriots and the Frenchmen who were also marching to the scene. During those cell-bound weeks when he was struggling to suppress his will to live, no form of auto-suggestion had proved more helpful than one simple and recurrent idea: if you'd been hit in the head at Kowno, not the shoulder, you wouldn't be in a death-cell today. The birds would have picked you clean, or you'd have been ploughed under long ago – or maybe buried in a grave – so look on the bright side: you had two whole years extra, and eighteen months of them were as happy as they could have been in war-time. No combat duty, decent treatment, an easy job, and a woman who gave you all a woman *can* give, short of a child. You've seen nothing of the world – just a week on the Baltic at Danzig – but what else could life have given you? Nothing more than you had, not if you'd lived to be a hundred!

He strove to shield this consoling simplification from every doubt that assailed it, uneasily wrenching his thoughts away, for instance, whenever he experienced a tug of homesickness for his mother and Lodz. At last he felt strong enough and sufficiently in command of his voice, which had begun to waver, to tell Victorowicz what had occurred to him long before, so that Victorowicz could write and tell his mother what he hadn't so far trusted himself to say for fear of being unable to say it calmly. Now he came out with it fast: 'Tell my mother I stopped feeling frightened once I told myself they couldn't inflict half as much pain on me as she suffered when she gave birth to me.'

A sudden jerk. The truck moved off, disrupting the mechanism that always restored his composure – thousandfold repetition had moulded these reassuring thoughts into a set formula – as soon as his mind triumphed over his fear: in other words, over his body. But his body was very, very strong. It had scarcely been sapped at all by imprisonment, poor food and mounting terror. The splendid vitality in which he had revelled with Pauline, who had revelled in it too, the libido that knew and wanted nothing save life itself – these forces were activated by the fear of death. They rose in revolt and tormented him. He felt strong enough to have knocked both policemen senseless, bare-handed, had his wrists been manacled together. With his arms spread-eagled and shackled to two different guards there was no hope – not the slightest – of enlisting his own strength and rage. As he saw it, his one remaining hope of survival rested with the four hundred or more compatriots whose hands were free. Surely they wouldn't just stand there idly when ...

But the truck was now leaving the village. The narrow lane and the farm track that joined it – how many hundreds of times had he taken this route when driving Melchior's two horses to the woods or the grassy uplands, singing and whistling as he went! In a moment they would leave the quarry behind on their left, and only a few hundred yards above were the outskirts of the forest – the forest that symbolized freedom because, instead of ending at the German border, it merged with its counterpart in Switzerland. Why should the truck be taking this road to freedom? Zasada stared at Victorowicz, insanely hoping against hope, and said, 'Where to?' Then the truck answered him by stopping at the quarry.

For something to do, Mayer lowered the tailboard himself, pale as the condemned man and so nervous that his every order became a bellow. The policemen got up off the coffin. Because three men manacled together could only have jumped by common consent, they squatted and prepared to slither to the ground on their rumps. But Zasada leapt from a standing position, as far as he could. The man on his left, jerked off balance like his companion, who staggered but didn't fall, landed on his knees with a jarring thud and toppled forwards on his face. Mayer helped him up. The constable, who had yelped with surprise and pain, rubbed one knee and glared at Zasada as if there were still some way of punishing him. 'You bloody fool,' he growled impotently, 'you goddamned stupid Polack!'

Mayer was already detaching Zasada from the victim of his sudden impulse. Now he released the constable on his right but kept hold of Zasada's wrists and handcuffed them quickly behind his back. The condemned man's eyes had grown as wide as his face looked small and shrunken. His head swivelled wildly in all directions, looking for his fellow-countrymen. They were nowhere to be seen. Zasada was alone with his murderers, their confederates and those of like mind. And up on the hillside, on the grassy slopes above the quarry, which the public could be prevented from entering but not from overlooking, hundreds of people from Brombach, Lörrach and neighbouring villages had gathered like blowflies round an open sewer. No Nazi had summoned them to attend. What had whetted their appetite was an innate but unassuageable blood-lust which had condemned the noncombatants among them to lifelong frustration ... Many others came – let no one doubt this – in the same way as they would have attended a funeral: drawn by a sympathy which only their physical presence could express. Some were inwardly riven with compassion and others – a very few – numbed by the certainty that their native land would have to pay for this – this too ...

'What are you waiting for?' Mayer shouted into the truck, and Victorowicz scrambled out. Get it over quickly, he told himself, but he couldn't. Mayer had to take him by the arm and hustle him along just as the constable on Zasada's right – the man who had fallen was still bent double – had to tow the prisoner on his first few steps towards the gallows. Beneath it stood a small cart belonging to Paul Alker, a pig-farmer and long-time resident of Brombach who was actually a Swiss citizen and had been born at Wettikon in 1892. Summoned here today because Zinngruber had estimated that the cart he used for collecting kitchen waste and field-gleanings as feed for his pigs would make a suitable platform for the condemned man to mount before it was driven away from under him with a 'Hup!', the stocky, bull-necked, bul-

266

let-headed, carrot-haired Swiss regarded the Pole, who was *his* victim too, with a kindliness which not even horror could banish from his face. There was no doubt about it: Alker didn't know what he was doing, only what he was expected to do, for that had been eloquently impressed on him. Zasada, white as the whites of his eyes, clung fast to the single resolution which he had enthroned above himself and all else, and which had not let him down so far: show no fear!

He looked round for Victorowicz, who hastened to join him, but he was too closely flanked by Mayer and another policeman. Zasada lowered his eyes. He had already caught sight of the noose dangling over Alker's ramshackle cart and scrawny horse from the gallows which Klages and Matzke had put together like a carpet rail. And so Stasiek Zasada took the few remaining steps that left him encompassed by murderers of whom all but Zinngruber denied, decades afterwards, that they had been present at the scene. Cowardice, remember, was the prime mover of their aggressive urges.

Zasada walked faster the closer he came to the gallows, but Mayer halted him beside the wheel of the cart. The prescribed formalities had still to be completed. In default of a judicial sentence, Reichsführer Himmler had personally devised a form of words applicable to those who violated his 'GV' edict. Because Mayer was on edge, Zasada being the first man he had ever executed, he read the brief paragraph from a prepared sheet. In his agitation, he forgot where he had put it and had to grope in his pockets. At last he was ready: 'The offender, Stasiek Zasada, has forfeited his life by engaging in sexual intercourse with a dishonoured German woman. In the interests of national and state security, he is to be consigned to his death. Sentence will now be carried out.' Horror had made one of the bystanders chuckle at the prosaic phraseology. He stifled his laughter with an effort. There was nothing callous about it – the same sound had escaped him at his mother's funeral. Like everyone in the circle of onlookers, he had failed to realize – for instance at home in bed with his wife last night, while explaining the vital necessity for his presence here today – how closely he was implicating himself in a foul murder. Like him, the rest avoided looking at the Pole, whose face had become pinched and moist, as he said something to his half-dazed companion – evidently a word of encouragement – before preceding him on to the upturned tub that served as a mounting-block to Alker's little cart.

The doctor, who thought it quite possible that the hangman would lose consciousness before his victim, nudged Mayer and gestured to him to mount the cart too. This was just as well because Mayer had, after all, forgotten to secure Zasada's ankles, and he took longer over it than anyone expected – longer than many could endure without turning away. But that was not the only hitch. The noose itself had been hung too high, and Victorowicz fumbled vainly with it until Mayer adjusted the rope to a suitable length. But although the Gestapo chief could tell that the doctor's misgivings about his 'hangman's' competence were only too well founded, the policeman in him triumphed and he declined to relieve Victorowicz of his appointed task. What happened next was not only predictable but doubtless intentional, since it had been Himmler's own sadistic whim to have such killings performed by any available compatriot of the victim rather than a public executioner. The result was a barbarous form of strangulation ... The noose was not where it had to be to kill Zasada outright, and the rope was too short to allow a drop that would have wrenched his strong young neck with sufficient force and violence to sever the spinal cord when Alker's little cart moved off, as it did at an unduly leisurely pace. And because Zasada couldn't die – not for a long time – a cry burst from the lips of the man who had retained his composure till the very last moment. 'Mother!' he screamed.

He screamed the word again and again.

The photographer who had turned up 'pursuant to instructions' had ample time to reload his camera.

Being exempt from the threat of having to pay for it, the perpetrators of this crime were at least ashamed of their failure to commit it in a regulation manner. Even they were so appalled at what they had done and the way they had done it that they unanimously claimed to have forgotten how it came to pass –

some measure of their inability *ever* to forget it. Only the wife of the district director, who hadn't actually witnessed this 'rotten business', could bring herself to speak of it at all. Recalling the incident after a lapse of thirty-six years, while the district director himself, now eighty, stared shamefaced at the floor, she declared that 'Father couldn't eat his dinner for a fortnight afterwards'.